KU-078-963

To the other Ed

THE
HOPE
THAT
KILLS

ALSO BY ED JAMES

DC Scott Cullen Crime Series

Ghost in the Machine
Devil in the Detail
Fire in the Blood
Dyed in the Wool
Bottleneck
Windchill
Cowboys and Indians

DS Vicky Dodds Crime Series

Snared

Supernature Series (writing as Edwin James)

Shot Through the Heart
Just Walking the Dead

THE
HOPE
THAT
KILLS

ED JAMES

THOMAS & MERCER

This is a work of fiction. Names, characters, organizations, places, events, and incidents are either products of the author's imagination or are used fictitiously.

Text copyright © 2016 Ed James
All rights reserved.

No part of this book may be reproduced, or stored in a retrieval system, or transmitted in any form or by any means, electronic, mechanical, photocopying, recording, or otherwise, without express written permission of the publisher.

Published by Thomas & Mercer, Seattle

www.apub.com

Amazon, the Amazon logo, and Thomas & Mercer are trademarks of Amazon.com, Inc., or its affiliates.

ISBN-13: 9781503936553
ISBN-10: 1503936554

er design by Stuart Bache

in the United States of America

Day 1
Wednesday, 16th December 2015

Chapter One

D I Simon Fenchurch leaned against the window frame, kneading his aching back. Rain battered against the glass, long streaks running down the pane. Outside on Leman Street, streetlights painted the stone buildings opposite a harsh white. Stray gusts of winter wind blew the last few leaves around, mixing with carrier bags and fast food containers.

He checked his mobile. Just after half past seven. No new messages. No new calls to action.

He went back to his desk and opened the case file. The brown card was ragged in places, a tear running up the inside.

Fenchurch took a long look at the cover.

01-AT-00748-04
Chloe Fenchurch (DOB 12-Jun-97)
Missing Person
17/07/2005

His fingers tore at the pages. Too few leads. Not much of anything. He swallowed and returned to the start.

The photo stared out at him. The last one they had, one of the best. Chloe's smile punctuated by the gap in her front teeth. Her school uniform ironed and pressed. Uneven blonde pigtails made her look like trouble. The flash had caught the dimple in her cheek, just like her mother's. Her shadow was cast against the matte painting pretending to be sky.

He shut the folder again. Fingers traced the edges of the rough sticker. Over ten years now. Where had the time gone?

He unlocked his desktop and entered the case number into the Police National Computer. The machine started processing the request, as if it was powered by a hamster on a wheel. He drummed his fingers on the fake-oak desk, watching the hourglass empty and refill. The screen flashed to the crime report. All it took was a quick glance, the contents of every field long since etched into memory.

Nothing had changed. Same as it ever was.

He let out a sigh and found a blank sheet of A4. He started a mind map, the same one he always drew. 'Chloe' in the middle. Then 'Leads', 'Witnesses', 'Suspects'. Still too few in each subcategory. Nobody had seen—

His desk phone rang. 'Fenchurch.'

'Simon, it's me.' Gruff London accent, like a forty-a-day taxi driver.

'Dad.'

'You're in her PNC file again, aren't you?'

Fenchurch returned the search to the home screen. 'Nothing's changed.'

'It tells me when you check, you know?'

Fenchurch's stomach rumbled. Acid reflux gnawed at his gullet. 'I knew I'd regret supporting your return to duty.'

Laughter rattled down the line. 'I'll tell you when there's something new, Simon. Don't you worry on that score.'

'Is this the only reason for your call?'

'Let's just say you jogged my memory.'

Fenchurch sat up straight. 'You've found something?'

'I need to speak to you, face-to-face.'

If Dad had something new, he'd be the one coming over. Would already be here. Fenchurch sighed into the handset. 'I'm pretty busy just now.'

'Too busy for your old man?'

'Too busy for anything.'

'I worry about you, son.' A pause on the line, heavy mouth breathing. 'Come out and see me in Lewisham, will you?'

'Let me think about it.' Fenchurch looked up at the office door as it juddered open. 'I've got to go, Dad. I'll maybe come see you soon, okay? Bye.' He slammed the phone down in its cradle. 'I was just about to send out a search party, Sergeant.'

DS Jon Nelson nudged the door shut behind him. Tall and black with the kind of suit a City lawyer would kill for. He dumped a brown Chilango paper bag on the desk and sat opposite Fenchurch. The table dug into his bulk, mostly muscle. 'That carpet's still not fixed, guv.'

'I can only chase up Facilities so many times.'

'Not fancying getting down on your hands and knees with a stapler?'

Fenchurch plonked a pile of expenses on top of Chloe's case file. He used his Airwave police radio as a paperweight. 'That's why I've got two Detective Sergeants.'

'Funny.' Nelson shrugged off his overcoat and frowned at the fresh heap of paper. 'What's that you're hiding from me, guv?'

'It's nothing.'

'It's never nothing with you.' Nelson nudged his chair back a few inches and unloaded the bag's contents onto the table. Took care with the tall, clear cups of lemonade, lidded with straws sticking out. He squinted at the long tubes of silver foil then tossed one over, marked with a 'C'. 'This is yours, I think.'

'My turn next time.' Fenchurch slowly unwrapped the top of his burrito to give a clear stretch of tortilla. He took a bite, closing his eyes as he chewed. 'Always a good burrito from there. Always lacking something, though.' He reached into his desk drawer for his bottle of hot sauce and tipped some on the exposed filling. Another bite and the fire started to burn. 'That's better.'

Nelson picked up a serviette from the pile and cleaned his fingers, nodding at Fenchurch's food. 'You're not worried about your acid reflux?'

'Like I've got a choice in the matter, Jon. Which one was that you went to?'

'Spitalfields.' Nelson unwound more foil and grinned. 'You're not still ranking the Chilangos in London, are you?'

'That one's still behind the one on Upper Street. Just.'

'Used to be your local, right?'

Fenchurch looked away. The rain had stopped battering the window with so much violence. 'I've not even been to the Leather Lane one yet.'

'You're something else.' Nelson laughed hard, his head and torso rocking.

Fenchurch took another mouthful and stretched out. The knot in his back started to unkink. 'I'm still sore from beasting it in the gym this morning.'

'You should give up the weights, guv.'

'What, at my age?'

'I don't mean that. Come running with me.'

'I'm not much of a runner.'

'And I am? Couple of lunchtime jogs out to Canary Wharf and back, you'll become more of a runner.'

'I'll be getting the DLR back from Shadwell after I do my ankle in.'

Nelson laughed before slurping his lemonade through the straw.

Fenchurch's Airwave chirruped on the desk. The display showed a familiar badge number. He tapped the screen to answer. A Scottish accent blasted out, softened by a few years in civilisation. 'DCI Alan Docherty to DI Fenchurch.'

Fenchurch held the device out and rolled his eyes at Nelson. 'Safe to talk, sir.'

'Get your arse over to Little Somerset House. That's just off the Minories, by the bus station. Got ourselves a body.'

Fenchurch's frown was mirrored on Nelson's forehead. 'Last I checked, boss, the Minories is City of London territory.'

'That building's just inside Met territory.'

Fenchurch glanced at his watch. 'Well, I'm off-duty, sir. I thought you'd want DI Mulholland there?'

'I'm asking you. Don't make me tell you twice. And bring some friends.'

'We'll be five minutes.' Fenchurch ended the call and stood up. 'Come on, Sergeant, look lively.'

Nelson waved at Fenchurch's burrito. 'You not finishing that?'

Fenchurch retied the stray fronds of foil. 'I'll take it with me.'

Chapter Two

'That's it here.' Fenchurch pulled off Aldgate High Street into the bus station and headed for the uniform manning the crime scene entrance. He wound down his window and flashed his warrant card. Rain sprayed into the car. He got a nod from the shivering soul. 'Poor bugger.' The window whirred back up as he parked behind the Scenes of Crime, the back looking even grimier in the sodium glare.

Fenchurch killed the engine and checked his burrito was secured in the door. He zipped up his jacket and got out. The bitter air smelled like half the Thames was pouring down. The breeze caught the vaguest whiff from a nearby kebab shop.

The dull arc-light glow bled across the wet tarmac. Lights flashed in the fourth-floor windows of the smallest of the three hulking brick buildings surrounding them. At least twenty floors of brutalist ugliness, the gentle curves betraying their recent construction. Eighties, by the look of it. Already obsolete and shut down.

'Come on, Sergeant.' Fenchurch led him over to the building. A slab of chipboard was dumped next to the entranceway. He waved at another shivering figure. 'Evening, Kay.'

'Nice night for it, guv.' DS Kay Reed cowered under a bent and battered umbrella. No chance it was keeping the rain off the red hair spidering behind her ears. Her navy pinstripe trouser suit was baggy enough to hide her wide hips. Essex accent from way out in the estuary. She handed him a clipboard. 'I need you to sign in.'

Fenchurch grabbed it and jotted their names on blank lines halfway down the page. 'Getting quite full in there already, I see.'

'And then some.' She took back the clipboard, nostrils twitching. 'Chilli and garlic. Mexican, I take it?'

'As if I eat anything else.' Fenchurch held up his Airwave. 'Just got the usual vague nonsense from Docherty. What's happened here?'

'Disused offices, guv. The security guard found the body of a girl just after six.'

'Were you First Attending?'

'First of our lot.' Reed tugged at her hair. A spray of water flashed out. 'Nothing on her. Just cash and condoms. No ID. Could be a prostitute.'

'How old?'

'I'd say sixteen, seventeen.'

Fenchurch swallowed. His throat felt a nanometre in diameter. 'That's no age at all.'

'IC1's about as close as I can give.' Reed exhaled, her breath misting in the air. 'Could be English, Polish, Bulgarian, Czech, American, Australian. You name it.'

Fenchurch nodded at Nelson. 'Let's have a butcher's.'

Nelson smiled at Reed. 'See you later, Kay.'

Fenchurch walked inside. The stench of mould and mushrooms mingled with a strong dose of aftershave. He followed the trail up the stairs, the footplates missing on most of the steps. Graffiti adorned the walls.

Fenchurch waited on the third-floor landing. Shouting cut through the crackle of Airwaves. 'I don't like the fact we've not got an ID, Jon. Gives me the feeling we'll lose Christmas to this case.'

'Tenner says we solve it by then.'

'Never take up gambling, Sergeant.' Fenchurch started up again, two steps at a time.

The shouting got louder as they climbed. Flashes of light blasted out, outlining a figure standing in the doorway.

DC Lisa Bridge was staring into a mirror, trying to restore her blonde locks to the usual rough bedhead look. The SOCO suit's blue mask hung behind her head. She stood up straight and held out her clipboard. 'Need you to sign in, sir.'

'Completing forms is my life, Constable.' Fenchurch grinned at her as he filled it in. He caught a suit Nelson threw over. 'Make sure you never get promoted beyond sergeant.'

'Will do, sir.'

Fenchurch got a leg into the suit. 'That was a joke.'

'Right. Sorry.' Bridge cleared her throat and fiddled with an earring. 'DCI Docherty's waiting for you through there.'

'I thought I could smell his aftershave.'

'Bit overpowering, sir.'

Fenchurch tugged the hood over his head and secured the mask around his mouth.

Nelson was struggling with his zip, caught halfway up. 'These things weren't designed with the larger gentleman in mind, were they?'

'Maybe you need more runs out to Canary Wharf.'

'Yeah, yeah.' Nelson yanked at the zip. 'That's got it.'

'Come on.' Fenchurch followed the flashes into the large chamber. Hundreds of wooden desks were rammed together in the middle, decaying IT equipment stacked on top. Ten or so Scenes of Crime officers combed the area behind, dusting and cataloguing, obscuring what they were investigating.

Two suited figures stood apart from the rest. Arms folded, locked in conversation, both clearly male. One of them broke off, holding an Airwave to his head, mask dangling free.

Fenchurch made for the other one. 'That you, George?'

'Wish it wasn't, but yes.' Mick Clooney tilted his head towards the other figure. 'Your guv'nor's around somewhere.' He gestured at the far wall. 'The body's over there.'

'Cheers.' Fenchurch peered through the group of SOCOs. A pale thigh, navy tights and pink knickers around the knees.

Bloody hell fire.

'Hoy!' Fenchurch stormed across the room, fists clenched. He nudged a pair of gawkers out of the way. 'Give her some dignity.' He pointed at a female figure holding another clipboard. 'And set up a bloody tent around her. Now.'

The SOCO gave a nod and moved off, head bowed.

Fenchurch shook his head. 'Bloody amateurs.'

A heavy-set man was kneeling over the body, his thick beard filling out his SOCO suit. Dr William Pratt. He was prodding the flesh with a metal cylinder. The needle was sharp enough to make your eyes water.

Fenchurch tapped him on the shoulder. 'William, this is a shambles.'

Pratt looked up, his mask puffing. 'Evening, Simon.'

'You've got the victim on public display here. Didn't think to cover her up, did you?'

'Sorry. Should've thought.' Pratt went back to the body. 'My kingdom for some peace and quiet to do my bloody job . . .'

Fenchurch gave up on him and switched his focus to Nelson. 'Jon, get this place organised.'

'Will do, guv.'

Fenchurch took in the body. The chilli heat felt close to climbing back up from his stomach.

Reed was right. Barely a woman. She lay on her back, open eyes staring up at the ceiling. Spatters of blood covered her neck and matted her hair. The beige carpet beneath her soaked up a red pool. A thick crust lined her blonde hair, partially obscuring her face.

Wait a second . . . Shit.

Fenchurch's heart started hammering, the blood thudding in his ears like drums beating a staccato rhythm. He reached out a gloved hand and pushed the hair away.

A face he didn't recognise. No traces of his ugly mug or of Abi's dimple. It wasn't Chloe.

He let out his breath and stood up. His mask was dripping with moisture around the eyes. 'You been here long, William?'

'Twenty minutes, give or take. Have a look at this.' Pratt knelt down and eased up the girl's top.

Her upper torso was a swamp of knife wounds. Gouges spread from her throat down to her ribcage. A ladder of cuts down her chest bisected her small breasts, deepening as they progressed to her flat belly.

Fenchurch sucked in cold air and blinked back the tears. 'Cover her over, for crying out loud.'

'Right, yes. Of course.' Dr Pratt pulled her top back down. He stood up with a groan. 'That's some impressive butchery there.'

'You think this is a pro?'

'It was a mere turn of phrase, my dear Simon. Has all the hallmarks of a rage attack.'

'Right.'

'Watch out!' Nelson dumped a desk on its side, blocking the view from the door. He panted as he got out his Airwave Pronto and tapped the stylus against the touchscreen. 'DS Reed said we're not sure if this girl's—'

'Good heavens.' Pratt pawed at the device. 'Where can I get my hands on one of those?'

12

'We're trialling it just now. Be a while before you're trusted with one.' Nelson raised an eyebrow. 'Now, is this girl a prostitute?'

'Right, right. Well, I'm not so sure. She's very young but…' Pratt brushed the back of his hand across his mask, the blue Nitrile glove squeaking. 'I've seen them younger, more's the pity. A telltale sign would be evidence of hard drug use, but her arms are clear of track marks and her gums are clean.' He pointed at a SOCO dusting a few metres away. 'We did find this, though, which confuses things somewhat.'

Fenchurch craned his neck around. A purple 'Hello Kitty' bag lay on the carpet tiles. The zip was open at the top, with a similarly branded notepad peeking out. 'That hers?'

'Could be.'

'I want no assumptions made here.'

'As if I would.' Pratt cleared his throat. Took another couple of attempts to dislodge whatever was in there. 'Assuming it's hers, though, it looks like she's a schoolgirl.'

'I'll get someone analysing the notebook.' Nelson clicked the stylus off the Pronto's screen again. 'You got a time of death?'

'I've got cause of death, blood toxicology, an ID and a list of all of her sexual partners.'

Nelson frowned at him. 'How've you got that?'

'I'm winding you up.' Pratt laughed. His suit crinkled as he raised a long thermometer. 'Body temperature is five degrees centigrade, which is a few degrees above what passes for room temperature in this place. That gives me . . .' He tilted his head from side to side, clicking his tongue. 'Sometime last night. Ten o'clock? Well, there or thereabouts.'

Nelson scribbled it on his Pronto. 'Anything else?'

'Think we've found the murder weapon.' Pratt held up an evidence bag. A Stanley knife. Congealed blood smeared the small triangle of blade sticking out of the grey-blue metal case. 'Our

American cousins would call this a boxcutter. Unfortunately, who-ever did this treated this young lady as a box.'

'And it matches the wounds?'

'They're consistent, but I shall arrange for Mr Clooney to con-firm it's our weapon, of course.'

'ASAP, please. And check for prints and DNA.' Nelson took the bag and stared at it. 'What a bloody mess. It's either what killed this poor girl or we've got another death elsewhere.' He handed the bag back. 'Any DNA traces on her?'

Dr Pratt waved at the body. 'Mixed in with the blood on her abdomen is what we think is semen.'

'Semen?'

'It would appear someone ejaculated on her.'

'Before or after death?'

'Impossible to tell.' Pratt drummed his fingers on his suit. 'Once Mr Clooney and his team are finished with her, I'll have a look in Lewisham. Then we'll run a blood toxicology and all that good stuff.' He knelt back down again and fiddled in his medical bag.

A tap on Fenchurch's shoulder accompanied by a blast of after-shave. 'Simon.' A Scottish snarl.

Fenchurch took a step back and twisted to the side. 'Boss.'

DCI Docherty was prodding a gloved finger at a vanilla Airwave. The blue SOCO suit hung loose off his skeletal frame. 'Just spoken to the City of London Police.'

'Told you they'd be sniffing round, sir.'

'Aye, looking for some bloody glory.'

Flashlights bounced off the ceiling tiles. 'This building's on the City boundary, boss.'

'Anything on Mansell Street's ours. Besides, they've got neither the resources nor the expertise to deal with this.' Docherty's voice echoed around the room. Too loud, as ever. Everything had to be shouted. 'Need you to get on with this while I argue the bloody toss with them.'

'No problem. There's a mother out there who's lost her daughter.' Fenchurch cracked his knuckles through the gloves and walked off. He took one last look at the victim, now surrounded by a gang of crime-scene photographers, and waited until Nelson caught up with him. 'Thanks for taking the bullets from our friendly neighbourhood pathologist, Jon.'

'Pratt by name, Pratt by nature.'

Chapter Three

Reed was leaning against the building's exterior wall, talking on her mobile. She raised a finger at Fenchurch and turned away.

A young uniform held out a clipboard to them. 'I need you to sign out, sir.'

'Did DS Reed pass the Crime Scene Manager role to you?'

'She did, sir.'

Fenchurch did the honours and pressed the form back into the officer's stomach. 'There you go.' He started off across the bus station.

Glowing City towers dominated the skyline. The lights of the Minories' pubs and bars twinkled in the distance, busy with Wednesday night after-work idiocy. Nearby drinkers were shouting into the night sky, howling at the moon.

Fenchurch stared back at the building and sighed. 'What the hell happened in there, Jon?'

Nelson just shrugged.

Reed appeared, clicking her clamshell phone shut and swapping it for her Airwave Pronto. 'That's my mother-in-law staying an extra three hours, guv. Anyway, I've got twenty officers on their way over from Leman Street and Brick Lane.'

'Good work.' Fenchurch held her gaze until she looked away. 'It goes without saying we need to identify the victim. Kay, you're managing the street teams.'

'On it.'

'Get a team going round the street girls down Commercial Street and Whitechapel High Street. Find out if our victim is a prostitute or not.'

'Already on it.'

'Good, good. Pratt reckons she was killed at ten o'clock last night. Someone could've been working late or out drinking and spotted those two enter that infernal place.'

'No problem, guv.'

'And I want you to check with the local schools.'

'Control are getting the out-of-hours numbers for me.' Reed pocketed her Pronto. 'If that comes to nothing, I'll get people into the schools first thing tomorrow.'

'Good work.'

A clatter came from over by the building. Pratt was lugging his medical bag out of the door. He splashed his foot in a deep puddle and waved his hands around like he'd just lost his life savings.

Fenchurch looked back at Reed. 'You said the security guard found her. Has anyone spoken to her yet?'

'Not in any detail.' She pointed over to a small hut at the edge of the bus station. 'That's her office, guv. Her name's Selma Burns.'

— —

Fenchurch knocked on the door and waited in the dank corridor. A tall gunmetal-grey cabinet dominated the space. The green walls were more chipped than painted. 'You lead in here, okay?'

Nelson nodded slowly. 'You think she could know something?'

'This is East London, Sergeant. Everybody knows something.'

Nelson tried the door. It swung open. Inside, the mid-grey wallpaper was torn and hanging off. Even worse than the corridor.

A woman sat at a wooden desk covered in CRT monitors. She was playing with an iPad Mini, a card game filling the small screen. Rolls of flab stretched the buttons on her white blouse close to popping. 'Yeah?'

'Selma Burns?'

'That's me.' She smiled at Nelson, her lines deepening. She ran a hand through her blonde hair, exposing grey roots. 'Can I help?'

'DS Nelson and this is DI Fenchurch.' He flashed his warrant card. 'We've got a few questions about the body you found in Little Somerset House.'

'I've already given a statement.'

'And we appreciate that. Unfortunately, we need to ask more specific questions.'

Selma gestured at a stack of chairs on the far side of the room. 'Take a seat.'

Fenchurch stayed by the door.

Nelson grabbed a folding seat and cracked it open. He sat next to her and got out his Pronto. Then patted down his suit. The stylus was in his trouser pocket. 'Can you start with finding the body, please?'

'This again . . .' Selma shook her head to the heavens. 'I found the girl when I was doing my rounds. I manage a few buildings in this neighbourhood. I visit them every night to check nobody's dossing there. My portfolio shrinks by the year. Supposed to be demolishing the whole lot.'

'And Little Somerset House is part of this portfolio?'

'That's what I'm told to call it. I manage Bain Dawes and Latham Houses as well. Done it since they shut them down ten years ago. Might be eleven now.'

'That's a long time.' Nelson waved at the banks of monitors. 'And I take it you spend the rest of the time watching the CCTV.'

'Well, I would. Problem is it doesn't work.' She tugged at a cable coming from a tape machine. 'The feed from the buildings died three years back. I've been nagging my supervisor to get it repaired. It's fallen on deaf ears like everything else in this bloody place. They just don't want to spend the money.' She blew air over her face. 'They're building a skyscraper on this site. Can't remember the name but it'll swallow up the bus station, too. Been at it for years but it's ground to a halt what with all that austerity business.'

'There are quite a few buildings going up around here, though.'

'Don't I know it. Used to manage half of them before they knocked them down.'

'Who do you work for?'

'Hutchison and Barker.'

'The security firm. I've heard of them. We'll need a contact there.'

Selma scowled at him. 'My supervisor's called Jason Smith.'

Nelson tapped a note on his Pronto. 'Who owns this place?'

'I've no idea.'

'You've worked here ten years and you don't know who owns it?'

'All I know is it's some big firm. I think it changes all the time. It's not my business to ask questions.'

'You got any idea who that girl might be?'

'The way you're talking, it's like you think I done it.'

'And did you?'

'Of course I bloody didn't!' She stabbed a finger on her iPad. 'Never seen her in my life.'

'Did you see anyone leave? Say last night, about ten.'

'Nope.'

'You ever find any used condoms in that building?'

'What's that supposed to mean?'

'It's a straight question. Did you find any contraceptives in there? Used or otherwise.'

'Sometimes.'

'What about near the body?'

'I found nothing.'

'Do you get many prostitutes in there?'

'A few. It's mostly kids from the flats on Mansell Street, though.'

'But you do get prostitutes in here?'

Selma sucked in a deep breath. 'My boss told me to keep quiet.'

'Keep quiet about what?'

'Between you, me and him.' Selma thumbed across to Fenchurch. 'Those hookers have been using this place for years.' She bared her teeth. 'If girls want to use this place for a quick bit of how's your father, I'm not stopping them.'

'You could speak to the police.'

'Been told not to.'

'This boss of yours tells you not to do a lot of things. You wouldn't be taking a backhander from the girls, would you?'

She slammed a meaty fist on the tabletop. Her iPad jumped in the air, flipping around ninety degrees. 'My orders are to keep any dossers out. That's it.'

Nelson got to his feet. 'I'll get a colleague in here to add all that to your statement.'

'Thanks for your time, Ms Burns.' Fenchurch left the room first and started off down the grimy corridor. 'You were a right charmer in there, Jon.'

'Learnt from the best, haven't I?'

'And you've learnt from me.'

'I was going to use that line.'

'Why I got in there first.' Fenchurch stopped at the top of the stairs. 'Think it's worth looking into her background?'

'Much as I don't like the fact she's been ordered to turn a blind eye, I don't think she knows anything.' Nelson put his hands in his pockets. 'I'll track down this Jason Smith geezer. And look into the ownership of that place. Doubt it'll give us much, but you never know.'

'Decent idea. I'm going back to base. I want to get to Docherty before Mulholland does.'

Chapter Four

Fenchurch turned right onto Leman Street, rain hissing off his tyres. The new tower climbed into the sky, its ground floor still not finished. Across the road, cranes dragged another new skyscraper up to ground level. The new London, climbing out of the worst parts of the old.

Ahead, Leman Street was dark and mercifully empty. He powered through the lights and passed even more new buildings. The painted white brick of the Garrick Theatre was now a rare antique in the area. He took a right then a quick left. *There we go.* A free space just by the red-brick station's rear entrance.

One of the civilian staff out on a smoke break gave a mock salute accompanied by a wink.

Fenchurch threw his ID lanyard around his neck and got out of his car. Still hadn't fixed the crack in the security door's glass. He entered the building and flashed his credentials at the desk sergeant. 'Evening, Steve.' A grunt and a buzz as the gate opened. Then he started the long climb up the back stairs. The light on the first floor was blinking. Almost a regular pattern. Just not.

A privately educated English accent bled through Docherty's office door. Mulholland had beaten him to it yet again.

Fenchurch stopped and stared up at the ductwork on the ceiling. Need to be faster next time. He opened the door and cleared his throat. 'Evening, boss.'

Docherty got up and tucked his baggy shirt into his loose trousers. Spiky white hair stood to attention, still dark in patches. 'Nice of you to join us, Simon.' He held out a bony hand to Fenchurch.

Fenchurch reached out to shake it.

Docherty snatched it away. 'Too slow.'

'You never get tired of that.'

'Never tire of seeing you fall for it.' Docherty sat back in his chair and ran a hand through his hair. 'Have a seat.'

Fenchurch stayed standing. Still couldn't make eye contact with Mulholland. 'Sir, I want—'

'Just a sec, Si.' Docherty pointed to Fenchurch's left. 'Dawn was asking to be made Deputy SIO.'

'Evening, Simon.' DI Dawn Mulholland tightened her black scarf then rubbed her hands together, her skin still holiday brown. Older than Fenchurch but looked about five years younger. 'Do you need me to repeat it?'

Fenchurch just folded his arms. 'You're on nights this month, Dawn.'

'And this case relates to prostitution.' She smiled. 'Ladies of the night, as you say.'

'Does it?' Fenchurch finally locked eyes with her. Dark brown pools, looked like a tunnel down to hell. 'That's a big assumption, Dawn. She looks more like a schoolgirl to me.'

'And you'd know?'

Fenchurch held her gaze then switched it to Docherty. 'Boss, why did you ask me to attend if I'm not Deputy SIO?'

'Fair point.' Docherty leaned back in his seat. The metal creaked and rattled. 'Dawn, Simon's deputising on this.'

Mulholland shook her head. 'But, sir—'

His eyes drilled into both of them. '*But* I expect you to work closely, okay?'

Fenchurch sat next to Mulholland and tried not to smile. 'As if I'd do anything else.'

Docherty raised his dark eyebrows at Mulholland. 'You okay with that, Dawn?'

She gave a shrug. 'The joys of being on nights, boss. I'll wait till it's Simon's turn.'

'The joys, indeed.' Docherty drummed his fingers on the desk. 'Anything else I should know from the crime scene, Si?'

'Jon and I just interviewed the guard who found the body.'

'You've got a team for tasks like that, you know.'

'DS Nelson led the interview. I just wanted to hear it first hand to see if we're missing any angles.' Fenchurch rested against the chair's arms. 'She reckons she was instructed not to report any prostitutes using the building. Jon's trying to get hold of her manager now.'

Docherty scribbled something on his Pronto. He stabbed the stylus against the screen a few times. Enough force to crack it if he kept it up. 'Bloody thing.' He clipped the stylus to the side and dumped it on his desk. 'Right, children, let's get a plan of attack together. As far as I know, we've got a girl in a derelict building with her throat sliced wide open. What else do we know?'

'Nothing so far. Literally.' Fenchurch put his hands in his pockets. Gripped his phone and his wallet tight. 'Still don't have an ID. She could be a schoolgirl, could be a prostitute. Determining which might help.' He folded his arms. 'We need to get a press release out while it's still fresh, boss.'

'It doesn't look good to go around asking who a dead body is, does it?'

Always wondering about how things bloody look.

Docherty tugged his hair down. 'Let's hold off until we've exhausted every other avenue. Anything else for now?'

'DS Reed's managing the street teams. Targeting businesses, pubs and schools in the area. Got a team speaking to the prostitutes to see if they know the victim.'

'Covering all the bases. Good.' Docherty nodded at Mulholland. 'Dawn, can your team take over?'

Fenchurch glowered at him. 'I've only just given them their orders.'

'Aye, and I don't want your team knackering themselves on day one by pulling an overnighter. There's a reason I've got my three DIs on rotation.' Docherty grabbed his suit jacket from the back of his seat. 'But the City of London lot are on their way over. I want you with me.'

———⌣———

The lights flickered on as Fenchurch followed Docherty into the top-floor conference room. As posh as it got in Leman Street. The place stank of marker pens and cleaning fluids. 'Know who the City are sending, boss?'

'DI Clarke and DCI Thompson.'

'Never heard of them.'

'You and me both, pal.' Docherty sat at the head. He locked his BlackBerry and spun it round on the table. 'You okay, Simon?'

Fenchurch let out a breath. 'What makes you think I'm not?'

'I heard about you kicking up a stink at the crime scene.'

'Pratt and Clooney had been careless. The girl needs some dignity.'

'Sure it's not because—'

The door slid open. A male officer in full City uniform stepped through the doorway, peaked cap under his arm. Heavy-set, looking like he belonged on a Dorset pig farm. 'DCI Thompson. Which one of you gentlemen is DCI Docherty?' The sort of accent that let you into private members' clubs.

'That's me.' He was spinning his BlackBerry on the desk again.

Thompson sat next to him. 'Nice to meet up, one Chief Inspector to another.'

'You are a Detective, though, right? The woolly suit's throwing me.'

'Our brass like us to dress up when we come out of our high castle.' Thompson adjusted his black tie before shrugging the jacket off onto the chair. 'That's better.' He frowned at Fenchurch. 'Who are you?'

'DI Simon Fenchurch.'

Another uniformed officer appeared, zipping up his flies. He dried his hands on his trouser legs. Muscular with a dark spray tan, hair even whiter than Docherty's. 'DI Steve Clarke.'

Fenchurch grinned. 'Didn't you just get sacked by Reading?'

Clarke rolled his eyes as he sat near Thompson. 'Never heard that one before.' Could've worked on Bishopsgate with that accent.

'Gentleman, if you're quite done?' Thompson let Fenchurch and Clarke settle. 'The reason we're here's twofold.' He pushed his hands together, forcing the fingers vertical. Pudgy little things, just little stumps covered in thick hair. 'Firstly, Little Somerset House is almost our jurisdiction.'

'Aye, almost.' Docherty sat back in his chair. Legs wide, like he owned the place. 'As you're well aware, it's outside the City of London boundary. Mansell Street's ours. I'd have been washing my hands of this case if it was either of the other two buildings.'

'This is on the fringe of the City and the East End, Chief Inspector. A few metres west and you're in our land. The area's of prime concern to us.'

'And I'm very pleased for you. That body was in Met territory, not City. End of. Okay? Done.' Docherty got up.

Thompson waved him back down. 'We're very far from done.'

Docherty took a few seconds before sitting. 'Any idea how many times a year I have this sort of dispute, whether it's with you lot, Kent or Essex?' He pinched his lips together. Thompson and Clarke didn't butt in. 'Last year it was seventy-three times. I'm surprised we've never locked horns before.'

'You're Scottish.'

'Well spotted. Ex-Lothian and Borders. That's Edinburgh, in case you're wondering.' Docherty pocketed his BlackBerry and flashed a smile. 'Listen, lads. We work in one of the most densely populated areas in the world. This kind of thing happens all the time. The way we sort it out is by looking at where our boundaries are. Little Somerset House is in our bit of London, more's the pity.'

'Before you two get into a "my dad's bigger than your dad" thing, I should make you aware of something.' Fenchurch tried to ease out the kink in his spine again. 'We don't have an ID on the body yet.'

He got Clarke's attention, Thompson just fluttered his eyes. 'Meaning?'

'Meaning it's not an open-and-shut case. If you're thinking you can swoop in and tick off another row on your spreadsheet, then think again.'

'Thanks for that input, Inspector.' Thompson held his gaze. 'My superiors have asked me to take an active interest in this case.'

'Have they now . . .' Docherty clicked his teeth together a few times. 'Listen, I know what you lot are like. If it's not the Uzi ninjas up on Bishopsgate, it's financial crime. Some wee lassie getting cut up in a disused building doesn't sound like your cup of Châteauneuf-du-Pape.'

'I'm more of a Bollinger guy. Krug at a push.' Thompson laughed, tilting his head back as he roared. He sniffed at the lack of reaction. 'We're concerned about the proximity of the crime scene to our jurisdiction. We need to be party to all investigations relating to the City and its denizens.'

Docherty winked at him. 'That's too many long words for a wee laddie like me.'

'I expect you'll find some way to stray into my territory. When that happens, you call us.'

'Deal.' Docherty shrugged, like he was ordering a sandwich. 'That us?'

'That's us.' Thompson raised an eyebrow as he gestured at his colleague. 'Inspector Clarke will be your primary conduit.'

'And DI Fenchurch will be the one calling him, okay?'

Fenchurch gritted his teeth. Here we go. Dragged into this shit now. He locked eyes with Clarke. The guy looked as bored by the pissing-up-the-wall contest as he was. Pair of pillocks still acting like they're in a bloody playground.

Thompson kneaded his ruddy face before picking up his jacket. 'I'll need to re-engage my superiors to ensure they're in accord with this, but I think we've got a working agreement.'

Docherty raised his eyebrows and flashed a grin. 'Wouldn't dream of doing it any other way.'

'Until the next time.' Thompson stood up and nodded at Fenchurch. 'Inspector.' He stormed out of the room, leaving Clarke to shut the door behind them.

'Christ on a bloody bike.' Docherty tightened his face. 'Pair of them couldn't tie their own bloody shoelaces.'

'Doubt it's the last we've heard from them, boss.'

'Never is, but thank Christ they've buggered off. This case is far too much like hard work for them.'

'They do have a point about the jurisdiction, though.'

'Whatever.' Docherty dug Fenchurch in the chest. 'Just don't make their dad call me up about it, okay?'

Chapter Five

Fenchurch pulled into the space right outside the flat. For once. He opened the car door. The second half of his burrito fell out, spilling some rice onto the tarmac. 'Bloody hell.' He picked it up as he got out.

The cold wind hit his face and he tugged his jacket tight. Above, Canary Wharf's towers twinkled in the night sky. A roll of thunder pealed down from a plane coming in to land at City Airport. He remote-locked the Mondeo and bounded up the five steps in one stride. His old man's thighs grumbled as he landed.

Inside, his pigeonhole was empty. Same as it ever was. He locked it and set off up the stairs. The vaguest whiff of marijuana from across the carpeted hall. Grinding hip-hop cannoned through the dark-grey door. Bloody City playboys monkeying about again.

Fenchurch opened his door and stepped inside the dark flat. He bumped his thigh off the ironing board. Bloody thing was still plugged in. Stupid, stupid bastard. He crouched down and turned it off. At least it had switched itself off.

He set the burrito down on the kitchen counter and searched for a clean plate. Nothing. The dirty dishes still filled the sink. He didn't need a cleaner so much as a mum.

He reached into the cupboard for some hot sauce. Not much left. Three splashes and that was it. Where did it all go?

He leaned back against the counter and ate a mouthful. Fire burnt his tongue as he took another bite.

He got a bottle of wine out of the rack. The last one. An Aldi Rioja. Need a lot more to get through Christmas. Maybe Nelson would be up for another booze cruise . . .

He uncorked it and poured some into the only clean teacup. Let it breathe for a bit. He put the corkscrew back in the drawer, almost the only thing in there, and sucked in the wine's aroma. Dark and chocolatey. Maybe it wouldn't need that much breathing, after all.

Sod the playboys next door. He cued up Morrissey's *Your Arsenal* on his Sonos and the bass line thudded through the flat. He raised the cup to the glam-rock stomp of 'You're Gonna Need Someone On Your Side'.

Anyone would do.

Fenchurch grimaced slightly and grabbed the burrito, bottle and teacup. He took them out onto the balcony, leaving the door open. A swift kick shook the rainwater off the patio chair. The side wall gave him the night view without the wind as the Thames sucked away London's daytime warmth.

He finished the burrito as he took in the night's activity, scattering rice and beans on the concrete between his feet.

What a pathetic existence. Shivering on a patio with cold food and cheap wine.

He reached into his pocket for his mobile and dialled Nelson.

'Guv?'

'Stand at ease, soldier.' Fenchurch smiled as he splashed out another glass with his free hand. He jammed the plastic cork on, his thumb wrestling with the catch. 'Just checking on progress.'

'And I could've sworn we had a briefing at seven tomorrow for that very purpose.'

Fenchurch couldn't help but laugh. 'Wanted to see if there's anything I can worry about as I struggle to get off to sleep tonight.'

'Nobody's got anything so far, guv. Tried that building manager but he's foxtrot oscared for the night. Just off home myself. Kate's put an M&S ready meal in the oven for me.'

'The oven? She's treating you?'

'I'm salivating as I drive, mate.' Nelson paused, engine sounds swelling up down the line. 'One of Mulholland's lads relieved me. Tell me she's not the Deputy?'

'I am, but I'm still counting my teeth from the fight she gave.'

'I love the friendly atmosphere you DIs have instilled. Sends an example to the rest of us.'

'It's not our atmosphere but that of our beloved leader.' Fenchurch took another drink. Delicious. 'I'll see you first thing tomorrow. Goodnight.'

'Night.'

Fenchurch ended the call and stretched out in the cool air. A rush of warmth hit his face. The open bottle stared up at him. He finished the second teacup and poured another.

A girl, blue eyes ringed by hair. Smiling, her cheek dimpled. Eight years old and hiding from her father. Chasing her, catching her, tickling her. Squealing out. Laughing.

He swallowed hard and gritted his teeth. Finished the glass. Didn't feel any better. Maybe felt worse. Just a trickle left in the bottle.

A dimpled cheek smiling at him.

A dimpled cheek dead. Stabbed, gouged wide open.

He reached into his shirt collar and grabbed hold of his chain. Unhooked it and let it dangle to the ground. He put his finger through the wedding ring, the gold long since tarnished. It still fit.

Would've been worse if it was pristine, like that geezer with the painting in his attic.

He picked up his phone and stared at the contacts page. Still the first one. He pressed dial. It just rang and rang. Bloody thing.

Second entry was a house number, North London area code. A few seconds of sipping. Then he hit the button. More ringtone.

'Hello?'

Caught him unawares. 'Abi. It's Simon.'

A pause filled with a deep sigh. 'Simon? It's twenty past ten.'

'Sorry. I just needed to speak to you.'

She yawned. 'Right?'

'I've been thinking about Chloe today. A case came in this evening. A young girl. She'd be Chloe's age.'

'A murder?'

He nodded. Couldn't force the words out. 'I don't know what to think.'

'Is it her?'

He wiped at his cheek – damp. 'No.' Blinked hard in the light. 'I don't think it is, anyway. Looks nothing like her, even ten years on.'

'Simon, why are you doing this to me?'

'It just hit me like a train.'

'You're finally trying to process it after ten years?'

He swallowed and shut his eyes. 'I'm sorry.'

'You're sorry? I lived with a zombie for two years and you're sorry *now*?'

A car pulled into a parking bay below. Someone he didn't recognise. Making a bloody mess of it. Better not scratch his car.

'You can't just phone me up out of the blue and do this.'

'Look, I shouldn't have phoned. I'll hang up, if you want.'

No response. Just breathing.

Fenchurch stared down at the car. Looked like a City boy in an Uber car. What was wrong with bloody taxis? 'I'd like to see you.'

Another deep sigh down the line. 'Simon . . .'

'Just for a coffee.'

'I can't. We . . .' Sounded like she gasped. 'I've not heard from you in years and now this? It's over, Simon. It's been over for years. You know that.'

Fenchurch took another glug of wine. Still fiddled with the ring. 'Do you want me to hang up?'

No response.

'Goodnight, Abi.' Fenchurch prised the phone away from his face and ended the call.

His breath hung in the air in front of him. Across the street, the couple were arguing behind the decorative trees on their patio. Same as it ever was.

His jaw tightened. He finished the cup and shivered. Glad there's no whisky inside. He got up and nudged the door open.

Day 2
Thursday, 17th December 2015

Chapter Six

Fenchurch took a gulp of builder's tea. Strong and milky. Those extra-strong teabags really cut the mustard. Wind rattled the token-gesture trees outside the station. The sky above the narrow corridor of Leman Street was still dark.

He turned to look across the Incident Room. Yawns, muffled phone calls and fingers caressing laptop keyboards. Mulholland was hovering by the whiteboard, filling in some detail. A whole night and she'd progressed bugger all by the looks of things.

The clock hit seven and he clapped his hands together. 'Come on, you lot. Briefing time.'

Nelson wandered over, flanked by a pair of DCs. Reed got up from her laptop and hugged her suit jacket tight. She perched on the edge of her desk and sipped from a can of Red Bull.

Another gulp of tea. 'I appreciate some of you have been in all night, so I'll keep this brief.' He focused on Reed. 'Kay, where have the street team got to?'

'Just been brought up to speed, guv.' She grimaced over at the female night-shift DS. Dark brown hair tied up in a ponytail. Icy stare. Jennifer something. 'We've got nothing of note, I'm afraid.'

'Define nothing.'

'Nobody in the pubs saw anything.' Reed yawned into her fist. 'We've checked the Minories, Aldgate High Street and the back streets round this way. That's all going on the assumption people drinking on Tuesday would've gone back on Wednesday. From what we can gather, Tuesday night was pretty quiet.'

'In that case, nothing's a decent summary.' Fenchurch went up to the whiteboard. Mulholland glared at him for a few seconds and shifted to the side. He scribbled a note in the *Actions* box. 'Make sure you get into the offices today. Look for anyone working late on Tuesday night.'

'Already on the docket, guv. Going to get onto it after we've cleared the schools.' Reed crumpled her can and rested it on the desk. 'We've spoken to all the prostitutes we could find in the vicinity.' Her fist covered another yawn. 'One of them saw a man walking down Commercial Street, asking anyone he came across if he could "buy them".'

'Isn't that common parlance for you know what?'

'Hardly. He wanted to own them outright.' She adjusted her hair, flicking it behind her ears. 'Sounds like this guy was approaching a lot of women. Including non-prostitutes. We've got a statement from a waitress in the Mexican restaurant halfway up.'

'That's a regular haunt of mine.' Fenchurch made a note of it on the board. Still didn't get what any of it meant. He put the pen down. 'Did he do anything else?'

'Not that we know of. We're taking detailed statements from these women. As detailed as it gets, anyway.'

'Extend the CCTV search to include Commercial Street, okay? If some idiot's trying to buy prostitutes, I want him excluded as soon as possible.'

'Guv.'

Fenchurch finished his tea and plonked the cup on the table under the window. He focused on the wide prairie of the white-board. 'Anything else?'

'One of my team's analysing the notebook.' Mulholland stabbed a finger on *Hello Kitty*, right in the centre. 'No DNA on it. There were prints, though. Bad news is they don't match anyone on the system.'

'So she's still unknown.' Fenchurch added the note, unsure why she hadn't bothered. Other than to get attention and show him up, maybe. 'We're still assuming it's our victim's book and bag. Anything in the content?'

'Well, the owner of the book seems mentally underdeveloped for her age. The handwriting is like a small child's, maybe seven or eight. Looked like she was practising spelling.'

Bloody hell. Fenchurch stared at Nelson. Kept his eyes off Mulholland. 'Jon, can you get people looking at similar cases with a lack of ID?'

'Sure thing, guv.' Nelson scribbled on his Pronto. 'While I've got my fifteen minutes, I've managed to track down Jason Smith, the building manager's supervisor. Nobody's spoken to him so far.'

'Then let's head out there after this.'

Mulholland narrowed her eyes, like a cat about to pounce on a mouse. 'Simon, I think we're at the point where we have to put out a press release. Don't you?'

Fenchurch held her gaze. Watch who you're attacking. 'It's the next logical step. I'll raise it with DCI Docherty again.'

'After you go to the post-mortem?'

'I'm awaiting instruction on that.' Fenchurch looked around the room. 'For the record, I'm the Deputy SIO on this case. DI Mulholland is covering for me in the hours of darkness. Clear?'

The old Southwark warehouses were now all designer apartments and offices. Ancient maritime frontage to modern shells. Audis and Mercs jammed the street. Not even the congestion charge discouraged the City boys from driving.

'Always hate going south of the river.' Fenchurch got out of the car. 'The traffic's a bloody nightmare.'

Nelson grinned over the roof. 'You're full of joy this morning.'

Fenchurch wrapped up against the biting cold. Still dark in the sky, just a faint glow to the east. 'Maybe I should let you run back to the station. You know the route, don't you?'

'Yeah, from Canary Wharf.' Nelson bellowed with laughter. 'Believe me, it'd be better than listening to you moan about the traffic.' He waved at an old wharf building across the road, a canal running underneath. The Hutchison and Barker logo shouted out in lime green on a grey background. 'This is us here, I think.' He darted between two idling BMWs and opened the building's front door. The wind almost tore it off. 'After you.'

Fenchurch led into a brightly lit corridor. Boards of rental properties lined the walls, some of them a cop's salary for a week's rent. He peered through the glass into the dark reception space. Looked a world away from Selma Burns' office in Little Somerset House. Stripped brick covered with vintage photographs of Southwark's prime days as a port. An old bread oven filled the far wall.

The lights flickered on. A middle-aged woman dumped her leather gloves onto the desk. Then a heavy overcoat.

Nelson rapped on the glass door and flashed his warrant card.

She hurried over and shifted her scowl from the card to him. A streak of grey lined her shoulder-length fringe. She unlocked the door and opened it an inch. 'Can I help, officers?'

'DS Nelson. DI Fenchurch. We're looking to speak to Jason Smith.'

'In you come.' She went back over and checked her computer. Grinding came from somewhere to the left, faint and distant. 'Mr Smith's diary's currently free, Sergeant. You can go through.' She nodded at a hole in the wall. Whoever had renovated the place hadn't bothered with the trivialities of putting a door in. 'It's on the right through there.'

'Thanks.' Nelson led, climbing a couple of steps. He pushed at a door recessed into the brick. The office wall was dominated by a large print of the Arsenal Invincibles team in a huddle. 'Jason Smith?'

A man was behind a tall desk, typing at an iMac as he marched on a treadmill. The whirring suggested it wasn't that happy supporting his massive body. He squinted at them. 'Who are you?'

'DS Jon Nelson. This is DI Simon Fenchurch.' Another wave of his warrant card. 'We understand your firm manages Little Somerset House.'

'That's correct.' Jason reached for a white towel on his desk and dried his fat face, breathing hard. 'I'll just give you the number of my building manager.'

'We spoke to Selma Burns last night.' Fenchurch hovered next to Nelson. 'We've got a few additional questions to ask you.'

'I see.' Jason started walking again, sucking at air. 'Shoot.'

'Do you mind stopping that?'

'Doctor's orders. I've lost six stone since I got this little baby. Down to twenty, aiming to lose another six by this time next year.'

'Your doctor won't mind you stopping for five minutes.' Fenchurch narrowed his eyes at him. 'Why did you tell her to let prostitutes service their clients in Little Somerset House?'

'Bloody hell.' Jason slowed to a halt and jumped off the machine. Another wipe then he draped the towel across his shoulders. Face like a smacked arse. 'Who told you that? Selma Burns?' He shook his head, the loose skin wobbling. 'She was to make sure nobody used the place as a squat, that's it.'

'So she never mentioned prostitutes to you?'

'Listen, I've no problem with that. They're in and out.' He smirked and raised a hand. 'Pardon the pun. I don't care so long as they don't stay there and it doesn't cost my client a bean. That's how we manage that place for our clients.'

'Who are they?'

'None of your business.'

'Not sure about that, sir. A young woman's turned up dead in their building. We'd appreciate speaking to them.'

'I assure you there's no connection between them and a junkie's corpse.'

'She wasn't a drug user, as far as we know. If you've got evidence to the cont—'

'Look, I just don't see them as being pertinent to your investigation.'

'Just tell us, sir.'

'No.'

Fenchurch barked out a bullet of laughter. 'We can get a warrant.'

A shard of sunlight flashed in the floor-to-ceiling windows and caught Jason's face. 'I'm not stopping you.'

'And I'm wondering why you're being so evasive. Turning a blind eye to prostitution probably warrants a word with one of our specialist units. They'll be here as soon as you get back on that treadmill.'

Jason ran the towel across his ruddy face again. 'Fine, fine. Darke Matter Capital own the building. That's Darke with an E. They're a hedge fund out in Canary Wharf.' He tossed the towel onto the desk. It missed, flapping to the floor like a seagull on a pile of chips. 'The contract's with a chap called Aleister Vaughn. That's with an E and an I.'

Bloody hedge funds. Love their obscure names as much as avoiding tax. Fenchurch scribbled it on his Pronto. 'Do you have many dealings with him?'

'I've met him once. That's it.' Jason bent down to collect the towel and dumped it on a radiator. 'They retained us from the previous owners. Operate very much at arm's reach. I send them an invoice every month and get a cheque in return.'

'This instruction about the prostitutes came from him, though, yeah?'

'It's not about prostitutes. Look, when they took it over, I went over to Canary Wharf to speak to Mr Vaughn. He explicitly instructed me to keep the budget tight. It'll be a struggle to get anyone as cheap as Selma if she ever left.'

'You're not a living-wage employer?'

'Bottom line's everything in this game.'

'Can you arrange a meeting with him?'

'I can try.' Jason fiddled with the mouse on his desk and glanced over. 'I'll make a call.'

'Be our guest.'

'I'd rather do it in private?'

'Would you now?' Fenchurch took a step forward. Just inches from Jason. His sweat stank like stale biscuits. 'I'd appreciate it if you set up the meeting now, sir.'

Jason opened his mouth to say something but stopped. He scratched at an eyebrow. 'Fine.' He picked up the phone and grinned as he spoke. 'Hi, Sara. It's Jason Smith. Yes, yes. Another stone. Yes. Listen, I've got some police officers here asking about Little Somerset. I take it you heard— Nasty business, I know. Well, I tried but they want to speak to Aleister. Yes, I think so. Yes. Okay.' He put a hand over the mouthpiece. 'How long will it take you to get to Canary Wharf?'

'This time of day?' Fenchurch let out a long breath. 'About half an hour, plus parking.'

Jason put the phone back to his ear and replaced the smile. 'They'll be there at quarter to nine. And if you could— Yes, the underground one. Thanks, Sara. Bye.' He lowered the phone and the smile. 'They're arranging parking.'

'I appreciate you doing that. Sounds like you're a regular there, though.'

Jason clambered onto the treadmill and stretched out the towel. 'I have other clients in that building.'

Fenchurch pushed the ice-cold handrail and spun through the revolving door. He marched across mid-brown flagstones towards the reception. Suited-and-booted office drones criss-crossed the open space. Chatter and clicking heels bounced off the hard surfaces, stone, chrome and glass.

What the hell was that?

Fenchurch stopped and leaned to the side.

In the far corner, a military helicopter crouched behind a Starbucks concession. The queue snaked around it, the propellers drooping down to head height. People checked phones, chatted about dates or childcare or bosses like a helicopter was normal.

Nelson chuckled. 'Quite some place this.'

'Tell me about it.' Fenchurch fumbled for his warrant card and flashed it at the security guard. 'DI Simon Fenchurch of the Met. Here to see Aleister Vaughn of Darke Matter Capital.'

'Darke Matter, eh?' The guard was a middle-aged Indian man. Grey streaked his black hair. He was missing the index finger on his left hand. 'Expecting you, is he?'

'His PA booked in the appointment.'

'Sara? Right, I'll see what's what.' The guard mumbled into a telephone handset, like he was incanting Satanic verse.

Fenchurch still couldn't take his eyes off the helicopter.

The guard smiled at them. 'Mr Vaughn will meet you upstairs. He's on the eighteenth floor.' He waved a hand across the foyer. 'The lifts are over there.'

Fenchurch nodded. 'What's with the helicopter?'

'The building owners bought it ten years ago. It served in Iraq, I believe.'

'So why's it here?'

'Now that I can't answer.'

Fenchurch marched across the flagstones to the lifts. All four doors were shut, mirror-perfect sheets of steel. He tapped their floor number on a keypad and it flashed up *Lift 1*. The door to their left slid open with a ping. 'Feels like I'm on bloody *Star Trek*.' He got inside.

The door just about shut on Nelson. 'Bloody thing.'

Fenchurch shook his head, laughing. 'Thing I love about London, Jon, is you've got millions of people stuffing themselves into a barely competent transport system every day. Forces them to get in at the crack of sparrow fart and work on late. All to avoid getting crushed on the bloody Northern Line. Means we can always speak to someone no matter how stupid the time is.'

'You should try getting from West London to Aldgate in the morning, guv.'

'Bollocks to West London.'

The lift doors slid open and Fenchurch stepped out onto a marble floor. Dark walnut lined the pale-blue walls. A window looked west to the growing collection of towers in the City. The teeming rain obscured much beyond the Gherkin, the Cheesegrater and the Walkie Talkie, with its car-melting concave glass. The Shard speared the sky on the south bank surrounded by its smaller children.

'It's quite some view, isn't it?' A man stood to their right, grinning at them. Tall, thin and pale. Blonde hair hung across his eyes in a side parting. He fiddled with his double-collared shirt, resting just so under the jacket's sleeves. He stretched out a hand. 'Aleister Vaughn, Darke Matter Capital.'

'DI Fenchurch.' He smiled as he shook his hand, eyes narrow. 'And this is DS Nelson.'

'If you'll follow me into my office?' Vaughn strolled down the corridor, leather loafers clicking off the marble. He held open a matt-black door, grinning like a vampire inviting them into his lair, and pointed at a flotilla of four cream armchairs by the window. 'Please, have a seat.'

Fenchurch took the one nearest the glass. His flat was just below as the Thames kinked around Greenwich and the Isle of Dogs. 'Another nice view.'

'We pay a lot of money for them. I'd say it's worth it.'

Fenchurch waved at the pale-green wall. 'And that's some picture.'

A colossal landscape painting, a quaint pastoral scene. Carthorses and a group of men threshing wheat in front of an imposing stately home.

'Ah, that.' Vaughn undid his suit jacket's top button and perched on the chair next to Nelson. 'Yes, it's the family seat.'

'You're of the landed gentry?'

Vaughn held up his hands and smirked, eyebrows arched high. Like he was in some seventies sitcom. 'Try not to hold it against me, officers.'

'Not something we tend to do, sir.' Nelson waved around the place. The office looked like it took up a large chunk of the building's floor. 'I take it business is good?'

'Always is in this industry. We've built DMC to eighteen billion pounds under management in ten years. From scratch.'

Nelson's mouth slackened. 'Impressive.'

Fenchurch gave a shrug. 'I wish that meant something to me.'

Vaughn flicked up his eyebrows again and shifted to a frown. 'Now, I'm afraid Sara neglected to capture any details of your visit?'

Fenchurch unclipped the stylus from his Pronto's case. 'We gather you own Little Somerset House in Aldgate.'

'This business does, yes.'

'You'll be aware of a young woman's body being found there last night, of course.'

'Excuse me?'

'Do you need me to repeat it?' Fenchurch let it hang in the air and watched Vaughn squirm. 'Wouldn't happen to know anything about it, would you?'

'We own that building. That's it. The history of our involvement would send you to sleep.'

'I'm all ears.'

'It's a long and dull story, I'm afraid.' Vaughn smoothed down his suit trousers. 'We bought that one and its siblings in 2011. They represent a very small portion of one of the Property portfolios under my management.' He reclined in his seat and did a bit of manspreading. 'We're a small firm. Six on the board and an army of bean counters like myself to manage our assets. Plus a team who perform due diligence on acquisitions.'

'And I presume these buildings passed with flying colours?'

'Not exactly.' Vaughn gave a nervous laugh. Followed it with a calm smile. 'The previous owners went into liquidation in 2010. I'm afraid the whole portfolio had been rather poorly managed. When they acquired them in 2004, the campus carried a rental income in excess of two million pounds per month. With all the development in and around the City, they haemorrhaged tenants. The firm went bankrupt before they could get through planning.'

'Are you responsible for any of their difficulties?'

'Indirectly, maybe.' Vaughn brushed some fluff off his otherwise pristine shirt collar. 'The investment management community swell my Property funds because the fringe area of the City has been very lucrative for us. Fewer listed buildings and a surplus of postwar ones awaiting demolition.'

'Why buy a building with no tenants?' Nelson steepled his fingers. 'I would've thought a Property fund needed rental income.'

'It does.' Vaughn grinned at Nelson. 'You seem fairly well educated for a police officer.'

'I worked in financial services before I decided to do something with my life.'

Vaughn pursed his lips. 'Well, I used one of our development funds to purchase those buildings. The investors for those vehicles are encouraged to take a long-term view.'

'What's that particular site's objective, then?'

'We're working with our partners to build another prestige development.'

Fenchurch poked his tongue into his cheek. 'Like London needs any more.'

'London can support an awful lot more, believe me. The rest of the UK?' Vaughn snarled. 'Not so much.'

'And Hutchison and Barker manage the estate until the bulldozers go in.' Fenchurch propped his elbows onto the arms of the chair. 'We gather you know they let prostitutes use Little Somerset House.'

Vaughn spluttered. 'Excuse me?'

'You instructed your factors to turn a blind eye on them.'

'Did we now?' Vaughn cleared his throat, a manicured hand covering his mouth. 'Inspector, I'm a fund manager. We outsource all of that frippery to a specialist firm. Hutchison and Barker manage day-to-day operational matters.'

'You're telling me this is their decision, not yours?'

'That's correct.'

'They didn't discuss the matter with you?'

'I instructed them to minimise spend on an empty property. I'm a slave to my investors. Every pound spent is closely scrutinised, believe me. There's very little point in us, for example, reglazing a condemned building.'

'You didn't even have chipboard up, though.'

Vaughn shifted forward in his seat to perch on the edge. Looked like he could just topple off. 'If the Metropolitan Police Force let prostitutes carry crowbars, then that's your decision.'

'When do the bulldozers move in there?'

'We're still in the planning stages.'

'So they'll be getting away with this for the foreseeable?'

'Officers, I don't know what else I can give you. That building's an asset, that's all. I suggest you pick up with Hutchison and Barker directly.'

'We have.'

'I'll apply some pressure to ensure they support your investigation. Believe me, I want this killer caught as much as you do.'

'Thanks for your time.' Fenchurch got to his feet and handed him a business card. 'Give us a call if the pressure leads to anything.'

'Most certainly.' Vaughn led them across his office and held the door open. 'I mean it when I say this is bad for business. A prostitute being murdered in our asset won't bode well for the planning process. Not to mention reputational damage to the City fringe.'

'Your concerns are duly noted.' Fenchurch smiled then left him to it. He led Nelson back to the lifts and hammered the button for the basement. 'What a bleeding arsehole.' He let out a sigh and took in the view again. 'What do you make of his story, Jon?'

'Well, it tallies with what Jason Smith said.'

'Almost as if they had half an hour to plan it.' Fenchurch got in the lift and collapsed against the side. The cage shook a little. 'This is a bloody dead end.'

Chapter Seven

Fenchurch opened the Incident Room door. The place was a hell of a lot quieter than it should've been.

Reed sitting at a computer. Next to her, Bridge was rubbing her eyes. Reed stood up tall, eyes wide, forehead creased. 'You need to see this, guv.' She spun the laptop around.

A grainy CCTV shot of Victorian tenements, cars streaming by. A pedestrian trudged past, talking on her phone. Could've been anywhere.

'What am I supposed to be looking at?'

Reed stared at the monitor. 'That's Commercial Street, guv. Just by the Ten Bells pub.'

'I know it. Not far from Spitalfields Market, right?'

'Right.' Reed tapped Bridge's shoulder. 'Run it again.'

She pressed a finger into the corner of the screen. The time stamp read *22.02, 15/12/2015*. 'This is Tuesday night, sir. Around the time the girl was killed.' She hit a key.

The footage ran on and a man staggered onto the frame. Looked like he'd gone twenty rounds with George Best. He propped himself against a shopfront. Then struggled on.

Fenchurch scowled at Reed. 'This is all very amusing, Sergeant, but what's the point in this?'

'This is the geezer who was trying to buy people. Keep watching.'

The view flipped to further down Commercial Street. After a few seconds, the man appeared. He stopped a pair of women walking up. Miniskirts and leather boots, shivering against the cold. The one on the left shook her head. He shouted something at them.

Fenchurch hadn't noticed he was holding his breath. 'Have we got any audio on this?'

'Just video, sir.' Bridge tapped the keyboard and the footage shifted to a camera just by Lupita, halfway up the road.

A woman paced around at the bus stop across from the restaurant. Looked like she was keeping herself warm. Kept checking her mobile, white earbuds dangling down. The man from before lurched over and spoke to her, head tilted to the side. She shook her head and stared back at her phone. He got out his wallet and waved some cash in her face. She shook her head again and took a step back into the bus stop. He put his face right up to hers and held it there for a few seconds. He clicked his fingers in her face and walked on.

Bridge hammered the keys. 'This is the big one, sir.'

The man staggered up the ramp to the hulking RBS building on Aldgate High Street and reached into his pocket for his wallet again.

Fenchurch jabbed the screen. 'Does he work there?'

Reed brushed his finger away. 'Keep watching.'

A woman stood up and stretched out. She must've been sitting on the concrete. He showed her his wallet. She looked around for a few seconds then nodded.

Reed circled the woman on the display. 'This is our victim, guv.'

Fenchurch screwed up his eyes and tried to resolve the pixels. Tried to reconcile the living flesh with the body in the building. She certainly fit the description but it wasn't conclusive.

Her bag bounced up and down as she walked, made it look like *Hello Kitty* was waving.

'Well, it's her bag, whoever she is.' Fenchurch swallowed. 'Is this the guy who killed her?'

'Keep watching.'

The woman pointed down the back lane towards Little Somerset House. Bridge hit a key and the view changed to a camera a few doors down. It looked across to the bus depot and the Subway sandwich shop. Must be on Aldgate tube station.

The girl looked around and led him down Little Somerset Street. Another slapped key and they cut to a split view. The bus station camera was joined by another two, the clock whirring in double time.

'This is from the Minories.' Bridge tapped the monitor. 'And this one's by the Duke of Somerset pub at the other end of the lane.' She let it run on. The whole room was silent, just their breathing. She tapped the screen again. 'The girl doesn't reappear.'

'How long have you checked?'

'Six hours, sir. Our friend came out, though.' Bridge pressed a button on the keyboard.

The man strolled onto the camera by the Duke of Somerset, like he was going to meet a mate.

Fenchurch leaned forward to get a better view. 'When was this?'

'This is half an hour later.'

'Can you follow him?'

'I tried, sir.' Bridge messed up her hair again, leaving tufts sticking out in all directions. 'The coverage is pretty thin down Mansell Street. Lots of back streets he could've gone down.'

Fenchurch stood up and huffed. 'Is this is our killer?'

'I think so.' Reed held up a sheet of paper. 'This is as good as we've got, guv.'

Fenchurch snatched it off her. A pair of blurry screen grabs of the man and their victim. 'Get them run through the automatic CCTV system.'

'I'll try. Wouldn't hold your breath, though.'

'Feels like I'm making a habit of that.' Fenchurch handed the sheet back to Reed, snapping the paper tight. 'And get these to the street team.'

'Already on it, guv. Looks like our victim might be a prostitute.' Reed shrugged. 'Or she's homeless and looking for some money.'

'I don't disagree, but I'd like some more evidence.' Fenchurch checked his watch. 'I think it'd be an idea to get an appointment with Vice.'

'They're called Trafficking and Prostitution now.' Reed raised her eyebrows. 'And I can take a hint . . .' She smiled as she made a note. 'Oh, Docherty was looking for you. Said you're due out at Lewisham for the PM?'

'Shit.' Fenchurch set off towards the corridor. 'Get those Vice buggers to meet us here.'

Fenchurch opened his eyes again and stared at the brilliant-white tiles on the wall. At the ceiling. Anywhere, just so he didn't look at the body on the gurney. 'So, in conclusion?'

Pratt kept his focus on the girl, his eyelids flickering in quick succession. His beard looked like small birds could nest in it. He wiped his hands on the apron covering his waistcoat, his bow tie hanging untied. 'I've performed a full genital examination and analysed her paragenital areas. Breasts, inner thigh, buttocks.'

Clooney looked as queasy as Fenchurch felt. Fingertips on his shaved head, skinny arms creeping out of a bright-yellow Brazil

T-shirt. Socrates the philosopher dressed as his seventies footballer namesake. 'Yeah, yeah, we get it.'

'I've noted some vulvar inflammations and open lesions. There's no sign of any discharge, but it's enough to convince me that this young lady has had a lot of sexual activity recently. And not of a recreational variety. So, it would appear she is, indeed, a prostitute.'

The door opened and DCI Docherty appeared in the doorway. 'Oh look, the gang's all here!'

'And you've missed all the fun.' Dr Pratt went back to watching his assistant, a frail-looking Asian man, carefully slice a sliver off the heart.

Fenchurch's gut lurched. Just as well he hadn't eaten any breakfast.

Pratt looked up at Clooney then settled on Fenchurch. 'Now remember, gents. We don't discuss the DCI's toilet problems in public.'

Docherty rested against the wall and looked around the attendees. 'CPS not send anyone?'

'Not yet.' Pratt looked disappointed nobody'd laughed at his joke.

'Because she's a prostitute?'

'It's because they're busy, Alan.'

'Believe that when I see it. They'll be wrapping each other's Secret Santas just now.'

'I presume you'll want a summary?' Pratt stood up and rubbed his chin with his wrist, waiting for a response. He gave up with a tut. 'Well, for those who couldn't bring themselves to turn up on time, we've identified signs of forced intercourse. The spermicide found in her vagina indicates the use of an extra-strong condom.'

'So our killer was Mr Careful?'

'He's not exactly Charlie Sheen.' Pratt snapped off his gloves. 'Hopefully not too careful.' He nodded at Clooney, like he was cueing him up. 'And I'll pass over to our forensics god.'

Clooney's ear piercings rattled as he waved his arms over the girl's stomach. 'The mucus on her abdomen was, indeed, semen.'

Docherty scowled at Pratt. 'Thought the boy wore a condom?'

'And he did.' Pratt grimaced. 'I suspect he decided to *finish* in that manner.'

Docherty smiled at him. 'Couldn't it be from a previous client?'

'She would be unlikely to wander around with that stuff on her. It'd dry and flake off. This was perfectly intact, albeit merged with some blood.'

'So it's our killer's spunk?'

'The only conclusion we can draw.'

'Any clues on who he is?'

Clooney ran a hand over the stubble on his head, smirking away. 'You're the ones with video footage of her.'

Docherty frowned at Fenchurch. 'News to me.'

He raised a shoulder. 'I sent you a text, boss.'

'Like I've got time to read bloody text messages.' Docherty clapped Clooney on the arm. 'That DNA check's your highest priority, right? Our guy's screwed up here.' He grinned. 'Pardon the pun.'

'We're already on it, Al.'

'Okay. Good.' Docherty massaged his forehead. 'So, take me through your results.'

Pratt waved a gloved hand around her neck area. 'There were sixteen separate stab wounds to her throat and a further twenty-six to her mammary glands.' He leaned forward and prised apart the flesh on her chest. 'As you can see, they were cloven in two.'

'How did she die, William?'

'A melee attack of this nature results in a number of injuries. Exsanguination is the most likely cause of death.'

Fenchurch shut his eyes, acid reflux fizzing. 'She just bled out?'

'I'm afraid so. Would've taken maybe twenty minutes, I expect. The blow to her skull would've knocked her out, if that's any consolation.'

'Not much. Anything else?'

Pratt indicated her left arm. A rough grid of scratches covered it from hand to elbow. 'These are defensive wounds, confirming the fact she was attacked. We're still running checks on the blade we found at the crime scene.'

Clooney held up a bagged Stanley knife. 'We've got a blood-type match between this and our victim. Also found some prints on the handle.'

'Sounds promising.' Docherty moved around to stand a few inches away from the SOCO. 'So, what's next?'

'Blood toxicology's running.'

'Simon and I are first to know, right?' Docherty pointed at Fenchurch. 'Right, laughing boy, let's get back to base.'

'Cheers, William.' Fenchurch smiled at Pratt and followed Docherty into the bleached white of the vestibule. 'Surprised to see you out here, boss.'

'Had to chase that bugger at the Archive about one of Mulholland's bloody cases. Thought I'd pop in to wind up our friends there.'

Fenchurch laughed. 'Wasn't I doing a good enough job of it?'

'You always try to get them onside, Simon, that's your problem.'

'It's my style, boss. Trying to make sure they don't make a mess in a monkey shop.'

'A what?'

'Never mind. I'll keep them focused, sir. That DNA could crack this wide open.' Fenchurch opened the front door and the biting air cooled his burning cheeks. A plane rumbled low in the sky. The lunchtime smells from the canteen made his stomach growl. 'Good to be back outside, anyway.'

Docherty took a cigarette from a plain packet and stuck it between his lips. 'So you do get squeamish.'

'I hate post-mortems, boss, you know that.' Fenchurch's stomach rumbled even louder.

Docherty clicked at his lighter. 'Come on, you bastard.' He got a flame on the third go. 'That you or me rumbling?'

'Haven't had lunch yet.' Fenchurch adjusted the buttons on his suit jacket. 'I think it's time to get that press release done.'

'I'll get round to it this afternoon.' Docherty lit his cigarette and sucked in smoke like it was fresh air. 'Text you once it's done.' A frown danced across his forehead as he looked behind Fenchurch. It turned into a broad smile. 'Ian Fenchurch, as I live and breathe.' He held out a hand. 'How you doing, Fenchy?'

'Doc.' Fenchurch's dad cackled as he shook his hand. His eyes still had a twinkle the rest of his body had lost. Liver spots were using his face as a chessboard. 'I'm doing okay, Doc. Doing okay.'

Docherty glowered at Fenchurch then at his old man. 'So what are you doing here?'

'I'm working here again.' Dad tapped Fenchurch's arm. 'My boy put in a good word with the registrar at the Archive and they took me back. Me and old Bert have been in the Cold Case Unit since August.'

'Can't keep you retired. Still looking at that old case that got away?'

'Like an itch I can't scratch, Doc.'

Docherty sucked in a deep drag and patted Fenchurch on the arm. 'Take your old man for something to eat, okay?'

'Thought you needed me back at base, boss.'

'Don't wait till I've changed my mind.' Docherty tugged at Fenchurch's cheek, blowing out smoke. 'Back by two, okay?'

Chapter Eight

'Dad, I can't tell you what I'm working on, so just drop it.' Fenchurch held the canteen door open.

'Suit yourself.' Dad meandered through the doorway, like he was in a bloody dream. 'I'll get it out of you eventually.'

The place stunk of chip fat. Steam billowed up from the counter at the far end. They joined the ten-deep queue, the guy in front muttering something about no more chips.

Fenchurch squinted at the small text on the menu above the hatch. A blackboard separated into six sections, the chalk writing barely legible. Fish and chips, baked potatoes. Nothing Mexican or Indian, even Thai at a push.

'Happens to the best of us, boy.' Dad laughed as he got a blue specs case out of his shirt's top pocket. 'Get yourself a pair of specs.'

'I don't need them.'

'You're so proud, my boy.' Dad put on his glasses, the clear frame and legs looking like something from a Chemistry lab. He nudged them up his long nose and sighed at the menu. 'I hate it when they over-describe everything.'

Was that nachos? Fenchurch tried to focus on it. Probably was. He frowned at his dad. 'What do you mean over-describe?'

'The special always has a description longer than the back of one of my pill bottles.' Dad pointed up at the menu. 'Why's it a "grass-fed tongue of ox"? What's wrong with just ox tongue? It's bloody soup. And what the hell's a "red wine moule"?' He shook his head. 'This is a police canteen, not the bloody Ivy.'

Fenchurch stepped forward in the queue. 'What can I get you?'

'No pie and mash today . . .' Dad twisted his head round to take in the full width of the menu. 'I'll have fish and chips. Hope it comes with lots of chips.'

'Is that a good idea?'

'I've been living off rabbit food for so long, son. Let me have a little treat for once, all right?'

Fenchurch smiled at the server. A young black woman, acting like she had to put up with Dad's shit every day. 'One nachos and one fish and chips, please.'

'Anything to drink, sir?'

'Diet Coke.'

Dad grinned. 'Bottle of water, sweetheart.'

She rolled her eyes and reached into a fridge. The bottles were stuck at the back like they were hiding from the law.

'You keeping well, Dad?'

'Don't reckon I've got much time left.'

Fenchurch's buttocks clenched. 'Don't say that. You're as fit as an ox.'

'One with a triple heart bypass, maybe.' Dad flashed him a cheeky wink. 'Never mind, my old house'll be worth a packet. Even without central heating.'

'Dad—'

'Five minutes stroll to the DLR. You and your sister will do well out of me and your old mum.'

'That's a bit morbid.'

'When you get to my age, son, it's all you think of. Being back here stops me thinking so much.'

The server returned and pushed a tray across the hatch's scarred surface. The heaped plate of nachos bubbled away. They shouldn't really do that.

Dad stared at his plate like a little kid who got a lump of coal on Christmas morning. A giant battered cod rested on top of four potato wedges. He tapped the plate. 'That's not a portion of chips.'

'That's a whole baking potato, Dad.'

'Even so.'

The server pouted at them. 'Want me to get you something else?'

'No, it's fine.' Dad wandered off, shaking his head.

She smiled at Fenchurch. 'Sixteen fifty.'

He stuffed his card into the machine and typed his PIN. 'Sorry about him.'

'He's like that every day.' She tore off his receipt and handed his card back. 'You get used to it.'

'Not sure you ever do.' Fenchurch picked up the tray and squinted around the canteen, looking for his dad. A waving arm near the window. He walked over and clattered the tray off the tabletop. Sat on the hardwood bench. Felt like it was giving him piles already.

Dad handed him a mismatched knife and fork then grabbed his plate. He cleaved his fish in two and steam spiralled up from the white flesh. He snapped off a chunk of batter and ate it. 'That's lovely.'

'After all that . . .' Fenchurch's plate was a big splodge of cheesy mess. Jesus. He dipped a couple of soggy nachos in the heap of salsa and wolfed them down. Not bad. He took a drink, panting. 'This is bloody hot.'

'Why do you like all that Mexican stuff?' Dad scowled at his son's dish. 'You never used to eat it. What's wrong with proper English food?'

'You know, Dad. Those LAPD guys I trained with at the FBI in Florida. All they'd eat was Mexican.'

'Waste of time that course, wasn't it?'

Fenchurch looked away. 'It didn't give me any answers, no.'

'I don't see what's wrong with good old English food, anyway.'

'Fat, carbs, lack of vegetables, too much protein, no fibre.'

'You've got me there.' Dad laughed and skewered a hunk of batter. 'Come on, what is it you're working on?'

Fenchurch fixed a glare on him. 'You free to go to Upton Park on Saturday?'

'You know I hate it when people call it that.' Dad glowered, like he'd eaten dog shit. 'You'd call a patch of grass Upton Park. West Ham play at the Boleyn Ground, son. It's got a grandness to it.'

'We're talking about West Ham, Dad.'

'You've changed your tune since last season.'

Fenchurch shrugged. 'Old Slaven's got them playing proper football now.' He dipped another tortilla chip into the congealed mound of salsa and guacamole. 'Anyway, the boy next to me is back in Scotland for Christmas. You can have his ticket. It's Sunderland.'

'Three easy points with the way they're playing. Shame I'm working.'

'On a Saturday?'

'Every week, son. Remember, I'm trying to find—'

'It's a quarter to one kick off. I'll pick you up from here.'

'That's fine.' Dad beamed at his son. 'Thanks for putting in that word. I'm having a lot of fun here.'

'I'll bet you are.' Fenchurch chewed on another tortilla. 'You're not here all the time, are you?'

'It's better than drinking whisky in front of the TV.' He swallowed down a forkful of peas. 'Any girls on the scene?'

'I'm not fifteen.'

'Yeah, but you've been a little hermit since Abi chucked you, haven't you?'

Fenchurch picked up his cutlery and attacked the soggy tortillas stuck to the bottom of the plate. 'What happened isn't the sort of thing you recover from.'

'Not a day goes by when I don't miss your mother, son. The last thing she wanted was for me to be miserable.'

'Is this your way of telling me there's a lady?'

'Actually, it's a bloke called Reginald. He's got a massive cock.'

Fenchurch dropped his cutlery onto the table. He covered his mouth as he laughed. 'That the truth, yeah?'

'No, there's nobody kicking around.' Dad stabbed half a potato wedge and stuffed it in his mouth. He swallowed it down without chewing. That'll bloody give him indigestion. Again. 'Last thing your mother would want was you moping round that bloody flat of yours, Simon. You're still a young man.'

'I'm forty-two. That's not young.'

'I'm just saying you should get out and play the field, son.' Dad grabbed his wrist. 'I am worried about you. So's your sister. The other day, when I caught you in Chloe's—'

'*Dad.*'

'You were in her file again. You've got to stop that. It's not healthy.'

'Says the man who's back in here, trying to find her.' Fenchurch finished his drink. Couldn't taste it.

'I'm still out in the world. Still see my mates. Your closest friendship is with that Scotch geezer at the Boleyn.'

'I've got friends.'

'Jon Nelson and Doc don't count.'

'I'm fine, Dad. Honest.' Fenchurch tried to outstare him. Knew within seconds he wasn't going to win. 'Drop it.'

The grip tightened. 'You're lonely and you're obsessed, son. You've been frozen for ten years. You didn't bloody cry at your mother's funeral.'

'Dad . . .' Tears burnt at the back of Fenchurch's throat. He blinked them away. 'Time I got back to work.'

'Son . . .'

'I'd love to say this has been fun, but . . .'

'You're not out here for something to do with Chloe, are you?'

Fenchurch got up. The bench almost toppled backwards. 'Would I tell you if I was?'

'Simon, there's something I need to—'

'Goodbye.' Fenchurch tore off across the canteen, hands in pockets.

Going to bloody kill Docherty.

Chapter Nine

Fenchurch wandered back into the Incident Room. The clock above the whiteboard read 14.06. How the hell did it get to that time? He dumped his coat on his chair and had a look around. Nelson was scowling at his laptop, teeth gritted. He walked over and tapped him on the shoulder. 'How's it going, Jon?'

'No further forward with an ID, guv.'

'I was hoping I'd come back here and it'd all be solved.'

'Fat chance of that.' Nelson slammed the lid of the laptop. 'Been looking into other cases with no ID. There's a hell of a lot out there. Just no way to pin them to ours.'

'Even if we narrow it to prostitutes?'

'Still leaves us a gap a mile wide.' Nelson leaned back and folded his arms. 'Some geezer's digital fingerprints are all over these cases, though. Guy called Ian Fenchurch.'

Fenchurch covered a burp. More acid reflux. 'Keep away from him.'

'What's your old man up to?'

'His own bloody thing, as ever.' Fenchurch looked around. 'Very quiet in here.'

'Everyone's out on the street teams while things are still fresh.'

'I hope it's not going stale.' Fenchurch perched on the edge of the desk. 'I told Docherty to get that press release out soon.'

'We really need it, guv. How was the PM?'

'Other than the DNA, we've got nothing much. Pratt reckons she was a prostitute.' Fenchurch nodded at the interview room monitor near the whiteboard. Reed and Bridge sat across from a woman in room three. 'Who's Kay in with?'

'Lisa Bridge.'

'Not her, you muppet. Who're they interviewing?'

'That's the prostitute who gave them the statement earlier about this geezer trying to buy her. Woman named Vicki, I think. Had a bit of a rigmarole getting hold of her again.' Nelson scratched at his neck. 'Don't think they're getting anywhere with her.'

'Then why's she waving at the camera?'

———

Reed smiled at Fenchurch as he hovered in the doorway. She stretched over the desk. 'Interview suspended at fourteen eleven.'

Fenchurch waited for her to come out before he shut the door. 'Why were you waving?'

'She's not speaking to us. I need Jon in here.'

'Can't I help?'

'Worth a try, I suppose. Come on in.' Reed shrugged and went back in. She sat and picked up the microphone. 'Interview resumed at fourteen twelve. DI Simon Fenchurch has entered the room.'

He stayed by the door, watching Bridge and their interviewee.

Vicki was in her thirties and heroin thin. She wore a tight blue miniskirt dress, arms tangled up in a black cardigan. She reached down to scratch behind her knee-high boots, eyes on Fenchurch. 'Getting a good look, are you?'

Fenchurch signalled at Bridge. 'Continue, Constable.'

Bridge slid a sheet of photos across the desk. 'Was this the man who approached you?'

The paper crinkled as Vicki picked it up. She stared at them for a few seconds, her mouth hanging open, showing a wad of pink gum. 'Is this who you think killed that girl?'

'Did he approach you?'

'Is it him?'

'We believe so, yes.'

'So I could've been killed?' Vicki tugged her cardigan tighter. Gave a look that could curdle cheese. 'You should be protecting people from the likes of him!'

Bridge tapped the page. 'What about her? Do you know her?'

'I don't go to the bingo with her, if that's what you're asking.'

'But you recognise the face?'

Vicki nodded. 'She's a new girl. Seen her out the last few nights.'

'Any idea who her pimp is?'

'What's a pimp?'

'Very cute.' Bridge groaned. 'I take it you don't know?'

'I've no idea who runs her, no.'

Reed got up from her chair and led Fenchurch back into the corridor. 'Well, that's a bit further forward. Thanks for the help, guv.'

'Not sure what I did.'

'She'd completely clammed up till then.' She checked her watch. 'What are you still doing here, anyway?'

'Working?'

'But I got you an appointment with Trafficking and Prostitution at three?'

'Gives me a chance to read up beforehand.'

'It's at the Empress State Building, guv. Across town?'

Fenchurch stormed out of the lift. The windows opposite showed the view back across London. Kensington's leafy opulence sprawled below them. Far away, the City and Canary Wharf skyscrapers sat apart on the horizon, like they'd fallen out over something. The cogs of the London Eye were stuck between them.

'How the other half live, Jon. Bloody Vice. They're all crooks.' Fenchurch walked up to the reception desk, shoes clicking off the flagstones, and showed his warrant card to the young woman. 'Here to see DCI Howard Savage.'

The receptionist checked her computer. 'Is he expecting you?'

'We've got an appointment at three.'

'Then you're late.' She flashed a cheeky smile. 'Just a moment, I'll see if he's still free.' She picked up a handset and turned away from them.

Fenchurch raised an eyebrow at Nelson. 'Remind you of anything?'

'Darke Matter?'

'This lot think they're running a bloody hedge fund. They're in this place and we're stuck in Leman Street.'

'You'll get used to it.' A man was standing at the glass doors behind them. His few remaining strands of grey hair were scraped across his head. He adjusted his tweed sporting jacket, one hand in the pocket of his black trousers. 'DI Fenchurch, I presume?' He had the voice of a dirty old pervert, nasal and smarmy.

He held out his hand. 'That's me.'

'Howard Savage.' He shook it. 'Pleasure to meet you.' He gave a thumbs up to the receptionist, still on the phone, and pushed through the glass. 'In you come.'

Fenchurch followed him into an office, glancing at Nelson as they sat. 'Thanks for seeing us, sir.'

'Not a problem.' Savage lowered himself into his chair. Took more effort than it should've done. His desk overlooked the white bulk of Earl's Court Exhibition Centre. 'Why do I know the name Fenchurch?'

'It'll be my father, Ian.'

Savage clicked his fingers, then pointed like a pistol. 'That's it. Anyway, thank you for making the trip across London.'

'We actually needed you at Leman Street, sir. That's where our case is.'

'I'm much too busy for that.'

'And we're not?' Fenchurch's chair creaked as he eased off his suit jacket. 'Have a look at these.' He reached into his pocket for the sheet of photos and tossed it on the desk just out of Savage's reach. 'The girl's our murder victim. The man's the prime suspect.'

Savage frowned at it before looking up. 'So?'

'We believe this guy picked her up on Whitechapel High Street. He had sex with her, then killed her. The guard discovered her body last night.'

'Well, it would appear you've had a wasted journey.' Savage turned the page over. 'I don't recognise either of them.'

'The autopsy indicated she was a prostitute.'

'Inspector, there are times I wish I knew every single prostitute in London so I could warn them. But I'm afraid I just don't know this girl.'

'What about Little Somerset House.'

Savage blinked hard. 'Excuse me?'

'Your eyes just twitched, sir, so I'd prefer the truth.'

'Ah, the joys of dealing with a murder squad.' Savage smiled, his eyes narrowing to slits. 'As I'm sure you know, Little Somerset House's a notorious den for prostitutes.'

'Why would I know that?'

'Well, it's your patch. Have you spoken to the building owners?'

'First thing. A company called Darke Matter Capital.'

'I've had meetings with Vincent Darke, the CEO.' Savage stared out of the window. 'We've been attempting to apply a modicum of pressure on them to accelerate the development of this new Minories skyscraper. While it means further gentrification of the area, it's three fewer derelict buildings in East London. All of which pushes our, shall we say, temporary tenants further out.'

'So you're cleaning up the City for Boris?'

'I can assure you the Mayor's office has had nothing to do with this initiative.'

'This girl's new on the streets.' Fenchurch tapped the photos. 'You sure you don't know her?'

'I said I didn't.'

'Know who might be running her?'

Savage wheeled his chair around to look out of the window. 'There are a few gentlemen out that way with thriving street operations.'

'Anyone likely?'

'Maybe.' Savage turned back and held up the sheet. 'Looking at her, I'm thinking Frank Blunden might know something.'

'Flick Knife?' Fenchurch groaned. 'Blunden's Mile End, isn't he?'

'Runs a cab firm as cover for a few other interests.' Savage patted down a strand of hair. 'Mr Blunden's been putting a lot of girls onto the street recently. Not all of them his usual MO, either.'

'Which is?'

'Blacks and Asians. Never whites.'

'Of course, it could be some new player.'

Savage let out a sigh. 'If it is, I've never heard of them.'

'I'm glad this hasn't been a complete waste of time.' Fenchurch got to his feet. 'Come on, Jon, let's get out to Mile End.'

'You're not speaking to him without my officers attending.'

'You've presented us with a lead, sir. Standard operating procedure would be to interview him.'

'We have several operations in play in that neck of the woods. I don't want a Major Investigation Team's blunderbuss antics jeopardising any of them.'

'So lend me some.'

Savage laughed. 'I can't just snap my fingers and magic them up.'

'This is a murder case, sir. We're already outside the first twenty-four hours.' Fenchurch kept his voice level. 'Give me a skull and I'll take him or her with me.'

Savage clenched his jaw, looked like he might crush a tooth. 'I don't appreciate the strong-arm tactics here.'

'Are you giving me an officer or not?'

'It's not as simple as that.'

Fenchurch gripped the edge of the seat. 'What if it's not Blunden? I'll need someone with access to your knowledge here.'

'We'll cross that bridge when we come to it.' Savage folded his arms. 'Feels like there's no way I'm getting out of this.'

'Send him to Leman Street, please.'

⌣

Fenchurch locked the pool car and stared up at the back of Leman Street. The brick was dyed yellow in the street lights. 'When I retire, I swear I'm moving to Spain.'

Nelson grinned. 'Don't you like a London winter, guv?'

'I had a winter in Glasgow one year, hunting down a bloody serial killer. That was brutal.'

'The weather, I take it?'

'And the people. Gets dark at half three and it pisses down all day.' Fenchurch started off towards the entrance. 'Other end of the scale, I had a winter in Miami and Louisiana shadowing the FBI Behavioral Analysis Unit. Now that's how to live. Beach parties on Christmas Day.'

Nelson held open the rear entrance. 'Still had your turkey?'

'Found a little English pub in Miami Beach.' Fenchurch entered the station. Despite how cold it was outside, it felt colder in. Bloody place.

'You think Savage is going to send a lad over?'

'I'm not holding my breath. Not that I think Flick Knife will lead anywhere.'

'I've dealt with him in the past, guv. Nasty piece of work.'

'Yeah?' Fenchurch swiped through the security. 'I don't like being babysat by those crooks.' His mobile rang — DS Reed. He answered it. 'Hi, Kay.'

'Got a witness for you in interview room one, guv. You'll want to speak him.'

Chapter Ten

A large man in a navy suit was sitting opposite Reed, scratching his curly hair. His thick chest strained the buttons of his stripy shirt. His sideburns touched his jawline, puffed up with flab.

Fenchurch whispered in Reed's ear: 'This isn't our guy.'

'I know that, guv.' She smiled at the man. 'Mr Quinn works at the RBS on Bishopsgate. I thought you'd appreciate hearing his statement first hand.'

Fenchurch took a step back and leaned against the wall. 'Let's hear it, then.'

'Now, where was I?' Quinn had a Scottish accent, slower and deeper than Docherty's. Less of a snarl. Made him sound a bit simple. 'Like I told the guy who came round, I was out for a few beers with guys from the office.' He prodded the printout in front of him — the man on the CCTV. 'I saw him on Tuesday night in Dirty Dick's on Bishopsgate.'

'Been there a few times.' Fenchurch tapped out an *Action* on his Pronto. *Call DI Clarke.* 'Do you live down here?'

'I'm based in Edinburgh. Came down for the Christmas night out.' Quinn coughed, eyebrows raised. 'Had a few meetings on as well.'

'I get it.' Fenchurch held out his own crumpled sheet of photos. 'You're sure it was this guy?'

'Positive. He was drinking at the table next to us. Similar-sized group to ours, maybe twenty people?'

'They look like bankers?'

'What does a banker look like?' Quinn soaked up the space Fenchurch gave him. 'Maybe. I didn't recognise them, though. They were all pretty hammered. Way worse than us. Most of them cleared off about nine.' He pointed at the photo. 'Except for him. He stayed around for another hour, I think. Flitting around tables, making a nuisance of himself. That's how I remember him. Had to have a word.'

'What sort of a nuisance?'

'He was trying it on with a couple of the girls. Asked Lauren if he could see her vagina.'

'Classy. What was this word you had?'

'Just told him to behave. He left not long after. I kept an eye on him as he went, just to make sure.'

'Which way did he go?'

'He headed right.'

Fenchurch tried to get his bearings. 'Towards Shoreditch?'

'I've no idea. Sorry.'

'If you turn right again, you're on Commercial Street.' Fenchurch cracked his knuckles. 'When did he leave?'

'Couldn't have been much before ten.'

'Did you notice anything particular about him?'

'The girl he was asking to see her, you know . . . He was really loud about it. I think he was a Geordie. Definitely from the North East.'

'How did he seem?'

Quinn focused on the photo. 'Well, he was banjaxed. All over the bloody place.'

'What was he wearing?'

'A work suit. Looked a bit grubby, though. Like he'd spilled something down the front.'

'Thanks for this.' Fenchurch stood up tall again. Knees didn't like all the crouching. 'I'll need you to give a statement to my colleague here.'

Quinn worried at his neck. 'Listen, I've got to catch a flight home at the back of eight.'

'That gives you four hours. You should be fine.'

'What if I miss it?'

'We'll put you on a train.'

Quinn bowed his head. 'Great.'

Fenchurch pushed his shoulders back. 'You should be proud of helping us. This could be the break we need.'

'Pleased to do my bit.'

Fenchurch thumbed at the door and let Reed go first. He followed her out, pulling it shut behind them. 'That's good work, Sergeant.'

'Thanks, guv. We're taking statements from his colleagues at RBS. Might be something, might be nothing.'

'What about at Dirty Dick's?'

'DC Lad's up there now, trying to get hold of CCTV or bar tabs, anything we can.'

'This is—'

His Airwave blasted out. A male voice spoke in a monotone. 'Control to DI Fenchurch. Over.' The desk sergeant downstairs. What did he bloody want?

'Safe to speak, Steve.'

'Got some officers from Traffic for you at the Leman Street front desk.'

Fenchurch scowled at Reed. 'Traffic?'

'Hang on.' Silence. 'Sorry, they're from Trafficking and Prostitution.'

Fenchurch wandered around his office. Where was best to sit?

Perch on Mulholland's desk at the far end of the room? Her coat was draped over her chair, meaning she might come in at any minute.

His own? The West Ham scarf on the top of his monitor was the only personalisation. The only sign a human being ever sat there.

Sod it. He collapsed into his seat and waited.

The door crept open, like there was a mouse coming through. Then a tall man strode into the room. Tight black pinstripe suit. White shirt gaping at the neck. Shoes with a high shine to them. He claimed the chair next to Fenchurch's desk, a smirk on his face. Looked like a punter at the average lap-dancing bar. 'Fenchurch, right?' Welsh twang to his voice — south, maybe Swansea. 'DS Chris Owen.'

'Right. Thanks for coming over. I met your—'

'DCI Savage briefed us as we drove out. Been doing an obbo out this way.'

'"Us"?'

'Should be along any minute.'

Another officer bundled in the room, just as seedy as Owen. His coal-black beard was trimmed to the jaw, pencil thin. Mid-blue shirt and beige suit jacket. 'Sorry, had to go drain the lizard.' Estuary accent. South Essex or north Kent, same neck of the woods as Kay Reed. He focused his blue eyes on Fenchurch and held out a damp hand. 'DS Paul Kershaw.'

Fenchurch didn't shake it. 'Why's Savage sent two of you?'

'Because we can't be trusted on our own.' Kershaw yawned as he settled down next to Owen. Twisted it into a grin. 'Can we cut to the chase here? What do you want from us?'

Fenchurch let out a sigh, maybe a bit more than he intended. 'I need anything you've got on Frank Blunden running new girls in this part of town.'

'That all?'

'You've been working round here, right?' Fenchurch pushed a fresh copy of the photo sheet towards them. 'Recognise either of these two?'

'Afraid not.' Owen passed it over to Kershaw.

He gave a shrug and slid the page back. 'Me neither.'

Fenchurch picked it back up but didn't look at it. 'First, I want you two to give a plan of attack on tackling Blunden. And if he's not this girl's pimp then we'll need a list of credible suspects.'

Owen sniffed. Better not have a cold on the way. Or a coke habit. 'Is Friday okay?'

Pair of bloody jokers. Fenchurch clicked his fingernails on the desk. 'You've got an hour.'

'Seriously?'

'This is just speaking to someone, right?'

'A murder squad detective might think that.' Owen stared into space, looking really pleased with himself. 'There are many subtle nuances to speaking to a character like Blunden.' He glanced round at Kershaw. 'Paul's got a lot of intel to review before we can even start.'

'We're speaking to him this evening. End of.'

Owen swallowed. 'We need to run everything by DCI Savage.'

'Let me make myself absolutely clear, DS Owen. You're both on secondment to my squad. You work for me until we charge some-one or drop the case. Okay?'

'DCI Savage just told us to get here for five. That's it.'

'Well, I don't care. I want a plan of attack for Blunden after the briefing in five minutes.'

Kershaw raised a shoulder. 'Sure thing. Boss.'

'I'm glad one of you gets it.' Fenchurch glared at Owen. 'In addition, can you both shake down your black books and find out if anyone knows anything about this girl?'

'We'll get someone onto it, *sir.*'

'Less of the attitude.' Fenchurch grabbed his suit jacket from the back of his chair. 'Right, I've got to brief the troops.'

Owen looked around the office. 'Can we use this room?'

Fenchurch clenched his jaw. 'There are two spare desks through in the Incident Room.'

Chapter Eleven

Bridge and Reed stood by the whiteboard, nodding at something Mulholland was saying. She was in bloody early. Like a shark sniffing blood.

'Gather round, you lot!' Fenchurch waited for the holy trinity to break up. 'First things first, we've got two secondees from the Met Trafficking and Prostitution Unit. DS Chris Owen and DS Paul Kershaw.' He left a pause for them to raise their hands, acting like they were guests of honour at a Presidential fundraiser. 'Given the obvious Vice angle on this case, they're joining us for the duration. They'll mainly be working on intel. Both report to me.' He gave them a space to fill.

Owen flicked his tongue between his lips. 'A pleasure.'

'Next, the press release has gone out. I believe DCI Docherty was speaking to the fourth estate this afternoon. Not aware of any leads coming back on it.'

Another gap, just a couple of shrugs from Reed and Nelson. Mulholland was pouting in that particular way, like she knew something but wasn't telling him.

'We'll have to play that one by ear. DS Nelson, can you allocate some resource to dealing with the influx of sightings and fake confessions?'

'Will do, guv.'

'DS Reed, how's it going up at Dirty Dick's?'

'No dice yet. We spoke to the bar staff. They did recognise the bloke, though. Reckon he's been in a few times over the last couple of months. Bought himself a drink after the rest of his party left. Bottle of Peroni.'

'Did he use a credit card?'

'No dice again. Cash. And the CCTV's bollocksed inside. Someone seems to have nudged the camera. All they've got is a view of the alleyway leading to the toilets. The only thing remotely useful is a guy pissing against the wall.'

'We've got a large collection of that already.' Fenchurch sneered. 'ITV4 might be interested in the footage.'

Reed smirked. 'Never pissed against a wall in my life, guv.'

Fenchurch waited for the laughter to subside. 'Anything else from the street team?'

'Schools are still a negative. Same with the offices. But we're not finished.'

'We are where we are, I suppose.' Fenchurch looked around the room. Blank faces stared back at him. Owen was tapping away at his phone. 'Dismissed.'

Fenchurch barged through the throng to Owen's desk. No sign of Kershaw. 'I've got to update my boss. I expect that plan of attack when I'm done.'

'Sounds like everything's in hand.' Docherty stretched out and yawned. His office was dimmer than a nightclub at one in the morning. 'Dawn, are you ready to take the bull by the horns?'

'On it, sir.' Mulholland got to her feet and smoothed down her long skirt. 'Like you say, I'll batter them into a result.' She winked and left the room, pulling the door shut behind her.

Fenchurch got up to follow her.

'Not so bloody fast.'

Fenchurch lowered himself back down. 'What's up?'

'Tell me what's really happening with the case.'

'I just did.'

'And you usually redact what you say in front of DI Mulholland.'

Fenchurch grunted. 'Right.'

'Come on, Simon, I know you two don't see eye to eye. It's why I made you share an office.' Docherty rolled his tongue over his lips, like he was about to tuck into a deep-fried chip roll. 'What's going on?'

'That's someone's daughter lying in Pratt's freezer.' Fenchurch cocked his head to the side. 'We've had this body for a day and we still haven't identified her. It's embarrassing.'

'You sure that's all it is?' Docherty ran a hand through his hair, frosted grass on a frozen beach. 'You've been miserable as sin since Abigail kicked you out. I watched you throw yourself into all this shite.' He shook his head, a bitter scowl betraying his disappointment. 'I lost my own marriage to the Job. All I've got to show for my thirty years is an ulcer and an AA sponsor.'

'I don't even have your extra stripe, boss.'

'You can still drink, Simon. Be thankful for that.' Docherty nudged the mug to the far edge of his desk. 'If you want to talk about—'

A knock on the door. Owen stood there, one hand in his pocket. 'You ready for us?'

'Give me a second.'

'We're down the corridor.' Owen turned and left them.

Fenchurch smiled at Docherty as he rose to his feet. 'Thanks for the chat, boss.'

'One day you'll call me Doc like everyone else.'

Fenchurch sat at the end of the conference-room table. Place stank of bleach and vinegar. The flip chart was blank. He fixed a glare on Owen. 'You got something for me, Sergeant?'

'We've been speaking to our guv'nor.'

'And what's Savage saying?'

'He okayed a light plan of attack.'

'Define "light".'

'He doesn't want us to go in there and cause a scene. Thinks it might not be worth speaking to Mr Blunden, after all.'

'He bloody brought him up in the first place.' Fenchurch had to fight the instinct to slam a fist on the table. 'Are you two mucking about here?'

A frown danced across Kershaw's forehead. 'What's that supposed to mean?'

'We all know you lot can be as dirty as the scumbags you're investigating. We've all heard of Vice cops taking backhanders.' Fenchurch gritted his teeth. 'Plan of attack. Now.'

'Frank Blunden isn't the sort of punter you mess around with.' Owen smoothed out his crumpled notebook. 'Hence the nickname Flick Knife. Only time he's been inside was when he stabbed a geezer in the eighties.'

'With a flick knife. Yeah, yeah, I get it. He's calmed down a bit since, especially where the Old Bill are concerned.'

'Look, he's a *potential* lead at this stage, okay?' Owen squinted at Fenchurch and sniffed. 'Our intel suggests he doesn't run girls in this part of town. Further out's his speciality. Mile End, Walthamstow, Lewisham. The guv'nor's wary about us going there and knocking his door down if he's not done anything.'

'So what are you suggesting?'

'We have to get him onside. This isn't his patch but he's got his ear to the ground.' Owen brushed down his suit jacket. 'Blunden's a racist, okay? He only runs blacks or Asians, no white girls.'

Fenchurch drummed his thumbs on the table. 'I'm not following you.'

'Way we hear it is he'll find some pretty little black thing out of some East End hellhole.' Kershaw traced a finger down the line of his beard. 'Get her on smack, then stick her out on the street, sucking cocks. Same with the Asian girls, though they're harder to snare. Get a lot more money for them, though, I understand.'

Owen raised an eyebrow at Fenchurch. 'This Jane Doe of yours is as white as you are. She's not one of his.'

'Listen, son. I was at this point about three hours ago with your guv'nor. He told me Blunden had switched his MO.'

'Hear us out, yeah?' Kershaw picked at stubble on his chin. 'We go to Blunden and tell him there's a new player in town. Geezer who's putting white girls on the street. Play to his racism. If he knows something, he'll want them off the street.'

'And if she works for Blunden?'

'Then we've got a bigger problem than a dead hooker.' Kershaw rocked forward in his chair, elbows resting on his knees. 'That'd mean he's changed his business model. It's never good when people do that. Makes things harder to police.'

Fenchurch tightened his fists. His fingernails bit into his palms. 'Right, gents. DS Nelson and I will let you know—'

'You can't take him.' Owen leaned across the desk, stabbing a finger in the air. 'Aren't you listening to us? Blunden's racist. He'll have Nelson shooting up by breakfast.'

'I take your point, even if I don't appreciate the way it was put.' Fenchurch loosened off his tie and slipped it from his shirt collar. 'DS Owen, looks like it's you and me, then.'

Chapter Twelve

Owen parked his pool Vectra on a Mile End street bisected by a Victorian railway bridge. A DLR train rumbled above them, lit up in the night sky. Skodas, Mercedes and black cabs littered the place, telltale signs of a nearby taxi business. Frank's Cabs was hidden under an arch between some old houses.

Owen let his seatbelt ride up and unlocked his door. 'I'm leading in there. Right?'

'Whatever gets the result.' Fenchurch got out and followed him across the road.

The gate screeched open.

'Shit.' Owen looked around. Got away with that one. He marched through the archway into a car park. A wooden hut cowered under a weeping willow, its flat roof covered in decaying leaves. He led inside and rapped his knuckles on the reception desk. 'Is Frank in?'

The receptionist looked like an extra from *EastEnders*. A blue pen tucked behind her ear, grey hair twisted into a ponytail. She gave a quick glance at them, then shut her ledger. A taxi radio crackled behind her, muttered speech garbled by the airwaves. 'Who's asking?'

'DS Chris Owen.' He showed her his credentials.

'Give me a second.' She knocked on the only door and stuck her head in. A late-eighties Page Three calendar hung off the white wood just above a handwritten sign for Frank's Cabs. She returned and held the door open behind her. 'Frank'll see you now.'

'Appreciate it.' Owen squeezed past her into the room.

Fenchurch's nose twitched at the stench of cigarette smoke as he followed him in.

Frank Blunden was a barrel of a man, his giant fists hammering away at a phone. His maroon cardigan was worn at the elbows. He tossed the mobile down and leaned back in his chair, sticking his crocodile-skin boots on the oak desk, and folded his arms. 'Evening, gents.'

Owen sat on a sofa against the opposite wall. He pointed at the cigarette burning in the bronze ashtray in the middle of the desk. The window behind Blunden was open a crack. 'You know you shouldn't be smoking inside a place of work, don't you?'

'Oh, that?' Blunden smirked. 'It was here when I came back here an hour ago. Thought I'd best leave it so you lot could do some forensic analysis on it. Maybe find the bugger who broke in and put it there.'

Owen rolled his eyes. 'We want to speak to you about a prostitute.'

'And here's me thinking you gentlemen were after a cab. Could get you a transfer to Heathrow for thirty quid. Cheapest round these parts by a country mile. I'm robbing myself.'

'If it's all the same, Frank, I'll just hop on the DLR and get to City Airport.'

'Suit yourself. The offer stands.' Blunden went to shut the window. Still had a boxer's gait, practically skipping over despite his bulk. He rested against the frame. 'Why have you come in here to ask about prostitutes?'

'Because you know an awful lot about them.'

'I'm an honest businessman.'

'And I'm Irish.'

'That's a funny accent. West coast, is it?'

'Yeah, of Wales.' Owen tossed some photos on the desk. Blown-up shots of their Jane Doe from the CCTV, the crime scene and the post-mortem. 'We found this girl in Little Somerset House on Wednesday night.'

'Those bloody eyesores down Aldgate way, right? Spitting distance from the Tower.' Blunden raised his hands. 'So?'

'She's sixteen, Frank. And white.'

'What's that got to do with a taxi business?'

'She's been out sucking black cock. Getting screwed by Arabs from the airlines, no doubt. You happy with that?'

Blunden sat back down and fingered the photos. 'Is she English?'

'We think so.' Owen raised his left shoulder. 'Know anything about it?'

Blunden traced the face on the page like it was his own daughter. He gritted his teeth and nodded. 'There's some new geezers putting white girls on the street down that way.'

'How does a mere taxi firm owner know about such things?'

'Because my drivers have got ears, you little shit. My boys tell me stuff. Loose lips in the back of a cab after a few too many shandies. You know how it is. Now, do you want me to play ball or are you going to clear off?'

'I'm listening. Promise I'll behave.'

Blunden narrowed his eyes at him. 'There's a titty bar up Shoreditch way. Place called The Alicorn. I hear they've got English girls working there.'

'A few places have English girls, Frank. That's not illegal. Is this a high-end place?'

'In that bit of Shoreditch? Do me a favour. They put some of these girls out on the street. Very cheap, too.' Blunden reached over and stubbed out the cigarette. 'From what I hear, that place does an out-of-hours service. If you like a girl who's dancing for you, you can take her back home.'

'That happen a lot?'

'Less than you'd think. If they don't make the grade they're out the door.' He whistled as he thumbed behind him. 'Out on the street but still working for them. I despise what they're doing. *Despise* it.'

'This isn't you just throwing us a bone, is it? A chance to shut down a rival.'

'I don't know what you're talking about.'

'You must take a couple hundred a night from each skull you've got walking the streets.'

'I run a clean business here, you little punk. Now, are we done here?'

'Just one last thing.' Fenchurch tapped the photo. 'This girl was working on the fringe of the City, just off Commercial Street.' He pointed to the post-mortem photos. Still made his gut churn. 'We found her in Little Somerset House but you're saying she's connected to a club on the arse end of Shoreditch?'

'I'm just relaying what I hear. Anyway, it's a quick stroll up the City Road to Old Street roundabout, sunshine.' Blunden scratched inside his left boot. 'White girls, English ones. What sort of place does that when they can get blacks for next to nothing?'

Owen looked like he was failing to hide a smile. Blunden implicating himself in all sorts of nasty things. 'You tell us what sort of place, Frank.'

'A bloody cesspit is what.' Blunden scowled. 'Charging less than for blacks or Pakis. Even Romanians. *Disgusting*.' He stabbed a finger on the photo. 'If this girl's sixteen . . .' He broke off, a tight grimace on his face. 'Give me ten minutes in a room with whoever it is.'

'Do you know who's behind it?'

'This is all intel from my boys in the cabs, you understand?' Blunden tipped the ashtray into a bin under his desk.

Owen tossed a business card onto Blunden's desk. It landed on top of the sheet of photos. 'Give us a call if "your boys" hear any more in the back of their cabs, okay?'

Owen pulled into one of the few free spaces outside Leman Street station and killed the engine. 'Get what you needed there?'

'I still don't see why we needed your expertise.' Fenchurch let his seatbelt ride up. 'Me and Nelson could've got what little you did.'

'Nelson? You think Frank Blunden would open up to a black man, no matter how nice a suit he wears or how eloquently he talks?'

'You think your wand-waving got us a result, do you?'

'As it happens, I do. Which is why I'm doing strategic work while you're stuck investigating murders.'

'Strategic?' Fenchurch laughed. 'Brilliant.'

'We're cutting down people trafficking in the whole of the UK.' Owen tugged the key out of the ignition. 'A murder investigation is the definition of tactical policing.'

'You're something else, Sergeant.'

Owen's mobile buzzed in the hands-free cradle. He checked the message. 'What do you want to do with this intel?'

'First off, is this just Blunden trying to score a few points?'

'It's legit.' Owen held up his mobile. 'I sent a text to one of my DCs. He's had a look at it for me. It all stacks up.'

'They trust you to manage people?'

'Just a couple.' Owen pocketed his phone. 'We've got some intel of our own on that Alicorn place. Most of what Blunden said matches our understanding. English girls, cheap as chips. Off-street whoring. Like he said, The Alicorn's dodgy.' He sniffed. 'Whether we go in isn't my call to make.'

Fenchurch swallowed and stared into the middle distance. Behind, a lorry trundling through the building site blocked the road. 'Oh, we're going in, all right.' He looked up at the station. Docherty's light was still on. 'I need you to round up a squad while I fast-track a warrant.'

Chapter Thirteen

Fenchurch left the car and walked across Shoreditch High Street onto Hackney Road. The old church was lit up behind the trees, fanning out in front.

The Alicorn occupied the ground floor of a four-storey block of brick tenements. Neon lights flashed above the blacked-out windows and dry ice smoked out of pipes. Nelson and Kershaw were opposite it, waiting in a long queue at the Tesco Express's cash machine.

He joined them and clapped his hands together. 'You pair get anything this evening?'

'We've just got a statement from a prostitute, guv.' Nelson sucked on a vape stick. 'Black girl called Lucy. She confirmed what Flick Knife told you.'

Kershaw tugged his collar up. 'Got her on the record and all. Backed up the whole thing. New player in town.'

'So it's all slotting into place.' Fenchurch glanced across the road. The grimy metal sign above the club's door was swaying in the breeze, the grubbed-over shape of a horse. 'What's an Alicorn, anyway?'

'Mythical creature, guv.' Nelson held up his phone. The large screen showed a picture of a horse with wings, a horn sticking out of its forehead. 'A flying unicorn.'

'Like Pegasus?'

'That's only a flying horse.'

'So Pegasus with a horn? Right.' Fenchurch nodded at Kershaw. 'You stay here, okay? Owen's pulling together a team. DS Reed's getting the warrant.' Then at Nelson. 'Jon, you're with me. Let's have a butcher's at this place.' He waited for a vintage Ford Capri to rumble past before trotting over.

A bouncer blocked the entrance, rubbing his gloved hands together. Hulking great black guy dressed in top hat and tails. Would make two of Nelson. 'Gents.'

Nelson grinned at him. 'Evening, squire.'

'That supposed to be funny?'

'Not in the slightest.' Nelson took a suck from his vape stick. 'Just want a drink.'

'You can't smoke that thing inside, sir.' The bouncer looked him up and down. 'We had some trouble in here earlier.'

'Well, we ain't looking to cause any.'

The bouncer stepped aside and looked away. 'In you go.'

Fenchurch followed Nelson in.

The place was crowded. The decor was pretty much all black. Tables, chairs, the painted floors. Blacked-out boards where the front window should've been. Everything except for the white woodwork and purple curtains.

On the stage, a girl strutted to a Lana Del Rey song Fenchurch knew. Her leather corset barely concealed her. White-blonde hair, slightly darker than her skin. She caressed the silver pole running down from the ceiling. Open mouth, licking her lips at a pair of lorry drivers at the front. Dirty beards and Bon Jovi jeans. They clutched their pints tight, shagging her with their eyes.

A bar ran along the right-hand side of the room, opposite a series of half-moon booths. Groups of girls occupied them, surrounding one or two men at each. A bare chipboard partition blocked off the far end of the room, not even attempting elegance.

Fenchurch whispered at Nelson: 'How's this looking?'

'Relax, guv. It's fine. Just gathering intelligence, right?' Nelson peered around the place. 'I'll get a round in. Make it look like we're here under normal circumstances.'

'Lager.'

'Lager it is.' Nelson swaggered up to the bar like he was wading through water. He started flirting with the barmaid. Her laugh filled a lull in the music.

Fenchurch joined him and scanned the faces near the bar. He thought he recognised a couple. Definitely the skinhead with the scar.

On the stage, the girl slid down the pole in slow motion, naked as the day she was born except for a pair of platform boots. The music cut off mid-line and she picked up her corset. She stepped into it and sashayed off the stage. Barely eighteen, if a day.

Another girl broke off from a group of men in suits. She held out a pint glass in front of Fenchurch, half filled with pound coins. 'Pound in the jar?'

He tipped two coins in. 'Don't spend it all in the one shop.'

'Okay!' She frowned at him and walked over to another booth, rattling the glass. Eight girls to four men.

'Here you go, gu— Simon.' Nelson handed him a pint of lager, barely fizzing.

Fenchurch touched it to his lips and pretended to take a sip. 'Cheers.'

'Cost nine quid so you better bloody enjoy it.' Nelson took a step back and let two girls join them. A brunette and a redhead. 'Evening, ladies.'

'Evening yourself.' The brunette leaned in close to Nelson, hands spidering all over his shoulder. Her leather bikini showed a knife wound running from her ribcage to her thigh. 'What are you boys looking for?'

The redhead made for Fenchurch. She stroked at his arm, hard and slow. Painted nails clawed at his shirtsleeve. 'Would you like to buy me a drink?'

Fenchurch raised his glass. 'Sorry, I just got a beer.'

'Later?'

He gave her a shrug.

'Later.' She strutted over to the man with the scar.

The brunette whisper-shouted in Nelson's ear: 'You're a big boy.'

'You'll be disappointed.' Nelson took a fake drink, eyes on the surface of his stout. 'Let me have my beer first then we can get a room?'

'I'd like that.' She swapped to Fenchurch, resting a hand around his waist. 'Mmm, I like you.'

Fenchurch settled his pint on the nearest table. 'You asking me for a dance?'

'You asking *me*?'

'Maybe later.'

She raised an eyebrow at Nelson and licked her lips. 'I'll be back for you both, boys.'

Fenchurch watched her go. 'Both of them were English.'

'London-shire, too.' Nelson put his Guinness next to Fenchurch's pint. 'I need a slash.' He swaggered across the place, checking everyone out like he was after a dance.

'Enjoy the show?'

Fenchurch swung round.

The girl from the stage stood there, brushing against his arm. Her blonde hair was wedding-photo perfect. Strong perfume wafted off her. A dimple puckered her cheek.

Not a million miles from Abi's . . .

Blonde hair . . .

The drums cut straight into a John Bonham smash. Acid reflux burnt at his guts. He moved away from her and focused on the floor. Anywhere but at her. 'Wasn't paying attention. Sorry.'

She fidgeted with her corset, a nipple close to popping out. 'Why not? You gay or something?' Her accent was somewhere north of London. Maybe Luton.

'Just came in for a pint.' Fenchurch shrugged and took a proper drink. Tasted like it went off during the Roman Empire. 'This isn't my scene.'

She held out a hand. 'Erica.'

'Erica?'

She spoke up: 'Are you hard of hearing.'

'No, it's just . . .' He shook it. 'Simon.'

'Got a surname?'

'Fenchurch.'

'You boys turned up as I was onstage. Means you got a show for free.' She smiled, half of her mouth not moving. Still had the dimple. She nodded at the bar. 'Would you be a gent?'

'You expect me to get you a drink?'

'It's kind of the main rule round here.'

'I wonder why. What do you want?'

'Hooch.'

'They still make that?'

'It's my favourite.'

'Watch those.' Fenchurch rested his pint on the table next to Nelson's. Bubbles fizzed up, not as many as there should be. He went over to the bar and did up the top button on his suit jacket as he waited.

His drums were rattling through a long fill. Tom-toms to snare, kick drum thumping away underneath. He glanced back at Erica and got a coy smile. The dimple . . .

No way it could be her. No way.

'What can I get you?'

He smiled at the barmaid. 'A bottle of Hooch.'

She grinned back. 'Ten pounds.'

'Sorry, just the one bottle.'

'Yeah, and that's ten quid.'

'Christ on a bike.' Fenchurch fished out his wallet and handed her a tenner. No chance of a receipt in this place. He collected the ice-cold bottle and returned to Erica. 'Here you go.'

She grabbed the drink and sucked at the straw. 'Thanks, Simon.' She stared at the floor. 'You interested in a dance now? See what you missed?'

'Not right now.'

'You've bought me this, though.'

'I like following rules.'

Nelson reappeared and picked up his pint. 'Evening.'

Erica smiled at him. 'Evening, yourself.'

He gave Fenchurch a wink. 'You two look cosy.'

'Don't start.'

Erica ran her fingers along Nelson's jacket. 'Do you want a dance, handsome?'

Nelson swallowed down some Guinness, covering his top lip in creamy foam. 'Later, yeah?'

'Suit yourselves.' Erica sashayed over to a booth filled with other girls. She cuddled into another dancer and locked her gaze on Fenchurch, raised up her bottle and winked.

The girl with the pint glass climbed onto the stage. 'Celebrity Skin' by Hole blasted out of the speakers.

Fenchurch turned to Nelson. 'Come on, Sergeant. Let's raid this infernal place.'

Fenchurch tied on the stab-proof vest and nodded at Nelson then at Owen. 'We ready to rock?'

'Think so.' Owen flipped his Airwave to mute. 'Serial bravo's in place on the back alley.'

'Have we got the warrant?'

Reed tossed over a folded-up sheet of paper and crossed her arms over her own vest. 'Just came though, guv.'

'Excellent.' Fenchurch unfolded it and checked it through. Looked sound. Thank God for Docherty's golf club membership. Worth every grand.

Hardcore punk thudded in his ears. He tried to keep his breath slow. Failed. 'Let's go.' He clutched the warrant tight and jumped out of the van.

Nelson jogged ahead and stopped outside The Alicorn. Another team approached from the opposite side.

The bouncer's eyes were bulging as Fenchurch arrived. He thumped the door behind him. A repeating pattern, twice in quick succession. It shut, leaving him alone on the street.

Fenchurch got in his face. 'Police.'

The bouncer took a step to the side. 'We're not open, sir.'

'We've got a warrant.' Fenchurch held it up to his face. 'Let us in.'

No reply.

'Sir, you're obliged to let us enter the premises.'

The bouncer frowned at them. 'You two were just inside, weren't you?'

'This warrant lets us search the premises. Is the manager inside?'

'He's not. Anyway, the door's locked.'

Fenchurch chopped his hand through the air. 'Then open it up.'

'No can do. I've not got the key.'

The din from inside the bar stopped, replaced with male voices shouting and female screaming.

'This is your last chance.'

The bouncer held up his hands and shrugged.

Fenchurch flicked his hands at the door. 'Go!'

Two officers ran past, one of them lugging the Enforcer battering ram. He hefted the large red tube in gloved hands and rested it against the door. Then swung back and let go. The steel plate crunched into the wood.

It stood firm.

He swung again.

Knocked the door clean off its hinges.

Nelson barged into the club first. Owen marched the bouncer inside, Fenchurch and Reed following.

Girls screamed out. Fifteen or so of them were cowering at the back near the chipboard. Half of them were wearing casual attire, the other in corsets and bikinis. At least one was fully naked. Erica was in the middle, standing with the redhead from earlier.

Fenchurch held out the warrant and spun around to take in the entire room. 'This is a warrant allowing us to access and search these premises! Every single one of you is going to be formally interviewed!'

'Let me see that.' The bouncer tore it from Fenchurch's grasp. He scanned down the page. 'We can't shut this place. We'll lose money.'

'You can and you will.'

The bouncer stepped closer to Fenchurch. 'I need a private word with you.'

'Take a step back, sir.'

'I'm serious.'

'Are you the manager here?'

'He's not in.'

Fenchurch waved at Owen. 'Cuff him, please.'

The bouncer lurched forward and grabbed Fenchurch by the neck. Sharp nails broke his skin. 'You think you can get away with this, you stupid bastard?'

Fenchurch kneed him in the balls and pushed him to the floor. 'Of course I do.' His throat was stinging where he'd been cut. 'Now who's a stupid bastard?'

Chapter Fourteen

The monitors in Leman Street's Observation Suite showed the interviews with girls from The Alicorn. A pair of detectives in each one, begged, stolen and borrowed from across half of London.

Fenchurch's throat was bloody agony. Had half a mind to take that bouncer and kick him down some stairs.

'This is getting us nowhere.' Owen glanced at him. 'All we've got is Nelson and Kershaw backing up Blunden's story from that prostitute.' He raised an eyebrow. 'A black girl.'

'One of Blunden's girls?'

'Kershaw didn't think so. Doesn't mean it's not possible.' Owen tapped at the leftmost screen. 'Turn the sound up on that one.'

Fenchurch reached for the remote and adjusted the volume.

DS Reed sat in a dingy room. She passed over the set of photos, minus the post-mortem shot. 'Have you seen this woman before?'

The girl leaned back in the chair and clutched her arms tight around her shoulders. Her baggy T-shirt had a cartoon picture of a squirrel on the front. 'Never seen her.'

'You sure about that?'

'Positive.'

Fenchurch turned it down a couple of notches. 'Why are we watching this?'

'That girl.' Owen drew a hand across his mouth. 'I know her from somewhere.'

'Where?'

'Don't know. I think she's got a scar.'

'You still wanting to watch it?'

'You're fine.'

Fenchurch muted it and looked at the next screen, the bouncer sitting opposite Kershaw. The Vice DS prowled the room like he was in an American TV show. Didn't seem to be working. 'He's called Winston Gooch, right?'

'Yes he is and he's still not talking.' Owen sniffed yet again. 'Wonder if his balls have descended back from his stomach yet.'

'He grabbed my throat.' Fenchurch stretched out his collar to let the wound breathe. 'Bastard scratched me, too. What kind of man—'

The door opened and Docherty stormed in, wearing full uniform for once. 'Evening, gents.'

'Boss.' Fenchurch stared back at the screen, Kershaw getting in the bouncer's face again. 'Thanks for chasing up the warrant.'

'I'm not as popular with our chums in the judiciary as I once was. Had to call in favours with the CPS.' Docherty tore off his leather gloves and tossed them on the table in front of the monitors. 'You'd better be getting something from this.'

Owen folded his arms and flared his nostrils. 'We're getting nowhere.'

'Nowhere?' Docherty scowled at Fenchurch. 'That's not what I want to hear.'

'It's not Simon's fault, sir. These are all just rank and file. That bouncer's the most senior and he's not talking.'

Docherty waved his hand across the monitors. 'There's no management in any of these?'

'None were there, boss.' Owen bowed his head. 'We don't even know who owns it, sir.'

Docherty walked up to Owen and lifted his chin. 'I'm paying through the nose for you pair and you're not sure who owns a bloody strip club?'

'That's why we're being cagey, sir.' Owen leaned back in his chair. 'The Alicorn is held by a series of shell companies. The only thing we can trace it to is a company called Dragon Entertainment Holdings.'

'But you've got forensic accountants following the money trail, right?'

'It leads offshore. Trail stops in the Cayman Islands.'

'This isn't good.' Docherty shot a glare at both of them. 'Remind me why we're doing this?'

Fenchurch held his gaze. 'We've got intel that our Jane Doe worked there. They kicked her out onto the street.'

'How solid is this intel?'

'Two whores and Frank Blunden.'

'So pretty bloody far from solid?'

Owen lifted a shoulder. 'Correct.'

'If we get nothing here, we're scubbed.'

Owen looked away. 'I don't know what scubbed means, sir, but I get the gist.'

'Well, I'm off to brief your boss.' Docherty opened the door and stopped halfway, twisting round to face them. 'I'll catch up with you two later. For the sake of your arses, I hope you get somewhere.' He slammed the door behind him.

Owen let out a breath. 'Charming.'

'Welcome to my world.' Fenchurch slumped in a seat, eyes drawn to the screen with Erica. She sat there, arms crossed, looking a lot younger than eighteen.

The drums started up again. Topper Headon hammering the kit in a Clash video.

Nelson handed her the set of photos. She picked them up then dropped them onto the table. Looked towards the camera, tears in her eyes.

Fenchurch reached across for the remote and turned the sound up.

Onscreen, Nelson tapped the discarded photo. 'I take from your reaction you know who this is?'

Erica said nothing, just sat there, sobbing into her hand.

'Ms McArthur, I showed you two photos. You started crying when you looked at the second. Who is she?'

Owen squinted at Fenchurch. 'Why her in particular?'

'Because she's crying.' Fenchurch gestured at the other screens. 'None of the rest of them are.'

'Is that all?'

'That not enough?' Fenchurch shifted forward, focusing on the monitor.

Erica clenched her jaw and tightened her arms around her. Like she was trying to turn into a ball.

'She knows something. Come on.' Fenchurch charged out of the room and jogged down the corridor. He burst into the interview room.

Nelson was prodding a finger against the photo. 'Who is she?'

Erica shook her head. 'I swear I don't know.'

Nelson looked up then sat back, adjusting his suit jacket. 'DI Simon Fenchurch and DS Chris Owen have entered the room.'

Fenchurch walked round to the other side and got in Erica's eye line. 'Who is she?'

Erica looked up at the ceiling and kept quiet.

'Why are you crying if you don't know her?'

'I hate being locked up. This is police brutality.'

'We've processed you according to the most stringent regulations. There's no brutality going on here.' Fenchurch crouched down. 'Who is she?'

'No comment.'

'Did she work at The Alicorn?'

'No comment.'

Fenchurch snatched up the sheet and waved it in front of her face. 'You blinked when you looked at the photos. Is it him you recognise?'

'When do I get out of here?'

'When we've finished with you. Who is he?'

'I've no idea.'

'So why the reaction, then?'

'I thought I recognised him, that's all.'

'Erica, has he been in the club?'

Her eyes looked up at him. 'A few times.'

'Now we're getting somewhere.' Fenchurch stood up and smiled. 'Did he ever dance with you?'

She nodded. 'I think his name's Robert.'

'Did you ever get a surname?'

'Never said.' She stared at the table. 'Might not even be called Robert.'

Fenchurch pinched his nose. 'Anything else?'

'He said he was a banker. Earned a packet. That's it, I swear.'

'When was he last in?'

'Tuesday night?'

Fenchurch walked over to the door. Sweat prickled his neck, stinging the cut. 'Thanks for your help.'

———————

'Aye, of course I'm aware of that. Aye.' Docherty stood in the office doorway, silhouetted against the light. Airwave clamped to his ear.

'Have to go, Howard.' He killed the call and entered the room. 'You look like you've got something?'

'We've got a name, guv.' Fenchurch shuffled through the papers on his desk. 'Robert.'

'That's amazing.' Docherty settled against Mulholland's desk and tilted his head to the side. 'I've just burnt through fifty grand in one night raiding that bloody club and all you've got to show for it is a name?'

'I appreciate the support, guv.'

'You're a cheeky bastard, Fenchurch.' Docherty laughed. 'You got anything on him?'

'Not yet. Jon's leading the hunt.'

'With some of Dawn's team, I hope?'

'We're keeping them updated.' Fenchurch flashed a smile that had more in common with a snarl. 'Obviously, this could be bollocks. Geezer could be called Ray or Al or Len or God knows what else. I've got them working on both bases, boss.'

'Great. Well, it's progress, I guess.' Docherty checked his watch. Giant gold thing that probably weighed more than both of his legs. 'Right, that's gone eleven. I need you to hand over to Dawn and piss off out of here. I want you in fresh tomorrow. Well, slightly less soiled, anyway.'

Fenchurch got up and shrugged on his coat. He yawned, one of those ones that didn't want to stop. 'I'll see you tomorrow, boss.'

'I mean it.' Docherty stabbed a finger at him. 'You need to be fresh, okay? I don't need you heading off looking for Chloe acting the bloody martyr.'

'Sir.' Fenchurch left his office, hands deep in pockets. Any deeper and he'd be grabbing his ankles. Might not be a bad position. He scuttled down the stairs and pushed through the ground-floor door.

'Guv.'

Fenchurch swung round.

Nelson. The rings around his eyes as dark as the stubble on his head, several shades darker than his skin. 'Still drawing a blank with this Robert geezer.'

'Okay.' Fenchurch rested against the door and yawned again. 'Pass it onto Mulholland's guys and bugger off home, okay?'

'But I'm confident—'

'Now, Jon. Get home.'

'Okay, guv.'

'See you tomorrow.' Fenchurch buzzed through the door onto the street. The bitter cold clawed at his face as he walked over to his car.

'Simon?'

He looked round.

Erica shivered in the shade of a street light. Her hoodie was tugged up over her hair.

'I can arrange for uniform to give you a lift home. Wherever that is.'

'It's fine.' She waved towards the new towers nearby. 'My flat's just up there.'

Fenchurch looked her up and down. Like a Barbie in urban gear. 'Well, goodnight.'

'Why were you watching my interview?'

He frowned. 'I watched all of them.'

'That right?'

'Of course it's right.' Fenchurch checked down the lane. Nobody about. Lazy jazz drums hissed. 'You're acting like you want to speak to me.'

She sighed. A cloud of mist floated in the air between them. 'I might have something for you.'

'What?'

She bit her lip, her turn to scan the street. 'Not sure I should tell you.'

Fenchurch handed her a business card. 'Well, call me if you think of it.'

'It's not that . . .' She ran a ruby-red fingernail across the print. 'Aren't you going to ask me what it is?'

'I've not got the energy.' Fenchurch took a couple of steps away then turned back. 'How old are you?'

'How old do you think I am?'

'I'll go for sixteen.'

'You saw me drink in the club.'

'So you're at least eighteen?'

Erica fluttered her eyelashes at him. 'I'm more than old enough.'

'You're old enough to be my daughter.' Fenchurch clenched his fists as soon as he said it. The drums cannoned in his ears.

'Is that a problem? Do you prefer women your own age?'

'There's a rule, you know? Half your age plus seven.'

She flashed her eyebrows up and bit her lip. 'What age would I need to be?'

'Goodnight.'

'No, seriously, what age?'

Fenchurch rattled through the calculation in his head. 'Twenty-eight.'

She arched an eyebrow. 'So you're forty-two?'

'That's quick.'

'I like sums.' Her eyelids flickered for a few seconds. 'Twenty years.'

'What is?'

'How long I'd need to wait until our ages match.' She smirked. 'I'll be thirty-eight, you'll be sixty-two.'

'Just have to take your word for it.' Fenchurch got out his key and hit the remote unlock. The Mondeo's headlights flashed in the quiet street. 'What you do isn't a great way to make a living. Your looks will only last so long.'

'You think I don't know that?' She stared into space. 'Most guys in there . . . But it's the only thing I've got.'

'What about your sums? You did an equation in your head. Two, in fact. That's impressive.'

'It's not like I can do anything with it.'

'You mean this isn't paying your way through university?'

'Why aren't you getting into your car?'

Fenchurch just shrugged.

'Do you want me to come with you?'

'You remind me of someone.'

'Your daughter?'

'Maybe.' Fenchurch let out a deep breath. Jazz triplets on a cymbal. 'I lost my daughter about ten years ago. She was eight.'

'I'm sorry to hear that. How did she die?'

'She's not dead.' He sucked in cold air. Someone was smoking upwind of them. 'Someone kidnapped her. Or she ran away. But eight-year-olds don't tend to run away.'

'I don't suppose they do.' She tugged her hair behind her ear.

'You've got the same hair as her.'

'I could pretend to be her for you.'

Fenchurch walked over to his car, jaw clamped tight.

She trotted after him, platform heels clicking on the pavement, and stuck an arm out to block him. 'You were interested in me in the club. Same as in that interview room. You like me, don't you?'

'You're really overstepping the mark here. Get back.'

'I could be your daughter.'

He grabbed her by the shoulders. 'Go. Home.'

'Simon . . .'

'Erica!'

She swung round.

A car pulled up. Driver-side window down, a dark-haired man behind the wheel. Close-cropped hair, sculpted beard, designer suit. Like George Michael, post-Wham!, pre-cottaging.

Fenchurch let her go. 'Who's that?'

'It's nobody important.' She wandered over to the car. As she opened the passenger door, she craned her neck around to Fenchurch. 'The offer still stands.'

Chapter Fifteen

Fenchurch leaned against the windowpane. The cold glass flattened his cheek, hot breath fogging the uPVC. No arguments across the street tonight. No need to show his warrant card again or call Control.

Another bloody martyr. Bloody hell.

He went over to the counter and opened the wine, sniffing it. It smelled okay. Thank God for the twenty-four-hour off-licence on Commercial Road. A twenty-quid bottle there was same quality as a tenner in Tesco, a fiver in Aldi. The ladder of booze.

He reached into the dishwasher for a glass and poured it up to the brim. Just over half left in the bottle. He took a glug and collapsed onto the sofa. Just about drinkable.

He fumbled around for the remote and flicked on the TV. Jim White was shouting at the camera on *Sky Sports News*. Nothing happening. Spurs and Liverpool drew in the Europa League. Like anyone cared. Not proper football. He switched it off and put Lana Del Rey on the stereo.

A flash of Erica dancing on the stage. Strutting, young and carefree. The age Chloe'd—

His mobile rang. 'Evening, Dad.'

'All right, my boy. You had another look today, didn't you?'

'Docherty hasn't briefed me on you policing me.'

Dad laughed. 'Listen, what are you working on?'

Fenchurch took another drink. 'You know I can't tell you that.'

'I'm ex-Job, son, of course you can.' Dad chuckled down the line. 'And I'm back!'

'Still can't tell you.'

'Is it something to do with—'

'Got a new case last night, all right. Prostitute with no ID.'

'I tell you, son—'

'Leave it, Dad. We'll get an ID.'

'And if you don't . . .'

'If I don't, I'll come knocking on your door. How's that sound?'

'I think I'm onto something, son.' Dad left a pause. Heavy breaths hit the receiver. 'I've found a few cases I think might be connected to Chloe. Me and Bert call it the Machine—'

Fenchurch shut his eyes, clamping them tight. 'Dad, we've been over this . . .'

'You're over it so much you check her PNC record every day? Can't I bloody look? I wanted to speak to you about it at lunchtime but you just buggered off.'

'You knew I'd be there, didn't you?'

'Might've done.'

Bloody Docherty. 'Dad, I appreciate the offer but—'

'But you don't need my help looking for your daughter. Right, right, I get it.'

Fenchurch felt a sting in his gut, not all from the chilli. Sharp thwacks at a snare drum. 'Of course I still miss her.'

'We all miss her. Chloe was a lovely girl. Abi said you called her.'

'What?'

'You know I talk to Abi about her, don't you?'

'I didn't.'

'Why did you call her, son?'

'I shouldn't have done that.' Fenchurch's landline rang. 1571 could take the brunt of whoever was spamming him. 'Did I get a reply about going to see the Hammers on Saturday?'

'You said you'd pick me up at eleven.'

'I did, didn't I? We'll get something to eat before the match, all right?'

The house phone rang again. Fenchurch picked it up and checked the display. Abi calling . . .

'Sorry, Dad, I've got to go. I'll see you Saturday.' Fenchurch killed the mobile call and stabbed the other phone's answer button. 'Hello?'

'Simon.'

'Abi.'

Silence. Sounded like she was smiling. Running a hand through her hair. 'I'm sorry for acting like such a bitch last night.'

'I was out of order. Shouldn't have called.'

Another pause. 'I'm glad you did.'

Fenchurch sat forward and put the wine glass on the coffee table. 'Really?'

'It's . . . It's been hard for us. I . . . It's good that you're at least thinking about . . . what happened.'

'I've never stopped.'

'You've never started, Simon. That's the problem.'

'What's that supposed to mean?'

'Obsessing isn't thinking about it. It's not processing it. It's not dealing with it.'

'How do you process your daughter getting kidnapped?'

'She was my daughter too, Simon. I've been in counselling for ten years and I speak to my friends. You pushed me and your parents away. Just threw yourself into your bloody job.'

'Fat lot of good that did me.'

The line buzzed. 'You called, Simon. Ten years too late is still better than never.'

Drums clattered, like someone had chucked them down a flight of stairs. 'I don't know what to do, Abi.'

'Speak to someone.'

'I've tried that.'

'No, you haven't. You sat in a counsellor's office and didn't open your mouth the whole time. Just sat there, angry with the world. That's not talking.'

'Going there's half the battle. That's what you said.'

'Only half, though. You need to do the rest, Simon. You can't go on acting like nothing's happened.'

'I know something's happened. Believe me, I know.' Fenchurch brushed tears from his cheek. His hand was soaked. 'I saw Dad at lunchtime. He just called me. Said you spoke to him.'

'He's worried about you. You won't talk to him about Chloe.'

'Well, I'm worried about him.'

A tut and more buzzing. 'What a pair you are.'

'What's that supposed to mean?'

'He said you're still looking at it on the . . . thingy. Police Computer.'

'PNC.'

'You're your father's son.'

Wasn't that the truth . . . 'I should've spoken to you years ago, Ab.'

'Well, you didn't. Things are different now.'

He swallowed more tears.

'Simon, I've got work in the morning. And a ton of marking to do.'

'How do you cope?'

'I didn't. I don't.' She gasped. 'Every morning I think of her. Skipping out to play on the road outside here. I look out, hoping she'll come back. Every morning, all I can think about is how I wanted to run and stop her.'

'Hey. That's the stick I beat myself up with. I want it back.'

She laughed. 'We couldn't have done anything.'

'I could've. Still can.' Fenchurch stared at the wall. The black-and-white shot of The Clash blown up to distortion.

'Talk to me, Simon.'

'I don't know what to say. No, that's not right. I don't know how to say it. How do you cope with it, knowing she's maybe out there somewhere?'

Her voice was thick and deep, sounded like she was crying too. 'Counselling makes it easier. Most days, the sting is like a ninety-nine instead of the full hundred. On good days, it's only a ninety.'

'I'm at two hundred all the time. Minimum.'

'You're always at two hundred, Simon. Three hundred. A thousand. I just wish you'd spoken ten years ago.'

Fenchurch clenched his teeth together. 'Me too.'

'I've got to go. I've still not wrapped my nephew's Christmas present.'

'You've got a nephew?'

'Jake's boy.'

Thought he was gay. Fenchurch clutched the handset tighter. 'Why did you call me back?'

The buzzing hung in the air between them. 'To give you another chance.'

The music changed to the track in the club. Tears welled in his eyes, drums sped up. 'This case, Abi. There's . . .'

'What?'

He brushed away fresh tears. 'Can we meet up?'

A long pause, Abi's breathing hard and fast over the buzz. 'What about coming round for dinner tomorrow? Say eight o'clock?'

'I'd love to. It's just . . . This case . . .'

'Is that you letting me down gently?'

'No, no. I want to. It's just . . . I might be late.'

'I can wait, Simon. Kind of got used to your unique approach to timekeeping. It's been eight years. Twenty minutes isn't going to kill us.'

He smiled. His muscles ached from it. 'Thanks for listening.'

'Thanks for talking. Goodnight.'

'Night.'

Day 3
Friday, 18th December 2015

Chapter Sixteen

Fenchurch sped up as he neared the end. Lungs burning, feet clattering off the treadmill, loud even through his earbuds. The Cure's 'Pictures of You' blasted his ears, drowning out the drums for once. He skipped up onto the sides of the machine and killed the program. Four miles, that'd do.

The song stung his heart as it always did. A song to beat yourself up to. He stabbed his phone to stop the music. The background was now a photo of Abi and Chloe sitting in a sunny park.

Weights.

He stomped across the empty room towards the row of Nautilus equipment. Sucked down some water as he set the weights high. He pulled down, the bar rough against his hands. Felt the burn in his shoulders almost immediately. Punished himself. Six reps, seven, eight. Nine. The tenth felt like it tore something. He let go and the weights clanked against the barrel. The bar shot up and rattled around the metal support.

He sucked in breath, almost doubling over. Sweat dripped off his forehead, pooling on the floor like the roof had a leak.

'Still got the old magic?' Docherty.

Fenchurch twisted round and tugged his vest. Thing was like a sponge. 'It's hardly magic.'

Docherty leaned against the adjacent machine. In full uniform again. 'Got a meeting with your pal from the TPU.'

Fenchurch pulled the bar again. One. Two. 'That explains the uniform.'

'Got him coming here, though. No way I'm heading out to bloody West London at this time. Hard enough getting in as it is.'

The burn started at the sixth rep. 'Didn't you get enough flirting from him last night?'

'Aye, very good. Just want to make sure we're tight, that's all. That pair are costing me an arm and a leg. Do we still need them?'

'We're not home and dry, sir.' Ten. Fenchurch let the bar up slowly and took another drink of water. 'Anything happen overnight?'

'Mulholland's made a nuisance of herself with the SOCOs. The Crime Scene Report's on your desk.'

'Could've read it on the treadmill.'

'You needed to focus on sweating.'

'Anything else?'

'Finished the interviews with the girls. Nothing salient came out of it. A few of them were a bit pissed off Dawn kept them till last.'

'They shouldn't have been there. Have they typed up the transcripts?'

'Most of them.'

'I'll get someone going through them.'

'That's my boy.' Docherty smoothed down his uniform. 'I'm not having a go but get them doing something, okay?'

'Fine. Savage likes to talk, by the way.'

'As if I couldn't be more excited.'

Fenchurch reached up for the bar. One last set. 'You'll get on like a house on fire.'

Fenchurch dropped the Crime Scene Report on his desk. Waste of bloody time. He ran a hand through his hair, still wet from his shower. The heating was at full blast again. Mulholland's doing, no doubt. He opened the window a crack and a cold breeze burst in. Still pitch-black outside.

A knock at the door.

'Morning, guv.' Nelson. He made a face at the gym kit on the radiator. 'You been working out?'

Fenchurch crossed his arms. His triceps felt tight. Overdone it again, you old sod. 'Keeps me out of mischief.'

'Tell you, you should come for a run with me.' Nelson held up the report. 'Don't tell me Clooney's pulled his finger out for once?'

'Not so's you'd notice. They've spent a day and a half combing that building and the surrounding area. All they've done is prove the knife was used to kill her. Blood types match.' Fenchurch sighed. 'The prints are a dead rubber, too. Doesn't match anyone on the database.'

'And you were thinking the DNA was going to solve this for you.'

'I'm ever the optimist.' Fenchurch scowled at the report. 'This is just a first draft. Still waiting on the DNA analysis.'

'Mind if I have a read?'

'Fill your boots. I need someone going through the interview transcripts from last night.'

'Already got DC Lad on it. How do you think it's going, guv?'

Fenchurch tapped the page of briefing notes. 'This link to The Alicorn has given us something on our guy. That's progress. Still a mile away, though.' He indulged in another sigh. 'So why the visit, Jon?'

'I know that TPU pair of old. Keep an eye on them.' Nelson sat on the edge of the desk and scratched his chin. 'Had a few run-ins with Owen back in my uniform days. He was a DC in the North MIT.'

'Anything dodgy?'

'Nah, he's just a little wanker.' Nelson fanned himself with the report. 'It's always bloody roasting in here.'

Fenchurch pulled his shirt away from his armpits. 'You're not sweating as bad as me.'

'Anyway, watch what you tell Owen. Worked a murder with him up Highbury way. Sneaky little git sent everything up the line to his boss. Got my Sergeant into hot water.'

'And Kershaw?'

'He was in my cohort at Hendon.'

'Another late starter.'

'Think he was a lawyer for a few years before he got the calling. He'd been a City of London hobby bobby since he was a student.' Nelson snorted. 'He's a flash git.'

'So are you.'

Nelson bellowed with laughter. 'It's Kate who brings home the bacon in our house. Owen's a single man. Spends a lot of cash for a police officer. Drives a Beemer. Posh flat up the back of Shoreditch. Splashing the cash always makes me suspicious.'

'Ergo he's dodgy. Noted. Just need to keep ourselves squeaky clean.' Fenchurch checked his watch again. 'Right. Time for—'

His Airwave pinged. 'Control to DI Fenchurch.'

'Safe to talk, Steve.'

'DCI Docherty's instructed you to attend a crime scene. There's another body.'

Chapter Seventeen

Fenchurch turned onto Hanbury Street. Parked cars had already rammed it, obscuring the pub and chip shop on the corner. 'Decent chips in that place.'

Nelson grinned. 'Mexican spices on them?'

'I can eat food without chilli, you know.' Fenchurch trundled past the brick monstrosity of the old Truman brewery, now subdivided into hipster boutiques. He pulled in behind a squad car, lights still flashing, dyeing the puddles blue. The tenements had been acid-cleaned, stopping at a seventies block with a row of scooters outside. 'Boris's gentrification machine's been down here.'

'Can't see a Pizza Express, guv, and there's only two Prets.'

Fenchurch grinned as he got out. Then put his straight face on. 'Here we go.' He strolled through the car park entrance, passing a silver mural of a lion someone thought was a good idea. The place was half-filled with market traders sitting around, none of them setting up any stalls or selling anything. Smelled like posh burgers and gourmet hot dogs.

He made his way to the male uniformed officer managing the cordon. Tall and thin with bright red hair. Just beside him was a van with *Mandy's Nuts* stencilled on the side. The windscreen was a cloud of blue SOCO suits. Looked like they were trying for a Guinness Book of Records attempt inside. That or they were dogging.

'DI Fenchurch.' He waved his warrant card at the uniform. 'This is DS Nelson.' He grabbed the clipboard and signed them in. 'What have we got?'

'A trader found a body first thing this morning.'

Fenchurch frowned. 'Thought they'd moved them all down to Petticoat Lane?'

'One of them pop-up things, sir. Paella, fajitas and lots of other foreign muck.'

Fenchurch clenched his teeth. 'Man or a woman?'

'The trader was a geezer, sir.'

'I meant the body.'

'Oh, right.' The uniform lifted his shoulders, his brows knitted together. 'A girl. Sixteen or seventeen?'

Drums started clattering in his ears. Fenchurch looked around the car park. The SOCO's tent peered over a brick wall at the far side. 'Is she over there?'

'Just follow the tent, sir.'

'Don't get cheeky with me, son.' Fenchurch marched off and covered the distance in seconds.

A female plainclothes officer guarded the entrance to the inner locus, clipboard out. Took one look at his warrant card. 'DS Alison O'Neill, sir. Thanks for attending.'

'Not like I had a choice.' He snatched the clipboard off her and scribbled their names down. 'I'd say it's a pleasure, but . . .' He grabbed a SOCO suit and started putting it on. 'Got an ID on this girl?'

O'Neill shook her head, her bobbed haircut dancing. 'Nothing we can find.'

Fenchurch's stomach fizzed as he hauled on the romper suit. 'Was there a bag, anything like that?'

'Found a handbag.' O'Neill held up a leather purse encased in a plastic evidence bag. 'Not sure it's hers. Either way, it's empty.'

Fenchurch yanked up the zip. A few cameras overlooked the car park. 'Can you get the CCTV footage sent down to Leman Street?'

O'Neill nodded. 'Will do, guv.'

He tugged the hood over his head. 'Jon, let's have a look.' He crouched down and entered the tent.

Three SOCOs were squeezed into the tiny space. The nearest one was dusting the cracked tarmac, another taking photographs. A figure looking very much like Dr Pratt was kneeling at the far corner.

'William, that you?'

He looked up, blinking rapidly through the steamed-up goggles. The throat of his suit was stuffed like an old sofa. 'So they've sent a grown-up.'

'Wouldn't go that far.' Nelson barged into the tent and hovered by the SOCOs.

Pratt's knees popped in a series of clicks as he stood up. 'Must be a world record in attending a request.' He put a medieval-looking thermometer back in his bag and took out a scalpel. 'The Brick Lane lot were first attending. I took one look at the body and thought I'd call you in.'

'Why?'

'It's reasonably similar to our other Jane Doe.'

Fenchurch focused on the girl's body, a SOCO dusting beside her. Nirvana drums thumped.

A young woman lay on her back. Her face pale, eyes staring up at the heavens. Bruising covered her throat in a deep-purple Rorschach pattern. Her dark hair had the thickness of being natural and not dyed.

He let out a held breath and unclenched his jaw. The drums faded out to silence, just his breath rasping against the mask. 'Tell me you've got an ID for her?'

'Afraid not. And there's no distinguishing features either.'

Fenchurch grimaced. 'And here was me thinking all teenagers these days had tattoos and piercings.'

'Not all of them.' Pratt knelt down to zip up his medicine bag. 'Cause of death looks to be manual strangulation. I've been wrong before so I'll need a full post-mortem to confirm the matter.'

'Today, I hope.'

'Won't be until tomorrow, I'm afraid. You're lucky I'm here, as it is.'

'Can you at least tell me the time of death?'

'Based on my initial assessment, I'd wager seven o'clock last night.'

Fenchurch scowled back at the tent entrance. 'When was she found?'

'Seven o'clock this morning. I've been—'

'How did nobody see her body in *twelve hours*?'

Pratt waved at the far side of the tent. 'This section of the car park's hidden behind a wall. Very easy spot for a quick knee-trembler.'

'Classy, William.' Fenchurch grimaced at him, like he'd see it through the mask. 'This doesn't look related to the other one to me.'

Pratt adjusted his beard through the suit. 'I'm not absolutely sure, Simon. I'm saying it's worth assuming so for now.'

'Then I'll see you at the PM whenever you bother to have it.' Fenchurch left the tent and tugged off his mask. 'Bloody hell.'

'This can't be connected, guv.'

Fenchurch frowned at Nelson. 'Is that hope or belief?'

'Hope, I suppose.'

At the outer locus, DS O'Neill was stabbing her finger at a uniformed officer. Male and leering like he was after something. She motioned for him to leave and smiled at Fenchurch. 'Get anything?'

'Not yet.' He pulled down his zip and let the cold air attack his shirt. 'Your mate over there said some pop-up café owner found her?'

———⌣———

Fenchurch leaned back in the chair. The standard of furniture in Brick Lane interview rooms seemed much higher than in Leman Street, though it stank like someone hadn't found a dead rat in the corner of the room. 'Mr Mantilas, I need you to go through your statement again.'

Stef Mantilas shut his eyes and groaned. 'I've already been through it with your colleagues.' His voice was deep and rich. Complete contrast to his tiny frame, almost skin and bone.

'We need to establish the chain of events. Like it or not, you're central to that.' Fenchurch cleared his throat. 'Besides, we believe this may be related to another inquiry.'

Mantilas swallowed hard, his Adam's apple like it was white-water rafting. 'That girl in the building?'

Fenchurch gave a tight nod. 'Please take us through the events surrounding your discovery of the body.'

'I run a van with my brother, Andrew. We sell gourmet Greek Cypriot doughnuts at these foodie fairs.'

'This is Mandy's Nuts, right?'

'Correct.'

'So who's Mandy?'

'That's a nickname Andrew got at work.' Mantilas scratched at his long neck. 'It's kind of stuck.'

'This isn't your living?'

'Well, it's our dream. My day job is in IT. I'm a coder.'

'Might want to consider making it clearer what you sell. I'd expect a handful of roasted almonds and Brazils.'

Mantilas stared into space. 'Never thought of that.'

'Please continue.'

'I usually get there early to grab a good pitch.' Mantilas licked his lips, thin and pale. 'As you probably saw, there weren't a lot of good spots left by the time we got there. Had to make do with that one by the wall. And that's when I saw her. I didn't think it was a person at first.' He chewed on a fingernail. 'Thought it was a fox. Seen a few rummaging around the bins at these things.'

'When was this?'

'Just after seven. It was still dark.' He caught a big chunk of nail. 'I freaked out when I saw it was a woman.'

'Did you touch her?'

'I checked to see if she was okay. Tried to wake her up.' Mantilas wiped a tear sliding down his cheek. 'She was cold and wet. It'd been raining.'

Fenchurch made a note on his Pronto. *Clooney: Mantilas prints/ DNA on body.* 'What did you do next?'

'I called the police. Felt like hours before they showed up. The rest's a blur, I'm afraid. They locked the place down and brought me here.'

Fenchurch scribbled a timeline on a blank note. From the likely time of death at seven p.m. to the discovery twelve hours later. 'I need your whereabouts for last night, Mr Mantilas.'

'I need to get back to my van.'

'I've got a team dusting it for prints. No harm's going to come to it.' Fenchurch smiled, eyes thin slits. 'Now, where were you yesterday evening?'

'Me and Andrew were making the batter for the doughnuts. It's usually best to let it sit for a few days, but we've both been pretty busy.'

'From when until when?'

'I got back from work at five o'clock. We were at it until about midnight.'

'Sounds like a lot of doughnuts.'

'We make good money from these fairs.'

'We will, of course, check with your brother.'

'I gave his details to the officers I spoke to earlier. He's doing the late shift today. This thing goes on till ten at night. Well, not today, I imagine.'

'No, it won't even start.' Fenchurch made a note to check the brother. 'Mr Mantilas, do you know anything about this girl's death?'

'I found her, that's it.' He closed his eyes. 'I'll never forget the way she felt. She was so cold.'

'That'll pass in time, believe me.' Fenchurch gave another smile as he got up. 'My colleagues will look after you. You'll be allowed to go once we've finished searching your van and verified your story.' He thumbed at the door, motioning for Nelson to leave first, and shut it behind them. 'Poor kid.'

'Don't think he did it, guv.' Nelson got out his vape stick and stared at it. He pocketed it without a puff. 'There's a Rough Trade record shop across from the crime scene and a few bars with late licenses round there. I'll get someone out checking them.'

'I really don't want this to be connected.' Fenchurch shook his head, like that'd change the chain of events. 'I'll get Kay man-marking Owen while you manage this.'

'Guv.'

⁓

'What's that?' Reed looked up from her desk, nostrils twitching. 'Bit early for a burrito, isn't it?'

'Never too early, Kay. Trying that place on the Minories.' Fenchurch took another bite. Gave it a couple of chews before swallowing it down. Not half bad. The Incident Room always seemed a bit too quiet when he was around. 'Thanks for running the briefing this morning.'

'Bit of a dead rubber without you.'

'I'm sure that's not true.'

'Well, this bouncer from the club still hasn't spoken. Even after we got him a lawyer. Clearly been trained, guv.'

'Give him another pass, okay? Then we'll need to think about letting him go.' Fenchurch perched on a desk. 'Anything on the press release?'

'We've still got nothing on our Jane Doe.'

'Right. Can you get the street teams to take the new info round the banks on Bishopsgate?'

'We did that last night.'

'Well, I don't want to look like a prize plonker because we've not asked someone a second time. See if this Robert name rings any bells that the photo didn't.'

'Guv.'

'Get back to Dirty Dick's when they open. Speak to the girls again and all the other pubs in the area. If he's been in one pub, he might've been in others. We've maybe got a name now. I want table bookings, bar tabs, credit card receipts.'

'Let me get this straight.' Reed raised her eyebrows as much as that morning's 'Croydon facelift' would allow. Shiny hair pulled tight into a ponytail, stretching her forehead. 'You want me to ask if anyone called Robert has bought a round in a pub in the whole of the City?'

'It's just a square mile.'

She chuckled, shaking her head. 'Don't suppose I can get any City of London officers to help?'

'They're still at arm's reach, Kay. I haven't spoken to them yet.'

'Well, let me know when it's clear.'

'Get on with it now. I'll call my contact soon.' Fenchurch leaned back against the wall. 'And speak to the local prostitutes, as well.'

'Guv.'

'How're Owen and Kershaw doing?'

'They weren't at the briefing. I'll see where they've got to.'

Cheeky bastards. Maybe Nelson was right. Fenchurch tore into his burrito.

'Jon said there's another body?'

'Starting to stretch us thin. I've lost Nelson, Lad and a few others to it. No idea if it's connected or what. I asked for the CCTV to be sent down here.'

'Lisa's watching it now.' Reed got up and skipped over to Bridge's desk. 'Have you got anywhere with that footage?'

She tapped her laptop screen. 'This is Dray Walk car park last night.' She smiled at Fenchurch. 'Guv.'

'Lisa.' Fenchurch sat next to her and tore the foil further down the burrito.

The crime scene was in darkness. Hard to make out whether it was paused or empty. A plastic bag danced across the car park. Wasn't paused after all.

'You got anything?'

'Nothing yet. Pratt reckoned she was killed just after eight, right?'

'Seven.'

'Shit on it.' Bridge screwed up her eyes. 'Sorry, guv.'

Easy mistake to make . . . Fenchurch used his tongue to work a bit of chicken gristle from between his teeth. 'Don't mention it.'

'Here we go.' Bridge jockeyed the footage back, the bag undoing its dance. She stopped at 18.53. After a minute, a couple walked in from the Brick Lane end at double speed.

'Pause it.' He shifted forward and squinted. 'That's not him. Is it her?'

Reed shrugged. 'Can't really tell, guv.'

Bridge switched the display to a high-resolution photograph of their second victim, dead eyes staring through the camera. The wonders of modern technology. 'Doesn't look like her. Agreed?'

'Keep going.' Fenchurch chewed down another mouthful, leaving just the messy end of the tortilla.

Bridge tapped the screen. 19.10. 'Almost caught up with myself. I started this after half past seven. Thought I was being—'

'There.' Fenchurch dropped the burrito carcass and stabbed a finger at the monitor.

A girl ghosted across from the far end, arms tight to her chest.

'Is that her?'

'I think so, sir.' Bridge slowed it down.

The woman walked towards them, passing the front of the camera's range. Just by the lion mural.

'Lost her.' Reed sighed. 'Have we got any other cameras?'

'This is the only one live, Sarge. The others are fakes.'

'Unbelievable.' Fenchurch balled up his foil and tossed it into the brown paper bag. 'Keep it playing.' He finished the burrito, managing to avoid spilling any of it down his shirt.

Almost a minute later, the girl reappeared at 19.13. A man followed her at a discreet distance. It could've been their guy. Just too unclear from this angle. She pointed to the wall at the car park's edge, almost looking at the camera. He followed her behind it, his head darting around.

Fenchurch stayed focused on the screen, again looking like it was frozen. The clock hit 19.19 and the man jerked up from behind the wall. He adjusted his flies and hurried off.

Bridge froze the playback and zoomed in. Blocky and grainy. She pointed at the screen. 'That's our guy. Definitely this Robert character.'

Reed got up and reached forward. 'Can you enhance it?'

Fenchurch frowned. 'I thought you only saw that on *CSI*?'

'What they do on that show is bollocks, sir.' Bridge was grinning as she clicked and typed. 'They're adding pixels, which you can't do. Must've inspired our guys, though, as they've started taking hi-res photos with the video. Crystal-clear snapshots every five frames.'

The display shifted to a different shot, both figures just moved slightly.

'Things you can zoom in on.' Bridge dragged a rectangle round the man's face and it filled the screen, sharp as a needle.

Definitely Robert.

Chapter Eighteen

'That's him?' Reed sucked breath over her teeth. 'He's done both murders?'

'Probably.' Fenchurch couldn't take his eyes off the frozen frame. 'But we need some harder evidence than this, Kay.'

'Come on, guv, he shagged her behind that wall just before she died. There's nobody else there.'

'Yeah, I get it, Kay.' Fenchurch shifted his gaze to her. 'The evidence is stacking up against him, and I'm liking him for the killer. I just want you to keep an open mind. I don't want us to ignore a good lead because we're obsessing about this Robert character. Might not even be his real name.'

'If it is him, guv . . .' Reed snapped off her scrunchie, letting her ponytail tumble down, frizzy and tangled. She struggled to get it behind her ears. 'He's killed two girls in less than twenty-four hours. Why?'

'Wish I knew.' Fenchurch stared at the image on the screen. He didn't look like a hot-blooded killer, but then who did? What was going on in that head? Having sex with his victims then killing them.

The drums smashed into a thumping rhythm.

Assuming it was him, like Kay said, Robert or whoever he is is still out there. Two victims now. Could be more they hadn't found.

And he could kill again.

Fenchurch clapped Bridge on the shoulder. 'This is good work, Constable.'

'Thanks, guv.'

'Get a look at the CCTV on the streets around there.' Reed was on her feet, twitching like that morning's Red Bull had finally kicked in. 'I want to see where he goes next.'

'Warn all of the prostitutes in the East End.' Fenchurch couldn't take his eyes off the face on the monitor. Evil hiding in plain sight. 'The last thing I want is someone thinking they're Jack the bloody Ripper.'

'Guv.'

Fenchurch's phone buzzed in his pocket. Dr Pratt.

'Simon, my morning schedule's just cleared up. I can do this second girl's PM now, if you're available.'

———

'Come on, William.' Fenchurch leaned against the wall, clutching his Pronto. The fake wood panelling was the relic of some previous mortuary transplanted to the modern space. He glanced at Clooney, then at Pratt's assistant. 'You've been at this for two and a half hours. Much as Mick Clooney and I love watching you work, I need to stop this guy killing again. If it was him.'

'Always the same story with you . . .' Pratt smoothed his thick beard. 'It's incredibly difficult to work under these conditions.' He stared into space for a few seconds. 'Okay, let's go through the time of death. Last night wasn't warm. Luckily for us, the body hadn't yet reached equilibrium with the surrounding environment by the time of my initial observation. Both livor mortis and rigor mortis confirm she expired at just after seven p.m.'

'Consistent with our video footage.'

'Quite.' Pratt traced a line down the girl's side, dusky blue lividity hovering above the pale flesh at the bottom. 'The livor mortis additionally shows us she wasn't moved. She was killed in situ.'

'Was she a prostitute?'

'I believe so. There are similar vaginal artefacts as with the other victim. No, erm, DNA trace on her abdomen this time.'

'Is there anything?'

'Not that I've noticed. Whoever did this had protected intercourse with her but didn't leave any pubic hairs, I'm afraid. The spermicide is the same brand of condoms as our other victim. There's a slight tear in her vulva, consistent with the time of death. And there are these little beauties.' Pratt pointed at the girl's throat, necklaced by six round bruises. 'These contusions are a result of the pressure applied by the killer's fingers.' He pointed at a large purple circle in the middle of her throat, covering her windpipe. 'His thumbs have pressed into the recesses containing the carotid artery.' His gloved finger tapped a flap of skin, now resealed. 'Her hyoid's been fractured. That shows the force and intention of our killer.' He caressed the neck where lighter blue bruises dotted the skin. 'There is significant injury to her neck muscles, showing signs of struggle on her part.'

Fenchurch's heart fluttered, something like hope swimming against the tide of disgust. 'Any skin under her nails?'

Pratt held up the girl's hand, struggling against the rigor mortis. The fingernails were clean. 'Sadly not.'

Fenchurch exhaled. 'I was pinning my hopes on that.'

'There is something, though.'

'Always save the best to last, don't you?'

'I'm nothing if not a showman.' Pratt floated his pen in the air just above a bruise. He motioned at a semicircular mark not even a pencil width, easily missed by the untrained eye. 'There are some minor cuts to her throat here.' He moved his pen to the other side, furthest away. 'And here. There's a slight chance her assailant has some of her derma under his fingernails.'

'Then we'd better find him quick smart.' Fenchurch stared at him. 'Anything to think it's the same guy?'

'Different killing method. But I'd say the general modus operandi's similar. Find a prostitute, get his money's worth, then kill her.'

'Any idea who she is?'

'I've got nothing.' Pratt nodded at Clooney. 'Mick was going to be a saint and run the usual battery of tests.'

'I wouldn't hold your breath, Si. It's a long shot.'

'What isn't on this case.' Fenchurch locked his Pronto and clipped the stylus to the side. 'We done here?'

Pratt tore off his gloves and clasped a hand on his assistant's arm. 'We'll start typing this up.'

'Thanks for fast-tracking this, William. I might be a cock most of the time, but I do appreciate the help.' Fenchurch groaned. 'Now, I need to speak to someone downstairs.'

Fenchurch's dad stared out of the open doorway, the strip light humming in the tiny room behind him. 'What are you doing here, Simon?'

Fenchurch smiled. 'I might need your help, Dad.'

'It's lamb stew on in the canteen today, I think. Better than—'

'Mind if I come in?'

'Sure, sure.' Dad led into the room, stooping over slightly. He collapsed into an armchair. God knows where he'd got that from.

There was a chaos of paperwork on the desk. Bookcases filled the room, rammed with case files. 'Have a seat.'

Fenchurch leaned against the wall instead. 'You alone?'

'Bert's at a funeral today.' Dad nudged some paperwork towards the desktop computer. 'What can I help you with, son?'

'There's been another one. We believe she's a prostitute. No ID on her. Strangled this time. Same killer. There are differing MOs, but there are a lot of similarities.'

'Two makes a pattern.' Dad whistled through his teeth. 'And you want to see if they match any of mine?'

'If that's not too much trouble.'

'Simon, this stuff I'm looking into . . .' Dad scratched his neck. 'It's not easy to stomach.'

'Dad, you take one look at a case and see a link to Chloe.' Fenchurch swallowed down mucus. 'Tell me what you've got isn't just wishful thinking.'

'Wishful thinking? Son, I'm trying to—'

'Yeah, Dad, I know what you're trying to do. I just need you to strip it down to the bare facts. No embellishments, yeah?'

'Right.' Dad rubbed his hands together, shivering. 'I've found some disappearances going back to the eighties. Some girls' bodies just turned up with nothing to trace them back to. Nobody's reported them missing, nobody knows who they are.'

'How many?'

'Five so far. All girls. No identities. Completely unknown. Nothing in their purses, where there was one.'

'Had any false positives?'

'Twenty-seven. Mostly where their handbags have been nicked. Lost property is a gold mine. Five girls without IDs and no Missing Persons reports. Their post-mortems identified them as prostitutes.'

'Have you got any leads?'

'Well, we've got some geezer over in—'

'So you don't know.'

'Well, no. But I think we're on to something, son.'

'Is there anything I can use in this case?'

'Isn't what I've found good enough?'

Fenchurch glared at his father. 'This is another bloody wild goose chase, isn't it?'

'Don't be like that, son. I'm trying to get you some closure. Get it for all of us.'

Fenchurch waved around the small room. 'Have you taken this to anyone?'

'I've tried proper channels and . . .' Dad gave a chuckle. 'Improper ones. Nobody's biting.'

'Who's seen it?'

'My superior officers here for starters. Told me to keep digging.' Dad closed a file on the desk behind him. 'That's why I took it to some geezers in Vice a couple of weeks ago.'

Fenchurch frowned. 'Wouldn't happen to be DCI Savage, would it?'

'That's the fella.'

'Do you know if he did anything with it?'

'I got an email back from him.' Dad stared into space, like he could access his Inbox through the air. 'Said something like it's on the active investigation pile, but he's been unable to allocate any resource to it.'

'So nothing, basically.'

'Why do you ask?'

'He's given me some officers for this case.'

'You couldn't ask him for me, could you?'

Fenchurch pushed away from the wall. 'Thanks for that, Dad. I'd better get back.'

'Sure you don't fancy some lamb stew?'

'Another time.' Fenchurch patted his dad on the arm and left him to it. Out in the corridor, his breath came in short bursts.

Fenchurch stared out of his office window. A few day-old *Metro*s danced around Leman Street. A passing taxi kicked up a fresh swirl. The sun had disappeared around the Bank of America building round the corner so it was pretty much night now at half past one.

He checked his phone — still nothing from Nelson. His stomach tightened around the lunchtime burrito. The hot sauce burnt in his guts. Acid reflux loomed.

A knock at the door.

Fenchurch swung around.

Kershaw and Owen let themselves in.

'Afternoon, gents. Nice of you to show your faces, finally.'

Owen sat on the edge of Mulholland's desk and sniffed. He spread his legs wide and let them swing. 'DS Reed said you wanted an update from us?'

Kershaw plonked himself into a seat opposite, scowling like a petulant teenager. Cheap aftershave started fogging the room.

Fenchurch draped his suit jacket over the back of his chair and took a gulp of tea. Almost scalding. 'You pair are mucking about here. Missing briefings is something I take seriously.'

Owen smirked. 'It's just you who gets to miss them, is it?'

Fenchurch gave each of the bloody idiots a long stare. 'What do you two bring to this case?'

Owen sniffed again. Blew air through his nostrils like he was trying to dislodge something. 'We didn't ask to be put on the case.'

'Well, you're on it. Now what have you got for me?'

'We've just spent a few hours freezing our nuts off on the streets of merry Shoreditch. One of the black girls said they'd heard something from someone about your Jane Doe working in The Alicorn. That's two now.'

'Oh, "something from someone"?' Fenchurch took another slurp. 'Sounds solid.'

'We've spoken to all the girls in the known daytime hangouts.' Kershaw was tracing the line of his beard with a finger. 'Nobody's recognised the name or the photo of the killer. That's us until DI Mulholland's team go back out tonight.'

'We've been speaking to the team back at ESB. The name's drawing a blank with our sources there.' Owen stretched forward on the desk. 'Of course, that name could be a load of bollocks, couldn't it?'

'We know that, Sergeant. I've asked you to investigate it as if it was his name.' Fenchurch finally focused on Owen. 'What about the management of the club?'

'We've got nothing.'

'Then you better have a fantastic strategy for getting them in here so we can identify those bloody dead girls out in Lewisham!'

Owen took a few seconds of sniffing before speaking. 'We've got that place under surveillance.'

Fenchurch straightened his tie. 'So this whole bloody case rests on the management paying a visit at some point today?'

'I've got some lads going through the footage for the last twenty-four hours.' Owen raised an eyebrow. 'Anyway, you've been gone a few hours and all you've come back with is tinfoil.'

Cheeky bastard. Needed taking down about seven or eight pegs.

'We've got another victim. Same killer.' Fenchurch tossed the CCTV photo across the desk. 'Picked up a girl on Brick Lane then killed her behind a wall in a bloody car park.'

'Christ.' Owen ran a finger across the page, jaw clenched. 'Why on Earth is he doing this?'

'I wish I knew, Sergeant.'

The Airwave on his desk blasted out. 'DS Reed to DS Fenchurch. Over.'

Fenchurch grabbed the device. 'Safe to speak.'

'Guv, it's Kay. Need you up at the River Poet pub on Folgate Street. Might have a sighting of this Robert guy.'

'Go on.'

'Only problem is, City of London police are threatening to arrest me.'

Chapter Nineteen

Fenchurch pulled onto Folgate Street, the car rocking as it trundled over the cobbles. Reed was outside the River Poet, a sprawling ground-floor bar taking up a few corner units. He parked opposite, next to a town house with Union Jacks stuffed into the windows, and got out. 'Where are they?'

Reed pointed at a silver Vauxhall just down the street. 'They're in there, guv. Thompson and Clarke. You told me it'd been cleared.'

'This is my fault.' Fenchurch stared at the car. 'I should've called him.' He set off across the side lane and hammered on the Vauxhall's roof.

The door opened and Thompson clambered out, sending the suspension rocking. He stretched out to his full height as he did up the buttons on his straining suit jacket. 'Good afternoon, Inspector.'

'No uniform today?' Fenchurch gave a broad smile, his brow creasing. 'What brings you out of Castle Greyskull?'

Thompson leaned against the pub's brick wall, seemingly unable to keep his hungry eyes off Reed as she joined them. 'The Met sending officers out on my manor, sunshine.'

'I hope you're joking.'

Thompson thumbed behind him. 'See that back there?'

'The boozer?'

'No, Bishopsgate. That's my jurisdiction.'

'Yeah, and it ends at Brushfield Street. This is Met territory. Nothing else to say.'

'Except for the fact you've got a squad crawling around the City. RBS, Santander, BES, HSBC. You name it you've been in there today. We've had a few calls from concerned businesses.'

'So?'

'So we had an agreement, or at least I thought we did. Any time you lot visit the City, you take my officers with you.'

'This is on me.' Fenchurch glanced at Reed and nodded. 'I'll ensure it doesn't happen again.'

'You're damn right it won't.' Thompson tapped the roof of the car. 'Give me a minute.' He got in and slammed the door.

Fenchurch looked down the street. 'When I started, all the prostitutes used to mingle here.'

'Shame they still don't.' Reed looked at the ground. 'Those girls might still be alive.'

Through the tinted windows, Thompson was stabbing his hand in the air to punctuate a point.

'Did that bouncer speak, Kay?'

'Still shtum.'

'We'd better let him go, then.'

'Will do. Still nothing from the street team, guv.' She loosened her jacket collar. 'Nothing from any of the businesses. Reckon that's us up to about sixty per cent on the second pass now.'

'So this is another bloody dead end?'

The window wound down and Thompson peered out. 'DI Clarke's going to shadow you.'

The car's street-side door opened and Clarke propped himself up on the vehicle's roof. 'Inspector.'

Fenchurch scowled at Thompson. 'Are you serious?'

'It's that or your subordinate's going into custody. Besides, I've cleared this with DCI Docherty.'

'You went over my head?'

Thompson sneered at him. 'And you shouldn't have let your officers swan around my patch without my express approval.' The window started winding up and the car roared off down the cobbled street, cutting left at the junction.

Fenchurch glared at Clarke. 'You're working with me, okay?'

'That was the idea before you bloody bulldozed your way in.' Clarke winked at Reed. 'Looks like we'll delay your detention for a while, sweetheart.'

'Don't you bloody call me sweetheart.'

Clarke held her gaze and grinned at Fenchurch. 'So, what's happening?'

Fenchurch focused on the pub then on Reed. 'I take it you've got something?'

'My team have been in the pub before with the photo, but I got them to come back here with the name. Jogged the barman's memory. Reckoned he'd been in for a pint in the evening a few times. Thinks he might've stayed next door.'

Fenchurch checked the adjacent brick building. The Note. Yet another central London hotel. Looked expensive, designer paint-work and pot plants on the pavement. 'And did he?'

'Let's find out.'

―――――⌒―――――

The manager's office was a tiny space rammed with catering boxes and paper files. DC Bridge was sitting at a small desk, typing into her Pronto. A tall man with dark hair squeezed in next to her, wearing an unflattering grey polo shirt. His fingers danced across a computer keyboard.

Bridge wheeled her chair back and frowned at Clarke. Then at Reed. 'Think we're finally getting somewhere, Sarge. This is Mr Cartwright. One of his staff has recognised our man. He's giving a statement over at Brick Lane.'

Fenchurch took a deep breath. 'So let's go speak to him.'

'Wait a second.' Cartwright tapped the screen of the computer. 'I think I've got him.'

Fenchurch squinted at it. Just grey windows and blurry text.

Cartwright reached down to a printer at his feet and collected a page. 'Corporate gig earlier in the year. His name's Robert Hall.'

Thank God that checked out. A few grand down the right plughole for once. Fenchurch sifted through the sheet. Meant nothing much to him. 'Has he stayed here recently?'

'No. That's why it took Khaled a while to remember his face. Sorry.'

Fenchurch nodded. 'When did this arrangement finish?'

'March, according to the system.'

'Any idea why?'

'Got a flat? Stopped coming to London?' Cartwright raised his shoulders. 'Happens all the time in this trade. Sorry, but I've no idea.'

'You been here long?'

'Since August. Not while he was staying here, though.'

Fenchurch folded the sheet in half. 'You say this was a corporate stay?'

'Paid for by his business, I think. Certainly booked it.'

'Who were they?'

Cartwright snatched the page back and unfolded it. 'Give me a sec.'

Fenchurch locked eyes with Reed, her baby blues turning to stone. 'He clearly didn't intend to kill. At least not initially.'

'Why, because he's using his real name?'

'Got it in one.'

Cartwright jabbed a finger at the bottom of his screen. '6DA45B is the client code for BES.'

'Snappy.' Fenchurch rolled his tongue across his teeth. 'That's a bank on Bishopsgate, isn't it?'

Clarke beamed at him. 'I know a few people in there.'

———⌣———

Fenchurch stormed across the atrium, drums clattering in his ears. Steel support columns cast long shadows across the flagstones, burnt coffee stung his nostrils. He flashed his warrant card at the receptionist, a young Asian man. 'DI Fenchurch. I need to speak to a Robert Hall.'

His name badge read Deepak. 'Is Mr Hall a BES employee?' Barrow-boy accent.

'I believe so. Can we have a word with him?'

'Just a second.' Deepak tapped the keyboard. 'Here we go.' He put a phone to his ear and looked away. 'Is Mr Hall there? Oh? Right. Okay. Is there anyone— When does the meeting get out? Okay. Thanks.' He gave a grimace. 'Unfortunately, Mr Hall's not in today.'

'Shit.' Fenchurch shut his eyes and let his shoulders drop. Reed and Clarke appeared, both of their faces flushed. 'What about his line manager?'

'He's in a meeting and I don't have the authority to drag him out of it, I'm afraid.' Deepak gestured at a row of black leather sofas to the side. 'If you could take a seat, please?'

'I told you, I need to speak to someone.'

'And I'm trying my best here.'

'This is a murder case.'

Deepak raised his hands in the air.

Clarke flicked up his eyebrows, a shit-eating grin on his face. 'Not going too well, is it?'

Fenchurch held his gaze for a few seconds, his stomach stinging. 'One step forward, two back.'

Clarke switched the smile to Deepak. 'Can you call Katrina Hardington for me?'

The receptionist nodded. 'Who shall I say is calling?'

'Tell her it's Steve Clarke.'

Fenchurch walked off, scowling. 'Bloody City wanker.'

Reed shrugged as she caught up with him. 'He seems to know people, though, guv.'

'Which is my main concern.' Fenchurch leaned over to whisper: 'Jon said something about Owen and Kershaw being bent.'

'Gay?'

'Corrupt.'

'Well, they're Vice.' Reed shot him a wink. 'Being bent's par for the course, right?'

'We just need to keep our eyes and ears open.'

'Paranoid much?'

'The way he keeps sniffing, it's like—'

A dog whistle squalled across the reception. Clarke was winking at them, like he was in a bloody *Carry On* film. A tall woman in a trouser suit was standing next to him. Maybe a bit too close. Her dark hair was scraped back into a ponytail, a couple of notches tighter than Reed's had been that morning. She held out a hand as he approached. 'DI Fenchurch?'

He shook it. 'This is DS Reed.'

'Katrina Hardington.' She smiled at Reed, but didn't offer a hand. 'I'm the UK HR director. If you'll just follow me?'

Hardington's office was at least double the size of Fenchurch's own shared space. Two floor-to-ceiling windows looked onto the opposite building's roof garden. A huge chrome and steel thing, growing out of Spitalfields Market. The church spires lurked behind.

Fenchurch glanced over at Clarke sitting next to him. 'I take it you two know each other?'

Clarke narrowed his eyes. 'We've had dealings on a number of cases.'

'Come on, Steve.' Hardington giggled. 'We go back further than that.'

Clarke let out a sigh. 'We're here to discuss one of your employees. Name of Robert Hall.'

'Is Mr Hall in some kind of trouble?'

Fenchurch jumped in before Clarke. 'We need to speak to him regarding an ongoing inquiry.'

'Before we get too far, I should point out we'll need a warrant for any information.'

'You should've told us you weren't going to play ball downstairs.'

Clarke leaned back in his chair. 'Katrina, my Met colleagues are working a murder.'

Hardington's eyes darted over to Fenchurch. 'What do you need to discuss with him?'

Fenchurch unlocked his Pronto. 'He's our main suspect in the murders of two prostitutes. One on Tuesday night, one yesterday evening. We've only just identified his full name.'

She fixed a gaze on Clarke. 'We need to keep the BES involvement out of the press.'

Clarke bounced her steely glare back. 'Kat, just give us what we want and we'll clear off.'

'Very well.' Hardington licked her lips as she typed, jaw clenched. 'It would appear he's not in work today.' She ran a finger across the screen. 'His pass hasn't accessed any of our London sites.'

'What about elsewhere in the UK?'

'We're only present in the City and Canary Wharf, Inspector.' Hardington tapped her monitor. 'Mr Hall appears to have called in sick yesterday morning, in accordance with policy.'

'What was wrong with him?'

'Stress is the code logged.' She tilted her head to the side. 'That can be unreliable, though.'

'Is he absent often?'

'That was the first day Mr Hall's missed since he started.'

'Have you got an address for him?'

'We have one in West Sussex and one in London.'

One Prescot Street was a giant art-deco building. Green balls of box climbed out of the pot on the top step. Etched stone surrounded the doorway. Red brick columns reaching up into the sky separated a grid work of windows. The upper floors had ornate beige stonework like something in Manhattan.

Fenchurch hammered the intercom and took a step back. 'Come on, come on, come on.' He jabbed the buzzer again and looked down the narrow tunnel of Prescot Street towards Mansell Street. The ancient church halfway down on the left sat among a cacophony of modern buildings. A gust of wind blew grit into his eyes. 'Shit.'

Reed hit the intercom again and waited. 'Doesn't look like he's in, guv.'

Fenchurch pressed the button marked *Concierge*. 'This bugger better answer.'

'Good afternoon. Number one Prescot Street. How can I help?' Sounded like a butler from a forties farce.

'Is that the building manager?'

'It is. To whom am I speaking?'

'Detective Inspector Simon Fenchurch of the Metropolitan police service. We need access to one of your flats.'

'Which apartment do you seek?'

'Number six. The occupant's name is Robert Hall.'

'Are you certain Mr Hall is in?'

'Well, he's not at work.'

'I'm afraid I'll need a warrant to provide access to his apartment.' His accent broke, fragments of gruff Cockney appearing at the edges.

'Come on, sir, this is important.'

Nothing.

Fenchurch hit a few other buttons. No response. He turned round.

Clarke was jogging down the street, flanked by two uniformed officers.

Fenchurch trotted down the steps to meet them. 'We need a warrant to get in.'

'It's not my patch.' Clarke wheezed out. 'I'm here to check you don't stray too far.'

Fenchurch stared at Reed. 'We need to get the Big Key round from Brick Lane.'

'Guv.'

Clarke frowned at him. 'You tried the old Criminal Evidence Act trick?'

'Good shout.' Fenchurch jogged up the steps and stabbed the intercom again. 'We require urgent access to the property.'

'And I said you need a warrant.'

'No, I don't. Under section seventeen, subsection 1b of the Police and Criminal Evidence Act, I may enter the premises to arrest a person for an indictable offence.'

'That sounds very American to me.'

'Trust me, sir, it's not. Murder is an indictable offence under English law.'

A gust of wind clattered into Fenchurch. More grit and a fug of cigarette smoke.

Still nothing from the concierge.

'We've reason to believe the tenant has committed murder.' Fenchurch pinched his nose. 'Listen to me. I'm justified in getting a squad of constables round here with an Enforcer battering ram. Should be two minutes at the most. We'll knock this door down first. Then we'll knock down Mr Hall's flat door. That's a lot of repair work to manage.'

A pause then the front door clicked open.

Fenchurch let out a breath. 'After you.'

Reed led inside the building. The foyer was dark and musty, the lights barely illuminating the space.

A jangle of keys came from the right. The concierge stood there, his belly hanging out of the bottom of a grey tank top. His greying hair was gelled into a Teddy-boy style. 'Are you Fenchurch?'

'I am.'

The concierge grunted. 'I'm not happy with you threatening me.'

'There's a murder suspect in one of your flats.'

'Still don't like it.' He started off down the corridor. 'Follow me.'

Fenchurch jogged across the maroon tiles, locking step with him. 'Do you know Mr Hall?'

'Just the usual crap. When his heating breaks or he's got a delivery from Amazon.'

'Not many buildings have a concierge.'

'The new ones do. Bloody city's turning into New York.' The guard stopped outside a door marked with six and slid a key into the lock. Turned it twice to unlock it. 'Here you go.'

Fenchurch stepped inside. The place smelled of burnt marsh-mallows. A tiny hallway, just a dark wooden staircase leading down. No other doors. He crept down, extending his baton as he descended. 'Mr Hall?'

There was a small lounge at the bottom of the stairs. Pale laminate flooring was coming apart in the middle. A chocolate-brown L-shaped leather sofa sat in the corner by the dark window. A children's book sat on top, a grinning cartoon seahorse carrying a pebble under the waves.

'Who the bloody hell is Charlie the Seahorse?'

Reed walked over and flicked it with her baton. 'My kids love it.'

'Things have changed since . . .' Fenchurch swallowed. He spun round and took in the rest of the room, his throat thick.

A small desk with a closed laptop sat next to a wall-mounted flat screen.

There was another door. He opened it. A bedroom. An unmade bed with stained white sheets, almost grey, the duvet hanging half off.

A man lay on the floor, a needle dug into his wrist. Arms by his sides, one tied off with a leather belt. Dead eyes stared out at them.

Robert Hall.

Chapter Twenty

A nother suited figure clomped through the tiny flat, the SOCO suit hanging off a skinny frame. Docherty.

The crinkling of Fenchurch's own suit drowned out his knees creaking as he got up. 'Boss.'

'Simon.' Docherty looked around the place. 'How're you doing?'

'Seen a few dead bodies in my time. Never gets any easier.'

'Anything to report here?'

'Not yet.' Fenchurch thumbed through to the bedroom. 'Pratt's still checking him over.'

'This doesn't look good. Guy turns up a day after he's bumped off your first Jane Doe and a few hours after number two.' Docherty's sigh was muffled by his mask. 'What do we know about him?'

'Bugger all, really. DC Bridge's gone to the other address. Might be his parents or something.'

'Good girl.' Docherty scratched at his mask. 'Bloody thing.' He got it to settle. 'Thought you said he was a banker. Why's he shooting up?'

'People who kill prostitutes don't tend to be rational, boss.'

'Think he's a serial killer?'

'In my experience, serial killers who focus on prostitutes are the mission-oriented type. In their eyes, they're ridding the world of a scourge.' Fenchurch grimaced, his eye caught on the Charlie the Seahorse book. 'I don't get that impression here. There's no message, no religious iconography.'

'Don't they say bankers and CEOs are all psychopaths?'

'Definitely CEOs.' Fenchurch loosened off his suit. The plastic was sticking to his sweating skin, the scratch still raw. 'What's happened to our Jane Does looks like rage attacks to me, not some logical slaying.'

'He could've killed them because they laughed at the size of his knob.'

'Maybe. The second one was more focused. Just squeezed the life out of her.'

'I don't like this.'

'Me neither. Come on, let's chase him up.' Fenchurch walked through to the bedroom and crouched down beside Dr Pratt again. 'So what do you reckon, William?'

Pratt brushed his wrist against his mask and nodded at Docherty. 'I'm still nowhere near anything useful. My initial assessment is he's died of an overdose. It's heroin in the syringe.' He waved a hand around the needle on the floor next to him. 'I'll confirm it when I open up his lungs back at Lewisham.'

Fenchurch breathed in stale air through the mask. 'Could it be deliberate?'

'You mean suicide?'

'No. Could someone have killed him?'

'Now that's something I just don't know.' Pratt stood up and clicked his back. 'Some good fortune, though. Unlike your Jane Doe this morning, there appears to be some skin under his nails.'

Fenchurch frowned. 'So he was attacked?'

'It could be he was the attacker. But I've asked Mr Clooney to check it against the victim from this morning.' Pratt waved over at a SOCO arguing with a colleague. 'He found an HTC thingumajig in the lounge.'

'Make sure he processes that ASAP. Get the skin stuff done first, though.'

'Thank God we're blessed with your insightful leadership, Inspector.' Pratt winked at Docherty through his goggles. 'Now, for time of death, I've had my magic thermometer out again.' He waved his arms around the room. 'It's a lot more temperate in here, thankfully, so I can say with a great degree of certainty that he died at ten p.m. last night. Give or take fifteen minutes either side.'

Docherty's goggles were still pointing at the body. 'So Mr Hall here's died three hours after he potentially killed victim number two?'

Pratt's suit squeaked as his head twisted between them. 'You know his name?'

Fenchurch held up the photograph Katrina Hardington had given them. 'Robert Hall. We suspect he's responsible for killing both of our mystery prostitutes.'

'Good Lord.'

'Can you dig out his medical records? We want to check if he's got a history of mental illness.'

'Of course. I'll need you to furnish me with someone to do a formal ID.'

'We'll try.' Fenchurch tilted his head at Pratt. 'I'll see you later, no doubt.'

'Look forward to it.'

Docherty beckoned Fenchurch away. 'Right, my reading of it is we're stuffed until Pratt and Clooney pull their fingers out. Correct?'

'Well, we can dig into his background, boss. See if anyone knew about the heroin, for starters. I'll start with the office.'

Docherty stared over at Clarke in the corner, facing away and speaking into his phone. 'Might have found a use for your shadow, after all.'

———— ⌣ ————

The old Truman brewery's chimney loomed in the middle distance, dirty brick climbing above the second victim's crime scene. Some blokes in Hackney had restarted the old brewery, a victim of some eighties corporate skulduggery.

Fenchurch checked his watch and sat down again in front of Katrina Hardington's desk. 'They're stalling.'

Clarke looked up from his mobile. 'Kat'll be in a meeting room somewhere talking through what they can and can't tell us.'

'Kat?'

'I golf with her husband.'

The door opened, sticking halfway. Hardington gave it a shove and swept into the room. 'Sorry for keeping you, gents. I've brought Mr Hall's line manager with me. He was in a meeting. I had to check a few rooms before I found him.'

A man strolled in like he was between classes at Eton. Navy three-piece suit with a beige shirt and grey tie. Hair shaved at the side, the top tapering into a Hoxton fin. He held out a hand. 'Christian Weston. Pleased to meet you.' A rich baritone. West London accent, Richmond or further out.

'DI Fenchurch.' He didn't shake his hand. 'This is DI Steve Clarke.'

'I'd say it's a pleasure, but, well.' Weston sat next to Hardington and rested his hands behind his head. 'Kat said you found Rob's body?'

'We believe so but we're in the process of confirming it now.' Fenchurch twiddled the Pronto's stylus between his fingers. 'We understand Mr Hall worked for you?'

'That's right. Rob started here in November last year.' Weston slackened off his tie. A sliver of tanned skin poked through the gap. 'Best guy on my team. I'm devastated to lose him.' He was struggling to control his bottom lip.

Fenchurch tapped the stylus off the screen. 'How's he seemed recently?'

West shrugged. Glassy-eyed, staring into space. 'Fine, I guess.'

'Nothing strange in his personality? No sudden mood swings?'

'He's been fine, like I said.' Weston crossed his arms. The light caught his wedding ring. 'We used to get a paella at lunchtime. Sometimes go for a couple of pints of Doom after work. Rob liked a beer, that's for sure.'

'Were you with him on Tuesday night?'

'We had a session with some key clients in Dirty Dick's on Bishopsgate. Finished up about nine, I think.'

'Did you leave with Mr Hall?'

'No, he stayed around. Said he wanted another drink. I've no idea what happened after he left. He was off ill yesterday.' Weston grimaced. 'There were a few jokes about his hangover.'

Fenchurch accessed the case files on his Pronto and pulled up the master timeline. 'And did you pay?'

'I did. Client entertainment.' Weston leaned forward in the chair. 'This is pretty tough to take.'

'We're almost done.' Fenchurch stabbed a few additional entries into the timeline. 'We found Mr Hall in a flat just down the road from here, but he's got another address in West Sussex. Is that right?'

'He lives in London during the week. Goes back to his family home at the weekend. Nice place in Three Bridges.'

Fenchurch tapped out a message to Bridge: *House you're heading for is family home.* 'That's commutable.'

'Not really. It's at least two hours each way, door-to-door. We work long hours here. We did put him up in a hotel for the first few months, but he moved into that flat in March.' Weston pinched his nose. 'Look, when you asked about how he'd been, well there was an incident a few weeks ago.' A quick glance over at Hardington before he continued. 'He didn't come back to the office after a client lunch. These things can get pretty boozy, but that's beyond the pale.'

'And out of character?'

'Quite. Rob'd been the model employee, but . . . I don't know. He's not been himself since then, now you mention it.'

Clarke caught Hardington's glare. 'Kat, did you know about this?'

'Well, we've been in discussions about this. Matters of employee discipline are—'

'Kat, come on.' Clarke had narrowed his eyes. 'What was going on?'

'We were investigating his conduct. I had scheduled a drugs test for him this Friday, masquerading as another appointment.' She raised a hand, fending off questions. 'All part of the standard contract.'

Fenchurch coughed, dragging Weston's attention up from the floor. 'So you thought he'd been using drugs?'

'It's not uncommon in this business. Coke, especially.'

'What about heroin?'

'God, no. Why would you think that?'

Fenchurch held his gaze until he believed Weston's shock was genuine. 'And you've been covering this up, have you?'

'Listen.' Hardington cracked her knuckles, practically pulling them out of the sockets. 'This is in the utmost confidence, okay? We've had to discipline more than one employee regarding this sort of behaviour. Steve, you said you found Mr Hall through his stay at The Note hotel?' She left a long enough pause for Clarke to nod. 'Well, back in April, we terminated the contract of a colleague of Mr Hall's who was also staying there.'

Why did it always come down to bloody threats with these people? Fenchurch decided to fill her next pause. 'For what reason?'

'Aside from his coke habit, he was using the hotel's front desk to book him an escort for the night.'

Chapter Twenty-One

Fenchurch followed Clarke up the backstairs in Bishopsgate police station. The walls were lined with portraits of senior officers going back to the nineteenth century, facial hair becoming less prominent as the years progressed. He checked his Airwave, still nothing from Bridge down in West Sussex. 'Thanks for letting us into the corridors of power.'

Clarke stopped at the landing and held a door open for him. 'Only way I can keep a proper eye on you, Fenchurch.'

'I've apologised for my earlier oversight.'

'Doesn't mean I trust a thing that comes out of your mouth.' Clarke powered down the corridor and paused outside an interview room. 'I'll be next door, making sure I record this for a training course. Show how the Met experts do it.'

Wanker. Fenchurch opened the door and plodded in.

Owen got up and screwed up his tie. He whispered in Fenchurch's ear: 'The hotel owner's in Dubai. He's the best we can do. Name's Derek Hateley, managed the place at the time.'

'Right, thanks for that.' Fenchurch sat in the vacant seat.

Opposite, Hateley played with a bum-fluff beard covering a sea of acne. He wore camouflage trousers and a plain black T-shirt. Arms like toothpicks.

Owen leaned over to the microphone. 'DI Fenchurch has entered the room at sixteen twenty.'

Fenchurch tried to attract Hateley's attention. He was looking around, an eyebrow arched. Didn't seem fazed by being in a police interview room. 'Thanks for joining us here, sir. We understand you worked at The Note hotel on Folgate Street. Do you recognise the name Robert Hall?'

'Sorry. It's not a first-name basis sort of place.'

'Well, Mr Hall stayed there for a few months. Up to March of this year, in fact. We believe your hotel had been arranging prostitutes for him.'

'I've no idea what you're talking about.' Hateley slumped against the back of his chair, the wood creaking. The overhead light caught on a gold tooth as he sneered. 'I've not worked there since August. I never met the geezer.'

'Listen, sunshine. Mr Hall was getting a home delivery of hookers. You were aiding and abetting, weren't you?'

'This is being recorded, right?'

Fenchurch tapped the machine. 'That's what this is doing, yes.'

'So anything I say could get me into trouble.'

Fenchurch whispered at Owen: 'Anything you can offer him?'

Owen cleared his throat. 'Mr Hateley, I work for the Met's Trafficking and Prostitution Unit. If you help us, I can put you on the books as a Covert Human Intelligence Source. You'll get immunity from prosecution.'

Hateley scratched at the wispy beard, eyes darting between them. 'This is on the level?'

'So long as you give us something.' Owen grinned. 'And that something turns out to be true, of course.'

Hateley let out a deep sigh. 'I was only following orders.'

'That old chestnut.' Fenchurch rolled his eyes. 'Whose orders? The hotel management?'

A slight nod. 'They wanted us to procure girls and boys, if asked.'

'Boys?'

'Rent boys.' Hateley grimaced, his lips parting to show yellowing teeth. 'I'm sure you've come across a few in your time.' He added a little laugh to the horror show in his mouth. 'We get all sorts of punters staying there. They're away from home. Lonely. Some of them want a bit of company. They'd get dropped off in a taxi, service their client, then leave. Some would stay the night.' He shrugged. 'I suppose some were only after the company.'

Fenchurch scowled at him. 'Do you have any idea whose taxis dropped them off?'

'No idea, sorry.' Hateley scratched at his neck. Skin flakes flew around the room, catching in the light. 'Listen, we had a problem when they installed the new Procurement system. We usually put them through as "Additional Cleaning" or "Flowers".'

'Flowers?'

'It's a luxury hotel. People want their rooms to look and smell nice.' He placed a hand over his thin beard. 'One of my team invoiced them as "Prostitutes (Male)" and "Prostitutes (Female)". Her name's Cindy.'

'Cindy.' Fenchurch noted it on his Pronto. 'And did she come in a box?'

'Hardly. Bloody dyke, if you ask me. Shaved head, piercings and tattoos. You know the sort. I had to have a word with her a few times after she confronted one too many of our guests about this . . . service.'

'Did Cindy have a personal beef against Mr Hall?'

'Like I say, I don't know the fella.' Hateley scratched at the back of his neck. 'Look, I know Cindy left there a few weeks back. I can give you her address, if that's any use?'

Fenchurch handed him a pen and a blank sheet of A4. 'There you go.'

Hateley scribbled it over four lines and pushed it over the table. 'She might've moved, of course.'

Owen took the sheet and folded it in half, smoothing out the crease with a fingernail. 'So where are the girls coming from?'

'All I know is it's somewhere out east.'

'East London's a very big place. Would any of your staff know?'

'I doubt it.'

'Interview terminated at sixteen thirty-one.' Owen rapped at the two-way mirror. 'I'm going to need you to give my colleagues a detailed statement, okay?'

'Right.'

Fenchurch waved at Owen and left the room. He stopped outside and leaned against the wall. 'Why did you stop that?'

'Because he doesn't know where this bloody knocking shop is.' Owen sniffed. 'Sadly, a lot of hotels do that particular sideline. It's even more lucrative than porn these days.' He stabbed a finger at the door. 'These lonely men in hotel rooms should just have a wank, if you ask me.'

The adjacent door opened and Clarke appeared. 'That do for you, Fenchurch?'

'It's a start, I suppose.'

'You really want one of my lads to take a statement from that clown?'

'Send him down to Leman Street if that's too much to ask.'

'You're welcome to him.'

'We'll take him. Are we cool?'

'Well, we're done here for now.' Clarke doffed his non-existent cap. 'I've got a proper case of my own to deal with up in Moorgate, so I'll trust you to behave yourselves.'

'We can be trusted.'

Clarke strode off down the corridor, shaking his head. 'Make sure me and DCI Thompson don't have reason to doubt that, okay?'

Fenchurch marched Hateley up to the desk at Leman Street's back entrance. 'Steve, can you arrange for someone upstairs to get a statement out of this bloke?'

The hulking Desk Sergeant tapped at his computer. 'Name?'

He gripped the edge of the counter. 'Derek Hateley.'

'Right, sir, I need you to sign this for me.'

'Cheers, Steve.' Fenchurch patted Hateley on the arm. 'Tell them what you told us and you'll get out of here, okay?'

Hateley just nodded, looking resigned to his fate.

Fenchurch followed Owen towards the stairs.

Steve gripped Fenchurch's arm. 'There's another thing, guv.'

Fenchurch stopped and frowned. 'What is it?'

'Got a Cindy Smith upstairs. Room two, your floor.'

'That was quick. Send my thanks to the Brick Lane lot.' Fenchurch grinned as he followed Owen into the stairwell. 'Tell me what you're thinking, Sergeant.'

Owen held open the door to their floor. 'There are quite a few brothels out east. We keep trying to shut them down but they keep popping up again. It's like playing bloody whack-a-mole.'

'You think he's on the level?'

'Don't have any reason to doubt it. On the other hand, it could just be escorts. Girls to slip an arm around at a corporate function.'

Owen screwed up his face. 'Most of them are also on the game, sadly. There's almost too many options here.'

'Well, what do we know?'

'Girls dropped off by taxis.'

'Flick Knife?'

'Not his style, guv. He keeps that taxi business cleaner than my teeth, you know. No, I think we should focus on the girls.'

'I'll let you get on with it.' Fenchurch stormed off down the corridor and made for the Incident Room. 'DS Reed.'

'Guv.' She looked up from a pile of reports. 'Lisa's just got to Three Bridges now. Doesn't look there's anyone in.'

'That's all I bloody need. Anyway, I need you in interview room two, now.'

'—and DS Kay Reed. Also present is . . .' Fenchurch frowned. 'Is that your full name?'

Cindy Smith was staring down at the table, her thumb fiddling with the many hoops in her right ear. Her collection rivalled Clooney's. Nowhere near as butch as Hateley led him to expect. Her green eyes were lidded with heavy eyebrows, three rings stuck in the left side. She blushed, the only colour on her milky-white face. 'Cinderella Jane Smith.'

Fenchurch had to cover his laugh with a cough. 'We understand you worked at The Note hotel on Folgate Street?'

'What of it? I'm at the Travelodge on Old Street now.'

'Why did you leave?'

'Nothing to do with you.' Cindy gave him a death stare. 'Why am I here? You've got me under interview and nobody's telling me why.'

'We're not accusing you of doing anything illegal.'

'Illegal? What the hell is going on?'

Fenchurch glanced at Reed. Looked like she was ready to jump in two-footed. 'We need to know whether you amended the invoice lines on the hotel's procurement system.'

'So what if I did?' Cindy folded her bulky arms. 'Has someone put me in the shit? Was it Hateley?'

'Did you make the changes or didn't you?'

Cindy just sniffed.

'Why did you do it?'

'They should've had tighter controls on the invoicing system, that's all I'll say.' She fiddled at a ring in her ear. 'I didn't think it'd let me put it live.'

'So you did do it?'

Cindy leaned back and focused on the ceiling. 'I changed "Flowers" and "Cleaning" to "Prostitutes", or something. Happy now?'

'Not just yet.'

She clenched her jaw and let out a breath. 'Do you agree with what they were doing there?'

'Not personally, no.'

'Can you blame me for what I did, then?'

'We're not questioning you with a view to prosecuting you. We just want to ensure we have the story straight.'

'We had to get hookers for the lonely wankers who stayed there.' She huffed out air. 'I wasn't going to stand for it any more. I was disgusted by those dirty bastards.' She shook her head. 'Anyone who exploits someone else for sex is subhuman.'

'So you saw your actions as a way of nipping it in the bud?'

'The bud was already a big flower by the time I did that.' Cindy wrinkled her brow. 'This was people. Prostitutes and rent boys. It's sickening.'

'They'd be lucky to even have a business after what you did.'

'It only affected a handful of clients.' She gave a shrug. 'If their wives or bosses found out, at least they know what they're up to.'

'Was Robert Hall one of those affected?'

'Who's he?'

'Just tell us if he was one of them.'

'I can't remember. Look, this wasn't personal. If he was doing that then it's his own stupid fault.'

'Do you know where they were getting the girls from?'

'I only dealt with a few of them. They were very discreet, as you can imagine. I think they came from somewhere in Shadwell.'

'Shadwell. You're sure?'

'There was one I saw a few times. Think her name was Parbatee.'

Chapter Twenty-Two

Fenchurch remote-locked the pool car. Its indicators pulsed in response. Wind sliced through the railway arches, a pair of DLR trains grinding past each other above.

Owen pointed down a dark lane. 'Parbatee's place is just down here.'

Ivy covered a red-brick building looming over some houses. The street lamp illuminated a mishmash of browns and greens — looked like wild buddleia, ash and hawthorn. Lights flickered inside a top-floor window, the rest in darkness.

Fenchurch tugged his jacket tight against the chill. 'Doesn't look like much.'

'Officially, it's an escort agency. Not particularly high class at that. We've got a pretty good idea what else goes on in there, though.'

'So why haven't you stopped it?'

'The girls aren't coerced. It's more like a sex cooperative than anything.' Owen pushed open a mesh gate. The metal rattled and a flurry of raindrops scattered onto the path. 'If we put a stop to this, they'd be off selling themselves on the streets.' He set off down the lane, barely wide enough for one man. Tall metal fences crowded them in on both sides. At the end, he pressed a buzzer set into a stout pillar. 'Police.'

'You sure you should be doing that?'

'Honesty's the best policy.'

'I'll be the judge of that.' Fenchurch scowled at him. 'What did this place used to be?'

'Primary school until New Labour merged it into a neighbouring one over the other side of the tracks.'

'So now the pupils work here?'

'They're all over age. Probably.' Owen looked around. 'This place is a classic inner-city slum, though, so you never know.'

'Take it they don't have an inner city where you're from.'

'Swansea has its fair share of hellholes, I tell you. More than, some would say.' Owen hammered the buzzer again. 'This is still the police and we're getting impatient.'

The speaker crackled and a woman's voice thundered out. 'You boys know you need a warrant.' Jamaican accent. Well, somewhere in the Caribbean at least.

'We just want a word.'

A blast of laughter burst from the speaker. 'It always starts with speaking and ends up with one of my employees in a police station.'

'We're investigating three murder cases.'

'A likely tale, Chris.'

Owen waved at a camera above them then pointed at Fenchurch. 'This is my colleague from the East London Major Investigation Team. That's the Murder Squad.'

'So why have they sent you, Chris?'

'Because we're looking at the death of a prostitute. You're not missing any girls, are you?'

'I keep telling you. My girls *aren't* prostitutes.'

'I'll take your word for it. Are you missing any, though?'

'Come on in, boys.' The buzzer clicked as the door swung open.

'Fancy set-up.' Fenchurch stopped Owen from passing. 'What's the play here?'

'We go in and we ask her questions. I want you to see if you can play nice. If we were here on Vice business, we'd need guns.'

'Guns?'

'Relax. They've got a lawyer on site, this is all above street level.' Owen nudged past Fenchurch into a tall room.

Mustard-yellow walls, red carpet tiles. Spotlights bounced off a huge chandelier slowly rotating in the middle of a spiral staircase. A few black girls sat around on couches. Glasses, blouses, skirts. Looked like they were models posing in an advert.

One of them walked over and pecked Owen on the cheek. Small and dark-skinned, looking more Indian than African. 'Hey, Chris, my boy.'

'Parbatee.' Owen kissed her back. 'Is there somewhere we could go?'

She grabbed a hold of Owen's cheek. 'I thought you were taking me dancing, boy?' She gave him a wink. 'Let's go to my office.' She patted him on the shoulder and sashayed over to a door. Sat on her desk and crossed her legs, some of the skinniest Fenchurch had ever seen. 'So, boy, what do you want to know?'

'Like I said outside, we need to ask you a few questions about some hotel visits made by your girls.'

Parbatee set her face straight. 'I run an office temp agency. You know that.'

Fenchurch cracked his knuckles. 'All three of us know that's not true.'

'I'm not going to bust your ovaries, Parbatee.' Owen rested the case photos on the desk next to her. Hall and the two Jane Does. 'Do you recognise this man or these women?'

She barely glanced at the sheets. 'No.'

'So why don't I believe you?'

'I've nothing to hide here.'

'So you'll be happy to do this down the station?'

'I'm saying nothing, boy.'

Owen hammered the table. 'Looks like you're coming with us, then.'

Parbatee got up and smoothed down her dress. She pushed up her cleavage. 'You won't mind if I bring my lawyer?'

'Listen to me, boy.' Parbatee puckered her lips. 'I've never sent any girls to that hotel.'

Fenchurch leaned against the interview room wall and shut his eyes. 'You're adamant about that?'

'You should listen to my client.' Nigel Edmonds clutched his fountain pen in one hand. His greasy hair was slicked back behind his cauliflower ears. 'She runs an office temping agency.'

Fenchurch grinned. 'Seems to do a roaring trade at night, oddly enough.'

'Let's cut the bullshit, shall we?' Owen opened a paper file in front of him. Black-and-white photographs of women in various states of undress, most of them co-starring middle-aged men. 'These are surveillance shots of her operations. Your client runs an escort agency with extras.'

'My client refuses to answer any questions relating to her involvement in these allegations.'

'We're investigating two murders. Maybe three.' Owen propped himself against the wall, a few feet from Fenchurch. 'Your client has ties to certain activities at The Note hotel on Folgate Street.'

'What would these activities pertain to?'

'Delivery of her agency staff to the hotel for something more than secretarial duties.'

'Don't play games with me, officer.' Edmonds reset a front of hair, slicking it like a twenties gangster. 'I'd like to see this evidence of yours.'

'Your client sent girls to provide sexual favours in exchange for money.' Owen sniffed. 'This was all put through their accounts.'

'So you've got evidence?'

'We've got a statement from an employee.'

Edmonds sucked on his teeth. 'This isn't a Vice investigation?'

'It's not, but I could get my forensic accountant to have a look at Parbatee's books.' Owen grinned like a little kid on Christmas Eve. 'Actually, that's a cracking idea.'

'That needn't be the case.' Edmonds brushed his hair back, plastering it to his skull. 'Suppose my client were to confirm these activities, what would she receive in return?'

'A clear conscience.'

'Very droll.'

'We'd be grateful for any information whatsoever.'

Edmonds made a note on a sheet of yellow paper. 'Can you please outline the evidence trail linking my client to these alleged activities?'

'A murder suspect procured prostitutes through The Note hotel between November of last year and March of this. Ms Holder here was linked to the prostitutes. Tell us what you know and we'll let you get back to your temping agency.'

Edmonds raised his hands. 'Very well.'

Parbatee picked up the sheet and stared at the photos of Robert Hall and their Jane Does. 'I don't know any of them, boy.'

'You sure?'

'I've definitely never seen those two.' She tapped a painted nail off each of the women.

'Mr Hall received visits from some of your girls.'

She smirked. 'I think he might've had help processing his corporate expenses.'

'Whatever.' Owen snatched the sheet off her and held it just in front of her face. 'Do you know him?'

'My girls might've visited him.' She lifted her left shoulder. 'Back in the day.'

'Twenty years ago?'

'Last Christmas, before I gave you my heart.' She fluttered her eyelashes at Owen. 'I sometimes chaperone them on the first visit to make sure they're not getting into anything dangerous. Mr Hall stopped receiving my services around March, I think.'

'Any idea why?'

'I don't like to ask.'

'He moved into a flat.' Owen scribbled in his notebook. 'Did you send any girls to another address for him?'

'His employers would've had corporate deals in place for temp staff, I'd imagine.'

Owen dropped his pen onto the table. 'So that's a no?'

'Correct. We had no dealings with him after March.'

'That's all we needed to know.' Owen spoke into the microphone: 'Interview terminated at seventeen fifty-five.' He got up and left the room.

Fenchurch nodded at the Custody and Security Officer. 'Can you escort Ms Holder and Mr Edmonds outside, please?'

Parbatee winked at him. 'Give me a call if you're ever lonely, sugar.'

Fenchurch grunted. He stormed into the corridor and thumbed back at the door. 'What's her story, out of interest?'

Owen arched his eyebrows. 'How much interest?'

'Just tell me.'

'She's from Trinidad.' Owen sniffed. 'Not common knowledge, but they didn't get all of the slaves from Africa. Her family came from India. Similar story with Portuguese slaves going to the sub-continent. Horrible business.' He sniffed again and attacked his nose with his wrist. 'Did you get what you needed there?'

'Not really.'

Owen started off down the corridor, twirling his BlackBerry between his fingers. 'Mr Hall had regular visits from Parbatee's girls until he moved into his flat. Then they stopped. Why?'

'You're supposed to tell me, Sergeant.'

'The girls there are all black. Caribbean girls like our friend Parbatee. Mostly second or third generation.' Owen frowned at a passing uniformed officer. 'Hall was getting black girls at that hotel up till March. Then he falls off the radar until now when he's picking up white girls off the street. What happened in the meantime?'

'Maybe his tastes just changed.'

Owen stopped outside the Incident Room. 'I'll chase up my DCs for some better intel on him.'

Reed waved from inside the room. 'Guv, I need a word.'

'What's up?'

'Two things. First, Pratt's done some of the post-mortem early. He's confirmed the overdose was the cause of death. Pure heroin, too, guv.'

Fenchurch leaned against the wall. 'Pure? Tell me your alarm bells are ringing as well, Sergeant.'

'You know me, guv.' She grinned at him. 'Pure heroin doesn't look like suicide so I got him to look into it a bit further. Turns out Mr Hall's been using a cocktail of drugs. Crack cocaine, Demerol, Viagra, ketamine. Looks like he'd been smoking smack, too.'

'Bloody hell.'

'I've told Pratt to do more tests and confirm it's murder. He'll have to compare answers with Clooney. Reckons he'll get back to me tomorrow.'

'Good effort. What's the other thing?'

'You know how we sent DC Bridge down to his other house? Well, Mr Hall's wife wants to speak to whoever's in charge.'

'I'm not going to bloody Three Bridges, Kay.'

'No need, she's in your office, guv.'

Chapter Twenty-Three

Mrs Hall was practically lying in the chair opposite Fenchurch's desk. She looked a lot younger than the photos of her husband. Mid-twenties at most, with shoulder-length blonde hair. A thick jumper was pulled up to her ears and her skin-tight jeans were tucked into beige Uggs. She barely looked up.

Fenchurch sat in his office chair and waited for Reed to sit. 'Mrs Hall, I understand you've been—'

'Please, call me Amelia.'

'You're Australian?'

She tutted. 'I'm from New Zealand. Just outside Wellington.'

'I take it you've not got any family over here?'

'Rob's mum treats me like family, you know?' She fiddled with her wedding ring. 'She lives nearby. She's looking after our girls.'

Fenchurch's stomach lurched. The guy had kids . . . Explained the Charlie the Seahorse book. 'What about his father?'

'He's very much alive. Retired last year. Christ knows what this is going to do to him, though.' She pinched her nose. 'They moved down from Durham when we had Susi, our youngest.'

'That's an upheaval.'

'It was a godsend.'

Fenchurch gave her his attempt at a warm smile. Didn't seem to cut through. 'Before we get started, we've got some admin we need to get out of the way.'

Reed smiled at her. 'Do you know his phone's lock code?'

'His HTC?' Amelia sighed. 'I think the code's two eight six eight.'

'Right.' Fenchurch picked up his Airwave and texted it to Clooney. He stretched across the desk, his cufflinks clunking on the wood. 'I understand he stays in his London flat during the week. I take it you hadn't seen him since Monday morning? Sunday night?'

'I haven't seen him for a couple of weeks.' Amelia slid the wedding ring almost to the nail. 'I asked him to move out.'

'I'd like to know why.'

Amelia pulled her ring back to the knuckle and ran a hand through her hair. 'Because I found something.' Back to fiddling with the ring, spinning it round on her finger. 'I was returning something, I can't remember what. Maybe something I'd bought for Katie. Whatever it was, I had to go through an old credit card statement. Before he got that flat, Rob was staying in a hotel.'

Fenchurch frowned. 'BES paid for it, didn't they?'

'They booked them, but Rob had to pay for them. Cheaper that way.'

'And these statements?'

'Well, the bills were higher than he'd told me, you know? Quite a lot higher. Hundreds more a week.' She took the ring off and it thunked onto the table. 'I went through his mail and found some invoices. It was all itemised. Some room service, breakfast, that sort of thing. But there were two items that just stuck out like a sore thumb. "Flowers" and "Additional Cleaning". Rob, cleaning? Flowers?'

Fenchurch glanced at Reed. She caught his gaze and flicked up her eyebrows.

'Anyway, one invoice said "Prostitute (Female)". I didn't know what to think.'

'So what did you do?'

'I looked through his other invoices. The flowers or cleaning amounts were mostly for the same amount as this.' She swallowed hard. 'This prostitute line. Sometimes double.' She pushed the ring away on the table. 'I picked up the phone and spoke to a girl at the hotel. Said it was her last day. Told me Rob'd been getting prostitutes delivered.'

'What was her name?'

Amelia brushed tears from her eyes, a bitter grin on her face. 'Cindy.'

Fenchurch smiled at Amelia as Reed hurried out of the room. 'Did you believe her?'

'She emailed me some pictures in my email of Rob kissing a couple of girls.' Amelia tore off another tissue and blew her nose. 'I couldn't believe he'd do that to me. After I stopped crying, I confronted him when he got home on the Friday.' She closed her eyes for a few seconds, reopening them with intensity. 'I asked him to leave. How do you Brits say it? Oh yeah, he caused a scene.'

'In what way?'

'Smashing things. Shouting. Screaming. It was like he was on something, you know?' She chewed at a knuckle. 'I called the police and some cops came out. They chucked him in the cells for the night.'

'And that was it?'

'Last time I saw him. He's been staying up here in that flat of his. I didn't want him to see our girls after . . .' She shut her eyes. 'After what he did.'

'I can understand that.' Fenchurch clasped his hands together. 'Did you speak to your husband at all during this time?'

'Just once or twice on the phone. He didn't seem like himself, you know? He was ranting and raving, asking me lots of stuff. How I found out about it.' Amelia bit her lip, staring into space. Her head fell into her hands and her shoulders started rocking. 'How could he do this to us?'

Reed appeared at the door, eyes on Amelia. She treaded over and leaned across the desk to whisper: 'Cindy's just confirmed the story, guv. Jon's hauling her over the coals about not telling us.'

'Thanks for that.' Then to Amelia: 'I'll need you or Mr Hall's parents to identify his body.'

'I'll do it.' Through gritted teeth. Eyes like fire. Forehead clenched. 'Look, you need to tell me what he's done.'

'Do you know if he's been using drugs?'

She looked up. 'What?'

'We believe the cause of death was a heroin overdose.'

'Heroin?' She lurched forward in her seat, knees almost buckling. 'Oh my God.'

Fenchurch raised an eyebrow at Reed and tilted his head towards Amelia. She placed a hand on her back. 'Do you need some time to yourself?'

Amelia brushed the hand off. 'Did he kill himself?'

'We don't know. We hoped you might—'

'This is bullshit.' Amelia pushed the ring right up to the knuckle. 'I mean, what evidence have you got?'

Reed clamped her hands to her knees, puckering the tights underneath. 'We've done a blood toxicology on your husband's body. He definitely died of a heroin overdose. We found traces of other drugs in his bloodstream. It's possible he was using lots of drugs. We'll check his bank account for withdrawals.'

Amelia reached into her handbag and tore off a paper tissue. She blew her nose with a loud honk. 'How could he do this to us?'

Fenchurch checked his watch and nodded at Reed. 'Kay, can you get a Family Liaison Officer to escort Mrs Hall out to Lewisham to ID the body? I need you in the briefing.'

Fenchurch shut his eyes and stared at the whiteboard. Drums clattered. Twenty or so eyes bore down on him. He just didn't have the words. How could he explain it? He was supposed to have the questions not the answers, but there were just too many. Far too bloody many.

He locked eyes with Nelson standing a few yards away. Gave him a nod then stared around the room. 'In summary, all we've got on Robert Hall is he's gone off the rails since his separation. Taking drugs. Uppers and downers, you name it. Just doesn't seem enough to make him kill two prostitutes.'

Fenchurch shrugged. Felt like he could just keep doing that and it wouldn't make any difference. 'He'd been using prostitutes while staying in London.' He gave a sigh. 'Two weeks ago on Friday, his wife found out about it. Kicked him out. We've got a black hole between March and now. Nine months where he appears to have behaved himself.' He tapped at the paper covering the wall. A new timeline in months instead of days had been added since he'd last looked, a giant question mark stuck in the middle. 'We need to nail down this timeline.' He looked around the room, making eye contact with Reed, the rest of them more interested in their shoes or coffees. 'He's killed two girls since Tuesday. Have we got any understanding of why?'

'I wish I had good news, Simon.' Clooney jangled a ring piercing the top of his ear. 'The second girl's crime scene isn't looking promising. The rain washed away all forensics off her body and the ground.' He shrugged, like he'd scored a last-minute own goal. 'We've just about finished at his flat. Should be done tonight. Got the team staying late.'

'I appreciate it.'

Clooney checked his spiral-bound notebook. Bits of multi-coloured paper hung out. 'I managed to get a result on the DNA markers from the semen on your first victim's abdomen. You're in luck. The semen matches his DNA. While the prints still aren't on there, it turns out Mr Hall's DNA's on file from this altercation in Three Bridges a couple of weeks ago.'

Fenchurch focused on the ceiling and let out a breath he didn't know he was holding. 'So he definitely killed her.'

Clooney wagged a finger in the air. 'All I'm telling you is he had sex with her that night. Whether he killed her is another matter.'

'This is solid, though.' Fenchurch wrote it on the whiteboard. *DNA Match*, a new line connecting the photo of Jane Doe 1 and Hall. 'What about the fingernails for our second victim?'

'I'm no miracle worker, much as you'd like me to be. That'll be Monday at the earliest.'

'Okay.' Fenchurch jotted *DNA Test 2 — MONDAY* on the board and put the cap back on the pen. He checked around the room. 'Anyone else got anything?' He stared at Reed, who avoided his gaze. 'Nothing?'

She frowned but kept quiet.

Nelson wandered away from the whiteboard and perched on the edge of a desk. 'I spoke to that Mantilas guy's brother. He pitched up to the car park just after eleven. I had a word with him in Brick Lane station. Story checks out.'

'Not sufficiently close to his brother's tale so as to arouse suspicion, I hope?'

'Nothing like that, guv. Used his own words and everything.'

Fenchurch looked around the room again. 'It's Friday night, so don't stay too late, okay? I need you to hand over to DI Mulholland's team and be in fresh first thing tomorrow. Dismissed.' He leaned back against the wall and kneaded his temples as they all went back to their computers and paper files.

Docherty strolled over, Mulholland following in his wake, pale fingers fiddling with her scarf. He picked at his teeth. 'You look done in, Simon.'

'Been a shit day, boss.' Fenchurch stood up straight and cracked his spine. 'Did you hear much of that?'

'None, sorry.' Docherty stabbed a finger on the whiteboard, smudging a couple of letters. 'Looks like you're getting somewhere, though.'

'The floodgates are still shut, though, boss. Just a bloody trickle.' Fenchurch put the cap back on his pen and tossed it on the table next to the board. 'We've still no idea who our Jane Does are, just who killed them.'

Docherty scratched his five o'clock shadow, a lot more salt than pepper. 'There's nothing else we can do, right?'

'Maybe. Maybe not.' Fenchurch felt his phone buzz in his pocket. 'Anything else for me, boss?'

'Their lawyer's asking us to let them reopen The Alicorn. Same guy who was representing that bouncer.'

'Are you going to do it?'

'Not got much choice.'

'But, guv—'

'But nothing.' Docherty waved his hand, dismissing him. 'Off you go, Simon. Have an evening for once. Recharge your batteries. Dawn'll chivvy Pratt along, don't you worry.'

Fenchurch marched across the Incident Room and checked his mobile. It was still ringing. Unknown Caller. He took a second to think then hit the answer button. 'Fenchurch.'

Silence on the line. Not even background noise. 'It's Erica.'

'Who?'

'You've got a short memory, Simon.'

He leaned against the wall outside the room, his shoulder pressing into the hard edge of the noticeboard. 'How did you get this number?'

'You gave me your card last night. I thought you'd be more interested in why I'm phoning.'

'What do you want?'

'I need to speak to you. Meet me at my flat.'

'I'm not doing that.'

'It's there or nowhere.'

'Then it's nowhere.'

'You'll be interested in what I've got to say.'

'Out with it, then.'

'It needs to be in person.'

'Goodbye.' Fenchurch killed the call.

It's a trap. Clear as day. Get round there and some big guys in balaclavas batter him in.

But what if she knows something? They were still nowhere near anywhere. And if she could give them something. Anything. Well . . .

He popped his head into the Incident Room, looking for Nelson or Reed. Couldn't see either of them.

Docherty was striding straight for him, looking very much like he wanted something. Another stupid insight into the case, no doubt.

Fenchurch spun round.

Reed was right behind him, dressed for the elements. 'Just wondered if you fancied a beer across the road, guv?'

'Now I know how Abi feels . . . ' Reed brushed her hair behind her ears. Dubstep boomed out of the pub speakers, loud enough to drown out the other punters in the bar. A passing taxi's headlights glinted in her eyes. 'We're here for a drink, guv. It helps if you do some talking.'

Fenchurch stared into his foaming pint of, what was it? Punk IPA? He'd barely touched it. Unlike Reed, now well below halfway on her Peroni. 'Right. Sorry. Where are your kids tonight?'

'Mother-in-law's. Give her an inch and she takes a mile.' She took another sip from her pint and winked at him. 'You looked like you were struggling in the briefing.'

'It's this bloody case, Kay.' Fenchurch gulped down some beer. That's better. Lovely, in fact. 'I just don't understand how he could go off the rails like this. How he could do that to his family.'

'Happened to a friend of mine.' Reed raised a hand. 'Not the murdering prostitutes part. Karen found her husband had been using . . . escorts, shall we say.' She grimaced. 'How could he bring something like that into their home?'

'Doesn't figure, does it? Makes me sick to be a bloke.'

'You've never been with a call girl, have you, guv?'

Fenchurch took another swig. Nice stuff. Really nice stuff. 'We're off-duty, Kay. Don't call me "guv".'

'Is that you avoiding the question, Simon?'

'I've never been with one, no.' Fenchurch took a big dent out of his pint. 'Was on a stag in Amsterdam years ago. Couple of the blokes went to the red-light district.' Bile swilled in his gut. 'Didn't speak to them for the rest of the weekend.'

'Good for you.'

Fenchurch shrugged. 'Bad for them. Pair of arseholes had their wives at the wedding a few weeks later.' He clutched both hands round the glass, like it would suck in all the rage and disgust. 'Feel like I'm letting those girls down, Kay.'

'What do you mean?'

'We've still not identified them. There's two mothers out there looking for their lost girls.'

'We know who killed them, though. That's a start.'

'I just don't get why, though. Why's he bloody killed them? Thinking about it sends a shiver up and down my spine.'

'People go off the rails sometimes. It happens.'

'Not like this.'

She finished her pint and clinked a fingernail off his empty. 'Sure it's not because you're reminded of Chloe.'

Fenchurch just took a drink.

'Simon, I know how you think.'

Another drink. Didn't even taste it. Might as well have been water. 'Can't stop thinking about her, Kay.'

'You never stopped. The number of times Abi called me up at night, you wouldn't believe.'

'Bloody hell, remind me to sack the next of her uni mates I inherit in a department reshuffle.'

'You missed your chance, Si.' She winked at him. 'Why's this bringing it home to you?'

'Chloe was eight when she . . .' He swallowed. His mouth was bone dry. 'When whatever happened, happened. Ten years ago. She'd be eighteen now.'

'Like these girls?'

'Like these girls.'

'You think this is related to who took Chloe? You're telling me you think Chloe's a prostitute?'

'I just don't know.' Fenchurch wiped away the tear from his cheek. 'She'd be eighteen now, going to university.' Another gulp of beer. 'I wish something else had happened, that Chloe was still with us. Maybe studying at, I don't know, Durham or Edinburgh, doing Philosophy or Law or Maths. Or working in a supermarket or anything. A hairdresser. Anything instead of . . . Instead of, I don't know.' He sighed. 'I've lost ten years of her life. Every day goes past is another one lost.' He shut his eyes, felt the tears sting. 'My little girl.'

Her hand stroked his arm, gentle and delicate. 'It's okay.'

The dubstep shifted to some old-school jungle. Worse than the stuff in his head.

He stood up tall and composed himself. Sucked in breath, puffed out his chest. Let the breath go, along with the tears. Felt a couple of stone lighter.

'Abi told me you phoned her the other night.'

'She tell you she called me back?'

'Yeah. And you're meeting her for dinner tonight.'

He laughed. 'I'm shitting myself, Kay.'

'Just think how she's feeling.' Reed clutched her glass tight. 'This big ugly brute comes storming back into her life.'

'I'm not that big, am I?'

'You are a brute, though. And God knows you're bloody ugly. I don't know why you can speak to me but not Abi.'

'There's less pressure with you, I guess.' He took the pint way below halfway. 'Every time I speak to her, I just feel these drums clattering in my head. Feels like I'm that bloke in that film. The geezer on the trapeze between those two buildings. I can't take one wrong step or I'm pavement pizza.'

'You really think that's how Abi sees it?'

'You don't know the arguments we had, Kay.'

She flicked up her eyebrows. 'Don't I?'

'She shouldn't have told you.'

'I don't think any less of you, guv.'

'That because you couldn't?'

'I'm being serious. Abi just wants to help. Like she used to. You pushing her away wasn't good for her. Put yourself in her shoes for a minute.'

Fenchurch stared out of the window. Horizontal rain. A gust of wind blew a man's flat cap off. Taxis slooshing the rainwater. 'Maybe you're right.'

'Course I'm bloody right. You ever thought about counselling?'

'A couple of times. Even picked up the phone and spoke to some clinic's receptionist.' Fenchurch lost himself in the beer's hops. 'I'm worried counselling will change me. That I'll come out of there as a different person.'

'Is that a bad thing?'

She had him there. Another wipe across his face. 'Kay, all I've got left is me.'

'Then there's nothing to lose, is there. If you let go, maybe you'll stop blaming yourself and stop trying to take it out on the world.'

'Maybe.'

'You think about it, yeah? Before you head up there for dinner.' She tapped his glass. 'Same again?'

'Go on.'

She got up and wandered over to the bar. Two cops he recognised stood either side of her. Both of them seemed interested.

Christ, she felt more like a sister than his own one.

And she was bloody right. Stupid bloody idiot. Blaming everyone and the world for everything. Not sharing anything. Never talking.

He took another slug of beer. Stuff was rushing to his bloody head. He probably couldn't even drive after this. Maybe he'd walk up to Islington. Two miles, maybe a bit more. Might clear his head. Let the rain wash away his sins.

Reed dumped another pair of pints on the table. 'Here you go, gu— *Simon*.' Her Peroni glass was tall and elegant, like that compensated for the price. 'Here's cheers, guv.'

'Cheers.'

'I was just thinking while I was getting served. Why do these girls remind you of Chloe?'

Fenchurch finished his first pint and gripped the second one tight, let it cool his palms. 'Thought you were just flirting with those uniform geezers?'

'Quit it.' She raised her plucked eyebrows. 'Talk to Dr Kay.'

He laughed and shook his head. 'Right. The thing is, the problem is the logical deduction. I'm trained in all that shit, right? Timelines and all that muck.' He gulped at the second pint, attacking the tangy foam. 'You interviewed this girl from the club, Erica. Right?'

'Right.'

'Well, she reminds me of Chloe. Roughly the same age, give or take. Looks a bit like she . . . might've done. Might still do. Same dimple as Abi.'

'I don't think it's her, guv.'

'I know that. Christ, of course I know that. It's just . . . Right before you asked me for a pint, she called me.'

'What, phone called you?'

'That's what spooked me.' Another biting drink. 'Said I should come round and meet her. Said she's got something.' He locked his gaze onto her. She was nibbling at her lip. 'Could be a lead, Kay.'

'Could be a trap.'

'I've thought of that. Why, though?' Another cold draught of beer. 'What if it's a lead? What if it's genuine?'

'Worth staking your career on?' She ran a hand across her face. 'Remember these girls are street smart. Any inch they can take, they will.'

'It's a bit more than an inch. Three when it's not cold.'

She shut her eyes and groaned. 'You know what I mean.'

'I do.' Another sip. 'Problem is, she's playing this lost father card.'

'Does she know about Chloe?'

Fenchurch stared into his pint. 'Maybe.'

'You told her, didn't you? Simon, you're a bloody idiot.'

He held up his hands. 'It was a moment of weakness.' Another drink. Could just about taste it.

Her mobile bounced across the tabletop. She held it up. 'That's Pratt's office. Mrs Hall was off IDing the body.'

'Take it.' Fenchurch watched her walk outside the pub into the flowing rain, resting in the doorway. He stared at his own phone, still on mute. The missed calls box obscured the photo of Abi and Chloe. Same number Erica had called from before.

What did she want?

Was it really a trap?

Reed made eye contact through the window. Gave him a thumbs up.

He let out a breath. It was definitely Robert Hall. He stabbed the screen and stuck his phone to his ear. Listened to it ringing.

'You decided to call back?'

'Where's your flat?'

Chapter Twenty-Four

'Sorry, Kay. Something came up. See you tomorrow.' Fenchurch killed the call and stopped by Christ Church Spitalfields. He gritted his teeth against the cold wind, stopping him chewing the gum. Mint just about overpowered the beer.

Heavy traffic flowed down Commercial Street. Horns honked at a jaywalker. The Ten Bells pub was glowing in the night, a huddle of smokers outside checking their phones as they puffed. Next door, a man in tight jeans rolled up the canopy of the hipster café. His curly beard blossomed a good six inches from his chin.

Fenchurch took another look at his mobile. Definitely Fournier Street. He walked towards Brick Lane, swimming against the tide of office workers lugging laptop bags. His quarry wasn't far down. He poked the intercom button and waited. Tugged at the collar of his overcoat. Thick wool, matted. Really needed a new one.

He checked his watch. Still had an hour and a half till he was supposed to meet Abi. Plenty of time.

'Hello?'

He leaned over, mouth dry. 'It's DI Fenchurch.'

'Top floor. Flat on the left.' The buzzer sounded and the door clicked open.

Fenchurch opened it and stood there, chewing. This was a bad idea.

He pushed through into a bright corridor. Cream walls and beige carpet. The stale smell of fried food. His stomach rumbled as he started up the stairs. The beer was heavy in his gut.

Two doors on the top-floor landing. He held his gloved hand over the left one and paused. He stared at the carpet tiles beneath his shoes, teeth gritted.

Then knocked.

It swung open. Erica was standing there, left hand on her hip. A cheeky smile showing her dimple. Baggy tracksuit bottoms, three Adidas stripes down the side. A few shades of grey lighter than her Abercrombie & Fitch T-shirt. Her hair was tied up and she looked young, like she'd just got back from school. Her eyes darted around the corridor. 'You alone?'

'For now.' Fenchurch tried to peer behind her. 'Are you?'

'For now.'

'Slipped your marker, have you?'

'All this chaos you lot are causing at my work has diverted their attention. It won't last.' She stepped away from the door.

'Come on in.'

He entered the hallway, same cream and beige as the stairwell. A modern-art print hung on the wall, all reds and oranges. Made him feel angry just looking at it. 'Out with it, then.'

She shut the door. 'Do you want a cup of tea?'

'I want to know what you've got me here for.'

'Come on through.' She led into a small but well-equipped kitchen. Brand-new units lined the walls at the far end, stainless steel gleaming under the spotlights. She collapsed into a leather dining chair and hugged her legs tight to her body.

'Nice pad you've got here.' Fenchurch pulled off his gloves and dropped them onto the pale glass table. The heat of the flat hit him. A trickle of sweat ran down his back. 'Nice address here. Really close to the City.' He gritted his teeth. 'Bit expensive for a lap dancer, though. I'd have thought you'd be out east somewhere. East Ham or Woolwich, maybe.'

'It's not my choice. There's another four girls live here. They work at the club, too. Sure you'd recognise them.'

Fenchurch sighed. 'So how do you afford this, then?'

'They put us up here.'

Fenchurch picked up a DVD from the stack on the table. *When Harry Met Sally*, one of Abi's favourites. 'The Alicorn?'

She nibbled her lip.

'Are you working tonight, Erica?'

'In about an hour and a half.' She swallowed. 'It's fine. The pay's okay.'

'But you don't enjoy it?'

'I don't enjoy a lot of things.'

'There are better ways of making a living.'

'I don't really have a choice.'

'Of course you do. You're still young. What's to stop you leaving?'

'I need the money.'

'Don't we all?'

She stared into space and shrugged a shoulder. 'Thanks for coming, Simon.'

'Don't call me that.'

'Thanks for coming, DI Fenchurch.'

He kept his distance. 'Why did you phone me?'

'My dad's name was Colin. I never knew him.'

'I'm not him.' Fenchurch kept his eyes on the door. 'I'm here to talk about the case. Nothing else.'

'Your daughter—'

'I shouldn't have told you that.'

'You did, though. That means a lot to me.'

Fenchurch stood up straight and put his left glove back on. 'You did actually want to see me about something, yeah?' Then the right glove. 'I'm going now.'

'Wait.' She sat forward. 'Some of the girls in the club were talking about cops.'

'Was it about me?'

'No, it was about the raid last night.' She tilted her head to the side. 'It was some of the newer girls. I don't know their names. They were talking about that girl they found the other night.'

'There were two girls, two different nights.'

'Two? I didn't know.' She sucked in a breath. 'Well, it's the one in that building. One of them said our boss knows—'

'The manager of The Alicorn?'

She gave a tight nod. 'His name's Bruco.'

'What sort of name's that?'

'Greek, I think. It was him who picked me up last night.' She shivered and ran her hands over her bare arms. Goosebumps dotted the toned flesh. 'The girls were saying Bruco knows something about what happened to this girl.' She swallowed. 'These girls.'

He took another step to the door. 'This is just hearsay.'

'There's something else. The man you're looking for. Robert? He was at The Alicorn last night. He was hassling some of the girls. Tried to buy them. So they chucked him out.'

'But not you?'

'I kept avoiding him.' She looked away. 'I'm good at getting what I want in that place.'

'Why didn't you mention this during your interview?'

'We were told not to say anything about it.'

'I need you to go on record about this, Erica.' Fenchurch did up the top button of his coat. 'Come to the station with me now.'

'Not happening.'

Fenchurch pinched his nose. The gloves were cold against his skin. 'How can I persuade you?'

'You remind me of my father.'

'This again.' Final straw snapping the camel's back in two. 'You said you never knew him?'

She just shrugged.

'Forget it.' Fenchurch left the room and slammed the flat door behind him. He stomped down the stairs and pressed his mobile to his ear.

'DS Reed.'

'Kay, it's Simon. Are you still around?'

'Yeah, thought I had a date but he buggered off when I was on the phone. I've come back in.'

'Can you pull up the CCTV from outside The Alicorn last night?'

———

Reed spun around and tore off her headphones. 'Christ, guv, you scared the shit out of me.'

'You knew I was coming, Sergeant.' Fenchurch sat next to her. The CCTV suite was a tight space smelling of armpits and Pot Noodles. 'Found anything?'

'Aren't you supposed to be somewhere?'

'I've got an hour at least. Have you got anywhere?'

'Maybe.' She tapped the monitor. 'Got Mr Hall here. This is him getting chucked out.'

The street was in black and white. Paused, 20.32 in the bottom-left corner. Two men argued in sharp contrast on the pavement. Faces pinched, hard to pick out. One white, one black.

Fenchurch screwed his eyes up and focused on the white guy. He was stabbing a finger while his other hand grabbed hold of his dance partner's dress shirt. He was definitely the club's bouncer. His top hat hung in the air as it fell to the ground. 'He'd already killed our second Jane Doe, hadn't he?'

'That's right, guv. An hour and a half before this.' Reed pointed at a figure in the background behind the bouncer. 'That's Erica McArthur there.'

Fenchurch swallowed hard as he leaned over and squinted at it. Just wearing her corset, bare arms hugging her shoulders, bracing herself against the cold.

Something wasn't right with the image.

'Is he stabbing his finger at her?'

Reed hit the play button. 'Watch this.'

The footage started up. Hall shifted his finger from the bouncer to Erica and back again. He was shouting something.

Fenchurch folded his arms. 'Why's he doing that?'

'Might've been why they chucked him out. Went over the score during a dance?'

The bouncer got behind Hall and put him in a hold. Looked like he was getting him to nod to something. He let go and pushed hard, sending Hall stumbling down the street. He righted himself and shouted silent obscenities back at the bouncer. Then retreated until he was off camera. The bouncer led the crowd back inside, eyes on where Hall had been.

Reed stopped it playing. 'Who's your source, guv?'

'It's a Covert Informant, Kay. I can't tell you.'

'Bollocks it is.' She burped lager fumes into her hand. 'This is that girl, isn't it? Erica, right? That's where you buggered off to in a hurry.'

Persistent bugger. Still, no point in denying it. 'She said Hall was in The Alicorn last night. That's it.' He shut his eyes. 'Shit, she told me he was kicked out because he was hassling the other girls. It was her, wasn't it?'

'Guv, I told you. You really need to be careful.'

'I've not done anything.'

'If you're sure . . .' Reed held his gaze until Fenchurch broke it off. 'What's the plan, guv?'

The CCTV door burst open, raising the light level and making Fenchurch blink.

Nelson stepped through, sucking on his vape stick. At least it looked like him. He switched his gaze from Reed to Fenchurch. 'Guv, sorry I'm late.'

'Have a seat, Jon.' Then at Reed: 'Is there any more?'

'Wait for it.' She skipped the footage forward from 20.32 to 20.55. 'Here we are.'

The door opened and a man left the club. Sharp suit, black shirt, shoes gleaming in the street lights. A hand slicked through his jet-black hair. He walked a few paces down the street and got into a silver BMW. The man who picked Erica up from outside the station.

Fenchurch screwed his eyes up. 'That's The Alicorn's manager. His name's Bruco.' He got out his mobile and rang Owen. 'You still at Leman Street?'

'No, Paul and I are back at ESB. What do you want?'

'I've got a sighting of The Alicorn manager. Geezer called Bruco.'

'Who?'

Fenchurch grinned. 'How long have you had that place under surveillance?'

'A year. We just never got his name.'

'Couple of days on this case and I've outdone you. The geezer's Greek.'

'How'd you get this? Who's your source?'

'Never you mind.' Fenchurch held Reed's gaze as it burnt into him. 'What have you got on him?'

'I'm warning you now, Fenchurch. However you've got this, you need to log it in the case file.'

'I'll get on with that tomorrow. What do you know about him?'

'Nothing much.'

'Well, given you're at Hogwarts, any chance you can dig out what you've got on him?'

Owen paused for a few seconds. 'Let's catch up first thing tomorrow, yeah? Just as you're logging your source.'

'Excellent. See you then.' Fenchurch ended the call and dumped his phone on the desk. Reed and Nelson were mucking about with the footage, mumbling to each other.

'Guv, hope you forgive me but I've got a hunch.' Nelson tapped at the monitor. 'This is just before Hall was killed, right?'

'Right.'

'Well.' Nelson reached across Reed and pressed a few keys. 'Have a look at this. This is last night as well.'

The video shifted to Prescot Street. Camera must've been just across the road from Robert Hall's flat. 20.55.

Fenchurch folded his arms and stifled a yawn. 'Why here, Jon?'

'Keep watching.'

The video crawled by in real time. A woman marched down the street, her Sainsbury's bags rustling in the wind tunnel. Cars and taxis trundled up to the lights at the end. A couple jogged along the pavement, like it wasn't a London winter evening.

Fenchurch sniffed. 'This isn't paying off, Sergeant.'

Nelson let out a sigh and sped it up to thirty times. A car pulled in outside the flats and reverse-parked. He wound the footage back and played it back slowly.

It was a silver BMW 3-series.

Bruco's car.

'There we go.' Nelson tapped at the time code on the screen. 21.15. 'It took him twenty minutes to get round there. It's a five-minute drive at that time of night. Ten, tops.'

'So, what, he picked someone up on the way?' Reed was trying to wrestle back control of the console. 'I hope it's not just stopping for cigarettes.'

Bruco stepped out of the car and crossed the road. Another figure got out of the passenger side, barely visible.

Nelson pointed at the screen. 'Who's that?'

'I don't know.' Reed paused the video. The street lights just missed whoever it was. Definitely a man. Hood tugged over his head.

Fenchurch sat back again, hands in pockets. 'Can you do that fancy CCTV thing you did earlier?'

Reed shook her head. 'Not on that street, guv. Sorry.' She let it play again. 'What now, guv?'

'DS Nelson and I are going to pay him a visit.'

'Let's get in and out, sharpish. I've got something on later.' Fenchurch strolled up to the entrance. A gust of wind blew down the street, rattling the trees. 'I'll lead here, Jon.'

'Guv.'

The bouncer came over. He'd added a purple cummerbund to his formal get up. 'Evening, gents. Becoming a habit.'

Fenchurch stood a bit too close to him. Let him smell the booze. 'Nice to see our colleagues let you out this afternoon.'

'I didn't say nothing.'

'But I bet you know something.'

'If this is a pleasure trip, gents, it's ten quid each.'

'Business.' Fenchurch held out his warrant card. 'Is Bruco on tonight?'

The bouncer swallowed. 'Mr Vrykolakas hasn't been here all week.'

Nice to know . . . Fenchurch nodded at Nelson. 'Is that the truth?'

'You think I'm lying?'

'Mr Gooch, isn't it?' Fenchurch took a step forward. The tips of his shoes connected with the bouncer's. 'Mind if I call you Winston?'

'You can call me Mr Gooch.'

'Mr Gooch, we still haven't spoken to Mr Vrykolakas yet. Feels like he's avoiding me.'

'He's not in.'

'Then you won't have a problem with letting us in, then, will you?'

Gooch stepped to the side and ushered them inside. His attention was already on a pair of approaching suits. 'I've still got my eye on you boys.'

Fenchurch entered the club. Dirty disco hissed out of speakers, all whoops, wah-wah and hi-hat. The place was quieter than the previous night, but the clientele looked like they had more money to spend.

Five girls and a man sat round a circular booth halfway across the club. One of the girls was the brunette who'd tried it on with Nelson. No sign of Erica.

The man was dark-haired and tall. His beard was a chisel line tracing out his jawline. Bruco.

Fenchurch glared back at the door. 'Lying bastard.' He plastered a smile on his face and marched up to the table. 'Hey, Bruco!'

'Hey!' His grin faded to a frown. 'Do I know you, man?'

'DI Fenchurch.' He took out his warrant card. 'Need a quick word with you, Mr Vrykolakas.'

'Girls, go make me some money.' Bruco leaned forward and stroked a finger down his moustache as the girls got up. 'Please, have a seat.'

Fenchurch sat opposite Nelson, making sure they blocked Bruco's exit. He glanced behind to check it was clear. His internal drums drowned out the club's music. 'We were here last night. Must've just missed you.'

'So I hear.' Bruco stuck a hand to his heart. 'I hope my staff were helpful.'

'Nobody seemed to know who ran the place. Funny that. What's funnier is one of them was just sitting on your lap.'

Bruco snarled at Fenchurch and flicked his tongue between his teeth. 'How can I help you?'

Fenchurch unfolded a sheet of photos, Robert Hall and the two Jane Does. He dropped it on the table, far enough that Bruco had to stretch over to collect it. 'Do you recognise any of these people?'

Bruco stared at it then pushed it back. 'I've never seen them in my life.'

'You sure about that?'

'Positive.'

'Well, the two girls worked here.' Fenchurch pointed to the one on the left, the first Jane Doe. 'She was only here for a couple of nights, way I hear it.'

Bruco held up the page and scowled at it. 'Now you mention it—'

'Why did you say you never saw her?'

Bruco waved around the room. The volume of the music turned up. 'You see how many girls I have in here? That's a lot of faces to remember. This piece here.' He tapped the sheet again. 'She didn't make the grade. Told a client where to go when he touched her a few too many times. I can't tolerate that. It's all part of the fun here.'

'She was murdered on Tuesday night.'

Bruco held his gaze, no emotion in his eyes. 'I don't know anything about that.'

'You didn't put her on the game, did you?'

'Girls who don't make it in here have two choices. McDonald's or walk the streets.' Bruco traced the line of his beard. 'If she doesn't serve me my organic cappuccino in the morning, well. That's her choice.'

'You don't take a cut of the money she earns out on the streets?'

'That's not the business I'm in.' Bruco adjusted his collar and grimaced. 'That geezer, though. Think he was in here last night.'

'And I didn't even have to ask.'

'Did he kill her?'

'We believe that's the case. What happened?'

'He was asked to leave. Politely. We get a lot of drunk men in here and it's usually fine. He was too drunk.'

'He's dead, too.'

Bruco swallowed. 'If you want any more out of me then I need my lawyer to see a warrant.'

Fenchurch checked his watch. Supposed to be at Abi's in half an hour. And this prick wasn't playing ball. 'Have you got any police officers on the books?'

'I know where I recognised your face from.' Bruco wagged a finger at Fenchurch. 'You were talking with one of my girls near the police station last night, weren't you?'

Fenchurch pushed himself up out of the booth. 'I need you to come with me, sir, to answer some questions about why you were in Prescot Street at quarter past nine yesterday evening.'

'Prescot Street?' Bruco gave a shrug then stood up, grinning. 'Very well.'

Fenchurch gripped his wrist and led him across the bar.

Nelson held the front door open for them. Raindrops spattered off the tiles outside. 'After you.'

Bruco held up his hands, wrists first. 'No handcuffs, gents?'

'Not unless you—'

Bruco elbowed Fenchurch in the face. His cheek exploded in a burst of pain. He stumbled to his knees. A kick tore into his side. Then another.

Something landed on him and pushed him flat down, squeezing the air from his lungs. Black skin, pinstripe suit. Nelson. A blow on the other side. Felt like it'd cracked a rib.

Fenchurch wrestled Nelson off and looked up.

Bruco was sprinting off down the street.

A boot on the arse knocked him forward, knees crunching off the paving slabs. His chin clattered off the pavement. He tried to roll over.

The bouncer stopped him. Pressed his knee into his spine.

Fenchurch grabbed Gooch's leg and pulled. Managed to jerk him over onto his side. He reached down and twisted an arm behind the bouncer's back. 'Will you bloody stay down?'

Nelson was on all fours, blinking hard.

'You okay, Jon?'

He did a slow blink. 'Did you get him?'

'No.' Fenchurch got up and started to run. 'Keep a hold of this punk.'

Chapter Twenty-Five

Fenchurch sprinted underneath a canopy of trees, his chest aching with each step. A dribble of rain hit the top of his head as he ran through an empty bus shelter.

Ahead, Bruco spun round the corner leading onto the high street. Still a few hundred yards away.

Fenchurch put the Airwave back up to his mouth. 'Repeat, I am in pursuit of a suspect on Shoreditch High Street. Request immediate backup!'

He sucked in air and tried to push himself harder. Tried to ignore the screaming from his knees and the cracked rib. Not being able to breathe.

He skidded across a pedestrian crossing slicked with rain. A taxi screeched to a halt just by him. His Airwave crackled static. The honking horn drowned out the message. The driver was leaning out of his window, shaking a fist at him. 'You stupid bastard!'

'I'm a police officer!' Fenchurch powered on and stepped around the Friday night drinkers as they hurried to the next bar, sheltering fresh haircuts from the rain. He bumped into a young man in a greatcoat and leather trousers.

Where the hell—

There.

Bruco shot across Old Street in front of a bus. He was heading into Hoxton Square. The narrow side road was choked with idling cars and smokers outside the pubs and restaurants. Another glance behind and he locked eyes with Fenchurch. Then collided with a small table outside a noodle bar. He tumbled over, sending plates flying over two smoking diners. The fourth leg of the canopy collapsed in.

Fenchurch pushed his legs harder. His lungs were burning.

Behind the chaos at the table, Bruco stood up. Eyes widened. He picked up the fallen table and hurled it.

Fenchurch twisted himself side on. Too late. His shoulder took the brunt of the blow, the table hitting him square on. He collapsed to his knees and toppled backwards. The rim landed on his thighs. He clutched his side, eyes shut. His rib screamed out again.

He sucked in breath and got up on one knee, hand still on his shoulder. No sign of Bruco. He started to jog, eyes darting around. Bruises were stinging up and down his legs like nettles.

Footsteps cannoned out from a side street. Bruco was hobbling, almost back onto the main road.

Fenchurch sploshed through a puddle and lifted the Airwave to his ear. 'Control, I need an update on the backup.' He weaved onto the tarmac, skipping around a fight starting in a bus shelter. Almost ran into a streetlight.

'Alpha one-niner are in pursuit, sir. Need a description of the suspect. Over.'

Fenchurch crossed the side street towards a Sainsbury's gleaming beneath a tower block. Bruco had started running again. 'Suspect is an IC1 male, wearing a black leather jacket. Dark hair. Beard. Just passing the Sainsbury's on Old Street.'

Fenchurch stretched his legs as the pavement widened out. He passed the fire station, two of the doors wide open. Round another bus shelter and past a row of old shops. The stench of kebab and frying chicken hit his nose, sucked into his lungs.

Where the hell was Bruco?

There — descending the ramp down to the tube station.

Fenchurch lifted his knees, trying to get more power, more speed. The bruises bit into his flesh, his rib feeling like it was gnawing into his chest. He slid on the sodden ramp and skidded down. Grabbed the handrail for support. Just about righted himself. Then tore off down, slower this time.

'Control, I need an update.'

'Still a couple of minutes away, sir.'

He pulled into the underground station and bombed past the small shops. A crowd of commuters ploughed towards him.

'Suspect has entered Old Street Tube.'

'Which service is he on?'

Bruco jumped over the ticket barrier and raced towards the down escalator.

Fenchurch barged people out of the way. Sent a large man in a navy suit flying backwards. 'Northern Line.'

'I'll get the units to Angel and Moorgate as a priority.'

Fenchurch shoved his warrant card out at the ticket guard. The guy was distracted by the security officers tearing off after Bruco.

Fenchurch took the decision out of his hands and pushed through the barrier. He stormed across the tiles towards the leftmost escalator. Slick shoes still in danger of slipping. He started down the escalator, bumping into passengers too stupid to stand on the right.

Bruco raced off into the tunnel. A security guard lay prone at the bottom of the escalator.

Fenchurch rushed on, taking the steps two at a time. He jostled an Asian family out of the way and lurched off through the tunnel and the second set of escalators, now swelling with the tide of passengers.

No sign of Bruco, just a security guard lying on the floor. It did give some clearance in the crowd, though. He vaulted over and tore off down the tunnel, watching for the north/south split.

Where was he?

Sweet, stale air blew in from the left side. Southbound, had to be. The queue was barely one passenger deep. Bruco was halfway down, wrestling his way onto the stationary train. Fenchurch raced along the tiles. The door alarm sounded and he threw himself through the doors. Two Chinese students staggered back onto the platform.

He put the Airwave to his head, chest heaving. 'This is Fenchurch.' Gasp. Breath. 'Suspect is on a train going south towards Moorgate.'

'Buggery.'

The train rumbled as it set off.

Fenchurch marched over and crouched down to peer into the next carriage. No sign of Bruco. 'Have you got anyone at Moorgate?'

'Not yet, sir.'

Fenchurch reached the end, disconnected from the other carriage, not even a door.

Bruco was only a few metres away.

His whole body rocked with each breath. Sweat flooded his forehead, soaked his hair.

The train flashed into a station and juddered to a halt.

Fenchurch barged over to the door and jumped onto the platform. He jostled a gang of hipsters out of the way and made for Bruco's door.

The alarm sounded again.

Bruco jumped off the train. His shoulder smashed into Fenchurch's chest. Knocked him flying across the dirty tiles. A boot cracked into the same rib. His Airwave clattered somewhere. A breeze whistled as the train trundled off. Footsteps rattled away from him.

Fenchurch hauled himself up again, clutching his side. Bruco was nowhere. He picked up his Airwave and ran down the platform. 'Suspect got off at Moorgate. Request urgent support in the tube station.'

'Message received—'

A blow smacked Fenchurch's skull from behind. He tumbled over the tiles, landing face down in a pile of used *Evening Standard*s.

'You're persistent, I'll give you that.' Bruco stepped forward, swinging out to kick him.

Fenchurch rolled over and grabbed Bruco's foot mid-stride. He pushed it upwards and tipped him over.

Bruco fell backwards. His skull crunched off the tiles.

Fenchurch locked Bruco's arm behind his back. Could barely breathe. Everything hurt. 'Mr Vrykolakas, I'm arresting you for the murder of Robert Hall. You don't have to say anything—'

'My client refuses to answer that question.' Gordon Edgar rubbed his thick beard, the mass of dark hair adding serious volume to the lawyer's chin. He took off his navy pinstripe jacket and dumped it on the back of his seat. Underneath, he wore a plain black T-shirt. Rainbow braces held up skinny-fit jeans. 'Next question, please.'

Fenchurch eased himself back. Still wincing at the sting from his ribs. If this wasn't cracked, then what would that feel like? His legs felt like one big bruise. 'We're asking Mr Vrykolakas to confirm he understands the fact he was arrested.'

'He has a right to remain silent.' Edgar grinned, the hand back on the beard. 'He intends to use it.'

'Mr Vrykolakas, please can you confirm your full name?'

Bruco glanced at his lawyer and got a shrug in response. 'My name is Sotiris Georgios Vrykolakas. My friends call me Bruco. I ask you to call me Mr Vrykolakas.'

'Where were you on the night of Thursday the seventeenth of December 2015?'

'I was at my place of work, Mr Fenchurch.'

'So your silence is only selective?'

Edgar leaned over, his beard almost touching the microphone. 'I'd like it noted for the record that, on the date in question, Detective Inspector Simon Fenchurch made a visit to The Alicorn, my client's place of business.'

'It's noted in the case file, which will be made available to you in due course. The visit was to gain intelligence to support a raid, which took place ten minutes later.' Fenchurch held the lawyer's gaze. 'We've so far established that Mr Vrykolakas was at his lap-dancing bar.' He waved his hand between him and Nelson. 'Neither DS Nelson nor I can validate that version of events. It should also be noted that his absence meant he wasn't brought in for questioning like his employees.'

Edgar itched the short stubble on his head. 'I've yet to see any evidence supporting my client's involvement in any murder.'

'We need to know his whereabouts from eight o'clock that evening.' Fenchurch focused on Bruco. 'Did you leave the club, Mr Vrykolakas?'

'No comment.'

Fenchurch tossed a screen grab onto the desk, showing Bruco getting into his car. 'We've got video evidence of you leaving the club at eight fifty-five.'

Bruco shrugged. 'I went to a garage to get some cigarettes.'

Fenchurch raised an eyebrow. 'There's a Tesco Express across the road. Open till midnight, too.'

'I needed cash.'

'The Tesco has an ATM. I suspect a lot of your punters get money out of there for just one more dance. So why go to the garage?'

'I like a drive. I've got a very nice motor.'

'Do you have a receipt for these cigarettes?'

'I never keep receipts. And I paid cash.'

'What brand were they?'

'Benson & Hedges Gold.'

Fenchurch held up the shot of Hall's stand-off with the bouncer. 'This was taken at eight thirty on Thursday night. Twenty-five minutes before your excursion. It shows Mr Robert Hall in a heated discussion with one of your employees.'

Bruco snorted. 'We chucked that geezer out.'

'Why?'

'You spoke to my girls last night and this morning, didn't you?' Bruco stuck his hands in his pockets. 'So why don't you tell me why we chucked him out?'

'You're playing a dangerous game here, Mr Vrykolakas.'

'I'm innocent.'

'Of what?'

'Whatever you're implying I've done.'

'We're investigating the murder of two prostitutes.' Fenchurch tapped the page. 'And Mr Hall here.'

'Do these girls have names?'

'Neither of them have been identified yet.' Fenchurch tilted his head to the side. 'We believe they were both sex workers, hence asking you whether you knew them.'

Bruco traced his finger down the thin pencil beard lining his jaw. He frowned, creases deepening across his forehead. 'Could Jack the Ripper be back from the dead?'

Fenchurch rolled his eyes. 'Oh, come on.'

'You never caught him, did you?'

'We know they worked for you. What were their names?'

'I've no idea what you're talking about.'

'That's the way you're playing it, is it?' Fenchurch tossed another sheet onto the tabletop. 'Mr Vrykolakas, this CCTV shows you on Prescot Street at nine fifteen last night. That's Mr Hall's address. Twenty minutes have passed since this previous one.' He prodded the photo outside The Alicorn. 'You showed up at his flat around the time he died.'

'No comment.'

'Is this you in the picture?'

'No comment.'

'What did you do when you left your club?'

'I went for a drive.'

Fenchurch grinned. 'What did you do between leaving your club and turning up outside Mr Hall's flat?'

'I told you, I went for cigarettes.'

Fenchurch drew a circle with his finger around the shadowy figure next to Bruco. 'Who's your friend here?'

'No comment.'

'Speak to us, Mr Vrykolakas.'

'My client has the right to remain silent. You might've heard of it?'

'More than enough times.' Fenchurch glared at Bruco. 'You're going to be charged with the murder of Mr Hall unless you start cooperating.'

'No further comment.'

'Gentlemen, we're done here.' Edgar started packing away his stationery. 'Do I need to stay to witness more harassment of an innocent man or can I go grab a burger?'

'Go get your burger.' Fenchurch nodded at the Custody Officer. 'Take Mr Vrykolakas downstairs and stick him in a cell, please.'

Chapter Twenty-Six

'Thanks for taking a back seat, Simon.' Docherty held his office door open to let Fenchurch through. 'I needed Dawn to focus on processing the whole lot of them. There's a lot of girls and punters in that bloody club.'

'I didn't see Erica McArthur there.'

'That's very specific, Si.'

'She was very helpful last time, that's all.' Fenchurch perched on the edge of the desk. He winced as the rib flared up again. Had bruises all over his arse. 'Did you watch the interview?'

'Caught the bit of his lawyer going for a burger. Cheeky bastard.'

'I wished I could've torn that bloody beard off.'

'I bet that's not the end of it.'

'Those braces were ripe for snapping, as well.' Fenchurch yawned. 'Been a long day, boss.'

'I suspect tomorrow'll be even worse. We had a shut case and now you've bloody opened it again.' Docherty leaned against the closed door. 'You think this Bruco character killed him?'

'Him or his accomplice.' Fenchurch slumped back, his hip touching the monitor. 'Hall's death isn't looking accidental or suicidal.'

'You honestly think they forced him to OD?'

'Only logical conclusion I can come up with.'

'Guy got turfed out of that club.' Docherty started fiddling with the doorknob, tightening and untightening. 'I can't imagine he did anything bad enough to warrant what they did to him.'

'They could've just paid him a visit and found him dead.'

'If that's their story, we can still do them with something.'

'I'm sure DI Mulholland's team will find out, boss.'

'Aye, well. Early report is the girls who were on last night are keeping quiet about what happened with Mr Hall.'

'Bloody typical. TPU had The Alicorn on their radar but didn't even have the manager's name.'

'You think they're bent?'

'I'm not saying anything of the sort, boss.' Fenchurch winked. 'That club's linked to prostitution and they've done nothing about it.'

'Well, Hall's PM is first thing in the morning. I want you out in Lewisham, okay?' Docherty stood up. 'I've had to move heaven and bloody earth to get Pratt to come in on a Saturday morning.'

'Fair enough.' Fenchurch walked over to the door. 'Will I see you at the briefing?'

'Aye, that'll be shining bright.'

'That'll be what?'

'Never mind.' Docherty laughed. 'Get out of here.'

Fenchurch went back into the corridor and fumbled with his phone as he walked. No messages from—

'Guv.' Nelson clapped him on the back. 'Good result, right?'

'I've had easier ones, Jon.' Fenchurch touched his side. 'My rib's bloody aching and I think my whole body's purple.'

'Seen anyone about it?'

'Duty doctor said it's just bruising.'

'Well, whatever. We've got him.'

Fenchurch stopped by the stairwell. 'That was some good work with the CCTV earlier, Jon. You and Kay have still got the chops. I've no idea what to do with all that stuff.'

'Can't use new technology?'

'Eh?'

'Never mind. Let's use the next one as a training exercise. Are you up for a celebratory beer, guv?'

'You know, I'd actually love one, but I've got another appointment tonight.'

———⌣———

Fenchurch shivered outside the tenement and pressed the buzzer again. Up on the top floor, the lights from inside bleached the brick. Back along Barford Street, the old-fashioned lamp glowed in the downpour, raindrops caught in the haze. 'Come on, come on, come on.'

'Hello?'

'Abi, it's Simon.'

'You're late.'

'I know, I'm sorry.'

'Well, you did warn me, I suppose.'

The door clunked open and he stepped inside, dripping rain onto the tiles. He climbed the spiral stairs, swallowing hard. Half eight wasn't that late. He reached her floor and knocked on her flat door. His old home. Same as it ever was.

The pale-blue door opened. Abi peered out into the hall. She'd lost weight and gained lines, her eyes ringed with dark bags. Her hair was much shorter, touching her earlobes instead of her shoulders. She still looked miles better than him. She grinned at him, dimpling her cheek.

He smiled back, his heart thudding. Drums cannoned in his ears. 'You've painted the door.'

She tilted her head, frowning. 'Is that all you've got to say?'

'It's good to see you.' He coughed. 'You're looking well.'

'And you.' She leaned forward and kissed him on the cheek. 'In you come.'

He followed her inside. She'd replaced the old red carpet with gleaming floorboards. The grey walls were now a stark white, like an art gallery. New spotlights, too. 'The flat looks good.'

'Finally got round to painting it in the summer.' She looked him up and down. 'My God, you're soaked.'

'It's tipping it down out there.'

'I'll get you a towel.'

'I'll be fine.'

'Ever the martyr.'

Bloody martyrdom. 'I was going to blame my lateness on the *Star Wars* queue.'

'You're old enough to remember it the first time round.' Abi led him into the kitchen with a cheeky grin on her face.

The dimple . . .

The extractor droned away above a steaming pot on the hob, garlic aroma filling the room. She stirred the pan and tapped the spoon on the side. 'It's just about done.'

'Smells good. But I thought it'd be ready an hour ago?'

'I knew better than that, Simon.' She reached over and pressed start on the microwave. The machine hummed as it spun around. 'Beer?'

'Better not. I'm driving.'

'I got them in especially for you.'

He smiled. 'Just the one, then.'

'Have a seat.' She pointed into the corner.

He sat down. Another new arrangement. Grey table and chairs almost matching the new subway tiles on the wall. They'd replaced the marks as Chloe grew up.

She poured beer into a glass. It foamed up. 'Here you go.' She dumped the bottle down and handed him the glass, half foam.

Fenchurch took it and tilted it up. 'Here's cheers.' Craft beer attacked his tongue. Hops turned up to eleven. 'God, that's good stuff.'

'Glad you like it.' She took a mouthful of white wine. The glass was way below anyone's measure of halfway. 'You look like shit, by the way.'

'Thanks. I feel like shit. Just had the pleasure of receiving a kicking from a nightclub owner. Feels like he cracked a rib.'

'Are you okay?'

'I'll live.'

'Did you catch him?'

'Eventually. Ended up chasing the bugger onto the Northern Line.' He held up a hand. 'Not the tracks.'

She sat opposite and flattened down her skirt. 'Take it you're busy?'

'Same as it ever was.' He grinned. 'Can't talk about it.'

'You mean you won't talk about it.'

'True.' Another pull of cold beer. 'Bastard of a case, Ab.'

'What is it?'

'You really want to know?'

'If it'll stop you being such a bloody nightmare, then yes.'

'Two dead girls, young women really. Both killed by the same geezer, only he's turned up dead.' He took another glug of beer. 'This is my life, Ab. Death and murder.'

'I take it you've closed it?'

'I wish. Still got a mountain of paperwork to get through. A load of interviews still taking place, not all of the evidence is collected. Not got a motive, either.'

She drained her glass. 'There's something you're not telling me, isn't there?'

'Like what?'

'I know you, Simon Fenchurch. What you don't tell me.'

'This case . . . It's a bit close to home, Ab. I really shouldn't talk about it.'

The microwave pinged and Abi went over to the fridge. She got out a bottle of wine and refilled her glass. 'Simon, the only way you'll bloody talk to me is about work. Spill.'

'There's a couple of things.' Fenchurch finished his glass and poured in the rest of the small bottle. A lot less foam with his trained hand. 'It reminds me a lot of . . . what happened.'

'Say it.'

The beer fizzed away, tiny sparks popping just above the surface. 'I mean what happened to us.'

'Say her bloody name.'

'Fine.' He let out a deep sigh and looked up. 'I mean Chloe.'

She took a big hit of wine and dumped the bottle on the counter, uncorked. 'How does it remind you of her?'

'There's this girl. Her name's Erica. She's eighteen, works in a nightclub. A lap-dancing bar. There's something about her. She thinks I'm her father.'

Abi slammed the glass down. 'Is it Chloe?'

'No.' Like he knew the answers. Like he knew anything. 'She asked if I want her to be my daughter.'

'You told her we'd lost Chloe? Why the bloody hell did you do that?'

'Because . . . I don't know. I just did. I was tired and . . . My head's so full of shit. This case. Seeing that girl. Wanting to do *something*.'

Abi reached into the microwave for a steaming bowl and tipped the contents onto two plates. She ladled sauce on top and handed him one. 'Here you go.'

'Looks brilliant.' Fenchurch put it on the table. Little bows of pasta, some sort of green filling inside. No appetite, no matter how good it smelled. 'I've pissed you off.'

She sat down and had another drink. 'It's fine.'

'Not even in the door five minutes and I've made you want to open a vein.'

'I did ask.' She stabbed a fork into a parcel. Didn't lift it up, just held it against the plate. 'What else do you know about this girl?'

'Nothing much.' Fenchurch stared at the ceiling. 'She doesn't remember her dad. What little she does, she said I reminded her of him.'

'I said evidence, not what you want to hear.'

'I swear I've not been putting words in her mouth.'

'What have you been putting in her mouth?'

'Abi, there's nothing going on. Bloody hell.' Fenchurch speared a pasta parcel with a fork and held it in the air. Steam twisted up from it. 'She got me in my weakest point.' He swallowed without eating it. 'Chloe'd be eighteen by now. Same age as Erica.'

'We both lost her.'

He put the pasta back on the plate, uneaten. 'I lost you as well. Lost my marriage, my bloody future.'

'You stopped speaking to me that day.'

'I didn't.'

'No, you didn't, did you? You asked me about cups of tea and where your socks were. Never talked about how you bloody felt.'

'I tried to. Believe me, I tried.' He took a slug of beer. The booze was flushing his cheeks. Took the edge off his ribs, though. 'I went looking for her. Every day, before and after work.' He bared his teeth. 'I'd sit outside here, watching for whoever took her.' He dug the heels of his palms into his eye sockets. 'Then you kicked me out.'

'I didn't want to, Simon. I still . . .' She took another drink of wine. 'I don't know what I still do or don't feel.'

'I still love you, Abi. Never stopped.'

'Right.' She shut her eyes and massaged her forehead. Then another sip of wine. 'This girl's playing you, but you're too blind to see it.'

He shook his head. 'But what if she knows what happened to Chloe?'

'Could you believe anything she said?'

'Maybe.'

'What does your dad say about it?'

Fenchurch scowled at her. 'Dad?'

'You know he phones me. He reckons he's onto something.'

Fenchurch reached into his pocket for his mobile. 'I'm going to tell him to bloody stop calling you.'

'No, it's fine. It shows someone cares.'

'He still shouldn't be doing it.'

'Why not? You're still hunting. Still checking her case file every bloody day.'

Fenchurch didn't have a response to that.

She reached a hand across the table. 'You need to move on, Simon.'

He gripped her soft hands, like silk, and blinked away a battery of tears. 'But what if she's out there, Ab? What if she misses us as much as we miss her?'

'Simon, stop. This is killing you.'

'I wish I could stop.'

She pulled her hand away. 'Why have you come here?'

'To see you. To talk.'

'If you want to . . . If you want to *talk*, you need to be prepared to move on.'

'I don't know if I can.'

'Simon, you need to let go of her. It's the past.'

Fenchurch shut his eyes. Tears ringed the lids. He sucked in a deep breath and opened them again. 'The pain's still at a thousand,

Ab. I can't just let go. All I bloody do every day is dredge up the past. Looking into other people's lives. Why did they die? Who wanted to kill them? Who'd benefit from their death?' He sighed. 'I haven't got any answers to those questions about Chloe.'

'Simon, this fire in your gut is killing you.'

'I'm sorry.' Fenchurch stared at his full plate, the red pasta parcel still on the fork. An inch of beer in the glass. He scraped the chair back and got up. 'Thanks for dinner.'

'Simon, wait—'

Fenchurch stormed out of the flat and thumped down the stairs, wiping at his wet cheeks. He bumped past Quentin, still Abi's neighbour and still in rude health. Same as it bloody ever was. He stepped out into the rain and let his tears merge with the deluge. He looked up at the flat.

Abi was in the living room, looking down at him. She gave a gentle wave, the other hand covering her mouth.

He flicked up his hand and set off for the car.

What a bloody idiot. Same old Fenchurch.

Day 4
Saturday, 19th December 2015

Chapter Twenty-Seven

'You're not listening to me.' Fenchurch crunched back in his seat and tightened the grip on the handset, the cord coiling away to the desk phone. He slurped his morning tea in its Christmassy Pret container, all reds and greens. Bloody enforced happiness. Rain battered against the windows, still pitch-dark outside. His legs felt like he'd spent all night squatting at the gym. 'That DNA could be the key to this bloody case.'

Clooney sighed down the line. 'You don't have to keep putting pressure on me, you know?'

'So when am I getting the results back?'

'DNA sequencing takes time. I can't just click my fingers and magic them up.'

'Not this long, though. It's 2015.'

'It's less than a week to Christmas, Simon. You know how many people die in suspicious circumstances at this time of year?'

'Enlighten me.'

'A shitload.'

'Is that a metric or imperial shitload?'

'Aztec.'

Funny bastard. Fenchurch shifted forward. 'Look, when can I get my results back?'

'I'll try and get them to you this afternoon.'

Fenchurch glanced up at the clock. 'It's half seven. You've got till lunchtime.'

'What did your last slave die of? Remember it's a bloody Saturday. I'm not even being paid double time for this. And don't bother chasing me up again. It's getting in the bloody way.'

'Cheers.' Fenchurch slammed the phone down and started easing the sleep out of the bags under his eyes, not that he'd got much. Legs felt weighed down in concrete like some Mafioso was ready to chuck him off a bridge.

Abi looking down at him, giving him a wave.

Not the best move he'd ever made. Second best use for a time machine, though. Just get back up the bloody stairs.

He typed out a text. 'Ab, sorry for being an arsehole last night. Give me a bell. Simon'. He sent it and put his mobile down. The previous day's files sat underneath Chloe's. He leafed through it again. Nothing new sprang to mind, even with the information they'd got on the case, even with unburdening himself to whoever would listen.

Still just a bloody dead end. A cold case he should've handed off years ago.

He checked his mobile again. Nothing. Then went into the call log and found Erica's mobile number.

'So this is how the master operates, is it?' A Welsh voice boomed from the corridor.

Fenchurch dropped his phone and fumbled Chloe's file shut, spilling a drop of tea on it. 'You're in early, Sergeant.'

'Wanted to get a head start.' Owen had propped himself against the doorjamb, arms folded. 'I found a couple of interesting things at ESB last night.'

Fenchurch adjusted himself in his seat. 'About Robert Hall?'

'Not as interesting as your evening, I gather.'

'I got Bruco, that's all that matters.' Fenchurch took another glug of tea. 'What did you get?'

Owen counted one on his thumb. 'First, on the intel. We've got nothing on a Robert Hall. I checked our surveillance log for the other brothels we're monitoring. Nobody even remotely matching his description.'

'So he's just dropped off the radar between March and now?'

'He's either been a very good boy or he's getting girls off the street.' Owen shifted over to sit in front of Fenchurch. He counted two on his forefinger. 'Second, I've got a DC going through our CCTV log. Might find him kerb-crawling in October or something.' He counted three on his middle finger. 'Third thing we found was something very interesting indeed.' He leaned across the desk, his face inches from Fenchurch. His breath stank of stale milk. 'I know what you did last night.'

Fenchurch mopped up tea with leftover lunch serviettes, dabbing at Chloe's file. 'I don't know what you're talking about.'

'A nocturnal visit.' Owen wagged his finger at Fenchurch. 'Naughty, naughty.'

Is he stalking Abi? Am I being followed?

Fenchurch dumped his serviettes in the bin. 'I had dinner with my ex-wife. That's hardly the sort of thing you should be concerning yourself with.'

'Not what I'm talking about.'

'Then what the hell are you on about?'

Owen tossed a pair of photos onto the table. 'You visited a monitored site, you stupid wanker.'

Fenchurch picked up the first still. He looked shifty as he spoke into the intercom outside Erica's flat. Even shiftier in the second one as he left, mobile clamped to his ear. 'What the hell is this?'

'That flat's under surveillance as part of our East London operations. Five sex workers live in that flat. Which one of them were you screwing?'

'I was speaking to Erica McArthur.'

Owen clicked his tongue a few times. 'One of the lap dancers at The Alicorn, right? Were you passing on information to her?'

Fenchurch was inches away from swinging for the little shit. 'Excuse me?'

'Intelligence on the raid. Giving her a warning, maybe. I notice she wasn't there.'

'She gave me the intel that put us on to Bruco. You might've heard that we got him for Hall's murder.'

Owen folded his arms. 'Have you logged your visit?'

'This is beyond a bloody joke.' Fenchurch tightened his tie. 'It's in the case file as part of my report into Bruco's arrest. It's all been filed and I've got nothing to hide.'

'On the back page of some sub-report, no doubt.' Owen tucked his shirt into his trousers as he stood. 'Docherty needs to know.'

'Are you threatening me, you little shit?'

'You're sticking to your story, are you?' Owen shook his head slowly. 'Either you tell him or I do. I don't like dodgy cops on my investigations.'

Fenchurch got up and grabbed his suit jacket. 'You're one to bloody talk.'

Owen sniffed. 'Excuse me?'

'You heard.'

⌣

Fenchurch pulled the door shut behind him. 'I need a word, boss.'

'Good morning, sunshine.' Docherty looked up from his desk, covered with sheets of A3 criss-crossed with a spreadsheet.

He checked his watch. 'You're not supposed to be here for another couple of hours.'

'Couldn't sleep, boss.' Fenchurch sat opposite, fists balled tight. 'There's something I need to make you aware of.'

'This sounds a bit formal for you.' Docherty pushed his paperwork to the side. A stapler fell to the floor. 'Spit it out.'

Fenchurch picked up the stapler and put it back on the desk. A staple hung loose. 'I spoke to Erica McArthur yesterday evening.'

'The girl who gave you the lead on the club?'

'Yeah, her. It was at her flat.'

Docherty sighed. 'You better not have been shagging her.'

'I'm not even going to dignify that with a response.'

'Is she on your CHIS log?'

'Not yet.'

'She bloody should be. So, if you weren't spooning and listening to Marvin Gaye records, what were you doing?'

'There's nothing dodgy here, boss.' Fenchurch frowned. 'Like I said, she told me our Jane Does had worked for this Bruco character. That led to us discovering the CCTV footage.'

'This isn't like you. What's really going on?'

Fenchurch got up and circled round the room. Felt like a caged tiger. 'Because DS Owen accosted me about it. TPU are monitoring that flat. I was flagged up.'

Docherty swallowed hard. Difficult to tell who he was more annoyed with — Fenchurch or Owen. 'What did he say?'

'He got me to tell you.'

'Were you going to anyway?'

'It's all in the case file.'

Docherty drummed his fingers on the table. 'What the hell are you up to?'

'Nothing, I swear.'

'So why do I feel like you're bloody lying to me?'

'Listen, DS Nelson thinks the TPU guys are dodgy.'

'What did they do? Steal some Jammie Dodgers from the Incident Room's biscuit tin?'

Fenchurch smothered a laugh. 'Nelson heard something back in the day about both of them.'

'Oh, for crying out loud.' Docherty rested his head in his hands. 'This is all just he said, she said. Is there anything concrete here?'

'When I was at that flat, Erica said there's talk at The Alicorn of some dodgy officers. Sounds like cops on the take.'

'You got any of this on the record?'

'She won't come in.' Fenchurch cracked his knuckles. Pretty much the only part of him not bruised. 'I'm only telling you this because he's trying to blackmail me.'

'How can he . . .' Docherty covered his eyes with his hands. 'Has he got photos of you shagging her?'

'I said I wasn't going to answer that.'

'People use that line when they've done something and don't want to incriminate themselves.'

'I. Never. Shagged. Her.' Fenchurch was on his feet again, fists clenched, ready to swing. 'Are you happy now?'

Docherty looked him up and down. 'Sit.'

Fenchurch stayed standing. 'Whatever Owen says, I didn't shag her and there's no evidence to say I did.'

'You're acting like you have.'

'He's just got me going inside the flat then leaving. That's it. I've done nothing.'

'There's something you're not telling me, isn't there?'

Fenchurch leaned against the wall. Felt like he might slump down it. 'She might know what happened to Chloe.'

'Oh God, Simon. Why the hell do you think that?'

'There's something not adding up about her. Keeps teasing me about it.'

'Right. You want to talk about it?'

'No.'

'Same as bloody ever.' Docherty picked up his spreadsheets and started putting them back in order. 'Why are TPU monitoring that flat?'

'The girls who stay there work at The Alicorn.' Fenchurch stood up tall. 'Boss, I think Owen might be bent.'

'Any evidence?'

'Not as such. Geezer's sniffing all the time, like he's got a bloody coke habit.'

'Superb. Another bloody hunch. Have you got anything to support this?'

'Not yet, boss. I've not started—'

'Simon, you're acting like a bloody idiot here. You want me to put Mulholland back on days?'

'I'm deadly serious, boss. Something funny's going on with this case. You think it's a coincidence that this geezer turns up dead?'

'If it's murder.'

'Oh, it's murder, all right.'

'You're so sure about that and you've not even been to the post-mortem.' Docherty shook his head. 'Bloody hell.' He lined up the edges of his spreadsheet stack. A tower of bullshit. 'Leave it with me. And shut the door on your way out.'

'I'll end by thanking you for all coming in on a Saturday.' Docherty beamed at the officers in the Incident Room. 'I know you're getting paid overtime for it, but I appreciate you not excusing yourselves. It shows commitment.' He smiled at Fenchurch. 'Simon?'

'Boss.' Fenchurch took a drink of tea as he scanned the faces. Looked like a full house, even Clooney had bothered to show. 'After we conclude here, I'll be attending Robert Hall's post-mortem. This will prove whether it was suicide, death by misadventure or murder. As it stands, we think it's murder and we have a suspect under arrest. Still a lot of open questions, though.'

A long stream of paper covered one wall, filled with the timelines for the three murders.

'I want us to tighten up our understanding of the events of Thursday night. The death of Jane Doe number two.' Fenchurch tapped the autopsy photos of the girl. Dead eyes that followed you round the room. 'Mr Hall's activities after he murdered the second victim are still shrouded in mystery. The Alicorn's manager, Sotiris Vrykolakas, left the club twenty-five minutes after Hall was kicked out. Twenty minutes later, he turned up at Mr Hall's apartment. Just before his time of death. He either killed him or knows what happened in that flat.'

He held up a photo of the blurry figure next to Bruco. 'He wasn't alone, either. While we've got Mr Vrykolakas in custody, we're still hunting for his accomplice. Our highest priority today is identifying him.'

He looked around the room. Yawns and slurps of coffee. Same as it ever was. 'Anything else? No? Right—'

'Si.' Clooney raised a hand. 'We're getting nowhere with this Hall bloke's mobile. The HTC job.'

Fenchurch frowned. 'But his wife gave us the code yesterday.'

Clooney glanced at his own mobile. 'Is that what you sent me?'

'What did you think it was?'

'Two eight six eight. I thought you were calling me a cun—'

'Just get the bloody thing unlocked, okay?'

Clooney shrugged. 'What's the point? We've got the messages and calls from the network.'

'Then there's nothing for you to do but polish your halo.' Fenchurch held his gaze. 'That's all for now. Dismissed.' He stared at the whiteboard for a few seconds. Bastard thing was in desperate need of reorganisation. More tea first, though.

'Simon.' Mulholland encroached on him, tightening her scarf as she walked. Dark rings shrouded her eyes. Thank God this case was eating into someone else's soul as well. 'I need a word.'

'And I need to get out to Lewisham, Dawn.'

Mulholland arced her arm around to make him stop. 'I've got a lead for you.'

Fenchurch stepped to the side. 'What?'

'You two need to hear this, as well.' Mulholland grabbed Reed's jacket as she and Owen passed, both clutching coffee cups. 'I'd follow this up myself but I've got to collect my daughter from my darling mother-in-law. Then try and get some sleep.' She yawned into her hand. 'My guys have been speaking to prostitutes in the area. One of them made a house call to Hall's flat at about nine p.m. on Thursday night.'

Owen took a slurp of coffee through the lid. 'A street girl?'

'She was wearing suspenders and a purple miniskirt in mid-December, so I'll let you be the judge. She's one of the unidentified people on the CCTV.'

'Hang on.' Reed sucked at her coffee. 'Did you say she got there at nine?'

'Yes, why?'

'That doesn't fit the timeline, does it? He was thrown out of The Alicorn at half past eight.'

Mulholland tied her scarf as tight as her pout. 'She says he picked her up in a taxi on the way to his flat.'

'We'll speak to her.' Fenchurch nodded at Reed. 'Kay, can you get someone to find the driver who took them there?'

'Why do I get the feeling this is going to piss all over my day?'

Chapter Twenty-Eight

The prostitute and her lawyer were still deep in conversation. Difficult to work out which was the lady of the night. Both wore short skirts, their chunky thighs crossed and arms folded. Thick designer glasses. One wore a blouse, the other a tight top. Only one of them was chewing gum.

Fenchurch shut the door again and leaned against it, still in the corridor. 'Looks like they need a minute or two.'

Owen finished his coffee with a grimace. 'They're still not ready for us?'

'I need you to act like a professional in there.'

'Me, act professional?' Owen pointed at his chest. He crumpled his cup and laughed, loud as hell. 'You're not exactly behaving like an innocent, are you?'

Fenchurch snorted. 'I'm leading this.' He opened the door and sat in the nearest chair. 'Playtime's over, ladies.'

The woman on the right ran a pudgy hand through her hair, mid-brown streaked with blonde. She stopped chewing her gum. 'We're not finished. You're abusing my client's human rights here.'

Fenchurch checked his notes. Kerry Hopkins was the lawyer, Norma Barclay the prostitute. Alleged prostitute. 'You've had your chance. Besides, this is just intelligence gathering, okay?'

'Look, Fenchurch. I need a word before we get started.'

Fenchurch whispered into Owen's ear: 'Start the tape for me.'

Owen stretched over to the microphone. 'Interview commenced at eight thirty-three—'

Fenchurch walked over to the open doorway and smiled at Hopkins. 'Go on, then.'

'My client's here to provide information. I don't want this resulting in a prosecution.'

'All we want is a witness statement to back up Mr Hall's movements. Besides, we've no evidence of her soliciting. She's here because she offered to help our murder inquiry. End of.'

Hopkins stared back inside the room. 'Fine.'

'We should be more than fine.' Fenchurch went back into the room and sat as Owen finished the interview spiel. He cracked his knuckles, grimacing as the tendons clicked, then pushed the usual sheet across the table. Robert Hall on CCTV. 'We understand you recognise this man?'

Norma had a long scar down her cheek. Looked like a knife wound. 'That's right. He's called Rob.'

'And how do you know him?'

Norma cleared her throat again, rubbing at her lymph glands. 'I was walking home from work on Thursday night. He started chatting to me on Commercial Street. Just by Spitalfields Market.'

'And what's your profession?'

Norma glared at him. 'I'm a cleaner at a chemist.'

'So you don't solicit sexual favours in exchange for money?'

Norma glanced at Hopkins, who gave a slight nod. She cleared her throat but kept quiet.

'That's how you're playing it, is it?' Fenchurch held up the sheet. 'Tell us more about your encounter with Mr Hall?'

'His taxi pulled over and he got out. Asked me to join him.'

'What was he talking about?'

'The price of potatoes in China.'

'I take it you joined him?'

She raised a shoulder. 'I got in the cab.'

'What kind was it? A Hackney carriage?'

'You mean a black cab?'

Fenchurch gave her a nod.

'It was a silver thing. Posh car. German, maybe.'

Fenchurch sent an Action to Reed to check it out. 'What happened next?'

'We went to his flat. Place down by the Tower. Can't remember the street. It was by the railway bridges, though.'

Fenchurch passed her a still from the CCTV, just showing the building and parked cars. 'Was it this street?'

'That's the one.'

'For the benefit of the tape, this is Prescot Street. What time was this?'

'Be about quarter to nine?' Norma exhaled. 'We went inside and we had sex. Then I left.'

'How long did this coupling take?'

'About fifteen minutes. I asked if he wanted me to stay but he didn't.'

'Did he pay you?'

'I'm not answering that.' She scowled at her lawyer. 'After that, I walked back up Leman Street.' She looked around the interview room's ceiling. 'Past this building, actually. Then onto Commercial Street, where I'd been earlier.'

'Did you happen upon any more men on your travels?'

Hopkins dropped her glasses onto the tabletop. 'My client doesn't need to answer any questions relating to anything other than her liaisons with Mr Hall.'

'Mr Hall was murdered on Thursday night.'

Norma's eyes bulged. 'What?'

'Around the time you were enjoying his company, as it happens. You see why we need to know your client's whereabouts, Ms Hopkins?' Fenchurch stared at Norma. 'Did you kill him?'

'My client refuses to answer that.'

Norma held out a hand in front of her lawyer. 'I told you, I left his flat and walked past here. That's it.'

'But you can't confirm it?'

'No.'

'You're in more than a little spot of bother here.'

'Listen to me. I'm here because I told one of you lot I recognised this geezer. I've done nothing.'

'But you can't prove it.'

'How did he die?'

'A heroin overdose.'

'What? You think I gave him the drugs?' She shook her head. 'Christ. Look, Rob offered me some heroin.'

'And did you accept?'

'Christ, of course I didn't. Listen, the buzzer went as I was leaving his flat.'

Fenchurch frowned. 'When was this?'

'Be about five past nine, something like that. Someone entered the building as I left. I didn't see where they were going, so don't ask.'

'How many were there?'

'Think there were two of them, but I only got a good look at the first one.'

Fenchurch sat forward. Drums firing double speed. 'Can you describe him?'

'Not really.' She traced a finger down her scar. 'He had a beard like that singer. You know, the one who did that song about days of the week?'

'Craig David?'

'That's him.'

Owen reached into a folder and produced a photo of Bruco. 'Was this him?'

She nodded. 'Definitely.'

Owen spoke into the microphone: 'I've shown the interviewee photograph P dash zero one four. Interview terminated at eight thirty-seven a.m.'

'You're free to go.' Fenchurch smiled at Norma. 'We can arrange transport to this chemist, should you wish.'

⁓

Fenchurch stared at the timeline on the Incident Room wall as he finished chewing. Norma's account added only a sliver of information. 'Still full of bloody gaps, Jon. Bruco's appearance at the flat is still circumstantial. We need to back up him going inside. That Teddy-boy concierge was asleep at the wheel and all. Bloody hell.' He scrunched up the foil into a ball and chucked it into his bag. 'And what's worse is that was a shit breakfast burrito.'

Nelson stayed focused on his mobile. 'Where does it rank, guv?'

'It's just rank.' Fenchurch dropped the bag into the recycling bin. 'We're getting nowhere here. Can drive a bloody bus through that timeline.' He scanned across the busy Incident Room. Reed and Bridge were sitting at a laptop. 'Kay, you got a minute?'

She got up and strolled over. 'Guv?'

'Kay, tell me you've found Hall's taxi driver.'

'Wish I could, guv, but I'd be lying.' She sighed at the list on the whiteboard. 'We've done just about all the cab firms in East London.'

'Bollocks.' Fenchurch avoided Nelson's gaze. 'Did you get my note?'

'I did, not that it helped.'

'You didn't find it?'

'No, we did. Lisa's got it on the CCTV now. It's a Volkswagen Passat. She—'

Bridge appeared, out of breath, holding a print. 'Sarge, I've found it.'

'What?'

'Have a look.' Bridge handed the sheet to Reed. 'That Passat, it's registered to Frank's Cabs.'

Fenchurch used his tongue to pick at some bacon stuck between his teeth. 'Bloody Flick Knife.'

'Good work, Lisa.' Reed folded the page in half. 'What's the plan, guv?'

'We go in there and speak to him. Cheeky bastard's lying to us.'

'Thought we weren't to go there without Owen or Kershaw?'

Fenchurch looked around the room. Neither were about. 'I don't trust them.'

'We've got two dead prostitutes and a dead banker, guv.' Reed shook her head. 'This isn't the time to be playing office politics, is it?'

'Maybe not, but I'm not waiting for them.'

A light switched on inside the wooden hut. A beat later, the door opened. Blunden beamed at Fenchurch. 'Second time in a week, Inspector. Heathrow transfer, is it?'

'Mind if we have a word?'

Blunden looked Reed up and down. 'This your missus, is it?'

'She's a colleague, Frank. Cut the bollocks, will you?'

'In you come.' Blunden ambled through reception to his office. Bandy legs like he had rickets. He sat at his desk and narrowed his eyes at Reed. The ashtray was empty this time. 'I much prefer your company today, Inspector.'

'DS Owen is otherwise engaged.' The metal groaned as Reed sat on the seat opposite Blunden and crossed her legs. 'That okay with you?'

'Let's get this over with.' Blunden couldn't take his eyes off Reed. 'I assume you're after something?'

Fenchurch leaned against the pillar between the two windows, Pronto out. 'Just a few questions for you, if—'

'You better not be recording me on that thing.'

'It's how we take notes these days.'

'That supposed to reassure me?'

'If I was recording this, it wouldn't be admissible in court without your permission.'

Blunden gave a scowl. 'Fine, I believe you.'

'We think one of your cabs had a pick-up in Shoreditch on Thursday night, near The Alicorn.'

'You've got a lot of interest in that place all of a sudden. Why are you asking?'

'It's part of this case.'

'Be helpful to get a bit more context around the question.'

'It's a fairly simple request, Mr Blunden.'

'What time we talking?'

'Be about half past eight.'

'This is to do with those girls, isn't it?'

'That's correct.'

Blunden stared at his computer monitor, eyebrows raised. The white glow lit up his face as he tapped his keyboard. He scratched his jawline, an angry rash crawling from behind his ears. 'Who was in the taxi?'

'I can't tell you that, Frank.'

Blunden unfolded a crumpled sheet. The photos of Robert Hall and the first Jane Doe. 'Was it either of these two?'

'It might've been.'

'If you pair are fishing to see what you can get on my innocent operation here, well . . .' Blunden clawed at the rash. 'Let's say I'll not be best pleased.'

Fenchurch walked over to the desk, forcing Reed to the side. 'A car picked this guy up at about half eight on Thursday night. Somewhere near The Alicorn. We know it was one of yours, so quit with the bullshit.'

More scratching at the rash. 'Why should I help?'

'Because you're a pillar of the community?'

Blunden waved at the door. 'Get out of here.'

'There's no need to take this tone with us.'

'Like I said, you're fishing. I've got no time for that. I'm running an honest business here. Until you've got something on me, piss off out of it.'

Fenchurch held his gaze. Neither looked away. He rested his left ankle on his right thigh. 'I'm not going anywhere, Frank.'

'Get out, you scumbag.'

'The Note hotel.'

Blunden frowned. 'Excuse me?'

'Nice little place just off Bishopsgate. Very expensive. Does a lot of corporate travel, you know? Lonely businessmen staying away from home.'

'This going somewhere, Fenchurch?'

'They had a little back-books deal. They'd arrange for hookers to come round. Taxis would drop them off.' Fenchurch smacked his lips together. 'Wouldn't be your firm, would it?'

'You've no idea what you're talking about.'

'Be thankful I brought Kay here with me this time. If it was DS Owen, well, it might be going high up in Vice.'

Blunden tapped his computer again. 'Looks like you're right, Inspector. One of my boys did get a pick-up near that place at eight thirty-two.'

'Did it come through your switchboard?'

'Street pick-up. But I make sure they put them all through the desk here. I don't want any double dippers.'

'So, who—'

'I'll send him down to Leman Street, okay?'

'Make it soon.' Fenchurch stood up tall and raised an eyebrow. 'You should get some cream for that rash. Looks nasty.'

Chapter Twenty-Nine

Fenchurch prowled along the timeline on the Incident Room wall. Still so many bloody gaps. The thrum of the officers working behind him didn't quieten the drums.

'There you are.'

Fenchurch swung round.

Clooney was marching across the Incident Room, arms full of evidence bags. 'Got something for you, Si.' He dumped the bags on the nearest desk. At least four mobile phones in there. 'Managed to have a look at Hall's phone.'

'Two eight six eight.'

Clooney looked around. 'Shut up.'

'Take it you've found something?'

'Well, yes. The texts and emails all checked out.' He shifted his hand to jangle his rings. 'Thing is, he'd been using Tinder. The app for no-strings sex.'

'I know what it bloody well is.' Fenchurch glowered at him. 'Log in, find a girl, find a boy. Meet up for a bit of how's your father.'

'How's your father . . .' Clooney laughed at him. 'Sometimes I think you've just beamed in from the Victorian era.' He held up the bagged HTC. Black and silver metal. 'Your Hall geezer has been liking three hundred girls a day on this, by the looks of things.'

'Anyone liking him back?'

'This girl here did.' Clooney passed him the mobile.

A woman's face filled the screen. Beth, Twenty-six. Not bad looking, though she didn't look mid-twenties. Four miles away. Active twenty-six months ago. 'My interests are stamp-collecting and trainspotting. Not looking for sex. Yeah, right. ;-)'

'These are their messages.' Clooney gave him a wad of papers, just like a load of text messages, and flicked through to halfway. 'Notice how quickly they get dirty? "I'm wet for you, big boy." "My P in your V." Unbelievable.'

Fenchurch felt sick to the stomach.

'Different from our day, Si. Don't even need to buy her a glass of white wine these days.' Clooney turned to the next page and held it up. 'This is the first message after they did meet.'

Fenchurch squinted at it. 'Had fun, but let's agree no more, yeah?' He gave a shrug. 'What, she's letting him down gently?'

'Problem is, your Hall fella didn't like that.' Clooney held up another sheet, no danger Fenchurch could read any of it. 'Because she didn't have sex with him, he asked for the money for the meal back. And it went downhill from there.' Through some more pages. 'By the sixth message, he's threatened to kill her.'

'Have you tracked her down?'

'We're trying to.'

'How many of these hook-ups did he have?'

'Fifty? Sixty? Trying to figure it out is going to take a long time.'

Fenchurch stared at the timeline on the wall. 'So, between February and this week, he's stopped using hookers and started using that app?'

'That's right. Have a look at this, though.' Clooney went to the last page. A set of messages with another user. Trina, twenty-nine.

She liked pizza and craft beer. 'She was supposed to be meeting up with him last week. No account activity since, though. Not even a follow-up message from either of them.'

Fenchurch's mouth had gone dry all of a sudden. 'What?'

'I've got an address for you, though.'

———————

Fenchurch got out of his Mondeo and did a three-sixty. A modern primary school behind him, the playground empty. The dark sky was brooding with the menace of a ton of hailstones.

He pointed a finger at Reed and the pair of uniforms. Then swung it in an arc towards the third house on their left. A row of brick boxes blessed with gardens, dwarfed by a towering sixties council block.

Fenchurch put the Airwave to his mouth. 'Jon, you ready?'

Nelson waved from the road over the other side, flanked by three uniforms. It crackled. 'Affirmative, guv.'

'Then we're go.' Fenchurch started off across the tarmac. His legs wouldn't let him go faster than walking. The house looked empty. Curtains drawn, lights off.

He motioned for Reed to lead.

She rang the bell and waited a beat. 'This is the police! We're looking for a Trina Gordon!' Eyes on Fenchurch. Narrowing as the seconds passed by. Then another thump. 'Ms Gordon? It's the police.'

Fenchurch held up two fingers and waved forward.

The first uniform lumbered up to the door. Bulky muscles, just in a standard-issue black T-shirt despite the bitter wind cutting in from the Thames. He took his sights and lurched forward with a size twelve.

The door snapped open. It bounced back off the inside walls.

Fenchurch barged past into the house. The place was dark and stank of burnt toast and beans. He followed the scents into a small kitchen. Glossy units and worktops wedged into a tiny space. A navy pot of congealed baked beans sat on the hob, an open tub of Flora on the counter. On the right side of the room was a lime-green melamine table. A plate with two pieces of toast covered in beans, one slice half-eaten.

Fenchurch swung back into the hall and locked eyes with Reed. 'Nobody here.'

Wait. Steam was rising up from the beans. He put his hand to the pot. Had to jerk it away. Still boiling hot.

Below the table. There. A pink slipper. Attached to a leg.

Drums picked up the tempo and volume. Smashing away. Fenchurch crouched to get a better view. His legs stung as he went down.

A woman balled herself up on the floor, her head wedged against the underside of the table. Gripping her knees tight. Deep-ringed eyes. Lank hair. Breathing heavily.

He raised his hands. 'I'm a police officer. It's okay.'

She twisted her head to the side and swallowed.

'Are you Trina Gordon?'

'Who are you?' Scottish accent, barely audible above the racket from the hall. Clumping feet and bellowing voices.

He spun round. 'Shhh.' Then back at her. He slowly unfolded his warrant card and let her inspect it. 'My name's DI Simon Fenchurch. I'm looking for Trina Gordon.'

'You think you can break down my door, do you?'

'We thought your life was at risk.'

'Well, you weren't interested last week, were you?' She pulled her legs tighter. Shut her eyes and gritted her teeth.

'Do you want to come out of there, Ms Gordon?'

'No.'

'It's safe.'

She paused, clenching and unclenching her fists. 'He'll be back.'

'Who will?'

'Robert.'

Fenchurch glanced over at Reed. 'Robert Hall?'

'I never knew his last name.'

Fenchurch held out his hand.

She stared at it for a few seconds. Then gripped it tight and used it to pull herself to her feet. She was almost as tall as Fenchurch. Pretty, but there was a darkness in her eyes. Like she wasn't in the room with them. Didn't look anything like the profile picture Clooney had shown him.

She collapsed onto a chair. 'What happened to Robert?'

'He's not going to hurt you.'

'Is he in prison?'

Fenchurch shook his head. 'We found his body yesterday. Are you hiding from him?'

She spread her feet wide, like she was ready to pounce at any second. 'How do I know you're not working with him?'

'We're investigating him.'

A frown knitted her forehead. 'What's he done?'

'He's killed two women.'

'Christ.' She lowered her dressing gown and tugged down her pink T-shirt. A line bit into her flesh, an inch deep. Dark brown. 'He tried to strangle me.'

'You met him on Tinder, didn't you?'

Eyes shut, tears streaming down her cheeks. 'He seemed nice. Friendly. Had a nice smile.' She shook her head slowly, gasping for air. 'We went for a drink in Covent Garden then went for something to eat. I invited him back here.'

'You make a habit of doing that?'

'That was the first time I'd used that bloody app.' She sniffed. 'One of my friends swears by it. I added lots of men but he was the only one who liked me back.'

'What happened when you got back here?'

'He attacked me. Tried to have sex with me.' She scratched at her face, unpainted nails chewing at the flesh. 'I pushed him away. But he punched me. Again and again. Just kept doing it.' She leaned forward in the chair. 'He said I was a whore. Said all women are prostitutes. Then he said something like he should go back to prostitutes. They never said no.' Her hands went to her neck. 'Then he got the cable from my computer and he strangled me with it.'

'But you got away?'

'I lashed out. My elbow hit him in the balls. He fell over and I just ran. Went to the police station on Brick Lane. They came round here, but he'd gone. They couldn't find him.'

Fenchurch shut his eyes. 'This was last week?'

'I've not left this bloody house since. My parents are dead. I've got nobody.'

'You haven't seen or heard from him since?'

'I deleted that app.'

Fenchurch stood up tall and cleared his throat. 'Do you remember the name of the officer you spoke to?'

'Smith. Didn't catch his first name.'

'I'll make sure he loses his job for this.' Fenchurch left her with the uniform and made his way into the hall.

Reed was giving orders to another officer. She waved him off as Fenchurch approached. 'This is a shitty business, guv.'

'Tell me about it. Can you babysit her for a while?'

Reed looked over at the slumped figure in the kitchen. 'No problem.'

'Get Clooney to dig into his use of that app, okay? This might plug some of the gaps in the timeline and—'

'And you want it closed off. Got it. I'll see if he's been picking women up online.'

'Thanks.' Fenchurch stared at Trina, needling fingers into her eye sockets. 'That poor woman . . .'

His Airwave chimed out. Docherty. 'Here we bloody go.' He strode off down the hall and stuck it to his ear. 'Boss, we've—'

'Simon, I need you at the PM out in Lewisham now.'

'I've been caught up in a few things, boss.'

'I don't care about any of that shite. You. Here. Now.'

Pratt's beard almost touched the naked corpse of Robert Hall. Pale skin, like he'd been in a crypt for months. Stubble dotted his legs, mossing over a tattoo of a bike.

Docherty swung round from chatting to Clooney and nodded at Fenchurch. 'There you bloody are.'

'You knew something came up.' Fenchurch rested against the row of gunmetal cabinets lining the room. 'What do you want, boss?'

'I want you to see this, Simon. You, not any of your underlings.'

Fenchurch swallowed. Like he had time for this bollocks right now . . . 'I assume there's something for me to see?'

'William?'

Pratt looked up from the body. 'Oh, Simon. Didn't notice you there . . .' He jolted upright, as if he'd just realised how close he was to a dead body. 'Nice of you to join us.'

'So, what am I here for?'

Docherty thumbed at Pratt. 'William's just confirmed that Mr Hall was, in fact, murdered.'

'You're sure?'

'One hundred per cent. Let me take you through the logic, as it stands.' Pratt ran a hand down the corpse's arm, lingering over the injection site. 'The cause of death was definitely an overdose.' He held up a finger. 'How do I know this, you ask?'

Always the bloody showman. 'Assume I've asked.'

'Aha.' Pratt pointed at the open ribcage. The bones had been yanked apart. 'We've had a look inside his lungs.' He rattled a silver tray. What looked like chicken tikka sat on the metal, sliced wide open. 'Telltale sign of an overdose is water in the lungs. Tick.' He flicked his finger in the air in a V-shape. 'Secondary evidence is the presence of small amounts of talc crystals and cotton fibres. Again, tick.' Another V. 'The blood—'

'Hang on.' Fenchurch scowled, still trying to keep his gaze away from the open chest. 'Talc and cotton? Thought this was pure?'

Pratt let out a deep sigh, like he was fed up having to slow down for mere mortals. 'You know as well as I do that they cut cheap heroin with said substances. Have a tendency to get trapped in the lungs after the heart pumps them out. Now, we thought it was pure, but it had tiny amounts of those substances. Way above trace, though. It's just very, very good stuff.'

'But it's definitely heroin?'

'Absolutely.' Pratt waved a hand over at Clooney, not bothering to look up from his tablet. 'As our learned colleague's blood toxicology report stated, Mr Hall had a large amount of monoacetylmorphine present in his bloodstream. As I hope you know, heroin breaks down into morphine fairly quickly. But in overdoses, not all of it gets the time to break down.' He swivelled around the room, like he was performing the very first autopsy in an ancient lecture theatre. 'Therefore, Mr Hall died shortly after he'd been injected with the heroin.'

Fenchurch frowned at Docherty. 'Been injected?'

'Well, yes.' Pratt brushed a hand over Hall's skull. The skin was peppered with bruises around a lobster-red lump. 'You see these contusions and this depression? They happened perimortem, but were non-fatal. In layman's terms, someone's clobbered him before injecting him.'

Fenchurch stared at the floor. Murder was the only conclusion he could draw. He looked up at Pratt. 'Did you get hold of his medical records?'

'Indeed.' Pratt propped himself up against the bed. 'I perused them before I started here. There's no history of mental illness, I'm afraid.'

'So he's just cracked. Great.' Fenchurch focused on Clooney. 'You've been very quiet.'

'You've set Kay Reed on me. You're lucky I've got time to attend this.'

'I'm lucky you've got a team to make you look good, Mick.'

'Yeah, good one.' Clooney fingered the gaping hole in his ear-lobe. 'I've managed to move heaven and earth for you. The skin under his nails came from the second girl's throat.'

'So he definitely killed her?'

Clooney wagged a finger at him. 'I don't connect the dots, Si, you do.'

Touché. Fenchurch stuck a smile on his face. 'Have you got anything on the victims' DNA? Anything that could identify them?'

'Job's running as we speak.'

Fenchurch flinched as his Airwave rang. A generic Leman Street number. He took a step away, eyes on Docherty. 'Fenchurch.'

'Si, it's Steve on the front desk downstairs. Got a Mark Osbourne here for you.'

'I'm out at Lewisham, kind of in the middle—'

'Quit it with that, will you? Geezer says Frank Blunden sent him.'

'Here you are.' Fenchurch handed a coffee mug to Reed and checked his phone for any missed calls. Still nothing from Abi. Such a bloody idiot. He necked half of his lukewarm tea in one go. 'He's been here half an hour. Must be stewed worse than this tea.'

Reed tasted her coffee and made a face like she'd drunk her own urine. She clinked a painted nail off her mug. 'I was thinking of offering him this but I'm sure the Geneva Convention mentions something about "own-brand instant coffee".'

'Let's keep that in our back pocket.' Fenchurch rested his free hand on the handle. 'You want to lead in here?'

Reed flattened down her skirt. 'I'll be good cop.'

'I expect nothing less.' Fenchurch opened the door. 'Good morning, sir.'

Mark Osbourne was tapping a nail off the tabletop. Jeans and a Fred Perry polo shirt. Early forties, had the look of a guy who only liked sports you could preface with 'the'. The football, the rugby, the cricket. Never tennis, squash or F1. He gave a grunt. 'Mr Blunden told me to come here.'

'I'm very pleased for him.' Reed towered over Osbourne as she started the recorder. 'Interview commenced at ten fifteen on Saturday, the nineteenth of December. Present are myself, DS Kay Reed, and DI Simon Fenchurch. Also present is Mark Osbourne.'

'Do I need a lawyer?'

'Have you committed a crime?'

'You saying I have?'

'The purpose of this interview is to gain some intelligence into an ongoing investigation.' Reed gave him a smile. 'I hope we can count on your cooperation without legal representation?'

Osbourne raised a shoulder. 'Fire away.'

'We understand you had a pick-up by The Alicorn bar on Thursday night.'

'That's right.'

'Can you describe your fare?'

'Bloke in a suit. He was in a state.'

Reed slid a photo of Robert Hall across the table. 'Was it this guy?'

'Think so. It was Hackney Road at the Shoreditch end.' Osbourne looked away. 'Bit of a scene going on outside that bar. Geezer looked glad to get away. Seemed jumpy, you know?'

'Was he drunk?'

'He was on something. Wasn't sure I should take him but it'd been a quiet night, you know? He was dribbling a bit.'

'Dribbling?' Fenchurch nodded at Reed. 'That confirms the heroin story, I think.'

She grimaced. 'How did he pay?'

'Cash. Looked like he had a lot of notes in his wallet. Dropped it on the floor of my cab, had to bend down to pick it up. Took a few goes, you know?'

'Did you pick up a girl for him?'

'Come again?'

'Did you procure a prostitute for him?'

'A prostitute?' Osbourne shook his head slowly. 'Are you having a laugh?'

Reed looked like she needed to sigh. 'Did you let a woman into the car?'

'Well. Geezer got me to pull in halfway down Commercial Street. I thought it was to get some cash out. This was before I saw his wallet, you know?' Osbourne tugged at his polo shirt's collar. 'Next thing I know this girl jumped in the back with him. Chubby. Not bad looking, mind, but she had a scar on her face.' He traced a line that matched Norma Barclay's wound.

Reed showed him a photo of her. 'Is this her?'

'I'd say so.'

'Where did you drop them off?'

'A flat at the start of Prescot Street. The geezer paid me and asked me to wait for her.'

Fenchurch glanced at Reed. 'What did you say?'

'I said the geezer asked me to wait for her. You not listening?'

'So you knew what they were up to in there?'

'It pays not to ask questions, okay?' Another sharp tug at his Fred Perry. Needed a good pressing. 'She came out about ten, fifteen minutes later. I had TalkSport on. It was one of them evening fellas who just shouts. Anyway, she comes back out and I took her back up Commercial Street.'

It almost tallied with Norma's story. Fenchurch sent a note to Bridge to get it checked. 'Did you see anyone when you were there?'

'Well, this motor pulled up, like it was from a Meatloaf album. You know, like a bat out of hell?' Osbourne smirked. 'It was a Beemer, I think. These two geezers got out and piled into that building.'

'You saw two of them?'

'Absolutely.'

'Could you identify them?'

'One of them was a real George Michael lookalike. Had a suit on. A cheap one trying to look expensive.'

Reed pulled out a picture of Bruco. 'Was this him?'

'Pretty geezer, ain't he?'

'Not my type. What about the other bloke?'

'Didn't get a good look at this other fella. Had a hoodie on, pulled up like a snorkel parka. But, I swear, he could've been his brother.'

A frown tore across Reed's forehead. 'In what way?'

'Had that same stupid beard. I don't get why geezers do that, must take ages to shave in the morning.'

'How tall was he?'

Osbourne nodded at Fenchurch. 'Your height, I think.'

'So, six-one?' Reed got her Pronto out of her pocket and fiddled with it for a few seconds. She held it out at arm's reach. 'Was this him?'

'That's the geezer.'

Chapter Thirty

Fenchurch crunched back in his office seat. The wood cut into his back and sent another wave of pain to his rib. He gasped. 'Bugger.' He picked up his Airwave, eyes locked on Reed. 'DI Fenchurch to Control. Over.'

'Receiving.'

'Do you have a location for DS Paul Kershaw yet?'

'Not at present. His Airwave's still off, sir. Over.'

'Let me know when he switches it back on.' Fenchurch tossed the device on his desk. 'This is a bloody disaster.'

Reed bunched up her hair at the back of her head. 'You think he killed him, guv?'

'That or he saw Bruco do it.'

The door opened and Owen stormed in, fists clenched. 'What's up?'

'Thanks for joining us, Sergeant.' Fenchurch waved at the spare seat next to Reed. 'A taxi driver just identified an accomplice in Robert Hall's murder.'

Owen stayed standing. 'It's not death by misadventure, then?'

'He identified your little mate, Paul Kershaw.'

Owen collapsed into the chair. 'What the hell?'

Fenchurch reached into his desk drawer for a cereal bar. He waved the box at Owen, got only a shake of the head. Reed took one. 'I'm assuming this is news to you?'

'You can't ask me that.'

Fenchurch stopped halfway through tearing open the wrapper. 'What?'

'I said, you can't ask me that.'

Another knock on the door. Docherty and Savage ploughed in, looking like they were competing in a scowling competition.

Docherty stood in front of the window. Light bent around his skinny frame. 'We've got a bit of a situation here.' He didn't seem to want Reed to clear out. 'As chance would have it, Simon, I was with Howard when you called me. Any sign of DS Kershaw?'

'Nothing yet, boss.' Fenchurch chewed his cereal bar, keeping his gaze on Owen. 'I was just asking his colleague here but he's keeping quiet.'

'Strict instructions, Fenchurch.' Savage hauled off his waterproof jacket and tossed it onto Mulholland's desk. He slumped into her chair. 'First chance this month of getting on the golf course and I've had to come into the bloody office.'

'This is a bit more important than a round of golf, sir.' Fenchurch chewed the last of the bar and dumped the wrapper in the bin. 'It looks like your officer was involved in the death of Robert Hall.'

'I see.'

Docherty snapped out a laugh. '"I see"? That's all we're getting?'

'That's all you're allowed to know.'

'Howard, you've got a bent officer who's making a cock and balls of my case.' Docherty's eyes looked like they needed a firearms warrant. 'Now you're telling me you knew?'

Savage stared at him for a few seconds. Then gave the slightest of nods. 'Let's say we had our suspicions.'

'Christ on a bike.' Docherty glowered at Fenchurch. 'What have you got on him, Simon?'

'We've got CCTV backed up with two statements. First, a prostitute paid a house call. She saw The Alicorn's manager enter the building. Mr Vrykolakas was with another man but she couldn't identify him. DC Bridge is trying to get her to ID Kershaw as we speak.'

'So far so good.'

'Then we spoke to one of Frank Blunden's drivers, who—'

'Frank Blunden?' Docherty twisted up his face. 'You're taking Flick Knife's word for it? Christ on a bloody bike.'

'Guv, this driver identified DS Kershaw.' Fenchurch waved over at Reed. 'Kay's had some uniform check with the neighbours and the concierge. Two of them have backed up his statement.'

Docherty paced over and grabbed Savage by the shoulders. 'Howard, what the hell's going on?'

Savage ignored him, instead locking onto Owen. 'Chris, what were DS Kershaw's movements on the night in question?'

'He was at home.' Owen opened a paper file. 'We had a surveillance team on his street.'

Savage nudged Docherty off and focused on Fenchurch. 'So how come he's at your crime scene?'

Fenchurch glared at Owen. Drums clattered in a Ringo Starr solo. Loose and imprecise. 'Were there any BMWs on the street?'

'Hang on.' Owen frowned at another page. 'Shit, there was one. Left at nine.'

Fenchurch grabbed the sheet off him. A log of cars but no location. 'Where does Kershaw live?'

'Top end of Shoreditch.'

Fenchurch folded his arms. 'So Bruco left the club at five to nine, drove to Kershaw's flat and picked him up. Then they drove to Prescot Street and killed Robert Hall.'

Docherty punched a fist on the desk inches from Savage. 'Howard, this is a bloody joke.'

Savage stroked his temples. 'We can handle this.'

'Whatever you're handling has just exploded all over my bloody murder case. You've got a nest of corruption in your team.' Docherty widened his eyes. 'Give us the truth. Now.'

'It's just a single bad apple. It's nothing worse than that.' Savage waved a hand at Owen. 'DCI Owen is undercover.'

Fenchurch swallowed. 'DCI?'

'I'm from Professional Standards. South Wales Police.' Owen puffed out his chest. 'You can call me "guv" if you fancy.'

'You're serious?'

'Deadly.'

Fenchurch couldn't decide which one to swing for first. 'Why is Kershaw still on the loose?'

'Because I want to catch him red-handed.' Savage bit into his knuckle. 'We've been running a sting on him for over eighteen months. Chris has been man-marking him all that time. We want who Kershaw's working for.'

Owen chewed the broken skin on his hand and looked at Fenchurch, Reed and Docherty. 'You three have really messed this up.'

'*We've* messed it up?' Docherty raised his eyebrows at Savage. 'You allocated dodgy officers to my case.'

'I couldn't risk exposing Chris's operation.'

'Did you know Kershaw was connected to The Alicorn?'

'That's the one good thing to come out of this, I suppose.' Savage puckered his lips. 'Means we're a step closer to identifying his paymasters.'

Fenchurch glared at Owen. 'You've been at this eighteen months and you've not even found that out?'

'Take a step back, tiger.' Owen winked at him.

Cheeky bastard.

'I'll not do anything like that.' Fenchurch got on his face. Could smell his coffee and aftershave. 'If you'd had your house in order, three people would still be alive. Why haven't you arrested Kershaw?'

'Because we lack a coherent evidence trail.' Owen was fiddling with the edge of his paper file. 'Your taxi driver witness is our first solid intel on him.' He gave Savage a nod, like he was still subordinate to him. 'What's the plan now, Howard?'

'We need to find him.' Savage stroked a hand across his face, eyes locked shut. 'But we need to confront him in a safe manner. I don't want him warning his handlers.'

'Hang on, hang on.' Fenchurch scowled at Savage. 'We can bring charges against him and Vrykolakas.'

'They're both small fry. There are bigger fish here.'

'Like who?' Fenchurch narrowed his eyes at Savage. 'You've been doing this even longer than laughing boy here and you've not got a bloody clue who you're up against.'

He pointed his finger at Fenchurch. 'Now just you listen to me—'

'Is this anything to do with what my dad's been looking into?' Savage was staring at the floor. 'Your father?'

'When I came over to ESB the other day, you knew my name from your dealings with him.'

'Right.' Savage stroked his chin, staring into space. He came to with a sigh. 'Well, I suppose there's a chance it could be linked.'

⁓

Fenchurch got in the lift and stabbed the button for B2. He wedged a foot in the door until Savage entered. His stomach lurched as they rumbled down. 'Why didn't you follow up on my dad's email?'

'It wasn't just one email.' Savage let out a breath and leaned against the wall. 'Four emails, eighteen phone calls and two paper memos. Usually means a particular brand of crazy.'

Fenchurch snarled and got closer to him. Tried to make the small lift even smaller. 'Watch your mouth.'

'Look, I'm sorry. This isn't easy for me.' Savage looked like he had something to hide, like a cat covering over its litter tray when everyone in the house had already smelled it. 'We simply don't have the budget to respond to every lead like that we receive.'

The lift thunked to a halt and the doors creaked apart.

Fenchurch left him and strode across the wide concourse. He knocked on the door.

It swung open and Dad squinted out into the corridor. 'Simon? You're early. I've left my Hammers scarf—'

'We won't be going to the match today, Dad.' Fenchurch barged past him into the room that felt even smaller than the lift. Case file boxes filled the shelves. The ceiling didn't give much clearance. 'Why aren't you answering your phone?'

Dad fished out his mobile. 'Bloody thing's on mute again. Sorry.'

Same as it ever was.

Fenchurch waved a hand at the door. 'I've brought a visitor.'

'DCI Howard Savage.' He stepped into the room, acting like he owned the place. 'Nice to finally meet you, Ian.'

'And you, sir.' Dad beamed at him as though he was meeting the Queen. 'Is this about my emails?'

'And your phone calls and memos.' Savage perched on a desk cluttered with paperwork and glanced at Fenchurch. 'Take us through your theory, from the start.' He raised a finger in warning. 'I want facts and no frippery. Am I clear?'

Dad's awe and wonder switched to bitter disappointment. 'So you haven't read them, then?'

'Let's pretend I didn't.'

Dad picked up a ring binder and chucked it to Savage with a bit more force than was necessary. 'That's my master file there. It's all indexed.'

Savage inspected the first page. 'I'm listening.'

Dad snatched the file back. 'You know the general gist of it, right?'

'Assume I know nothing.'

'Where the bloody hell do I start?' Dad stared up at the ceiling. 'Right, I was working cold cases here with a few old mates. We came across one which just nagged at me. Looked similar to one I worked back in the eighties when I was a DS.' He pulled out another case file. 'We'd found a girl in Canary Wharf when they were building the first tower. They call it One Canada Square now.' He tossed the file over to Savage. 'She was a sex worker. Couldn't identify her.'

Savage thumbed at the file. 'But you got someone for it?'

'Caught this geezer. Not quite red-handed, but he was guilty. Worked at Billingsgate Market, gutting fish. Ten months later, he got off. The jury didn't like our evidence trail, though. My DI got busted to traffic for it.'

Savage was flicking through the file at speed. 'How does this connect to your son's case?'

'Well, we've found another four girls. All sex workers with no identification. All shuffled off to the Cold Case Unit.'

'But you think they're linked?'

'Well, it's still early days, but yes.'

'So, you're saying this fish gutter is a serial killer?'

'I wish. That'd be easy.' Dad snorted. 'Geezer died three weeks after the verdict. And these others are all after that. Hanged himself. Official verdict was suicide.'

'And I take it you think it wasn't?'

'He was suing the force. The commissioner at the time wanted a lid put on it, so he settled out of court just after the verdict. The sort of payout that'd make your eyes water. That geezer had a lot of cash, no real reason for him to do himself in.'

Savage took a few seconds to digest it. 'Tell me about the other four.'

'Here's the thing.' Dad leaned against the shelves. 'Like our fish gutter, anyone fingered in these murders usually came to a sticky end not long after. Accidents or suicides.'

'And you're saying they're something else?'

'They were murdered. Maybe not clear as day but someone's killed them. They're clearing their tracks. There were no missing persons reports for any of these cases, no ID. Nobody's missed them. Just like they were ghosts.'

Savage nodded at Fenchurch. Looked like he was holding something back. 'It's fitting your pattern, Inspector.'

'Tell us what you know.'

'I'm not finished listening.' Savage took a step towards Dad. 'Let me get this straight. In your first case at Canary Wharf, a man murdered a prostitute. You've charged him and the case fell apart. Then this fish worker was killed.'

'Glad you've been listening, sir.' Dad rolled his eyes. 'But the bodies turn up earlier with the other cases. Most don't even go to court. This fish gutter was guilty as sin. He tore out her guts, left them all over that building. He did it.'

'So someone on the case leaked information?'

'Way I see it, whoever's behind this sees these girls as their property. Someone harms them or kills them, they enact Old Testament vengeance on them.' Dad slumped back against the shelves. Looked like the whole lot might topple in on him.

Fenchurch walked over and patted his dad's arm. Felt like he was the only thing stopping him from falling apart. He focused on Savage. 'Do you know anything about this?'

Savage put the binder down on the desk and stared at the wall for a few long seconds.

Fenchurch went over and picked up the ring binder. 'Tell me what you know. If there's something in all this, something related to our case, I need to know.'

Savage glanced at Dad. 'Ian, who do you think is doing this?'

'The sixty-four-million-dollar question.'

'What names have you got?'

'Me and Bert call them the Machine. Someone damages their property and they kill them, make it look like suicide. Effortless, like a machine.'

'Very droll. I meant suspects.'

'Oh, right.' Dad stared at the floor, looked like a little puppy who'd shat his bedding. 'We've got nobody, I'm afraid.'

Fenchurch shuffled through the ring binder. 'How does Robert Hall fit in this? He was just another rowdy customer at The Alicorn. Pissed out of his skull, pushing it too far with the girls.'

'Both of your victims had worked there.' Savage sat on a chair, the metal clicking with his weight. 'And unfortunately for Mr Hall, you identified him as the killer of their girls. Well, you got some footage of him fairly early on.'

'So you think Kershaw's leaked it?'

Savage nodded. 'Not only that, but they clearly knew who Hall was. And far earlier than you.'

'Shit.' Fenchurch's back stiffened. Drums thumped in a deep tribal rhythm. 'Hang on, are we at risk here?'

Savage snorted. 'It's a distinct possibility. Loved ones, especially.'

The drums clattered louder.

'Dad, I need you to stay here, okay?'

He shrugged. 'I was quite looking forward to going to the Boleyn.'

'It's not happening, okay?' Fenchurch went out into the corridor and fished out his phone. He called Abi's mobile. No answer, just straight to voicemail. Another call and the same. The drums beat out of time, cannoning off hard walls. 'Abi, it's Simon. Something's come up and I need to speak to you.'

He ended the call and hammered out a text. 'Abi, give me a call. It's urgent. S'

He stomped back into the room.

Dad was holding the master file again, looking like he wanted to stick one on Savage. 'What I was trying to tell you in that email is there's something else at play here. Something going back years. Where women have disappeared and MisPers *were* filed.'

'I'm not following you.'

'These girls, their bodies turned up years later. Only nobody recognised them.'

Savage tossed a file over to Fenchurch. 'Have you seen this?'

He caught it and checked the cover.

01-AT-01087-03
Michaela Carr (DOB 07-May-66)
Missing Person
01/09/1982

Michaela Carr looked like a typical teenager, only the eighties camera blur and haircut dating it.

Fenchurch gave a shrug. 'Never heard of her.'

Dad took the file off his son and flicked through it. 'Michaela went missing in Canning Town. September 1982. She was just sixteen. Parents had no idea where she'd gone.' He passed the file back, open at a Crime Scene Report.

The skeletal body was naked, sprawled across a Paisley patterned bedspread.

'Eleven years later, a maid found a body in a hotel in Hammersmith. Overdosed on pills. They put it down as a suicide. Didn't even to bother to look.'

Fenchurch handed it back, acid burning his gut. 'But you don't think she was killed?'

'They thought she was homeless. Do homeless people kill themselves in hotel rooms?' Dad waved the file around. 'They didn't ID the body. She was . . . just a girl when she was taken. When she died, she was a woman. Nobody bloody cared.'

Savage scowled and grabbed hold of Dad's shoulder. 'How does this have anything to do with the Billingsgate case?'

'We noticed this one when we were looking at the other cases.' Dad shrugged him off. 'They had a lead on some geezer who paid for that room with a credit card. Looks like he'd been at it with her. Geezer hanged himself three days later. Left a suicide note and everything.'

'But, of course, you think it's murder.' Savage snapped the binder shut. 'That's not exactly evidence.'

'Me and Bert have paired three definite bodies with MisPer reports from around that time. Most of them died at least ten years later. They've all had kids as well.'

Savage frowned. 'What?'

Dad sifted through the master file and held up a typed list. 'There's another eight we think are likely.'

Savage stared at the floor, massaging his thighs. Skin as white as his shirt. 'Well, I've listened to your theory, Mr Fenchurch, but I'm struggling to see any evidence.'

'Evidence? I'll bloody give you evidence.' Dad stabbed a finger at the door. 'We've got the clothes and DNA for these old cases in the Archive. They didn't start doing all that testing jiggery-pokery till the late nineties.'

Fenchurch folded his arms. 'Why haven't you done it now?'

'Believe me, I've asked.' Dad shook his head, his mouth twitching. 'Nobody's bloody letting me do it. When did policing become about budget? These samples are just sitting in this geezer's office.'

'Whose?'

'Some bloody muppet.' Dad looked, smacking his lips together. Then he clicked his fingers. 'Clooney, I think.'

Fenchurch stood in the corridor in Lewisham, waiting for a squad of laughing SOCOs to wander past before getting out his Airwave. 'Control, this is DI Fenchurch.'

'Receiving.'

'Can you check on the whereabouts of one Abigail Ormonde, please? Lives on Barford Street in Islington. Number two, flat six.'

'Is this urgent? We're stretched to breaking with the West Ham game just now.'

'It's urgent.'

'Noted. I'm sending a car round now. Over.'

Fenchurch put his Airwave away and sucked in a breath. He entered the room. The place was roughly twenty metres by thirty and filled with contraptions of varying sizes.

Clooney was sitting behind his desk opposite Dad and Savage. He wandered over, fiddling with his piercings, and grimaced. 'Any danger you could call off Kay Reed, Si? She's busting my balls about this Tinder stuff.'

'That's exactly what I want her to be doing.' Fenchurch patted his old man's arm. 'Now, I understand you've got some DNA my dad's asked you to look at?'

Clooney wouldn't even look at Fenchurch. 'This isn't part of your case, Simon.'

'I'll be the judge of that. Where are you with them?'

263

'Awaiting budget.'

'Can you process them under Docherty's cost code?'

'Is he authorising this?'

'I think they're linked to our Jane Does.'

'Here we bloody go again.' Clooney let go of his earring. 'Fine, if it gets you off my back.'

'This could seriously help.' Fenchurch grinned at his father. 'See, Dad, you just need to ask nicely.'

'And give me a bloody nickname.' Clooney marched over to a floor-to-ceiling machine and started pressing buttons on the front. 'Once I've done the magic with the dropper, this'll take about an hour or so.'

'I appreciate it.' Fenchurch made to leave. Then stopped, frowning. 'Has that DNA profiling finished yet?'

Clooney had a fiddle with the adjacent machine and stuck his hands into his trouser pockets. 'Not had a chance to look since Kay nailed my balls to the wall.'

'Well, get on with it.' Fenchurch went back out into the corridor and dialled Abi's mobile number. Straight to voicemail again. 'Abi, please call me. Bye.' He let out a sigh and stared up at the ceiling. The raw ductwork snaked deeper into the building. Drums battered his head.

Where the hell was she?

He got out his Airwave. 'Control—'

'Still no confirmed location of Ms Ormonde, guv. Serial bravo just left her flat, sir. No sign of her.'

'Shit.' Fenchurch ended the call and clutched the phone tight. He stabbed another number.

'Guv?'

'Kay, have you heard from Abi today?'

'I was going to meet her for a coffee after work to talk about you.'

'When did you last speak to her?'

'I got a text at about half ten this morning.'

'Nothing since?'

'Has something happened?'

Fenchurch leaned his forehead against the wall. 'I hope not.'

'Guv, are you being paranoid again?'

'Just because you're . . .' He caught himself. 'Look, give me a ring if she gets in touch, okay?'

'Sure thing, guv. Look, do you—'

He killed the call. Got his car key out of his pocket and jogged down the corridor.

Chapter Thirty-One

'Still nothing, sir.'

'Thanks.' Fenchurch dumped the Airwave onto the passenger seat and pulled off City Road onto Upper Street. He bombed past the Angel tube on his right and battered through the changing light, tearing off down Liverpool Road. The giant cinema complex skulked over to the right, the Angelic on the left, an old haunt now turned into a gastropub. He swung a right into Barford Street and double-parked by a Subaru.

Fenchurch got out and sprinted across the pavement, wincing at the pain in his legs. He bounced up the steps and hammered on the entrycom, his heart thumping.

No answer.

Where the bloody hell was she?

He checked through the listing. There we go. He stabbed another button.

'Hello?'

'This is DI Fenchurch. I need access to the property.'

'Simon?'

'Yes, Quentin, it's Simon.'

'Why didn't you just say?'

'Can you let me in?'

The door thunked open. Fenchurch raced inside and took the stairs two at a time.

On her floor, Quentin was still in his dressing gown. At this time. He tilted his shaved head to the side, his intense eyebrows now flecked with grey. 'What's up?'

'Have you seen Abi today?'

'Yesterday.'

'Morning or evening?'

'Evening. She'd run out of milk and I'd just got some in. Had a nice little natter. About you, as it happens. Strange how I bumped into you on the stairs last night.'

'You've not seen her today?'

'Sorry, I've been dead to the world. I flew back from Munich yesterday afternoon. Been away all week on busi—'

'Did you hear anything?'

Quentin fiddled with the gown's belt. 'There were raised voices last night.'

No guessing who that was.

Fenchurch hammered the door. 'Abi?'

'Doesn't look like she's in, Simon.' Quentin tied up his belt again. 'How are you keeping, anyway?'

'How do you think?' Fenchurch hit the pale-blue wood again. 'Abi!' He crouched down and peered through the letterbox. 'Abi!'

Quentin grabbed his wrist. 'Simon, what the hell's going on?'

Fenchurch stared at him. Saying it out loud might make it real. 'She might've been abducted.'

'Oh my God.' Quentin put a hand to his mouth. 'Are you sure?'

'I don't know what to think. This case I'm working . . . Let's just say the people I'm investigating don't play fair.'

'Well, I've not seen her today.'

'Watch out.' Fenchurch got up and took a step back. He launched himself shoulder first. The door crashed open and he tumbled across the carpet. He picked himself up and looked around. 'Abi!'

Her bedroom door lay open. The bed was made, her side upturned. Typical Abi. No signs of a struggle.

He raced through to the kitchen. The kettle was cold. Same with the hob.

Where the hell was she?

Sunlight poured into the living room. A copy of that morning's *Times* sprawled over the sofa.

Quentin stood a good distance back, still in the flat's entrance, staring into space.

Fenchurch walked over and slipped him a card. 'Give me a call the second she comes back, okay?'

'Will do.' Quentin inspected it. 'It's nice seeing you, Simon. We should catch up for a beer sometime.'

'We should.' Fenchurch tilted his head at the fallen door. 'Tell Abi I'll get that fixed for her.'

A clatter in the hall. 'Simon?'

Fenchurch frowned at the flat entrance — Abi stood there, two Waitrose bags at her feet. 'Where the bloody hell have you been?'

She blinked in the light. 'My door!'

'Where have you been?'

'What does it look like? Shopping, you idiot.' Her look could melt steel. 'Has something happened?'

'I sent squad cars round here to check where you were.' Fenchurch pinched his nose. 'I've been calling you!'

'You can't have been. My phone's been on.'

'What? I've been texting you all morning. Left you voicemails.'

'Simon, I've had nothing from you since you . . .' She glanced over at Quentin. 'Nice to see you.'

He waved at them. 'I'll leave you to it.'

Abi watched him go. Then forced her scowl back at Fenchurch. 'Right, what the hell are you playing at?'

'I've been phoning you all day. I swear.' He let out a sigh. 'Someone threatened me. I thought they'd taken you.'

'I was shopping. What number have you been calling?'

'Eh?'

'I got a new phone two years ago.'

Fenchurch shut his eyes. 'Shit.'

'You're a bloody idiot, Simon.'

Fenchurch picked up the door and swallowed hard. The hinges were bent backwards but the wood looked intact. 'I'll get this fixed.'

'Too bloody right you will.' She gripped his arm. 'What's happening?'

'This case. It's . . .'

'It's always a case. I know you, Simon. It's okay. I'm fine. Nobody's kidnapped me.'

'I thought . . .' He rested the door against the wall. 'Jesus.'

'You're not paranoid much, are you?'

'Look, I'm going to get some uniforms to come round here, make sure nothing happens.'

'What?'

'It's not safe, Ab. It's that or you go to the station.'

'I'll take my chances here.'

'Good. And I'm sorry about the door.' He reached into his wallet. Fifty quid. He held it out. 'Call me if it's more than this.'

She winked at him. 'I'll make sure I call the right number.'

———

Fenchurch returned to his father's office, carrying two teas in paper cups. He took a drink through the lid. Bitter and sharp, nowhere near enough milk. 'Here you go.'

269

Dad was flicking through a file in his little room, like a hobbit in his hole. Stupid old goat bringing all this shit back up. He picked up the other cup, the steam billowing through the hole, and took a glug. 'Lovely cup of tea.' He gasped and smacked his lips together. 'Where did you run off to, son?'

'Long story.'

'Isn't it always that way with you?'

Fenchurch tapped the file on the desk. 'What's that?'

'Just been doing some thinking. Your geezer killed two girls then they faked his suicide. It's got the Machine written all over it.'

'Not sure Savage agrees with you.' Fenchurch took another drink. 'How could they do this to other human beings?'

'People do lots of horrible things to people every day.'

'Where's Savage?'

'Don't know.'

'Think he buys your theory?'

'No idea, son. Maybe.' Dad blew on his tea, staring into space. His gaze resolved on Fenchurch. 'They could've taken Chloe, son.'

Fenchurch tightened his grip around the cup. 'What?'

'This is why I started looking. It fits.' Dad placed his cup on top of a report near the edge of the desk. Looked like an accident waiting to happen.

'You said this Michaela Carr went missing in 1982.' Fenchurch swapped his cup for the case file. 'Chloe . . . She went missing ten years ago, not thirty.'

'What if they'd lost so many over the years that they needed to replenish their stocks?'

'We don't know that.' Fenchurch flared his nostrils and narrowed his eyes. 'We don't bloody know anything, Dad.'

Dad reached out a hand. 'I'm sorry, son.'

Fenchurch slapped it away. 'You don't have anything solid, do you?'

'Not on Chloe, no. I don't know what to say, Simon.'

Fenchurch took a drink of tea. 'You did what you thought you had to, Dad. You need closure as much as me and Abi.'

Dad picked up a file and shifted it to the other side of his desk. 'You still think we'll find her, don't you?'

'I don't know.' A shiver crawled up Fenchurch's spine. 'This stuff . . . I can't think what kind of life she's had.'

'You've been to hell and back, son.'

Fenchurch gave a laugh. 'Who says I came back?'

'You're all right, son.'

What if Dad was right? What if Chloe had spent ten years working the streets. How could he have failed her so badly? Fenchurch wiped at the tears burning his cheeks.

'Do you still love her, son?'

'Of course I still love Chloe.'

'I meant Abi.'

Fenchurch finished his tea. Burnt his throat. 'I never stopped.'

'Do you want to give it another go with her?'

Fenchurch stood up, clutching his mobile. 'I'd give anything. Anything.'

'Simon, need a— Oh.' Clooney came to a halt in the doorway. His eyes bulged. 'Sorry, I'll come back.'

Fenchurch wiped his moist cheeks. 'It's okay.'

'Right. Well, the results have come back.' Clooney handed them both a sheet of paper, dense with tables and data in a small font. 'Good news, Simon. As you can see, your old man's cases match the victims.'

Fenchurch tried to resolve the data into some sort of clear picture. 'What do you mean, they match?'

Clooney pointed at a table. 'Across the five original cases, there are two mothers. All of them share a father.' He grimaced. 'Your two victims share one of those mothers.'

'What?'

'I've checked and checked again.' Clooney leaned back against the wall, looking like he wanted to collapse. 'They're half-sisters, Si.'

Fenchurch held the paper away from him, struggling to focus on the print. He folded the sheet. 'So we've got seven dead women with no ID, most of them related. What the bloody hell does that mean?'

Neither of them seemed to know.

Fenchurch rolled his shoulders back. 'Suppose I'd better go and break this to the big boys.'

'Savage and your boss were going at it hammer and tongs in the canteen. No way I'd be getting between them.' Clooney took a step back towards the door. 'Now, I'll get back to preventing Kay Reed battering my nuts.'

'That'll save you a fortune in some Soho back alley.' Fenchurch's phone rang. He checked the display. DS Reed. 'Speak of the devil.' He put it to his ear. 'I'm kind of in the middle of something here, Kay. Is it important?'

'Guv, I've got something for you. While I'm waiting on Clooney to do his bloody job, I've been doing PNC checks on the women from The Alicorn. You know, the ones we brought in the other night.'

'Can't this wait?'

'There's a problem, guv. We started with Erica McArthur because of what she told you last night. Trouble is, we can't find her records.'

'What?'

'According to General Register House, she doesn't exist.'

———

Dance music thudded out of the brick building. Almost drowned out the drumming in Fenchurch's ears. He hammered the buzzer and shivered. Bloody freezing despite the winter sunshine. 'Come on, come on, come on.'

Reed still had her phone clamped to her ear.

A bearded man dumped a chalkboard on the pavement outside the café next door. He flashed a frown at them before he went back inside.

Fenchurch tried the buzzer again, giving it a few seconds. 'Any ideas?'

'I'll call you back.' Reed pocketed her phone. 'DC Lad's been up at The Alicorn. Place is empty, guv.'

'So where the hell is she?'

Reed's nostrils twitched. 'Can you smell hash?'

Just bacon and coffee from the café. Hang on . . . Gotcha.

'Yeah, can definitely smell something.'

'Come on, then.' Reed got out her wallet and pulled out a Nectar card. She slid it behind the edge of the door and it clicked open. 'There we go, guv.'

'Good luck using that next time you're in Sainsbury's.' Fenchurch followed her inside. He took the stairs two at a time and marched across the tiles. Then banged on the flat door. 'This is the police! We have reason to believe you are in possession of a controlled substance!'

'We've got nothing!'

'I need you to open this door!'

'You can't do this!'

'This is your last chance! Open up!'

The door down the hall opened. An old man squinted out, looked like a hedgehog emerging early from hibernation. 'What's going on?'

Fenchurch hammered the door again.

'This is a police matter, sir.' Reed held out her warrant card and took a step towards him. 'Please go back inside your home.'

The door shut. Back to hibernation.

'What do you think, guv?'

'Try that card again.'

273

She shook her head. 'There isn't a Yale, guv.'

'Shit.'

'You could do what you did to Abi's door.'

Fenchurch's cheeks started burning. 'She told you?'

'You really do need to talk to someone, guv.'

'We're coming in!' Fenchurch kicked at the spot just below the handle. The wood splintered but it stayed solid. Another kick. There we go. It toppled in.

Fenchurch burst into the flat.

A green-and-white-striped dressing gown flashed into the room on the left. The door slammed.

A crash from the closed door to his right.

'We're looking for Erica McArthur!' Fenchurch motioned for Reed to guard the front door then tugged the right-hand door open.

A bedroom with three single beds. One against each of the bare walls. Justin Bieber, One Direction and that actor who crashed his car. Stupid haircuts and rippling abs.

A girl cowered behind her hands on the bed furthest from him. 'Get out!'

'I need to speak to Erica.'

'I don't know her.'

'She lives here.'

The girl pushed herself further away, crumpling the pillow against the wooden headboard. Didn't speak.

'Does she sleep in this room?'

'I haven't seen her since last night.' She sat up and hugged her legs tight. Her tracksuit bottoms rode up, showing tanned ankles. 'I swear I haven't.'

'Where is she?'

'All I know is a man came here. I heard them talking.'

Fenchurch swallowed. 'Was this last night?'

'No, this morning. Just after ten.' She drew a line down her chin. 'He had a beard like that, just like Bruco?'

Kershaw. Bloody hell.

'I'll need a statement from you.' Fenchurch went back into the hall.

Reed was leaning against the closed bathroom door. 'And you swear you haven't seen her since then?'

'I swear.' The voice was muffled through the door.

'She's not here.' Fenchurch thumbed at the bedroom door. 'Sounds like Kershaw has her.'

'What's the play, guv?'

'I don't know.' Fenchurch stared at the bare wall. Just a water-colour of flowers in a vase, the kind you'd get in a pound shop.

CCTV.

He clicked his fingers. 'I got caught on a TPU surveillance obbo outside here last night.' He dialled a badge number on his Airwave. 'Fenchurch to DS Chris Owen.' Had to swallow down the DCI.

'Safe to talk.' Sounded like he was driving.

'We're at Erica McArthur's flat. She's gone missing. Looks like our friend's taken her.'

'I'm just off with our surveillance team. Kershaw was at that flat this morning.'

'Where is he now?'

'I'm en route to a possible sighting.'

Chapter Thirty-Two

The Arsenal logo on the Emirates Stadium was bigger than Fenchurch's flat. Across the road, a squad of armed officers prowled behind a brick building. Blue sky above, though dark clouds hung south of the river, looking like they'd send their rain back north at any point.

'Guv, we're still waiting on Owen.' Nelson, out of breath.

A purple Jag pulled in down the street, just outside a town house plastered with fresh stucco. Savage got out of the driver's side and Owen the passenger's.

Fenchurch jogged across the road. 'Been calling you.'

'Well, we're here now.' Owen met them halfway. 'Right, your team is providing operational support, that's it.'

'You're the DCI. Which house is he in?'

'That one there.' Owen waved at the town house behind Savage. Three storeys of bare Victorian brick. 'It's a buy-to-let rental job as far as we can tell. Owned by a shell company, by the looks of things. CCTV flagged his car. Street cameras showed him going inside.'

'Was he alone?'

'I don't know. I've not seen it.'

'What's he doing here?'

'Laying low, maybe? Until I haul the wanker over hot coals, we don't know.' Owen clapped Fenchurch on the shoulder. 'Come on, if you're coming.' He trotted down the street and stopped outside the building. Then held a hand out behind him to stop the black-clad officers inching towards the house. He pointed at Fenchurch then walked down the path. Drew three sides of a square in the air. Door.

Fenchurch tried it. Thing just slid open. He raised an eyebrow.

Owen swivelled round and pulled back his raised hand. Come. The armed officers followed. Then he made Bugs Bunny fingers at Fenchurch. Approach in column formation.

Fenchurch entered the building first. Carpeted stairs, a hall just to the right. A door looked like it led to the back. Three others led off into the house. He spun around.

Owen was circling a raised finger above his head. Rally point. He motioned for Fenchurch and Nelson to take the other two internal doors.

Fenchurch took a breath and entered his room.

An L-shaped lounge which widened out towards the windows. A black leather sofa sat below a giant TV mounted on the opposite wall. On screen, Xherdan Shaqiri did some step overs, trying to outsmart Winston Reid, his claret-and-blue West Ham shirt rippling in the wind. Just like the vertical blinds — a patio door hung open. The room was ice cold.

Fenchurch crept along the line of the boxout, two black-clad officers following. He adjusted his stab-proof vest and stepped around the corner to check in the cubbyhole.

Kershaw was sitting on a cream armchair, fiddling with a mobile. He glanced up and did a double take. 'What the hell?'

'DS Kershaw, we have a warrant for your arrest.' Fenchurch held up a closed fist, stopping the supporting officers. 'I'm asking for you to come quietly.'

Kershaw lurched forwards and jumped at the open patio door. He tumbled through and slammed it behind him.

'He's gone out the back!' Fenchurch pocketed his Airwave and followed. He tried the handle. Bastard thing wouldn't budge.

Kershaw was climbing a fence at the far end, fingers clawing the horizontal slats.

Fenchurch thudded his fist off the handle and got it to move. He stormed across the grass and leapt through the air, aiming for Kershaw's left foot. Just missed. He toppled onto the grass, landing on his rib.

Kershaw cleared the top and disappeared over. A crash boomed out from the other side.

Fenchurch got up and started climbing the fence. He stopped at the top, above a back lane. University buildings towered over them. No sign of Kershaw.

No, there — haring off to the right.

Fenchurch bumped down onto a compressed bin and set off. His lungs started to burn as he turned the corner into an open courtyard. 'Stop!'

Kershaw made eye contact. Then ducked his head and sped up, arms like pistons.

A pair of officers appeared at the end of the lane. They both drew their Glocks.

Kershaw barged into the one on the left, pushing him against the brick wall. A gunshot cannoned out. The other officer collapsed to the ground, clutching his chest. Kershaw grabbed a gun and set off.

'Man down! Man down!' Fenchurch held up his Airwave as he sprinted after Kershaw. 'Get a medic into the lane behind the house! Suspect is armed! Repeat, suspect is armed!'

He burst out onto the main road, feet pounding over the tarmac.

Kershaw was scurrying across the road, weaving between two cars queuing at the roundabout. Horns blared out. He slipped on the brick roundabout and tumbled over. The gun slid over to the road. Kershaw righted himself and darted over the carriageway towards the football stadium.

Fenchurch held out his warrant card as he crossed the road. The honking got louder, faster.

Owen was racing over from the front of the house, flanked by two armed officers.

Fenchurch passed the two cannons. He was losing Kershaw. Wait. He arced his run, trying to catch Kershaw by the stairs leading into the stadium.

Kershaw was taking the steps two at a time. His head twisted back to check.

Fenchurch tackled him from the side, knocking him against the steel handrail. He spun him onto his front and pinned him down with his knee. Then slammed the heel of his palm into the back of Kershaw's skull. His nose thwacked off the ground. 'You're under arrest, sunshine.'

Kershaw spat blood onto the concrete. 'What have I done?'

'I'm arresting you under section fifty-eight of the Sexual Offences Act 2003. Do you understand?'

Kershaw slumped forward. 'I don't know what you're talking about.'

'You do not have to say anything, but it may harm your defence if you do not mention when questioned something which you later rely on in court. Anything you do say may be given in evidence.'

Kershaw pulled his legs into a ball as Owen and Nelson appeared at the top of the stairs.

Fenchurch bellowed in his ear: 'Where's Erica?'

'No comment.'

'Where is she?'

'No comment!'

'We know what you're doing, Paul.' Fenchurch hauled him up. Kershaw was a good few inches taller but he slumped his shoulders.

Owen grabbed him and sat him against the handrail. He slapped on handcuffs. 'Who do you work for, Paul?'

'I don't know what you're talking about.'

'Who are you working for?'

'No comment.'

'You better hope they can pay to keep you out of prison. Police officers are usually very popular inside.' Fenchurch pointed at an armed officer. 'Get him down to Leman Street and get him his bloody lawyer.'

'Sir.' The officer grabbed Kershaw by the wrist and led off.

Fenchurch stared at Owen then Nelson. He let out a deep sigh. 'Have we searched that house?'

Nelson nodded. 'No sign of Erica, guv.'

Fenchurch squinted at Kershaw as he was led away to a waiting meat wagon. Blue lights flashing, reflected in the puddles on the pavement. He got out his Airwave. 'Fenchurch to Savage. Over.'

'Safe to talk.'

'Have you found anyone in that house?'

'Negative.'

'Erica McArthur should be there.'

'Well, there's a hatch in a back bedroom.'

Fenchurch raced off down the steps and sprinted along the street. He entered the house and stormed up the stairs three at a time.

Voices came from a room to the back left. A uniformed officer was boosted up on another's shoulder. He crawled up into the roof space and let his colleague breathe again.

'Have you got her?'

Savage spun around. 'Jesus, you frightened the life out of me there.'

A ladder shot down from the attic. The second uniform rested his hands against it. 'Come on down, you're safe now.'

Grey tracksuit bottoms stepped out onto the top step. Adidas three strip. Erica peered into the bright room. 'Simon?'

———— ‿ ————

'Here's what I don't get, Erica.' Fenchurch brushed the stubble on his chin. The overhead lights cast long shadows into the corners of the interview room, space occupied by Owen pacing around. He focused on Erica again. 'Why don't you seem to exist?'

'I'm right here.' She pinched herself on the arm. 'See?'

'That's not what I mean.'

Erica hugged herself tight. 'I don't understand any of your questions.'

'We don't have a register of your birth.'

'I'm English born and bred.'

'So why aren't you on any system?' Fenchurch cleared his throat. 'Is Erica McArthur even your name?'

She looked away and focused on the other wall. 'Only one I've ever had.'

'Whatever mess you've got yourself into, we can help.'

'Oh, really?' Erica shook her head, eyes shut. 'I'll believe that when I see it.'

Fenchurch got up and leaned against the interview room door. The steel was cold against his back. 'What really happened at The Alicorn on Thursday night? Why did Robert Hall get chucked out?'

'I don't know.'

'You sure about that?'

'Positive.'

Fenchurch tossed the screen grab across the table. Erica shivering behind Winston Gooch as Hall pointed a finger at him. 'This is you, right?'

She shrugged a shoulder. 'What's this got to do with anything?'

Fenchurch placed the next still down. A few frames on from the last. 'Why's Mr Hall pointing at you?'

'I was working, that's it.'

'Sure *you* weren't the reason he'd been kicked out?'

'Maybe.'

'Now we're getting somewhere. What happened?'

'He had a dance with me.'

'That's it?'

'He tried to buy me.'

'Buy you.' Owen rolled his eyes. 'Right.'

Fenchurch held up a hand, trying to stop the tirade of sarcasm. 'You told me it was two other girls he tried to buy.'

'And he did.' She flicked her hair. It'd lost some of its sheen but still glowed under the lights. 'But he offered Winston a grand for me. He turned him down and this Robert guy started shouting at him.'

'And this is why he was chucked out?'

'He punched Winston.'

'Not a wise move.' Fenchurch sunk his hands deep into his pockets. The panelling on the door dug into his back and gave a satisfying ache. 'Does the name Paul Kershaw mean anything to you?'

'Should it?'

'Mr Kershaw never approached you?'

'I don't know who he is.'

'He's the man who abducted you.'

'I've never seen him before.' Erica kept playing with her hair. Hadn't shown the dimple all interview. 'I thought it was Bruco at the door. That's the honest truth.'

'Fascinating.' Fenchurch couldn't keep his eyes off her.

Owen took his seat again. 'Why aren't you talking to us? We've just rescued you.'

'Because they'll get me.'

'Who will?'

'Them.'

'We need something a bit more than that.'

'I can't say anything.'

'Why?'

Tears bubbled in her eyes. She swallowed, eyes screwed tight, and gasped in air. 'They've got my mother and my sister.'

Fenchurch crouched down next to her. His bruises flared up again. 'We can help.'

'You can't.' Erica tugged her hair, pulling it into long strands. She wiped her eyes with the back of the other hand. 'If I help you, they'll kill them.'

'Who will, Erica?'

Her gaze gouged at the tabletop like a power drill. 'I. Can't. Tell. You.'

'I hear you.' Fenchurch held up a hand at Owen. 'Is Kershaw helping you with this situation?'

'He didn't really talk to me. Just put me in a car and told me to shut up. Then he stuck me in that attic.'

'When I visited your flat last night, you told me there was some chat in The Alicorn about dodgy policemen. Your colleagues didn't name Mr Kershaw, did they?'

She blinked hard a few times. 'Is he a policeman?'

'He is.' Fenchurch stood up straight. Knees jolted. 'What's the story here, Erica?'

'I can't tell you anything.'

'You don't need to worry about Kershaw finding out you're talking to us any more.' Fenchurch looked away, focusing on the wall. 'He's next door, waiting on his lawyer.'

'Well, let me know when you've charged him.' She gave a slight chuckle, her nose bubbling with snot. 'They've told us to keep quiet.'

'Who has?'

She looked up, glassy eyes narrowed to tiny slits. 'Bruco.'

'Sotiris Vrykolakas?'

'Him.' She dragged a sleeve across her face. 'I heard there was a cop working for this group that owned us. That's it.'

Fenchurch frowned at Owen. 'What do you mean by owned you?'

'Nothing.'

'You mean owned the club?'

'No.'

'What, then?'

'No comment.'

Fenchurch tried to stare her out, waiting for her to look away. He turned to Owen. 'Can you leave us for a minute.'

'Why?'

'Just do it. Watch from the Obs Suite, if you need to check I'm not up to anything. Sound down, please.'

'Your funeral.' Owen left the room, taking the Custody Officer with him. The door clicked, resting on the rim.

'Interview paused at one thirty-six p.m.' Fenchurch stopped the recorder and sat in his chair. 'Erica, were you taken from your home when you were a young girl?'

'Is this because I said you remind me of my father?'

'Tell me about him.'

'I can't remember much. Last time I saw him was twelve years ago. He was in a wheelchair.'

'A wheelchair?'

She stared at the table. Her painted nails scratched the laminated surface.

'Where were you brought up?'

'I don't know.'

'Erica, I need to know.'

'Why?'

Drum rolls cut across Fenchurch's hearing. 'Because I think my daughter might be there.'

'What's her name?'

'Chloe.'

'It means nothing to me. Sorry.' She frowned at him, like a parent telling a child their dog was sleeping now. 'I'd tell you if I knew, Simon. Trust me.'

'Wish I could.' He shifted on the seat. 'I want to stop what's happened to you. I need you to be completely honest with me. Will you do that?'

She stared into space for a few seconds, then gave a light nod.

Fenchurch flicked his fingers at the camera.

The door flew open and Owen sat down next to him, eyebrow arched. 'What did I miss?'

'Interview recommenced at one forty p.m.' Fenchurch gestured for Erica to continue. 'Who owns you?'

'I can't tell you anything.' She swallowed something down. 'I was born on a farm somewhere. No idea where. I lived with my mother and sister in this house. They fed and clothed us. Took care of us.'

'And they brought you to London?'

'Two years ago. To The Alicorn. They wanted to see if I could work there. Dancing.'

'Had you been trained?'

'I slid down that pole every day since I was five.'

'You never went to school?'

She shook her head.

Fenchurch took out the photo sheet and passed it to her. 'I showed you this before. Tell me the truth now.' He tapped at the first Jane Doe. 'Erica, you said she worked at The Alicorn with you.'

She took her time inspecting it. 'She did. I didn't know her, though. She lasted a couple days before she scratched some guy's face.'

'What happened to her?'

'I never heard.' She gripped the edge of the table with her free hand. 'If we don't dance, they threaten to stick us on the street.'

'As prostitutes?'

She nodded.

'Why've you never run away?'

'Don't you understand? They'll kill my family.' She rubbed at her eye. 'I had to nick a phone from a punter just to call you.'

'Were you ever put on the street?'

'I was a good girl. Played by the rules. Kept the fat men in suits happy.' She swallowed again, staring into space, her lips twisting into a snarl. 'Their hands all over my body. Their fingers inside me.' She made eye contact. 'Do you know what that's like?'

'I can only imagine.' Fenchurch smiled, his eyebrows inverted. 'Erica, is there any way we can corroborate this story?'

'Not that I can think of.'

'What about the other girls?'

'They won't talk.'

'We'll have to see about that. Interview terminated at one fifty-three p.m.' Fenchurch wrapped his hands around hers. 'Listen. I'm not sure what's happened to you, but I'm stopping it. The people who did this to you are going to pay for it. Okay?'

'Okay.' A tiny whisper, barely any sound.

Trumpets blared over the drums now, atonal and distorted. Fenchurch was leaning against the wall, the corridor stretching off to infinity in both directions. He ran a hand over his face. His cheek was damp.

'Something in your eye?' Owen was grinning at him.

'Don't start.' Fenchurch stabbed a finger at him. 'I'm warning you.'

Owen raised his hands. The smile had disappeared. 'I'm really sorry, Simon. Genuinely.'

'I'm finding it pretty hard to believe anything coming out of your mouth, *Chief Inspector.*'

Savage appeared beside Owen, his face grave. 'What's going on here?'

Fenchurch pointed at the door. 'You watched that?'

Savage gave a tight military nod. 'Me and your guv'nor reviewed it in the Obs Suite.'

'What she's talking about. That's the Machine, right?'

'You're not cleared to know that.'

Fenchurch got in Savage's face. Foreheads almost touching. Coffee breath up his nose. 'I'm this close to kicking the living shit out of the pair of you. I want the full story.'

'Give him it.' Docherty was in the corridor now. Didn't seem to want to split Fenchurch and Savage.

'Easy, easy.' Owen pushed them apart, keeping his hand on Fenchurch's chest. 'Howard, I don't give a shit about protocol, you need to tell them everything.'

Savage shut his eyes and snorted. 'Very well.' He stormed into a vacant interview room and sat nearest the window.

Fenchurch followed Owen in and rested against the wall. 'Well, I'm listening.'

Savage waited for Docherty to join them. 'Your father's theory is pretty much on the money. Back in the early eighties, the European

Commission started flexing its muscles, tightening up immigration, particularly from behind the old iron curtain.' His nose twitched, taking his upper lip with it. 'They now knew exactly who was coming and going.' He scratched at his cheek. 'Problem was, it made it much harder to get cheap girls into the country from Eastern Europe and China.'

He stroked his chin. 'At the same time, my predecessors were turning over half of Soho on a weekly basis. The Machine, as your old man calls them, had their fingers badly burnt. They'd expanded into semi-legal operations like The Alicorn but they were becoming short-staffed as they grew. And they were making too much cash.'

'So they started kidnapping girls off the street?'

Another curt nod. 'They took them from areas where they didn't think they'd be missed. Sink estates in the East End. And Brixton, Tottenham, that kind of place. Got them hooked on drugs and forced them to work. They had absolute control over these girls.' Savage hugged his arms tight around his body. 'And that's just the first generation.'

Fenchurch frowned. 'What does this have to do with what Erica just told us?'

'They breed sex workers, Inspector.'

Fenchurch scowled at him. 'In this day and age, people can be treated like that. Really?'

'It's easier than you'd imagine.'

'And this is what Kershaw's involved in?'

'We think so.'

'Is this your big fish?'

'The rod just started twitching.' Owen let out a shallow breath. 'These girls they were kidnapping in the eighties, the ones your father's been looking into. Well, instead of putting them on the streets, they stuck them on a farm in the middle of nowhere. They bred from them.'

'How do you know this?'

'We've had some anecdotal evidence to that effect. Nothing concrete. These girls can be fairly loose-lipped when they first get picked up, but as soon as a lawyer gets in there, that's it. End of evidence trail. And they always ask for one.'

'How can they get away with this?'

'Because, like Howard said, they've got absolute control over their *property*. Their leverage is along the lines of "you tell anyone about what's going on and we'll kill your parents and your siblings". You see?'

Savage filled the space Fenchurch wasn't going to. 'And they throw the girls who don't make it out onto the street. Sink or swim. The Machine's a very good name for them. They're brutal. Efficient.' He bared his teeth. 'They make a lot of money. That cash pays for things. People like our friend Kershaw.'

'How much money?'

'Let me spell it out for you. Assume there's forty working at The Alicorn. Four hours of dancing in an eight-hour shift. That's forty dances a night per girl on average. Twenty pounds a dance. Thirty-two grand a night. Pure profit. They don't pay the girls. Over a year? Twelve million pounds. For *one club*. They've got *six*.'

Docherty curled his lip. 'We're in the wrong bloody game.'

'You can see why they'd run the risk, though, Alan.' Savage gripped the table edge tight. 'We reckon they take in over sixty million a year from the girls alone.'

Fenchurch pointed at each of them in turn. 'No more lies now, okay?'

Owen exchanged a glance with Savage. 'Absolutely.'

'Do you know where this farm is?'

Owen gave a slight shake of the head. 'We haven't a clue.'

'You're telling me you've no idea where they're breeding these girls?'

'The whole point in me man-marking Kershaw was to find out what he knows.' Owen folded his arms. 'We were operating on the assumption he'd lead us somewhere.'

'And did he?'

Owen looked away. 'No.'

'Fantastic.' Fenchurch waited for them to nod. 'Is his lawyer here yet?'

'Force Rep's been in the car park for the last hour, waiting for his lawyer.'

Savage went out into the corridor and grimaced. 'We've got company.'

A middle-aged man trudged towards them. Dicky bow and tweed jacket. Face like the world owed him an apology for existing.

Fenchurch joined them by the door. 'Right, let's get this started.'

Savage held out a hand, palm splayed. 'Not you, Fenchurch.'

Chapter Thirty-Three

'—and here I am watching bloody TV.' Fenchurch was standing, hands in pockets, staring at the screen.

Kershaw was focusing on the grain of the interview room table, squashed between the Force Rep in full uniform and his lawyer. Gordon Edgar, same one as Bruco. He'd lost the beard, which now made him look like a walking buttock. Huge rounded cheeks squeezed his features into a tiny space.

Savage sat opposite, grimacing as though the chair was inducing piles. Owen was against the wall, playing to the camera like a matinee star.

'They're getting nowhere with him, boss.'

'Didn't think they would.' Docherty looked up from his BlackBerry. 'Lad like that knows when to keep quiet. Probably got a nice tidy sum waiting for him somewhere tropical.'

'Think we've got enough to convict?'

'He's either murdered this boy or he's accessory to it. An ex-cop, too. He'll be going away for a long time.'

On screen, Kershaw winked at Owen. 'I knew you were in the Complaints.'

'You can't have.' Owen started drumming a finger against the wall behind him. The sound rattled through the speakers. 'You wouldn't have been such a careless bastard if you knew.'

'Who says I've done anything?'

'Quit it, Paul.' Owen smiled as he raised his shoulders. 'We know you're bent. You're up to your bollocks in shit. Only hope for you is telling us everything.'

Kershaw leaned back in the chair and stretched. 'There's nothing to tell.'

'You're a lying shit, Paul. You sold our secrets to the highest bidder. You think that's on? You think you can get away with talking out of school?'

'No idea what you're on about.'

'This isn't selling stories to the papers, you hear. This is much, much worse. You're working for some evil, evil people.'

Fenchurch glowered at the screen. 'He's more likely to twat him one than get him talking.'

Docherty frowned at him. 'So what do we do about it?'

'This.' Fenchurch hauled the Obs Suite door open.

'Simon, wait.'

'Boss, they're making a mess in a monkey shop here.'

'You keep saying that. What the hell does it mean?'

'Look, boss, I can get him talking.'

'How?'

'Just let me show you.'

'Fine.'

'Cheers, boss.' Fenchurch sprinted down the corridor and crept into the interview room. He stood near the back behind Savage.

'I'm saying nothing because there is nothing.' Kershaw made a zip motion across his lips. 'Nothing.'

Owen bent over, hands behind his back, his mouth right by Kershaw's ear. 'You know that house you were in beside the Emirates? Well, we found a woman in the attic.'

'I was looking after that place for a mate.'

'Why did you kidnap her?'

'No comment.'

Fenchurch cleared his throat. 'We've got a statement placing you at her flat this morning.'

Kershaw didn't even dignify it with a response.

Savage darted a glare at Fenchurch and twisted back round. 'Paul, we know you killed Robert Hall.'

'No comment.'

'We've got you on CCTV turning up with Sotiris Vrykolakas.' Owen folded his arms, grinning. 'Two witness statements confirm your presence. In about half an hour, you're going into a line-up with a load of other guys with stupid beards like that. You'll be on a murder charge by the time Swansea beat Liverpool at quarter to five today.'

'No comment.'

Owen stood up and reclaimed his spot against the wall.

Fenchurch took the chair. 'You know what the Machine is?'

Kershaw sniffed. 'Rage against or Florence and?'

'Comedian.' Fenchurch cracked his knuckles. 'They have a farm where they breed people, much like you would pigs or cows. They employ them in the sex trade in London.'

Kershaw went grey, his face losing all colour. 'What?'

'Did you think you were getting kickbacks from a couple of pimps? You stupid bastard.'

'I didn't know anything about that.'

'Just following orders, were you?'

Kershaw stared at his lawyer. A bead of sweat dripped down his forehead. 'Is there a deal on the table here?'

'Thought you didn't know anything?'

Edgar whispered in his client's ear. Kershaw shook his head. 'I don't care. You heard what he said.'

'Paul.'

'I said I don't care.' Kershaw nodded at Owen. 'Is there a deal?'

Savage clicked his tongue a few times. 'Paul, you know full well it depends on what you tell us.'

'Well, you've got the what, a bit of the where, a lot of the why and all of the how and when. All you're missing is the who and the rest of the where.'

Edgar crunched back in his chair and folded his arms. Looked like he was going to go running to teacher as soon as he got out of there. 'Paul, Paul, Paul.'

Savage ignored him. 'You're saying you can give us the ringleaders?'

'I can give up who I know.'

Savage ran his tongue around his gums. 'Go on.'

'I want immunity from prosecution and a new identity.'

'That's quite a lot.' Savage leaned forward, his teeth bared. 'I'm not going to make this easy for you, Paul. You're dirty and you're ignorant. I'm not sure what's worse. Names. Now.'

Kershaw fiddled with his beard.

Savage got up. 'Come on, gents, this is getting us nowhere.'

'Wait.' Kershaw tugged his stubble. 'Sotiris Vrykolakas.'

'Nice try. We've already got him in custody.'

'He killed Robert Hall. A lethal injection of heroin. Some uncut stuff he'd just got from Holland.'

Fenchurch rested against the desk. 'And how do you know this? You're denying you were even there.'

'When we got to his flat, the guy was lying on his settee, smoking smack off tinfoil. A very distinct smell, you know? Like marshmallows.' Kershaw grimaced. 'Bruco smacked him in the chops with a baseball bat. Knocked him out. He tied him up and stuck the smack in his veins. Made it appear that he'd injected it.'

'And you just stood there watching, right?'

'I did.'

'It's your word against Bruco's.'

'I know.'

'You're accessory to murder.'

'And I want immunity from that.'

'Well, let's see who else you give us.' Savage's tongue flicked across his crooked teeth. 'More names.'

Kershaw let out a breath. 'Not until there's a proper deal on the table.'

―――

Fenchurch shut the Observation Suite door. 'Were you watching that, boss?'

'Not quite a masterclass.' Docherty looked up from his BlackBerry. 'Take it you're not giving him a deal, Howard?'

Savage sat opposite Docherty. 'Not if I can avoid it.' His nostrils flared. 'I want him inside for what he's done.'

'Where does that leave us?'

Savage shrugged. 'Well, we know they've got a farm and that's it.'

Fenchurch perched on the edge of a desk. 'You said they've got a few other clubs. Where are they?'

'There's two in London. A club in Mayfair and a bar round the corner from here.'

Docherty scowled. 'Near Leman Street?'

'Right under your very nose, Chief Inspector.' Savage nibbled his lips. 'There are others in Nottingham, Ipswich and Leeds.'

'We should shut the whole thing down. Cut off their money.' Fenchurch adjusted himself on the desk. 'What about a coordinated raid on all five places. You reckoned there's a few hundred people working for them, right?'

'At least a hundred and fifty. Could be as many as two hundred.'

'Well, then. The odds are stacked in our favour. One of them might break.'

'They won't talk, Simon.' Owen grimaced. 'All the girls are under the same threat.'

'I remain to be convinced of this plan.' Savage narrowed his eyes at Fenchurch. 'I can't sanction it and I doubt a judge will.'

'Boss?'

Docherty cleared his throat. 'Howard, I'm afraid I'm with Simon here. You've had your turn with this lot. We should just fire in there.'

'This isn't the end game, Alan.'

'Then what is?'

'Bringing down the ringleaders.'

'If we raid these clubs, we can liberate hundreds of people.'

'They live in constant fear of their loved ones' lives.' Spit hung from Savage's mouth. 'They will not talk.'

'All the more reason to get in there.'

'Believe me, I know a thing or two about this.' Fenchurch folded his arms. 'I think they're better being free than imprisoned there.'

'Okay, fine.' Savage let out a breath. 'I'll get onto the other forces, see what we can rustle up.'

The unmarked van felt like a coffin. Reed's face was hidden in the gloom. Her Airwave chirruped and she stuck it to her ear. Waited a beat. 'That's them ready to go, guv.'

Fenchurch held his fist in the air. 'Go! Go! Go!'

The armed officers clambered out of the meat wagon and made their way through Berkeley Square. Mayfair opulence, a row of stone town houses with flower boxes in unnatural midwinter bloom.

Fenchurch stopped outside the Dragon & George and waited. Drums skittered in his ears. Deep thudding bled through the doors.

Three of the black-clad ninjas secured a perimeter on the tarmac, rifles raised in the direction of the club. Two squad cars pulled in at either end of the street and blocked the exits. Six armed officers took position in the park.

Fenchurch gestured for Nelson to follow. 'Let's go!' He trotted across the road and followed the officers inside the club.

The place was a riot of noise. Girls screaming, feedback squealing from the PA, music turned up full blast.

Fenchurch had to cover his ears. He spun around, looking for anyone of note.

Girls were crowding round the bar at the far end, like a surge at a metal concert. A topless dancer cowered in the corner of the stage, eyes screwed tight. Corseted girls snuggled up to men in jackets, shirts and jeans in the circular booths. One of the men nearby started tapping on his BlackBerry until an officer grabbed it off him.

A bouncer was spreadeagled on the floor, wearing the same get-up as Winston Gooch in The Alicorn. One officer pointed a rifle at his skull, another twisting his arm behind his back.

Fenchurch nodded at a uniform. 'Start processing everyone. Dancers *and* punters.'

'Will do, sir.'

Fenchurch stormed up to the bar, warrant card out. DC Bridge was blocking the barmaid's escape. 'We need to speak to the manager.'

'Well, he ain't here.' The barmaid looked him up and down. 'He was earlier. Don't know where he went.'

Fenchurch gripped the edge of the bar. 'Is there an office here?'

'Not to my knowledge.'

'Where do you put your handbag when you clock in, then?'

'I don't have one.'

'Your jacket?'

The barmaid leaned back against the counter. 'Through the back. The girls have a changing area. There's a room off that.'

'Show me.' Fenchurch waved for her to lead, beckoning for Reed to follow.

The throng of girls trying to escape was under control now. A group of uniforms had kettled them into the corner.

The barmaid pushed through, leading them deeper into the club. The Gents was on the left — no sign of a Ladies. Five doors on the right, all hanging open. In the nearest, an officer stood over a man on his knees. Hands behind his head, trousers round his ankles, a girl kneeling in front of him.

Reed pointed at the room. 'At least we'll get some arrests out of this, guv.'

The barmaid opened the final door on the right. 'In here.' Inside, another ten girls stood around. Most of them looked late teens or early twenties.

Fenchurch followed the barmaid across the room and waited by the door. 'What's the hold-up?'

The barmaid raised her hands. 'The door's locked.'

'So the manager is in there?'

'I don't know.'

'You said he wasn't here.'

'I don't know anything. I swear.'

'What's his name?'

'Matthew.'

'Does he have a surname?'

'If he does, I don't know it.'

'Well, you'd better learn it pretty quickly.' Fenchurch turned away, scowling at the girls as he spoke into his Airwave. 'Control, get the Big Key round here.' He hammered a gloved hand on the door. 'Matthew, this is DI Fenchurch of the Metropolitan Police Service. We need to speak to you.'

Nothing.

He focused on the barmaid staring at the carpet. 'Is there a back entrance or a window?'

'Yeah, but it's a twenty-foot drop down to the yard.'

Fenchurch gritted his teeth as he held up the Airwave again. 'How are we getting on with securing the rear perimeter?'

'Officers are still in place, sir. No movement.'

Fenchurch gestured around the room. 'Might be worth getting the birth certificates of these girls. Not sure all of them are legal.'

'Nice turn of phrase, guv.' Reed spun round and got out of the way of the pair of officers lugging the Enforcer. She pointed at the office door. 'That one there.'

The lead uniform got in position, securing the Big Key against the lock. He swung it and the door collapsed, the wood splintering. It took its time tumbling over.

Behind the door was a small room. A large CCTV display almost filled one wall, the rest of it crowded by huge storage cupboards.

'Glamorous.' Fenchurch grabbed the barmaid by the arm. 'Where's the manager, then?'

'I told you he's not here. Why don't you believe me?'

'Let's have a look at this, shall we?' Reed bolted over to the CCTV console. She jockeyed the footage back.

On the screen, a man entered the room and locked it behind him. He opened one of the cupboards and stepped inside. It clattered shut.

Fenchurch spun round. That one there. He tried the handle. Locked. He rattled the metal frame, nothing. 'What the hell?'

Reed clicked a finger at the uniform holding the Big Key. 'Get that open.'

'Stand back.' The officer hefted it up to lock it in place. Then swung it.

The navy steel buckled inwards with a deafening thud.

Fenchurch pushed him aside and opened the door. A staircase led down, a dim light shining. 'Kay, you're with me. The rest of you, keep this secure.'

The top step creaked as he put his weight on it. He took it slow, descending to an L-shaped bend, and raised a clenched fist. The stairs were empty, just flickering light. He crouched to look and listen. Nothing. He opened the fist and continued down. At the bottom, a steel door blocked the way. A light hung from the ceiling. He closed the fist again and tried the door. It swung open.

A deep and wide room with a vaulted ceiling, dim in flickering candlelight. The floor was filled with mattresses. Looked like an orgy. Nearby, an overweight man thrust away at a woman on all fours. White hair drenched with sweat, her eyes dead. Next to them, a middle-aged woman knelt in front of a young man, running her tongue down the length of his penis, while he checked his watch.

Fenchurch gulped in air. 'Christ.'

Chapter Thirty-Four

'We're getting nowhere.' Fenchurch scowled at his watch. 17.34. Then at Reed, eyes trained on the Charing Cross station's Obs Suite. A bank of ten monitors flickered in front of him, interviews in progress on all of them. 'How many have we done now?'

Reed looked up at the ceiling. 'Seventeen on our side, guv. Leman Street have processed twenty-two, last I heard.'

'And still nobody's biting.' Fenchurch fiddled with a cufflink and scanned through the screens.

There, in room six.

A young man, twenty-one at most, sat alone in a room. His body language was at odds with the trained refusal on display in the others. His right hand cradled his left shoulder, flexing his meaty bicep for an unseen audience.

'We've found our weakest link, Kay. Come on, let's have a word with him.' Fenchurch picked up his unopened can and paced out into the corridor. Had to stop to let another column of interviewees past. He rapped on the door and got the Custody Officer to come out. 'Is he ready?'

'If by ready, you mean not even giving a name, then yeah.' Looked like he'd shaved the patchy stubble on his head himself. Without a mirror. 'You mind if I take ten minutes, guv?'

'Be my guest.' Fenchurch led Reed into the room and took his time getting settled. He put his suit jacket on the back of the chair. Undid his tie. Adjusted his cufflinks again.

The kid was staring at his lap, stroking a thin soul patch below his bottom lip. Hair shaved at the sides, his long fringe tugged over. His ear had enough studs to rivet a battleship. He looked up, grey eyes tapering into a frown.

Fenchurch locked eyes and didn't let go. He sat opposite and handed the kid a can of Coke. 'You got a name?'

He curled his hands round the drink and flicked the ring pull with his thumb. 'You can call me Mr Howell.'

'What sort of name is that?'

'Mine.'

'Well, thanks for speaking to us, Mr Howell.' Fenchurch rested his Pronto on the table. 'It's difficult for us to get this interview on the record.'

'Why?'

'Because you don't exist, Mr Howell.'

He let his arm go. His T-shirt rippled as it dropped. 'None of us do.'

Finally . . . 'The way I understand it is you were born on a farm.'

Howell picked at the ring pull. The can hissed and brown foam filled the lid. He bent forward and supped it up. 'That's correct.'

'And, if you talk to us, they'll harm people close to you.'

Howell glugged down the drink, must've cleared half the can in one go. 'My mother and my two sisters.'

'Where are they?'

'I can't tell you.'

'But you do know?'

Another drink. 'Not exactly.'

'Mr Howell, you were caught engaging in illegal sexual activity. That club is an unlicensed brothel. Leaves you in serious trouble here. Name or no name, you're going to prison.'

'I want to help but I can't.'

Fenchurch huffed and got to his feet. 'Come on, Kay, let's see if the next one's willing to speak.'

'Wait.' Howell held up his hand. 'I can't speak to you directly but there's something that might help.' He scratched his soul patch. 'There was an event a few weeks ago, round the corner from . . .' A sharp tug at the V of stubble. 'From where you found me. Where I work.'

Owen snuck into the room, holding up his hands.

Fenchurch settled back in his chair. 'Go on.'

'We got taken to this hotel. Some sort of business was laying on a treat for their employees. There were men and women there, dressed up all fancy.' Howell swallowed. 'A South African woman took me to a room upstairs.' His palms dug into his eye sockets. He let go, blinking hard. 'She had a wedding ring on. She put it on the bedside table before she made me screw her. After I finished with her, they made me go back downstairs. Ding ding, round two.' He hugged his arms tight. 'A man claimed me as soon as I sat down. We went up to the same room upstairs. They'd already changed the sheets.'

'I take it this was for more sex?'

Another yank at the soul patch. 'I was supposed to . . . take it from him.' Howell let go of the mini beard. 'I lay on my back. Before he got his pants off, he apologised for the size of his thing. And I don't mean like it was going to hurt.'

Fenchurch tilted his head and lifted his eyebrows just enough. 'What did this man look like?'

'He was a big guy. I think he was from Northern Ireland?' He nodded at Fenchurch. 'He had hair like yours, though.' His cheeks rose as his forehead creased. 'He had his way with me and then . . . tried to strangle me.'

Fenchurch leaned forward. 'Did you fight him off?'

'I couldn't. He was twice the size of me. Two men in suits burst in. They dragged him off me and just took him down. It was well brutal, man.' Howell was stroking his soul patch like it was a pet. 'These guys started kicking at him. Just kicked and kicked and kicked. Split his face open. It was just blood, man. Then they carried him away somewhere. I don't know where, before you ask.'

Fenchurch looked round at Owen. 'This sounds like the Machine.'

His skin had turned paler than snow. Looked like he'd found fairies at the bottom of his garden. 'How did they know what he was doing to you?'

'They were filming us at it. This company wanted to blackmail their employees.'

So many rabbit holes this case could go down. 'What did these men look like?'

'They had beards like this.' Howell drew a line with both fingers from ear to chin, where they met. Went back to fiddling the soul patch. 'Pencil thin, you know?'

Fenchurch shut his eyes. 'Kershaw.'

Owen pulled the door open. 'I'll make sure his lawyer hasn't left the building.'

Fenchurch watched him go. 'Where was this hotel, Mr Howell?'

'They didn't tell us.'

Reed scowled at him. 'Did they stick a blanket over your head on the way there or something?'

'They drove us there in a coach. The windows were blacked out.'

'Do you remember anything about it, at all?'

'No, man, we couldn't see shit.'

'What about at the other end?'

'I remember a tall building.' Howell waved his hands in the air, making a shape like a vase. Bulbous in the middle, tapering to a point.

Fenchurch got up and grabbed his jacket. 'The bloody Gherkin.'

'I don't care, I'm seeing him anyway.' Fenchurch shrugged off the secretary and pushed open the office door. 'I need a word.'

DCI Thompson looked up from his glass desk. It took a few seconds for his jowls to stop wobbling. 'My, we are blessed today.' He swept a hand around his office, indicating a cream leather settee opposite. 'Please, gentlemen, have a seat. Would you like a coffee and a Danish?' He narrowed his eyes at his PA. 'That'll be all, Debs. Thanks.'

'This place really does remind me of a bank.' Fenchurch collapsed into one of the armchairs. 'Or a gentlemen's club.' He waved for Reed to take the other chair. 'You're making this place look crowded. The Chief Inspector likes his minimalism. This is DS Reed.'

Reed nodded at Thompson and perched on the front of the seat. 'Have you got my work request?'

'Work request?' Thompson spread himself out on his settee. His tie dangled down to his gleaming brogues. 'Care to refresh my memory?'

'There's got to be a reason you're in on a Saturday.'

'The City sleeps on a Saturday, Sergeant. It's my time to catch up.'

'Thought you'd be on the golf course?'

'I'm more of a rugby man, as I'm sure you can tell.' Thompson flashed a grin at her. 'Now, what does this work request pertain to?'

Reed handed him a sheet. 'We got this off the PNC. Took us a while to find it.'

As Thompson checked it, his smile twisted into a frown. 'This is a suicide. What the hell's this got to do with you lot?'

'We know it's suicide. This guy hung himself in a luxury hotel just by Liverpool Street station.' Fenchurch snatched the page back and thwacked a fingernail off the paper. 'We got a description of this man from a rent boy way out west. This guy tried to kill him after they had sex.'

'I fail to see how this relates to that girl in the Minories?'

'It's a very long story, but there's a pattern.' Fenchurch passed the sheet back. 'This guy fits it.'

'So what do you want from me?'

'DI Steve Clarke was the Senior Investigating Officer.'

Thompson picked up an Airwave and stabbed at the screen with his trotter. 'DCI Thompson to DI Clarke. Over.' He held it up until it crackled.

'Sir?'

'My office, now.'

'Sir.'

Thompson put the device back on the table. 'We're in on a Saturday doing work for a load of Scottish cops. Lost a few hundred million in the Caymans. Don't know their arses from their elbows, that lot.'

The door swooshed open behind them.

'Ah, DI Clarke.' Thompson smiled.

Clarke joined him on the sofa, his beady eyes darting about the room. He raised an eyebrow at Reed. 'You want me to arrest her, sir?'

'Not yet.' Thompson rested the print on the leather. 'Have a look at this, Inspector.'

Clarke picked up the page and cleared his throat. 'Oh, I remember this one. Edmund Watson. Died a couple of months ago, right? Suicide.'

Reed raised an eyebrow. 'Is that your final answer?'

Clarke let the sheet float to the floor. 'What, you're auditing my work now?'

'Not as such. You said this was a suicide?'

'That's right. Standard protocol is to investigate as if it was a murder. The pathologist ruled that out. We had a suicide note about his secret gay life. Guy hung himself. End of.' Clarke shrugged and got to his feet. 'It's a dead end.'

'Not so fast.' Fenchurch leaned forward in the chair. 'We've found a string of cases like this. Suicides that are really murders. It's a gang covering over its tracks.'

'Tastes like shit, Fenchurch, but sometimes a suicide is just a suicide.'

Fenchurch stood up and paced over to the window. Bishopsgate below was darkening and weekend quiet. 'Who did you speak to in Northern Ireland?'

'Come again?'

'The victim was from there. I assume you spoke to the Police Service of Northern Ireland?'

'Why would we?' Clarke's frown deepened. 'The guy lived in Wembley. We had a Met liaison. Lot friendlier than you lot, too.'

'What was the officer's name?'

'Kershaw, I think.'

Kershaw rasped his hand across the stubble on his chin. 'Look, I'm not speaking to you without a deal. Sorry.'

Fenchurch was sitting next to Owen, like a coiled-up spring. Fizzing with energy. 'We might have some progress on that front.'

Kershaw smirked at his lawyer. Edgar, the same arse-faced gimp as before. 'Bit late for that, isn't it?'

'Not sure, Paul.' Fenchurch tossed his head from side to side. 'You're complicit in two murders.'

'Two?'

Fenchurch slid the print across the table, leaving it between lawyer and client. Neither went for it. 'Edmund Watson. Grew up in the town of Lisburn in County Antrim. Lived in London since he was eighteen.'

'That supposed to mean something to me?'

'Cast your mind back a few weeks. The Legionnaire's Hotel by Liverpool Street. Lovely place. You and a friend, I'm assuming it's Bruco, hauled him off a rent boy.' Fenchurch tapped the sheet. 'This guy was strangling said rent boy. What did you do to him?'

'What do you want to know?'

'I want you to tell us everything.' Fenchurch folded the sheet in half. 'The only way you're getting out of this heap of shit you're in is by dropping other people in it.'

'So the deal's back on?'

'It depends on what you know and what you tell us.'

'Right.' Kershaw stared at Edgar. 'Get out.'

Arse face started twitching. 'Excuse me?'

'I told you to leave.' Kershaw put his mouth up to the mic. 'I am terminating the employment of Gordon Edgar with immediate effect. He no longer represents me.'

The lawyer was on his feet, grabbing hold of Kershaw's shoulder. 'You can't do this to me!'

'Get out!'

'No!'

The hulking custody officer picked Edgar off his feet, like he was a small child. He wrestled the scrambling lawyer out of the room.

Kershaw let out a deep breath. 'He works for them.'

'The Machine?'

'That's very cute.' Kershaw shrugged. 'Works, though.' He smoothed down his hair, making him look like a choirboy. 'What do you want to know?'

'Names. Faces. Places. Audit trail. Everything.'

'I can't.'

Fenchurch pointed at him. 'Paul, you're involved in the cover-up of at least two murders. This stuff at the hotel, how did you even get involved?'

'I know people. A few quid here or there is enough to change a form.'

'Were these people going to pick you up from that house?'

'The heat was getting too much.'

Fenchurch glared at Owen. His man-marking job wasn't Premier League standard. 'We know you killed this fella, then disposed of his body.'

'I didn't do anything! It was all Bruco!'

'Who do you work for?'

'I can't . . .'

'You're as bad as your paymasters. Worse, maybe. You betrayed the trust people placed in you.'

Kershaw nibbled at his lip. He'd cut it, blood staining his teeth. 'I need a deal.'

'Doesn't sound like you've got much to give us, then.' Fenchurch folded his arms. 'DCI Owen, what do you think?'

A shrug. 'I've got authority to offer a deal. It just depends on what we get in return.'

Fenchurch stared at Kershaw, waiting until he got eye contact. 'Well, what's it to be?'

'Other than Bruco, the only other person I've met is my handler.' Kershaw crumbled in his chair, defeated and alone. He slumped back and covered his eyes. 'His name is Alistair Barraclough.'

'And who's he?'

'Don't know. Just met him the once. Most of the time he sends me iMessages on my iPhone. They're encrypted, so nobody can intercept them.'

'And this is the guy who pays you?'

'Not that you're getting hold of any of that money.'

'That'll have to be part of any deal.'

Kershaw lurched forward, like he was going for Fenchurch. 'Come on, you can't—'

Owen grabbed his wrist and forced him down, face against the table. 'That's enough of that.'

Fenchurch picked up his Airwave. 'Kay, it's Simon. Are you at a computer?'

'Just sat down with a coffee, guv.'

'Give me a PNC check on an Alistair Barraclough. Two Rs.'

'Got it. One minute.'

Kershaw smirked at Fenchurch, his cheek rubbing against the wood. 'You know, you could check the PNC yourself.'

The line crackled. 'Here we go, sir. No priors against him.'

'Got an address?'

'One second.' A pause filled with the clattering of a keyboard. 'Place near Sudbury, on the Suffolk-Essex border.' Another pause. 'Bloody hell.'

'What?'

'I've got an AKA for him. It's Aleister Vaughn.'

'What?' Fenchurch's stomach lurched. 'The geezer from Darke Matter Capital?'

'Just a sec.' Seemed to take weeks. 'Same guy, guv.'

'Get units round to Canary Wharf. Now!'

Chapter Thirty-Five

'Still nobody at Canary Wharf.' Fenchurch dumped the Airwave in the footwell and glanced over at Owen in the driver's seat.

The car rocked back and forth across the uneven road, Biblical rain hammering against the windscreen. Bare horse chestnut and oak lined both sides of the lane, smaller trees plugging the gaps. A small sign pointed back to Sudbury.

Fenchurch waved to the right. 'Think it's down that lane.'

The road forked by a sprawling thatched cottage, bright pink walls beneath the golden canopy.

'You think?' Owen swung right and turned the wipers up full. 'We're bloody lost, aren't we?'

'The map says it's this way.' Fenchurch tutted, eyes on the rear view for the convoy of other vehicles. A meat wagon trundled behind them, its indicator matching theirs. The rain obscured the other two lorries.

Owen waved at a copse of modern houses sat back from the road, trampolines filling the front gardens. A church spire speared the clouds in the middle distance. 'Rural England as I live and breathe. Sure beats my flat in Clapton.'

'A DCI living in a flat?'

'It's cover. Got a massive house back home in Swansea. That's my place during the week.'

'And the Met pick up the bill?'

'All part of the service.' Owen steered down an even narrower lane, signposted for Griffin Farm. 'He certainly likes his Greek mythology.'

They passed the lane for the farm and pulled in. In the rear view, the two vans blocked it.

Owen turned off the engine. He reached into his pocket for his Glock semi-automatic pistol and chambered a round. 'I love these things.'

Fenchurch couldn't stop looking at it. 'You ever killed anyone?'

'Never fired in anger. You?'

'Not even firearms trained. Never saw the point. Until Paris.' Fenchurch looked out of the window, breathing hard. 'Got my training next month.' He motioned for the four squads to wait. Thirty officers, most of them carrying. Reed and Nelson hopped down from the last van.

The farmhouse had clearly received a recent facelift. A lattice-work of steel mesh encased the crumbling stone. Painted girders and wooden panels jutted out. The original building wasn't even a quarter of the new monstrosity.

Owen led up the drive past a Maserati and two Range Rovers. 'Lot of money in hedge funds.'

'Lot more in sex farms.' Fenchurch stopped at the front door. He held out a palm to keep the black-clad officers at a distance.

Owen knocked on the door and waited, gun ready.

Through the window to the right was a colossal lounge, a grand piano sitting in the corner.

A bolt unclicked, followed by another three. The door swept open. Aleister Vaughn peered out of the doorway. Green Barbour jacket and red trousers, navy hiking boots. He frowned, head tilted to the side. 'Yes?'

Fenchurch nodded. 'Do you recognise me, Mr Vaughn?'

'Should I?'

'We met at your office on Thursday morning.' Fenchurch took out his warrant card. 'Aleister Vaughn, I'm arresting you under suspicion of human trafficking for the purposes of commercial sexual—'

The door bounced off Fenchurch's toes. 'Bastard!' He pushed forward, opening it.

Inside, Vaughn was running down a hall, cutting left across a red carpet. He disappeared round the corner.

'Not again.' Fenchurch set off and twisted round the tight bend in the hall. An oak door slowly swung open on the rebound. He stopped, waiting for Owen to raise his weapon, and entered.

It was a snooker room, the giant table covered in balls midgame, two cues rested on the baize. It overlooked a sprawling lawn, the mesh fence of a tennis court just behind.

The left-hand patio door hung open, curtains flapping in the breeze.

Fenchurch shot off again. He cut round the table and raced through the door. No sign of Vaughn in the garden. Tall walls surrounded the lawn on both sides, edged with mature bushes, creepers covering most of the stone.

Owen shouted into his earpiece: 'I need a report from officers behind the property now!'

Fenchurch ran into the middle of the lawn, spinning around to get a better view.

A metal gate at the far side rattled as it bounced back. Behind it, Vaughn was jogging down a narrow lane between brick buildings.

Fenchurch raced over and wrestled with the sharp edges of the metal. He tugged the gate open and stomped towards a wall. Another lane, leading in both directions, covered by a corrugated iron roof. Farm buildings at one end, a courtyard at the other. 'Which way?'

Owen pointed at the ground. 'There we go.'

A trail of damp footprints led left.

Fenchurch sprinted off. Footsteps thrummed somewhere ahead of them. He stopped at another T-junction. A squad of police ninjas were bombing in from the left. He darted off to the right, leading Owen deeper into the farm, and broke into another wide-open space.

Vaughn was crunching over the pebbles towards an Infiniti sports car. Water dripped from the silver metal.

Owen knelt down, raised his gun and aimed. 'Freeze!'

Vaughn twisted round and stumbled. He fell face first onto the ground. 'Don't shoot!'

Fenchurch slid to a halt beside him. Stones kicked across the drive, chipping the car. 'You're under arrest, Mr Vaughn.'

'I've done nothing!'

'So why are you running from us?' Fenchurch took a look around. They were surrounded by brick farm buildings on three sides. Large doors in each one, all shut. They looked industrial. Another small lane led further on, just wide enough to get the car through. 'What's down there?'

Vaughn closed his eyes, pain etched on his face. 'You can't just—'

'Shut up.' Owen aimed his Glock at Vaughn's head. 'You're going to pay for what you've done.' He cocked the hammer. 'Now, get up.'

'Okay, okay.' Vaughn had his hands in the air, behind his head. He pushed himself to his feet, eyes on the gun. Then ducked low and rabbit-punched Owen in the chest. Vaughn grabbed the gun as Owen toppled backwards, sprawling all over the car's bonnet.

Vaughn pistol-whipped Fenchurch, the barrel of the gun cracking off his temple. He collapsed face down, groggy as hell but still awake.

A gunshot. Then another. An armed officer flew backwards, a red snail-trail behind him.

Vaughn sprinted off down the lane.

Fenchurch got up, dizzy as a boxer after twelve rounds. He pointed at Owen then the fallen officer. 'Stay with him!' Then he waved for two of the armed officers to follow. He raced over to the lane. The tight space broke into another open courtyard, footsteps cannoning off the walls. Fenchurch followed them. A chain-link fence towered over one side, blocking the way. Razor wire coiled over the top.

Vaughn was on the other side, sprinting away. He dodged into a row of chalets before anyone could get a shot off. There were at least forty or fifty of them. All stone-blue paint and white woodwork. Like a retirement village.

Fenchurch scanned the fence for an entrance. A gate was cut in halfway across. The padlock hadn't quite shut. He kicked it and the gate tottered open. He crunched over more pebbles.

A shot rang out, scorching the ground at his feet. He dived full length, rolling to hide behind the first chalet.

One of the ninjas lay prone, face down on the ground. Blood spattered his black vest.

'Officer down!'

Another shot hit nearer, the report echoing around the space. A head popped up over the lip of one of the farm buildings. It wasn't Vaughn.

Fenchurch pointed up, Airwave in his hand. 'On top of that building!'

A third officer knelt down by the discarded gate and took aim. A shot came from above and he dropped to the ground.

'Another man down! Repeat, man down!' Fenchurch lowered his Airwave and scanned around for other shooters. Looked like just the one.

There was only one entrance to the chalet Vaughn was inside, the curtains drawn.

'Cover me!' Fenchurch got a nod and sprinted over to the chalet. A bullet hit the side of the building, ricocheting away from him. He dived low and crawled backwards, right back to where he started. 'I'm going again.' He waited for the officer to reload his magazine. Then shot off towards the building.

A bullet clipped his jacket.

He screamed out and tumbled over. Shit. He scrambled to safety, hiding under another chalet's windows, clutching his shoulder. He looked at his fingers. No blood but it stung like buggery.

He got up and vaulted up the steps to the front door.

A shot splintered the wood halfway down.

He spun around. A man fell from the roof, tumbling into a heap on the ground just by the chalet.

Fenchurch took a deep breath. He snuck a look at the back of the brick building then at the armed officer. 'Any more of them?'

The police marksman shook his head. 'Looks clear, guv.'

'Get someone to check your mates.' Fenchurch turned his attention to the chalet Vaughn had gone in. Another large padlock, this time actually securing the door. He rattled it. No chance he was—

Something battered into Fenchurch's shoulder. He clattered into the door, screaming, and caught his eye socket on the padlock. He rolled over, his shoulder blade burning.

The armed officer was sprawled over the pebbles, face down. His Glock lay a few metres away.

Another blow hit Fenchurch in the shoulder. A deep thud. Felt like it reopened something. He tried to get up but couldn't.

A boot pressed down, choking him. Fenchurch clawed at the leather and twisted round, gasping. A man stood over him, clutching a baseball bat. Black, heavy. He put more weight on his foot, digging down on Fenchurch's windpipe.

Fenchurch gargled as he pushed against the shoe. Raked at the purple laces.

The man pushed the other foot on.

Fenchurch felt like he was going to collapse. He swung up with a leg. Missed.

His attacker's eyes bulged as he toppled forward, trying to brace himself against the house.

Now. Fenchurch lashed out with his left foot and cracked his opponent in the balls.

He squealed like a pig and landed on Fenchurch, squeezed the air from his lungs.

Fenchurch lay there, sucking breath in short gasps. He scrabbled around, trying to nudge the man off. A dead weight. He dipped to the side and managed to roll him off. He sat up. His back and shoulders were on fire. Rain battered against his face. He clambered up to his feet. His throat was so tight it felt like he had the flu.

The fallen officer sat up next to him, groaning. 'What the hell just happened?'

Fenchurch helped him to his feet. 'Did you see him coming?'

The officer pointed to the farm building. 'Think he came from in there.'

Another squad of officers arrived, Reed leading. She got them to stand firm, while a medic started inspecting their fallen comrades.

Fenchurch cupped his hands around his mouth. 'Over here!' His throat hurt like a bastard.

Reed gave a wave and sent a couple of officers jogging towards them.

Fenchurch directed them round the back. 'Secure it!' He raced up the steps and rattled the padlock again. Then reached over to the nearest officer and snatched his rifle. 'Give me that.' Barely sounded like a human had spoken.

The ninja's eyes bulged at the padlock. 'Don't shoot it!'

'I'm not stupid.' Fenchurch clattered the butt of the gun into the padlock. It snapped open. 'Follow me.' He nudged the door open and crept inside. His boots hit plush carpet. Beige. Blue and orange artwork lined cream walls. Three doors led off the hall, all shut. The smell of fresh coffee and scones. A childish sing-song came from behind the furthest away door.

Vaughn came through a door to the left and fired the Glock. The bullet fizzed past Fenchurch's head. He dived at Vaughn and pushed him against the wall. Vaughn grabbed his hair and smacked his head off the floor. Bone crunched off wood. The rifle tumbled towards the door. No chance of reaching it with Vaughn pummelling him.

Fenchurch lashed out with his feet, trying to connect with something. Anything. He missed.

'Freeze.' Vaughn was standing in the doorway, aiming Owen's Glock at him. 'You're my ticket out of here. On your feet.'

Fenchurch got up, wincing with the crack in his ribs. He leaned against the door. The sing-song voices were louder now. Definitely not in his head. 'That's not going to happen. You're going down.'

Vaughn shrugged. 'If that's the way it has to be.' He cocked the hammer and aimed the Glock at Fenchurch's chest.

Then he slumped forward, clutching his head. The gun tumbled to the floor.

Reed stood in the entrance, shrouded by misting rain. She was holding the rifle, butt pointing out the way. 'Take that you bastard.'

Fenchurch dropped to his knees, chest heaving. 'Thanks for the save, Kay.'

'Don't mention it.'

Fenchurch stood up tall and motioned for two of Reed's officers to guard the other doors. He got Reed to follow him towards the singing voices. He twisted the handle and eased the door open.

A woman and three girls sat on two sofas. A cartoon flickered on a large TV set, all primary colours. The music was deafening.

The woman was late thirties, dressed in black trousers and a cream blouse, the short sleeves designed to show off toned arms. She got between Fenchurch and the girls. 'What's going on?'

'It's okay.' Fenchurch fumbled to open his warrant card, his breath seeping out. 'It's okay. I'm a police officer.' He tried to smile at them. 'You're safe now.'

She scowled at him. 'What do you mean we're safe?'

Chapter Thirty-Six

What the hell? Fenchurch frowned at the woman, guarding her kittens like a mother cat. 'You're safe. They've been exploiting you.'

'Exploiting us?' She reached down to pick up the nearest child and cuddled her tight. The girl was pretty and dressed like she was in a beauty pageant. 'We're not being *exploited*.' The other two girls scampered over. She crouched down and put her arms around them. 'I want you to get out of here.'

Fenchurch stared at the kids. They didn't even look like teenagers but wore skimpy outfits. Skin-tight tops, lycra leggings barely containing overdeveloped buttocks. 'What's your name?'

'Karen.'

'Okay, Karen. I need you to—'

She pushed the kids back towards the sofa and took a step closer. Fists clenched, nostrils flared. 'Do we look exploited to you?'

Fenchurch tried to blink away the fatigue and pain. This was too much. 'We believe you've been the victim of sexual exploitation under the Policing and Crime Act 2009.' He let it settle. All it did was reinforce her steely glare. 'I need you to come with me.'

'I'll do no such thing.'

'It's not safe for you here.'

'And police officers firing guns in private homes is safe, I suppose?'

'You need to—'

She slapped his face. Felt like she'd pressed an iron to it. 'Get out!'

He grabbed her wrist and held a hand up to the ninja in the doorway. 'That's enough of that.' He nodded at the three girls. 'Are they yours?'

She wriggled against his grip. 'Of course they are.'

'How old are they?'

'Fourteen, twelve and nine.' Karen patted the oldest child on the head, hugging her hip again. 'I had Emilie here when I was seventeen and she's my little darling.'

No age at all . . . Fenchurch grimaced. 'Can I speak to their father?'

She looked away and kept quiet.

'What's going to happen to Emilie when she turns sixteen?'

Karen shut her eyes. 'Nothing.'

'Sure about that? They're not going to take her away?'

She glared at him, eyes full of fire. 'Nothing is going to happen to my babies!'

'Have you lived here all your life?'

'Of course I have.'

'You weren't abducted as a child?'

'Get out!'

Fenchurch sucked in breath. He waved at the officer behind Reed. 'Stay with them. Get IDs and don't let them leave.'

'Sir.'

Fenchurch left the room and led Reed through the chalet. He let the rain soak him and reached a finger into his shirt. It came out red. The bullet hadn't broken the flesh but the baseball bat had.

Pretty much all of the other chalets' doors were now open, the verandas filled with police officers and women. No men. The oldest woman looked mid-thirties at most.

'What a bloody place, Kay.'

She didn't say anything, just stared at the rain battering the nearest chalet's felt roof.

'They've got her!'

Next door, a twenty-something woman was hammering a finger at Owen's chest. It bounced off him like bullets off Superman.

Fenchurch trotted across the pebbles, trying to ignore the pain in his shoulder and rib, and clambered up the steps onto the veranda, Reed following him. 'What's going on?'

Owen took a step back. 'She says her mother's been taken.'

'You've got to hurry!' The woman was medium height with striking cheekbones. Desperate eyes blinking furiously, her gaze darting between Fenchurch and Owen. 'They take them as soon as . . .' She burst into tears.

Reed made eye contact with her, brow furrowed with concern. 'As soon as what? What do they do?'

'As soon as they get old, they take them away.' She waved a painted nail across the stones to the tall building. 'They go into the forum there, then we don't see them again.' A tear slicked her cheek, quickly lost to the rain. 'Please, you need to hurry!'

'What's her name?'

'Alison.'

⌣

'DS Reed and I are going in.' Fenchurch muted his Airwave and stepped out in front of the brick building. One of the great barn doors lay open. 'Be careful, Kay. This is where that bastard with the bat came from.' He put a finger to his lips and waved for the uniforms to follow.

Grey lino led inside. A partition was cut into the cold white walls with a small security-glass window.

Fenchurch crept up and swung his head up and down again. An office with computers and desks. Baseball bats filled a case behind. The place looked empty.

He whispered into his Airwave: 'Fenchurch to Control. I need a Forensics unit to report to what looks like an office. About ten yards inside the building.'

'On it, sir.'

Fenchurch swirled the air around his head, getting the support unit to stay put. He snapped out his baton and started off down the corridor, Reed following. He came to a wooden door hanging open and he let her go through first.

Inside, the walls were bare brick instead of whitewashed breeze blocks. He stepped down the corridor. Reed got on the other side of the door off to the right, back to the wall.

The door opened and two men strolled out, wearing black guard uniforms. 'I still think *Reservoir*—' The nearest guard's eyes bulged. 'Holy fu—'

Fenchurch lashed out with his baton. The man fell backwards. The other guard swung at Reed, his fist cracking into her jaw and sending her flying.

Fenchurch swung the baton again, missing his guard by tiny fractions of an inch. The guard elbowed Fenchurch. He tumbled onto the ground. Two kicks into his still-aching ribs. He rolled away and tucked himself into a ball.

The guard screamed and collapsed forward. Reed knelt behind him, brandishing her baton, chest heaving. Trying to click her jaw. 'Making a habit of saving you, guv.'

'Thanks for that. Again.' Fenchurch got up and braced himself against the wall. 'Bastard got me in the ribs again.' He got out his Airwave. 'Control, I need more support. Armed.'

'Two units on their way, sir.'

Reed rested on her baton. 'Shall we wait for them, guv?'

Fenchurch took a look at the two guards, both unconscious. He prodded them with his baton. Neither stirred. Footsteps and equipment rattled down the corridor. 'Come on.' He used his baton to open the door.

No other guards lurked inside, just computers and paperwork. A CCTV station hung on the far wall, looked like it was showing other rooms in the building. Only three people on the screen — a guard patrolling a corridor and a doctor inspecting a young woman.

'Come on.' Reed raced down the corridor and turned hard right. It stretched into the bowels of the building, twisting to the right again twenty or so yards away. She waited at the corner and motioned past it. 'Should be a guard round here somewhere.'

Fenchurch listened closely. 'Can't hear anything, Kay.' He set off round the bend.

Nothing, just more corridor, darker.

Wait.

A varnished pine door on the right, almost at the end before the next turn. And a window.

Fenchurch tiptoed down the lino. Vertical steel blinds obscured the glass. He put a hand on the door. 'What's the play here, Kay? Wait for backup?'

A woman screamed inside the room. 'No!'

Shit. Fenchurch looked back, still no sign of support. He twisted the handle. Bloody thing was locked. 'On three.'

'You sure?'

'We've not got a choice, have we?' Fenchurch sucked in a breath. 'One, two, three.' He opened the door and went inside.

High-end medical equipment lined two of the walls. A tread-mill filled another, next to an open door.

'Freeze.' A pistol appeared to the right, followed by its owner. A black guard, the spitting image of The Alicorn's bouncer.

Fenchurch lowered his baton, trying to crunch the probabilities in his head.

'No!'

Through the open door, the man in a doctor's coat held a syringe over a woman's neck.

Eyes back on the guard. 'Police. This place is surrounded.'

'I don't believe you.' The guard crunched his thumb down on the hammer. The chamber clicked round. 'I'm going nowhere.'

'You're going to prison. Drop the gun.'

'Help!' The woman tugged against her restraints.

The guard glanced round.

Fenchurch slashed forward. His baton smacked the gun out of the guard's hands. He followed through with a second strike. The guard collapsed to his knees, one hand cradling the other.

Reed got him in an armlock and pushed him face first to the ground.

Fenchurch raced over to the doctor. He still had the syringe against the woman's throat as she squirmed on the bed. 'Whatever you're doing in here, it's over.'

'You try anything and I'll inject her.' The doctor sneered at him, his bulbous nose flaring. He pressed his thumb on the plunger. 'This'll kill her quicker than you can take me down.'

Fenchurch lowered the baton and held out his hand. He smiled at the woman, his heart thudding. 'It's Alison, right?'

She nodded furiously. Eyes red, streaked with tears.

'Alison, we're going to get you out of here, okay?'

She blinked a few times. Looked worn out, worse than Fenchurch felt.

Fenchurch focused on the doctor again and took a step forward. 'Let her go and we'll see what we can do about not prosecuting you.'

The doctor swallowed. 'I'm a smart man, I know it's over. I just want to get out of here.'

'So why not let her go?'

The doctor pressed the needle into her throat. 'There's nothing you can—'

A shot tore at the doctor's arm. The report cannoned off the wall, screaming in Fenchurch's ears like a drill.

The doctor staggered backwards, clutching his wrist and screeching.

The syringe dropped from the woman's neck and tumbled onto the floor. Fenchurch caught Alison, stopping her following it down. He spun round.

Reed was staring at a gun, smoke curling up from the end of the barrel. She said something Fenchurch couldn't hear.

'What?'

Reed swallowed hard. 'I said, I've never done that before.'

'First time for everything.' Fenchurch grabbed the screaming doctor and forced him to the ground. Blood was pooling on the floor. He snapped a cuff on his right wrist, still intact, and stuck the other one on the radiator. He got out his Airwave. 'I need urgent medical attention in the main building. Location is secure, repeat, location is secure. Send a medic now!' The ringing in his ears blocked out the response. Someone was screaming. Alison. He stood up and hugged her tight. 'It's okay, you're safe now.'

She gripped him so hard he might turn to diamond. 'Thank you.' He felt it through her body more than heard it.

Moaning came from somewhere. There was another door behind her.

Fenchurch frowned at it. 'What's through there?'

Alison pulled away and stroked her bare left shoulder where the doctor's needle had been. She tugged the gown back up. More garbled sound in time with her lips.

'Wait here.' Fenchurch walked across the room, heart beating double time, and nudged the door open with his baton.

The room was dim, just a shaft of light crawling across the shiny floor. The moaning grew louder.

He reached around for a switch and clicked it on. Overhead strip lights flickered into life, each flash showing wheelchairs in all directions. Must be twenty or thirty of them. It stayed on. The walls were filled with men in wheelchairs, eyes wide, looking at him.

A hand grabbed his arm, gripped it tight. He swung round.

It was a man in a wheelchair, eyes pleading with him.

Chapter Thirty-Seven

The black-clad ninja helped the groaning guard to his feet and led him off down the corridor.

Fenchurch glanced over at Reed then crouched down to look the doctor in the eye, almost touching foreheads. 'You're going to talk to me.'

'I don't know anything.' The doctor spat on the floor. Bloody spittle spattered on the lino next to the pool of blood. The handcuffs rattled as he reached around to ease his shoulder. 'You're wasting your time with me.'

Fenchurch stood up tall, his ribs aching worse than ever. Drums thumped four-four time. 'Looks like there's a couple of hundred people here. We need to identify them.'

'You're getting nothing out of me.' The doctor sneered. 'I can help if you'll spare me from prosecution.'

'If you help, I'll get a doctor to look at that bullet wound. That's it. Someone needs to be prosecuted for this.'

The doctor stared at his hand, swabbed in bandages already soaked through, and grimaced.

Fenchurch was tempted to stick a pen into his wound. 'Is there anything like a register here?'

'Not that I know of.'

'Who might?'

The doctor narrowed his eyes. 'Who are you looking for?'

Fenchurch spoke in an undertone. 'Ten years ago, a little girl was taken from outside a flat in Islington. Her name was Chloe. She'd be eighteen by now.'

A frown danced across the doctor's face. He didn't say anything.

Fenchurch growled at him. 'I could stick something in that wound to make it a lot worse. Chilli powder for starters. Do you rename the girls you bring in?'

'What would be the point in that?'

Fenchurch swallowed. 'So you're still taking kids off the street?'

'Shit.' The doctor screwed his eyes tight. 'Yes, we are.'

'And what happens to them?'

'I want a deal.'

'Talk first.'

'Okay.' He spat out a laugh. 'The guys who take the kids do it indiscriminately. They're like bike thieves, just grabbing whatever they can get their hands on. Some pretty, some . . . not so.'

'What happens when they come here?'

'We inspect the merchandise. Grade them. Prize-winning cattle or substandard dairy herd.' The doctor grimaced. 'Pretty boys and pretty girls make pretty babies. The girls get treated like little princesses.'

'I've seen. And the others?'

He ran a tongue over his thin lips. 'They've never had a problem selling a small child.'

Fenchurch grabbed his arm and twisted it. 'Who do you sell them to?'

'I don't get involved in that.'

'But you know who does?'

'You're hurting me.'

'Good.' Fenchurch loosened his grip. 'Who knows?'

'It's only something I've heard about. There are groups who meet to buy and sell small kids. Do what they want with them and then dispose of the bodies.'

'This doesn't disgust you?'

'It's a tough world out there. Got to earn a crust somehow.'

'I'm going to ask again. Do you know a Chloe?'

'The only Chloe I've seen came in two years ago. She was ten.' The doctor groaned. 'I really need someone to look at this bullet wound.'

A queue snaked around the sodden yard, converging on Bridge and Lad as they led the groups of women to the waiting coaches. Teams of officers were processing their identification, umbrellas up and clipboards out.

Reed walked out of the first chalet and held up her Airwave. 'Aleister Vaughn's just arrived back at Leman Street.'

Fenchurch couldn't clench his fists any tighter. 'How much would it cost to have five minutes alone with him?'

'Already asked, guv. Owen said we had to join the queue. Same with Kershaw.'

'Get the duty doctor to check his head. You cracked him a good one there.'

'Cheers, guv. My jaw's fine, by the way.' She snorted and folded her arms. 'Story here's the same as The Alicorn and the George. Nobody showing up on any database. Nobody speaking.'

'Christ. This bloody place . . .'

Reed clapped him on the shoulder. 'We've done a good thing today.'

'It's not over yet. Those women in the chalets . . . I was expecting mud and pig huts. They're like pedigree dogs at Crufts.'

Reed flicked damp hair out of her eyes. 'There's a couple of women who we haven't processed yet. Won't leave their rooms.'

'Let me know how it goes.' Fenchurch paced off, fists clenched. He hauled the mobile crime unit's door open.

Nelson stood over the guard from the office, Owen lurking behind. 'Again, what's your story?'

'Again, I'm not telling you nothing.'

Fenchurch crouched down. 'It's Orson, isn't it?'

'What of it?'

'We've met your brother. Winston, right?' Nelson glanced over at Fenchurch. 'I'm guessing you were both taken years ago. Why didn't they break your legs, though?'

Orson looked away, rubbing at his neck.

'You can see your brother if you help us.'

'Sod it.' Orson gave a slight shake of the head. 'They spared us because Winston made one of them laugh. That's it. They let us help out. We're pretty high up now.'

'Who was it spared you?'

He looked at the ground. 'There's a good reason you've not found this place or the others until now. We don't speak.'

Fenchurch grabbed him by the throat. 'Where are the other places?'

'Easy, easy!' Owen nudged him away.

Fenchurch glared at him, tempted to swing for him and get Orson to open up. He pointed at Nelson then stormed outside.

Two paramedics wheeled moaning men out of the building while Clooney led a team through the mud, taking care as they crossed the puddles.

Nelson let out a deep breath and pointed at the brick building. 'The paramedics reckon they've got better gear here than most hospitals. Important to keep your cattle in good nick, right?'

'It's beyond barbaric, Jon. Beyond—'

'Guv!' Reed was jogging across the yard towards them. One arm waving at them, the other cradling an umbrella. 'We've got one.'

'One what?'

Reed came to a halt. Rain slicked off the brolly in a wide arc. 'We've got a woman with a name on the system.'

'What?'

'Susan Frost. I checked it with General Register House. She exists.'

'What?'

'She said she was abducted a few years ago and brought here.' Reed held up her Pronto. 'Just did a PNC check, guv. There's a MisPer report matching her name. She was taken from Nottingham in 1998.'

'Bring her out here.'

'That's the thing, guv, she's one of the ones not coming out of her room. Come on.' Reed jogged across the pebbles and entered a chalet. She led them through to a bedroom. 'It's okay, Susan, it's DS Reed. My boss wants a word.'

A woman sat on the bed, right up against the wall. Early thirties, blonde hair tied in a ponytail. A single-strap black cocktail dress fanned out around her legs.

Fenchurch crouched in front of her, struggling to control his breathing. 'You're safe now, Susan. Okay?'

Didn't look like she thought she would be. 'They'll hurt them.'

'Nobody's going to hurt anyone. Okay?'

She sniffed and adjusted the strap on her dress.

'Susan, what happened when they took you?'

'I was sixteen, working in a clothes shop. I'd left school, thought I was it, you know?' Her accent still had tinges of the Nottingham grit. 'I was shutting down for the night and this noise came from behind me. Bang. I turned round and a bloke grabbed me. Stuck me in a van and drugged me. Next thing I know, I woke up here.'

She nibbled at her lip. 'A doctor had a look at me. Did some tests and injected me with stuff.' She looked away. 'Then they made me have sex.'

'With the men who kidnapped you?'

She shook her head, her hair dancing around. 'With a boy. Thomas. He was pretty.' She bunched up a handful of her tights. 'He was in a wheelchair.'

Fenchurch clenched his jaw. 'What happened next?'

'I had a girl called Margaret.' She scowled. 'And another one, Tabatha. Then Diana. Then a boy called David.' She let go of her tights. Her fingers twitched in the air. 'They took David away from me when he was a baby. Diana's the only one who stayed. She's got three girls now.' She bit her painted lip. 'They already took two of them.'

'What about your other two children?'

'They took Margaret and Tabatha years ago. Margaret was seventeen. Tabby was only fifteen.'

'Where did they go?'

'I don't know. Someone said London.'

'Where are the men who did this to you?'

'They never speak to us.'

'I need you to help me.' Fenchurch waved Reed back and leaned forward. 'Does the name Chloe mean anything to you?'

'Should it?'

Fenchurch exhaled slowly. 'What about Erica?'

Susan looked up, eyes wide. 'Erica?' She swallowed. 'Diana had a daughter called Erica. They took her away. Do you know where she is?'

Fenchurch got out his Pronto and showed her a photo of Erica. 'Is this her?'

'Oh my God.' Her face collapsed in on itself. 'My baby. What's happened to her?'

'She's safe. We've got her in protective custody.'

Susan let her head fall. Tears streamed down her cheeks. 'When can I see her?'

'Soon.' Fenchurch found the case photos on his Pronto. He'd cracked the screen somehow. Both Jane Does, one grainy CCTV, the other a crystal-clear morgue shot. 'These girls are connected to a case in London.' He held it out to her. 'Do you know them?'

She looked away. 'You need to speak to Alison.'

———

Alison was inside the medical facility. A male paramedic was checking her out, listening to a stethoscope against her chest. She smiled when Fenchurch entered the room.

'Finally getting some reaction from you, eh?' The paramedic glanced at Fenchurch. Then did a double take. 'Oh, didn't see you there.'

Fenchurch nodded at the door. 'Could you give us a second?'

The paramedic tore off his gloves and let the stethoscope dangle free. 'Be back soon.'

Fenchurch perched on a metal chair next to the bed. 'How are you doing, Alison?'

She pulled her cardigan tight. 'He was going to . . . euthanise me.'

'Why?'

'I'm too old.'

'How old are you?'

'Thirty-two.'

'You're ten years younger than me.'

She clenched her jaw and gasped. 'I can't have any more children. Lord knows they try to make me. My girls are all gone. They say I'm useless now.'

Fenchurch swallowed hard and got out his Pronto. He found the CCTV image of their first Jane Doe and held it out. 'Do you recognise this woman?'

'Oh, my little girl.' Alison put a hand to her mouth, eyes wide. 'That's Ursula. My oldest daughter. Where was she?'

'London.' He held out his Pronto again. No CCTV screen grab this time, just the morgue photo. 'What about her?'

Her eyes filled with tears. 'That's Yasmin. Her sister.' She couldn't control her forehead. Great twitches flashed across it. 'What's happened to them?'

'I'm afraid I've got some very bad news for you.'

She lashed out and threw the Airwave against the wall. It clattered and the back fell off. 'My babies!' Her head collapsed, like it weighed a ton. Her whole body shook. She looked up, eyes full of fury. 'Who did this to them?'

'He's dead now.' Fenchurch bent over to pick up his Pronto. The back didn't quite fit any more. The paramedic was tapping his watch by the door. 'We'll get you back to London and start from there, okay?'

The paramedic came in and beamed at Alison. The metal chair groaned as he sat. 'Now, Ms Carr, let's get you sorted, shall we?'

Carr?

Fenchurch frowned. Shit. He spun back round. 'Did you say Carr?' He barged the paramedic out of the way. 'Alison, what was your mother's name?'

'Michaela.' She smiled, bittersweet and wistful. More twitching on her forehead. 'She's not here any more.'

'What happened?'

'She tried to escape. A long time ago.' Alison put her hand to her face and let out a breath. 'She tried to take me with her. They caught me, but she got away. She left me behind. I thought she'd come back for me.' She covered her eyes. 'That's the last time I saw her. I was ten. Do you know what happened to her?'

'My father's investigating something . . .' Fenchurch grimaced as he reached back into his pocket for his Pronto. He pulled up the PNC report. 'Her body was found in 1993. Her parents reported her missing in 1982, aged sixteen.'

'I was born the next year. Oh my God.' Her panting breath sounded like laughter but her face gave lie to it. She put a hand to her mouth, eyes watering. 'Are they still alive?'

'I don't know. We'll find out.' Fenchurch put the Pronto away. 'Did anyone else try to escape?'

'A few years ago, Pauline and Joan tried. They were my friends. They killed them and punished the rest of us for it. They did this to me.'

She held out her arm. There was a deep gouge just below her wrist.

Chapter Thirty-Eight

'Mr Vaughn, I'm asking you a question here.' Fenchurch stared at the blotchy white wall of the interview room. A fresh weal of graffiti was near the bottom, no sign of its creator.

Docherty let out a deep sigh and motioned to Fenchurch to continue.

'At least you could do me the courtesy of answering.'

Vaughn ran a hand through his hair and revealed a bald spot. Like lifting a car's bonnet to find the engine gone. He reset the elaborate comb-forward and restored the parting. 'What do you want from me?'

'A full and frank confession.'

'That's not going to happen.'

Fenchurch leaned over, scowling at him. 'Before you shot one of my colleagues, you ran away from us at your farm. Why?'

Vaughn gave a thin-lipped smile. 'Because I feared for my life.'

'Right. You ran into a chalet. There's a whole lot of them. We found over a hundred people living in them. What were they doing there?'

'I've no idea what you're talking about.'

'These people either don't officially exist or they've been missing for a very long time.' Fenchurch gave a mock frown. 'Here's a funny coincidence. A lot of the girls who worked at The Alicorn grew up on your farm. Can you believe it?'

'The where?'

'The Alicorn. It's a lap-dancing bar. Owned by a business called Dragon Entertainment Holdings. Problem is, it's all offshored. Needs someone with a lot of knowledge of high finance to do that. Now, what does a hedge fund do? Offshoring's certainly part of it.'

'Not the part I do.'

'Mr Vaughn, do you own this company?'

'I don't know what you're referring to.' Vaughn flicked his hair again. 'This feels like you're expecting me to give something up.'

'Were any police officers working with you?'

Vaughn clenched his jaw. 'No comment.'

'Did you have any part in the murder of Robert Hall?'

'None.'

'Did you have any part in the murder of Ursula Carr?'

'Who?'

'You know who I'm talking about. The girl who was found at your building on Wednesday night.'

'No comment.'

'What about Yasmin Carr? She was found in a car park just off Brick Lane.'

'No comment.'

'Shall I tell you our theory?' Fenchurch left a long gap. Vaughn wasn't looking like he wanted it filled. 'These girls were bred for use in the sex industry. You farm people like cattle.'

'Are we any better than beasts?' Vaughn rolled his shoulders. 'The world's full of cattle, people whose only role in life is to consume. You're not important.'

'And I'm sure you think you are?'

'I'm someone. I've achieved a lot.'

'You're a criminal, Mr Barraclough.'

'What did you say?'

'We've had a look at your background.' Fenchurch sifted through a wad of papers. 'Vaughn's not your real name, is it?'

He looked daggers at Fenchurch. 'It is.'

'Not according to your birth certificate, Mr Barraclough.'

Vaughn pushed himself to his feet and leaned over the desk. Breath hissed at Fenchurch. 'How dare you?'

'How dare I?' Fenchurch sat back and folded his arms. 'Mrs Thatcher must've been proud of a miner's son from Wakefield rising to a senior position at a hedge fund. And in just a few years.' He licked his lips. 'City of London police are sifting through your financial history as we speak. Your hedge fund's going to come under a lot of close scrutiny. Is anyone else at Darke Matter Capital involved in this?'

'No comment.'

'Is Vincent Darke involved?'

'No. I've only met him twice.'

'Is that all? You told me the other day how small the company was.'

'Doesn't mean we're living in each other's pockets.'

'Does he know about your lowly background?'

Vaughn laughed. 'I believe he used to work in a supermarket in Ealing before he got into finance.'

'So you're all barrow boys made good?'

'Quite.' Vaughn sat down again and tilted his head to the side. 'You know I'm not on the board at Darke Matter. I'm a salaried employee. I don't own a share of the company. My stock options are taken as cash. Do you know how much I make in a year, officer?'

'Enlighten me.'

'Last year, I took home over three hundred thousand pounds. After tax. I'm worth over ten million.'

'Impressive.' Fenchurch glanced at Docherty. 'Boss, what would you do with that sort of money?'

Docherty exhaled. 'I'd buy an island off the west coast of Scotland and never see another living soul again.'

'I'd move to Spain. Mr Barraclough here would spend it on accumulating more wealth.' Fenchurch slapped his hand on the desk. 'Until it all came tumbling down.'

Docherty sucked in air across his teeth. 'Why did you bother? Why not live in a big house and just do your job? Why all this sex trafficking shite?'

Vaughn just sat there, inspecting his nails.

Fenchurch tried to make eye contact, but Vaughn wasn't having any of it. 'How about Mr Sotiris Vrykolakas?'

'I've no knowledge of this man.'

'You may know him as Bruco. He used to run The Alicorn.'

Vaughn's gaze shot up.

'So you do know him?'

'Just you wait.' Vaughn folded his arms and smirked, a lizard grin on his face. 'Mr Fenchurch, Mr Docherty. You should be very careful which enemies you take on.'

⌣

Fenchurch opened the interview room door. 'What the hell?'

Gordon Edgar was fiddling with his mobile. 'Evening, Inspector.'

'What are you doing here?'

'Waiting for my client.' Edgar locked his phone and dumped it on the desk. 'Given he's in police custody, I hope you know where he is?'

The door burst open and Bruco staggered in, followed by Nelson and a Custody Officer.

Fenchurch nodded at Edgar. 'Do you need a moment with your client?'

'That'd be good.'

'Tough. You're not getting one.' Fenchurch reached over and started the recorder as Bruco and Nelson sat down. 'Interview commenced at six fifteen p.m. on Saturday the nineteenth of December 2015. Present are myself, DI Simon Fenchurch and DS Jon Nelson. The suspect, Sotiris Vrykolakas, is also present along with his lawyer, Gordon Edgar.' He tapped the stylus against the screen of his Pronto as it unlocked. 'Mr Vrykolakas, why did you kill Robert Hall?'

'No comment.'

'I'll stop you right there. We've got evidence that you did. The best you can hope for is to be as helpful as possible. One of our friends in the CPS might fast-track your case and the judge might minimise the sentence.'

'Inspector.' Edgar stretched out his braces, like some old-time vaudeville act. 'Can I just confirm you're speaking for the judiciary with approved authority?'

'That's correct.'

'Then why aren't they in here?'

'They're keeping at arm's reach. Standard procedure. One of their agents is watching this as we speak.'

'Why don't I believe you?'

Fenchurch ignored him, instead focusing on Bruco. 'Mr Vrykolakas, like I said, your only option here is to cooperate with us. Why did you kill Mr Hall?'

'My client has stated his desire to remain silent.'

Bruco put his hand on Edgar's arm. 'I never killed him.'

'Jesus . . .' Edgar shook his head. 'My client denies his involvement in the strongest terms.'

'Does he now?' Fenchurch crunched back in the chair. 'Anything to support his innocence?'

Bruco rubbed his hands together slowly, like a tramp at a brazier. 'Paul did it.'

Edgar collapsed into his seat. The braces popped back. 'Paul Kershaw?'

'He killed Robert Hall. Injected him with smack.'

Fenchurch crossed his arms. 'Let's start with what happened between you and Mr Hall at the bar on Thursday night. He'd been all over your girls so you chucked him out. Right?'

'He was going over the score with young Erica. He was trying to buy her. My bouncer had to intervene.' Bruco picked at something between his teeth. 'I had to help him take Mr Hall outside. He started ranting and raving.'

'What about?'

'It was just gibberish. Guy was on something.' Bruco smirked, hand smoothing down his beard. 'Guy was loco, you know? Lost the plot. He kept trying to score drugs off my girls.'

'Did they sell any?'

'My girls are clean, man.'

'So why kill him? Seems a bit extreme.'

'I didn't kill him. You should be speaking to Paul Kershaw.'

'Well, you were at Mr Hall's flat.' Fenchurch held up a hand. 'Don't even try to deny it. At the very least, you're an accessory to murder.'

'I wanted a word with him, that's all.'

'You're saying you helped Mr Kershaw have a word? That's it?'

Bruco rasped his hand across his stubble, almost as long as the trimmed beard. He switched his gaze between Fenchurch and Nelson. 'Listen, Paul told me this geezer had murdered two of my girls. Said we should sort him out.'

'Which girls?'

'I don't know their names.' Bruco stared up at the ceiling. 'Both of them only lasted a few nights before my superiors moved them on. This Hall geezer knew them from the bar. Guy was a regular. Two or three nights a week.'

'You told us you didn't have any idea who these girls were.'

'Shit.' Bruco swallowed hard. 'Shit.'

'I don't get why you had to kill him.'

'I didn't, man. Paul did it. Must've killed this guy because he killed two of ours.'

'Were you protecting your property?' Fenchurch left him enough space to fill. He didn't even try. 'You'd bred these girls. Fed them, raised them and Mr Hall butchered them.'

'What are you talking about?'

'He killed Yasmin Carr in Dray Walk car park on Thursday night, just before he'd been chucked out of The Alicorn.'

'What?'

They didn't even know about the second victim. Hadn't had enough time to figure it out. The retaliation was purely for the first girl. 'He killed Ursula Carr in Little Somerset House on Tuesday night.'

'That place is notorious, man. It's where all the girls in that part of town take their johns.' Bruco rasped a hand across the fine stubble on his cheek. 'You should check the CCTV in that building. See what really happened in there.'

Fenchurch frowned. 'There's no CCTV in there.'

'The guard tell you that? Well, Selma's lying. I've seen the video from that place. What Robert Hall did to that girl.'

'Ursula.'

Bruco shrugged. 'Ursula.'

'And I'm supposed to believe you?'

'Paul had it on his phone, man. He thought it was funny.'

Selma Burns sat at her bank of monitors in Latham House, one piggy hand in a giant bag of crisps, the other clutching a tall can of energy drink. Her mouth hung open as she stared at the screens.

Fenchurch waved a hand in front of her face. 'Ms Burns.'

She jumped to her feet, sending crisps flying and toppling her can over. 'Jesus Christ!' She dabbed at the spillage with a paper tissue. 'What the hell do you want?'

'I'll give you two choices.' Fenchurch perched on the edge of her desk, crunching a crinkle-cut crisp. He stuck his thumb out. 'One, you cooperate and we review what we'll charge you with.' He added the index finger. 'Two, you can do this down the station with a lawyer.'

'A lawyer. What?'

'You've withheld evidence in a murder case.'

'I've done no such thing.' Selma wheeled away from him, nearer Nelson and Owen by the door. 'This is police harassment.'

'You told us the CCTV in your buildings were broken.'

'Right?'

'So how come Sotiris Vrykolakas saw it?'

'Who?'

'Bruco.'

She scowled. 'That piece of dirt.'

'Ms Burns, he told us he saw some footage from Tuesday night. Footage of the girl being murdered. The girl you told us you found.'

She stared at the floor. 'They told me not to show it to the police.'

'Was it Paul Kershaw?'

She glared at him. 'What if it was?'

'What power does he hold over you?'

'We've been told to help him out. Let his girls in the building. Keep an eye on things getting out of hand.' Selma stared at the floor again. 'I'm really sorry. I knew the girl was in my building. They weren't clearing her away. I saw it happen. Paul made me send him the video.'

Nelson folded his arms, stared at her long and hard. 'Just show us the bloody video.'

Selma fiddled with the controls on the desk.

The machine in front of her rattled and clanked as a video machine sucked in a cassette. Some mid-eighties vision of the future. The bottom-left monitor switched on. The screen turned black then filled with footage of the building's interior.

Selma wound it forward and two figures danced across the display, slowing as she adjusted the dial.

Robert Hall was thrusting away at Ursula as she lay on a table, grimacing. He shifted back slightly, obscured by a cabinet. His knees buckled and liquid squirted onto her stomach.

Ursula lay there panting and dabbed at her belly. A mucus spider web trailed away from her hand. She reached down for her knickers.

Hall grabbed her by the throat. He pushed her onto the floor and kicked her. Then again. And again. He got something out of his jacket pocket. A blade shone in the dim light. He kneeled on her chest. He stabbed her in the neck. And again. And again. Kept going, down and down.

Fenchurch swallowed. 'Ursula Carr.'

Nelson glanced over from the display, his dark complexion slightly paler. 'Excuse me?'

'Her name. Our first Jane Doe. She's called Ursula Carr. We finally got them justice.'

Chapter Thirty-Nine

Fenchurch tore the foil from his burrito and sniffed the moist tortilla. Heaven. Outside his office window, rain fluttered in the sodium glare across the road. A taxi splashed a puddle on a couple as they hurried home.

Couldn't get his mind off Robert Hall's taxi trip. Picking up a prostitute and dying twenty minutes later. Did he deserve it? Hard to say.

He set his food down. He took a drink of lemonade instead. Tasted like rat piss. 'What a bloody case.'

'Agreed.' Nelson finished chewing a mouthful, scraping at his fingers with a serviette. 'You owe me a tenner, guv.'

Fenchurch waved a hand across the spurned burrito. 'But I fetched these?'

'I said it'd be over by Christmas.' Nelson tapped his watch. 'Five days to spare.'

Fenchurch reached into his wallet and dumped the money onto the desk. 'Don't spend it all in the one bloody shop.'

Nelson pocketed the tenner. 'How about the one pub. Tonight?'

'What about next week?'

'Why not now?'

Fenchurch tried another mouthful of the burrito. Barely tasted it. 'Because I need to sort something out.'

Nelson looked like a little boy who'd been told to go to his sister's friend's birthday party. 'You're a barrel of laughs.'

'I can't get the video out of my head, Jon. The way he killed her. It was so brutal. Stabbing like that. Complete overkill.'

'I worked a case like this years ago. A gay guy had come home to find his boyfriend in the bath with another man. This was like that, brutal. He just kept on cutting. Over two hundred stab wounds in the pair of them.' Nelson put his own burrito down, a lump of steak rolling onto the desktop. 'Christ, I'm off my food now.'

'Welcome to the club.' Fenchurch massaged his temple. 'Michaela Carr was fourteen when they forced her to have children.'

'Jesus. What's next for them? How do they cope in the world?'

'I don't know, Jon. This shit is the thin end of the wedge. Every single girl dancing is being exploited.' Fenchurch swallowed. 'Maybe not as much as Erica, Ursula and Yasmin. But they're being exploited, even in the posh clubs, even if they're taking a ton of cash home.'

'I can't believe how they got away with it for so long.'

'Their luck ran out eventually.'

'It's not the end, though, guv. There might be other farms. Do you really think Vaughn was behind it?'

'I just don't know, Jon.'

The door opened. Reed stood in the doorway, Erica lurking behind her. 'Thought I'd find you two here.'

Fenchurch smiled at Erica. 'Hello.'

She didn't smile back, just stared at the floor instead. 'Simon, I'm sorry.'

'What for?'

'For everything I've done. I could've stopped what happened to Yasmin.'

'You couldn't. Nobody could.' Fenchurch pointed to the seat next to him. 'You ever had a burrito?'

'Has it got potato in it?'

'They probably do in Ireland.' Fenchurch looked at Nelson and Reed. 'Can you give us a minute?'

'Sure thing. I'll see where we are with her paperwork.' Reed followed Nelson into the corridor.

Fenchurch swallowed. 'Did you see your mother?'

'And my grandmother.' Erica looked a lot younger than eighteen. 'They're both okay, thank God.' She nibbled at her bottom lip. 'I'm sorry about all that dad stuff.'

'I'll try and forgive you. You were desperate.'

'I shouldn't have tried to exploit your kindness.'

'I understand why you did it. You should probably stop doing that, though.' Fenchurch pushed his burrito away. 'So what are you going to do now?'

'I'm giving up dancing, that's for sure. Aside from that, I don't know.' Erica shivered. 'They say they're going to get us a house somewhere.'

'I'd avoid London, if I were you.'

She smiled, her cheek dimpling. It sent a jolt down his spine. 'Could I join the police?'

He propped his elbows on the desk. 'I wouldn't recommend it.'

She frowned, lines spreading across her smooth forehead. 'Remember earlier, you asked me about your daughter? What was she like?'

Fenchurch swallowed. 'Chloe had blonde hair. Looked a bit like you.' He tapped his cheek where the dimple would be. 'She was a lovely girl. Could be a little minx at times, but . . . Well.'

'I've asked around for you. Nobody's heard of her. And that's the truth.'

'Thanks.'

'I want to help.'

A knock on the door. Nelson stood there, holding up a black jacket. 'Erica, we need to get you to your new home.'

'Thanks.' She took the coat and stared at Fenchurch for a few seconds. 'Can I see you again?'

'I'd like that.'

'They say it'll be a few weeks.' She waved at him from the doorway. 'Bye.' She followed Nelson down the corridor.

Reed sat down and picked up Fenchurch's burrito. 'You feeling okay, guv?'

'Not really.'

'There's no way it'd work, guv. Too big an age gap.'

'Piss off, Kay.' Fenchurch watched her take a mouthful of burrito. 'I've given someone their family back. That's a good thing.'

'Going to take a lot of healing.'

'It never heals. You never stop thinking about it all the time. When I saw Erica, I—' Fenchurch clenched his jaw. 'Seeing Ursula lying there in Little Somerset House it just . . . It set something off in me.' He sucked in air. 'Erica was looking for a father figure. It's not me. Even if Chloe's been a lap dancer and lived in that kind of hellhole for ten years, I want her to be alive. Someone's got to know something about what happened to her.'

Reed sighed. 'You really need to speak to Abi.'

Chapter Forty

Fenchurch knocked on the pale-blue door. The stairwell stank of fresh wood shavings and the bitter tang of glue. Looked like it'd never been battered down by an idiot.

It swung open. Dad stood there, smiling. 'Hello, Simon.'

Fenchurch glared at him. 'What the hell are you doing here?'

'Abi asked me to come round.' Dad frowned. 'She said you smashed her door in.'

'Did she?' Fenchurch took a step back and stared up at the dark skylight, all mossed over. 'Dad, I was shit scared she'd been taken by the Machine.'

'Calm down, son.' Dad raised his hands. 'She told me what happened, I'm just winding you up.' He laughed, magic sparking in his eyes. 'Like I say, I'm helping Abi. She's a bit upset.'

'Is she—'

'Simon?' Abi appeared in the doorway. 'What are you doing here?'

'I wanted to talk.'

Dad reached inside the door and collected his jacket. 'I'll leave you both to it.' He pecked Abi on the cheek. 'See you later, love.'

He grabbed Fenchurch as he passed. 'Oh, Doc called me. Said something about a commendation. What's that for?'

'We took down the Machine today.'

'You're kidding.'

'Maybe not the whole thing, but a huge chunk of it.'

'That's my boy.' Dad hugged him tight, putting a bit too much pressure on Fenchurch's aching ribs. 'I'll see you later, son.'

'Maybe tomorrow. I taped the Hammers match. Still don't know the score.' Fenchurch watched him trudge down the stairs. He turned round, his heart thumping. Drums pounded in his ears as he tried to make eye contact with Abi. 'Hey.'

Abi bit her lip, hands on hips. 'The bill for the door repair's inside.'

'How much do I owe you?'

'It's fine.'

'Abi, I'm really sorry. I just—' He clenched his jaw and shut his eyes. 'I thought they'd taken you.'

'I know.' She smiled, her cheek indenting. 'It's really sweet.'

'Sweet?' Fenchurch tried to swallow down the lump in his throat. 'This case has brought a lot of stuff home to roost.'

'I can see that.' Her nostrils flared as she loosened her shoulders. 'Chloe's not coming back, Simon. You need to let go.'

'I can't.' Fenchurch rubbed at his eyes. 'Even if she's not out there, someone knows what happened to her. I need to find them. I've got to have some hope.'

'I gave up on hope a long time ago. Simon, you need to channel your anger into something constructive.'

'Finding our daughter isn't constructive? Getting closure?'

'It's destroying you. Your own hope is crushing you.'

His face crumpled up. All he could do was shake his head. 'It's all I've got.'

'You used to have so much more.'

'I used to have Chloe. I used to have you, but you chucked me out.' The crack on the hall ceiling still hadn't been fixed after ten years. 'I should go.' He took a step back. 'Listen, Abi. I . . .'

'Simon, you can't have me back.'

'But I thought . . . After this week . . . That maybe.'

'Simon, you're still hunting for her. I can't have that back in my life. If someone could tell me right now that she's dead, I'd take that. It's closure.'

'I've got to hope.'

'And the hope's killing you.' She stepped forward and placed her hand on his cheek. 'You're clinging to the past, Simon. You need to let it go.'

Fenchurch let her stroke his face. Felt like he was thirty-two again. He expected Chloe to run out and charge into his thigh. Wrap her arms around his waist.

But she wasn't there.

'We found this . . . this farm today. A gang had been kidnapping people. They took them there and raised them. Bred them, used them as prostitutes and dancers. I thought Chloe might be there. She wasn't. Nobody knew her.'

'Simon . . .' Tears slicked Abi's face. 'Simon, why are you here?'

'Because I want you back, Ab. I feel like I died ten years ago.'

Abi put her other hand on his cheek. 'You need to start living again.'

'You're right. I'll—'

'Simon.' She bit her lip. 'Okay.'

'What?'

'I want to help you get over this.' She reached over and pecked him on the cheek. 'Simon, you've got to let go.'

Fenchurch put his arms around her and pulled her tight. 'I know I do.' He sucked in the smell of her hair. Wildflowers and fresh water. His tears soaked into it. 'I just don't want to let her down.'

'Hey, hey.' She stroked a hand over his back. 'You're not letting anyone down if you get on with your life.'

'You really think that?'

'I do.' She wriggled free and took a step back. 'So?'

'So what?'

'Are you going to stop looking for her?'

He nodded. Slowly. Then faster, putting more into it. The drums stopped beating, just a cymbal crash dying away to nothing. 'I'm going to stop.'

She looked him up and down. 'I believe you.' She rested a hand on the doorjamb. 'There's still pasta in the fridge from last night. You can come in, if you want.'

Acknowledgements

Thanks to Rhona for the beta reading, pointing out the rather obvious flaws in the first drafts.

Infinite thanks as ever to Al Guthrie for being both a brilliant agent and the most aggressive editor a guy could ask for — you not only saved this book but showed me how to turn it into what it became.

Special thanks to Jenny Parrott for all the brutal editing and encouragement as I tore my hair out during December 2015.

Huge thanks to Emilie, Sana, Eoin and all at Thomas & Mercer for taking another punt on me with this book, but also being a brilliant publishing team over the last eighteen months.

And, finally, thanks to Kitty for all the help throughout the various stages of the book, putting up with a grumpy sod (me) and being awesome.

About the Author

Photo © Kitty Harrison 2014

Ed James writes crime fiction novels. His Scott Cullen series features a young Edinburgh detective constable investigating crimes from the bottom rung of the career ladder he's desperate to climb. *The Hope That Kills* is the first in a new series featuring DI Simon Fenchurch, set on the gritty streets of East London. Formerly an IT manager, Ed began writing on planes, trains and automobiles to fill his weekly commute to London. He now writes full-time and lives in East Lothian, Scotland, with his girlfriend and a menagerie of rescued animals.

17776946R00213

Printed in Great Britain
by Amazon